W9-CDN-213

DOWN AND OUT IN
Beverly Heels

ALSO BY KATHRYN LEIGH SCOTT

The Bunny Years: The Surprising Inside Story of the Playboy Clubs: The Women Who Worked as Bunnies, and Where They Are Now

My Scrapbook Memories of Dark Shadows

Dark Shadows Memories

DOWN AND OUT IN
Beverly Heels

KATHRYN LEIGH SCOTT

The characters and events portrayed in this book are fictitious. Any similarity to real persons, living or dead, is coincidental and not intended by the author.

Published by Montlake Romance
P.O. Box 400818
Las Vegas, NV 89140

ISBN-13: 9781611098860
ISBN-10: 1611098866

For Cynthia, my wise agent and truest of friends

Prologue

I rang the bell before unlocking the front door, even though I knew Paul wasn't home. Otherwise he'd have bounded down the walkway as soon as my car pulled up. I would have seen him striding toward me, tanned and grinning, his shirttails flapping over well-worn khakis, eager to sweep me up in his arms. Instead, I was greeted with newspapers yellowing on the front steps. I pulled the key from the lock and stepped inside to dense silence and the mustiness of a house shut up, unoccupied—how long? Three weeks?

Still, I ran up the stairs, calling, "Paul? Darling, I'm home!" I paused on the landing, about to call out again, but my voice was no more than a whispered "Where are you?" Paul should have arrived back from Mexico in the early afternoon and had a bottle of bubbly on ice to celebrate our homecoming. That was the plan.

I quickly walked the length of the hallway, passing the open door to a guest room and the closed door of the upstairs laundry and linen closet. I stopped at the threshold to my office, registering the sun-filled room, its walls hung with film posters and framed photographs. Only a single sheet of my notepaper, pale vanilla with MEG BARNES in red block letters, lay on the blond wood surface of my desk. In haste I'd written, *Love you, Paul—see you soon!* before leaving for the airport and a flight to North Carolina.

I hurried into our bedroom, a suite of rooms overlooking the garden. My eyes swept the cozy sitting area near the fireplace, fixing briefly on Paul's favorite camel-colored leather armchair. There was no sign of his Top-Siders, usually kicked off and left by the footstool. Nor was there so much as a pucker in the snowy linen coverlet on the California king, banked with an assortment of plump white and crème pillows. I pushed open the French doors to the balcony, breathing in evening air scented with eucalyptus. My eyes scanned the pool, bathhouse, and outdoor grill area, all as I had left them: the cushions stacked under the awning, everything covered. I glanced again at my cell phone. No messages, nothing from him since the night before.

Then, cutting through the silence, the two-note chime of the doorbell. *Paul!* I slipped out of my sandals and broke into a run, racing barefoot down the stairs to the front door, relief mixing with a jumble of explanations. *Lost his briefcase! Phone! No keys!*

I yanked the door open to find the stocky, middle-aged limo driver on my doorstep, a sheen of sweat on his brow, my two bags at his feet. "So sorry, Miss Barnes. Your luggage. The door swing shut before I catch it." I heard the rush of words in a foreign accent and realized that aside from introductions at the arrivals terminal, we'd barely spoken during the drive from LAX.

"I'm so sorry. I completely forgot. Here, just leave them in the entry."

I stepped back as he set the two suitcases on the floor. "Thank you so much." I reached into my shoulder bag and handed him a bill from my wallet.

"Thank you very much, Miss Barnes." He brushed his hand through his dark hair and glanced at the luggage, looking doubtful. "So this is good? I leave here? Is heavy."

"Yes, yes, fine. Perfect. My husband will take them up."

Still the driver hesitated, giving me an anxious look. "Really, this is fine," I assured him. "Thank you." Then I saw the manila envelope tucked under his arm. "Was there something else?"

"If you don't mind, Miss Barnes, my wife and I are big fans. I tell her I never do this, but when she hear I drive you, she make me promise." He whipped a photograph from the envelope and held it up. "Is you, yes?"

I nodded. Indeed, I'd signed copies of this eight-by-ten glossy of a leggy and oh-so-young version of myself—wearing a black swallowtail jacket with satin shorts and a top hat—many, many times before. The driver pulled a Sharpie from his pocket, uncapped it, and presented it to me with a flourish. "Awfully good of you, my dear."

I smiled at the popular catchphrase from the *Holiday* series that had become a national fad for a while. "All in a day's work," I said, just as my character, Jinx, would have responded to her partner in crime solving, played by Winston Sykes. The two-hour *Holiday* specials were part of a rotating "wheel" of detective shows that had aired for five seasons. Each production was geared toward a holiday: Valentine's Day, Halloween, Mother's Day, even Groundhog Day. Winston Sykes, faking a British accent and sporting a monocle, played a character known as The Magician. I was his assistant, Jinx Fogarty, and together we solved crimes, all holiday-themed, setting the trend for bickering, opposites-attract television sleuths.

I took the Sharpie and placed the photo on the hall table. "It's Tony, right?"

"You remember! Yes, please, if you could sign it to Tony and Joyce. You big in Italy, too. My whole family watch."

"Really? Well, there you go." I handed Tony his signed photo and the Sharpie. "All in a day's work," I repeated.

"Thank you. Thank you. My wife, she be thrilled."

"Happy to do it," I said with a finality intended to stanch the flow of gratitude. Tony was still grinning as I gently closed the door behind him. I heaved a sigh and looked down at the two heavy suitcases. *Where was Paul?*

I headed to the kitchen, idly picking up the wall phone as I reached the pantry. The dial tone sounded in my ear, but then I wasn't expecting to hear the *bip-bip-bip* indicating voice mail; I'd forwarded all calls to my cell phone. I dialed the code to discontinue the forwarding service, while my eyes roamed the kitchen, breakfast nook, and adjoining dining room.

Everything was in order, just as the housekeeper would have left it three days ago. The French doors stuck a bit as I unlocked and pushed them open. I leaned against the doorjamb, hugging my arms against the autumn chill. *Even if Paul had lost his keys, wallet, and cell phone, he'd find a way to reach me.* Fading sunlight cast mauve shadows on the patio and glinted off the stainless steel cover on the barbecue. A slight breeze ruffled the surface of the pool and sounded the wind chimes.

Abruptly I slammed the French doors closed and turned the lock. I was getting annoyed, of course, and didn't want to give in to it. *How could he spoil things like this!* It was the first time in our nearly one-year marriage that we'd been apart for any length of time. He knew how anxious I was to see him. *Why would he disappoint me?* Was it a client? A meeting that ran late, and he missed his flight? I didn't want to be angry when he finally walked in the door. I'd regret it—and what was the point? It wasn't like him to be uncaring.

I opened the fridge and grabbed a bottle of Pinot Grigio, half-empty and at least three weeks old. It would do. I poured a glass and took a long sip, grateful the wine hadn't gone sour. What to do? Unpack? Go through my mail and wait patiently? Call Sid? No, not even Sid Baskin, our attorney—although he would be the most likely person to know. He was the one who'd introduced me to Paul, and the two had become, more or less, business partners. But he was also married to my best friend, Carol, and I wasn't about to call and ask if they knew where my husband was. *No!*

I set my glass down on the granite countertop a bit too sharply and reminded myself to calm down. Paul could walk in any minute with some crazy would-you-believe-what-happened-to-me story that we'd laugh about. *So stop worrying! Do something useful.*

I settled on taking a long, hot bath. What better place for Paul to find me than up to my chin in scented bubbles? I poured the last of the Pinot Grigio in my glass and headed for the stairs. Midway down the hall, the phone rang. Retrace my steps to the pantry, or race for the phone in the entryway? I grabbed the pantry phone. "Hello? Paul?"

"Baby, you gotta listen." His voice was low, urgent.

"Paul, where are you?"

"Listen to me. I can't talk long. I'm okay, but I've been kidnapped down here."

"Kidnapped? C'mon, what happened?" I laughed. "Has your flight been delayed?"

"Meg, this is serious. Whatever you do, don't call the police. Don't call anyone. Not even Sid. Just wait. You'll get a call. They'll tell you what they want. Just do it!"

"Wait, what are you saying?" My throat tightened at the urgency in his voice. "Who'll call? What do I have to do?"

"My desk drawer. You'll find a piece of paper with a name and a phone number. When you know what they want, call that number. He'll know what you need to do. Gotta go, baby. I'm counting on you. I love you. Love you!"

"I love you, too—wait!" But the line was dead. "Wait, please!" I cried as I checked caller ID. "BLOCKED" flashed on the handset. "Please, please!" I tried to remember the code for last-call return. "No!"

My recollections of the tense, hurried exchange with Paul when he told me he'd been kidnapped come to me in scattered fragments. But I remember that he told me to wait, to call no one, not even Sid. It sounded so sensible at the time. He was counting on me. He trusted me to know what to do: Find the piece of paper in his desk drawer and make the call once I knew what the kidnappers wanted. My fear was real, and so was my icy calm as I waited for his abductors to present their ransom demand. I would follow their instructions and save my husband, just as Jinx had done when Winston Sykes had been kidnapped. That had felt real, too, and earned me my first Emmy nomination.

Hours later, when nothing seemed real anymore, when I was already struggling to remember what Paul had said and wondering if I'd imagined everything, a man with a gruff, heavy accent called. He gave me instructions, and I followed them to the letter. I made the call to Paul's contact and did as he directed. What else could I do? Any pretense that I was Jinx, or that rational thought guided my actions, vanished. I may have thought I was functioning on all cylinders, but that turns out to be part of the blurry mess I barely remember.

Throughout long nights and days I sat on the edge of our bed—his side, not mine—hugging his pillow and smelling his musky scent. My mind kept going back to the last time I saw Paul. A limo was parked at the curb, its driver waiting to take me to the airport to catch a flight to North Carolina for a three-week location shoot. Still in his bathrobe, hair tousled, Paul stood on the doorstep to kiss me good-bye, promising that if he could close his deal in Mexico, he'd fly out to join me in Wilmington.

"Please try, Paul. We could drive down the coast—"

"I'd love it, baby. I miss you already." Then he scooped me up and marched across the lawn, his slippers squishing in the dewy grass. I'd laughed, clinging to his neck as he carried me in his burly arms to the waiting limo. After depositing me in the backseat, he closed the door and leaned in the open window to kiss me again. Then, his eyes solemn, he ran his finger down my cheek. "Call me before takeoff, okay? I love you, baby. You take care of yourself."

"I love you, too. See you soon."

The driver pulled away. I waved to Paul until the car turned the corner at the end of the street. We spoke together many times after that, but it was the last time I saw him. It seems like yesterday, yet a lifetime ago.

Chapter One

ONE YEAR LATER

My husband and his mistress are dead—offed by a hit man the cops think I hired. I shift in my chair, trying to look calm. My lips stick to my teeth, but I manage to keep smiling as my mind grapples with the inane plotline of the script.

"So you worked with Alan Resnick?" The casting director teeters back and forth in his black leather chair, peering at me with the face of a boy playing at Daddy's desk. It crosses my mind that he's swinging his feet because they don't reach the floor.

Smiling still, I clear my throat and manage to peel my tongue from the roof of my mouth. "Who?"

His mouth twitches. He eyes me indulgently as though I'm his addled auntie. My mental Rolodex spins like a slot machine, but I'm out of luck. The name Alan Resnick does not come up—nor, for that matter, does the name of this infant casting director.

With his thumb and index finger, young whatshisname—Todd something?—plucks a corner of my eight-by-ten glossy from his desktop and dangles it before my eyes. I squint—I know it's my photograph and résumé he's holding, although I can't actually see either against the glare of sun blazing through the office window.

It's January, and this is Southern California at its seasonal best. But weather is only one reason actors migrate to Hollywood for the winter months. Another, not the least of them, is pilot season. Like the rest of the multitude, I need a job—desperately.

"Alan Resnick?" Todd repeats, enunciating clearly and a trifle louder than strictly necessary. "Like, *Easy Street*?"

"The sitcom? I don't think . . ." I'm about to admit I've never watched *Easy Street*, another smutty half-hour of brainless one-liners pickled in canned laughter. Mercifully I keep my mouth shut. *But why does he think I worked with Alan Resnick?*

I squint at Todd through the haze of white light but can make out only the silhouette of a slim torso, narrow shoulders, and a bobbing head with tufts of hair spiked in some sort of shiny goop. He looks like a newly hatched bird.

A cloud momentarily shades the blinding sun, and I glimpse a furrowed brow as he flips over my photograph to scan my résumé. "It says here . . . let me see . . ." Suddenly it all becomes clear.

"You mean Alain Resnais, the French director?" I say with giddy relief. "Yes, I did a film with him in Paris back in . . ." *Don't say it, Meg. It was before Todd was born.*

A look of alarm ripples across Todd's baby blue eyes. "French?" My résumé flutters from his fingertips onto the desktop. "No, that wouldn't be him. Never mind. I took it for a typo. Besides, this isn't comedy."

I stifle a groan, but just barely. Alain Resnais may not have a sitcom to his credit, but his latest film screened at Cannes not that many years ago. I'm reminded of the tale of multi-Oscar-winning director Fred Zinneman (*High Noon, A Man for All Seasons*) taking a meeting with a young producer, who asks the elderly filmmaker what he's done. "You first," Zinneman says.

Meanwhile Todd flips the script open and swipes his hand across the page as though clearing it of dust. "So, ready to read? Let's take it from the top of page fourteen."

"Read?"

"You don't have a problem with that, do you?" He cocks his head, his eyes frozen ponds. "Because I read *everyone*. No exceptions. You need more time?"

"No, thank you. I'm fine." Unaccountably intimidated, I've now committed myself to reading the scene virtually cold.

"Good. Okay, remember a dead body's been found, a link to your past. Your husband and his mistress were both killed, and the police now suspect you hired a hit man. I'll read the detective. Ready?"

Todd plants his elbows on the desk, utters the first line, and stares at me with fixed intensity. Despite his unnerving gaze I manage to respond. He nods encouragingly and, sounding like a robot on auto-speak, says his second line. I'm force-marched through two pages of dialogue while choking down an urge to flee. I *have* to get this job.

"Very good," he says. "Very nice. Can I get you back here at three to read for Lenny Bishop, the director?"

Of course, this is a *pre-audition*. "Sure," I answer. "Three o'clock. Great."

Todd is already on his feet, dropping my photo on top of a mound of glossies. *Next.* I ease myself out of the chair, my eyes falling on my head shot, a relic of the *Charlie's Angels* era, with me sporting shoulder pads and Farrah Fawcett hair. Across the bottom my name is printed in block letters. MEG BARNES. My heart sinks. These must be the only head shots my agent has left. *At least I still have an agent.*

Flustered, I thrust my hand across the desk, dip my chin, and flash a flirty smile that I immediately regret. Judging by the wince on his face, I must strike this kid as a Miss Havisham on the make.

He blinks and brushes my fingertips fleetingly before tucking his hands into the safety of his armpits. "Thanks for coming in, Meg. Great to meet you. Remember, keep it straight and real, and you'll do fine. See you this afternoon."

"Thank you," I say, not trusting myself to call him Todd in case I've got his name wrong. I slide the script in my bag and make my way to the reception room. Another actress paces the holding pen waiting for her turn to audition. *Pre-audition.*

"Good God, Meg, do you believe this?" she whispers as she walks past me.

"I know." I smile and touch her arm. "Good luck in there." I remember the days—not that long ago!—when neither one of us had to audition, let alone pre-audition. On my way out, I smile at the pretty receptionist. She might be the next casting director if Todd is tapped to head the studio in another month or two.

Keep it straight and real, and you'll do fine? Why not remind me to wear shoes?

I ride the three floors down to ground level making faces at the fun-house image of myself in the shiny elevator panels. I shift slightly, and the squat, wide-beamed image morphs into a pinched, elongated semblance of myself. With another slight shift, I appear almost normal. But even with some wavy distortion, I look pretty good. My auburn hair, blunt-cut, chin-length (I'm my own best hairdresser) gleams in the stainless steel. My Armani suit (a good five years old, but I'll take it to my grave) flatters my still-slim hips. How could I not pass for a rich society murderess? I'd cast me in a minute.

I step off the elevator and pause to get my bearings. There was a time, pre-tourist trolleys and theme park, when this lot was home to me. In those days this was a scene of bungalows and makeshift trailers, not flashy office blocks. I was a contract player then, and spent most of my waking hours on one of the soundstages.

When I first arrived in California, a somewhat snotty New York actress wondering if I'd made a terrible mistake signing on as a "Hollywood starlet," Clint Eastwood, James Garner, and Steve McQueen were starring in television Westerns. Rod Serling was still producing *Twilight Zone*. Alfred Hitchcock dined in the commissary. My photograph, a Technicolor confection of a pert and perky nineteen-year-old version of myself with big, brown eyes and a bouffant flip, hung above the booth where I took my lunch every day. I was in a picture with Jimmy Stewart, another with John Wayne. Now I barely recognize the buildings, let alone any of the people I pass. Yet the excitement churning my stomach is real—and all too familiar: *I got a callback!* I made the cut. Some things never change.

But other things do. I live on a strict budget these days, my wallet even leaner than it was in my salad days. Back then, salad actually meant a can of tuna, some lettuce, and a handful of saltines for supper, a feast in my present economy. Seeping sweat inside my beloved Armani, I stop for a moment in a patch of shade next to a soundstage. I'm hungry, and somehow I have to stay fresh while killing four hours until my afternoon audition. I head for the air-conditioned commissary.

The dining room that once sported red leather banquettes and miniature lamps on each cloth-covered table has seen many studio heads come and go—and undergone almost as many renovations. Today, it's an upscale cafeteria with salad and soup bars, latté stations, and pasta made to order. I settle on coffee, tomato soup, and a fistful of crackers, the cheapest nourishment available. With hours to waste, I manage to look as harried as everyone else trying to grab a table.

I spot an empty one near the wall and move fast, not waiting for a busboy to clear the debris. Before pushing it away, I glance at the tray of food left by the previous diner. Next to a bowl with the swampy remains of salad and blue cheese dressing, there's a plate with a half-sandwich of ham and cheese that appears untouched. A toothpick with a fringe of red cellophane sticks out of the whole-grain bread, an unopened packet of mustard beside it on the plate.

With my hand still poised over the tray, I wrestle with temptation. Waste not, want not. *But it's the remains of someone's lunch!* Who will know? I edge the tray closer, my fingers hovering within grabbing distance just as someone brushes my arm.

"Meggie? I don't believe it. Where you been, gal?"

My hand snaps back like a sprung rattrap. I look up at the weathered face of Doug Haliburton, wondering if his rheumy eyes have caught me scavenging leftovers.

"Dougie, my God! How're you doing?" I throw my arms around the frail, sagging shoulders of the man who directed most of the episodes of the *Holiday* detective series I filmed on this very lot.

"Not so bad. Mind if I join you?"

"Please do. Here, let me clear the table."

"Wait, don't forget your sandwich." I watch without protest as he lifts the plate off the tray and sets it next to my soup bowl. "You finished with this salad?"

"Yes, thanks. I was going back for some water. Anything I can get for you?"

"Just a napkin. Hey"—Dougie juts his chin and affects a snooty British accent—"awfully good of you, my dear."

"All in a day's work," I say, then give his thin shoulder an affectionate squeeze. "Awfully good of you, too, Dougie," I whisper to myself on the way to the water cooler. He cast me as Jinx, and I've probably worked with Doug Haliburton more than any other director in my career. I grab a handful of bread sticks and a napkin from the soup and salad bar before heading back to join him.

"So where you hangin' these days?" he asks as I bite into my secondhand ham-and-cheese. "Same place up in the hills?"

I shake my head. "Not anymore. Actually, I've been traveling. Stopped off in Nebraska for a while to visit my mother. I just got back a few weeks ago."

"Good for you. Not a bad idea to blow town once in a while." He catches my eye and smiles. "Ever see Winnie?"

"I think ol' Winston's back in Canada, retired. We used to exchange Christmas cards until a few years ago."

"Man, those were the days." Doug shakes his head. "Are you working?"

"I just read for a guest role in a new murder mystery series. I'm up for the bad guy, a rich society matron."

"Did you get it?"

"Don't know yet. First I had to meet the new casting director. He's twelve." I laugh as Doug rolls his eyes. "I've got a callback at three."

"You? A callback. Man, what next?"

"Are you kidding? What actress isn't hankering for a series these days? I expect to see Meryl Streep sweeping in this afternoon hauling one of her Oscars in her handbag."

"So? Don't sell yourself short. You had a couple of good series and took home an Emmy."

"The embryo casting this wouldn't remember, Dougie."

He laughs. "You'll land it. Trust me." He sips his coffee, a grizzled native in his trademark worn-out safari jacket and two-day stubble.

A wave of emotion engulfs me, remembering how kind Dougie was to me years ago when I was still married to my first husband. When I needed a favor, Dougie was there.

As though reading my thoughts, he says, "Say, I was just reminded the other day—whatever became of your husband, if you don't mind me asking?"

"Dirck? I don't know. I haven't seen him in years. Probably still back in New York teaching acting."

"No, not him." Dougie gives me a quizzical look. "C'mon, Meggie. The property developer—aren't you still married to him?"

"Paul? I am, only—sorry. I try not to think about him."

"I'm not surprised you want to forget him, all things considered." I hold my breath, hoping Dougie will move on, but it's not the case. "I probably shouldn't bring this up, but Edie and I were down near San Diego visiting her niece, and, damn, I coulda sworn I saw him coming out of a restaurant as we were going in."

"Couldn't have been. It's almost certain he's dead."

"Dead? I'm sorry, Meg. I didn't know that. I just remember hearing he was missing. Well, sure looked like him. Handsome devil. Big, broad-shouldered. Of course, I didn't get to know him like I knew Dirck, but—"

Dougie gazes at the space around my left ear, the way he always did when he took me aside on the set to give direction. Still not looking me in the eye, his voice soft, he says, "I sort of lost track when Edie got sick, but I remember reading about it in the newspaper last year. He was kidnapped or something, right?"

My throat tightens. "It might've been a hoax. But who knows? The FBI seems to think Paul set it up himself." Anxious to move on, I pat his hand. "I'm so sorry about Edie's stroke. I should've kept in touch, but so much was going on the past few months—"

"I know. Me, too. I kept thinking about calling and just never got around to it. You must've been going through hell. I'm sorry, kid."

"So how's Edie doing?" I ask, determined to change the subject.

"Hanging in there. Never complains."

"Maybe I could drop by for a visit one day—"

"Please. Anytime. You need any of those boxes you stored in my garage?"

"Yikes, I almost forgot. It's just books and stuff. You want me to get them out of there?"

"Nah, leave 'em. They're not in my way." Doug sips his coffee, then shakes his head again. I can see he's not finished with Paul. "Of course, I only met the guy a couple times up at your place. Funny thing is, he sort of hit me up, too."

"Dougie, you never told me you invested with Paul!"

"Turns out I didn't. It was right around the time Edie started going downhill, so I backed off. It kinda scares me now to think how I would've got by if I'd invested, you know?"

I nod. Ice masses in my chest. I know only too well how it feels to lose everything. But it's even worse to think about the friends that Paul roped in. Facing some of them in the aftermath was painful, often ugly, but the living hell of it was knowing there was nothing I could do to help make it right, to give back what they had lost. Paul disappeared, vanishing without a trace, leaving nothing behind to recoup.

Dougie pushes his plate away and licks his thumb. "You know, despite all the bad stuff that came out about him, the guy had a lot of charm. I guess that's how they get away with their schemes."

I tuck the last of my sandwich in my mouth, hoping to avoid having to comment. Dougie watches me chew, waiting until I finally swallow before speaking again. "Then again, maybe he didn't."

"What?"

"Get away with it. You say he's dead?"

"Most likely. They never found a body, but—"

"You're not sure, then?"

"No, but what does it matter? He's gone. Dead or alive, he's out of my life." Even to my own ears, it's a bad line reading. I tense, knowing Dougie won't buy it, either.

He looks out the window, then slowly back at me, his head cocked to one side in a gesture I remember well. "Jinx wouldn't let it go at that. She'd wanna get to the bottom of it, don'tcha think?" His eyes flicker. He's heard my breath catch.

"Sorry, Dougie. Without the swallowtail coat I'm not Jinx." My smile is so tight my cheeks ache.

"I only meant she'd want to know. Wouldn't you like to know?"

"Sure. So would the FBI, the U.S Attorney's Office, and a whole slew of people out a helluva lot of money. Personally, I'm just glad it's not front-page news anymore. Maybe everyone will forget. I'm certainly not going to be the one to dredge it up again." I can feel Dougie pulling in to a close-up, so I play it small, keeping it light. "Crime-busting is a lot more fun when it's scripted and you're the one solving it. I can handle my share of media attention, too, but not when it's camped on my doorstep. I was praying one of the Kardashians would pull a trigger, or at least shoplift."

"Hell, maybe even Alec Baldwin acting up again, you know?" Doug smiles, and we exchange a look. We've both worked with Alec Baldwin. "Sorry, kid. I'm sure there were people who thought you were in on it."

"Probably still are. Notice I'm not flashing any diamonds. Maybe I should've just kept traveling."

"Nah, running away never works." Dougie's face softens. "I'm glad you came back. If you don't deal with it, you can end up feeling like something on the sole of a shoe."

I nod. Feeling like a piece of crap is nothing new to me these days.

"It's a good thing Edie was with me that day, or I'd probably have said something to that S.O.B." He gives me a look, then pushes his chair back. "Anyway, gotta hit the road. They've got me editing another retrospective. What the hell, everything's a compilation now. Cheap and fills air time." He stands, and I rise to give him a hug.

"Take care of yourself."

"You bet. Good seeing you again, kid." He pats my arm, then reaches for his tray.

"Leave it, Doug. I'll get it."

"Yeah?"

"All in a day's work."

"Guess I'm jinxed again," he says, mimicking Winston's closing line of every episode. "Awfully good of you, my dear."

Dougie shuffles toward the door. Once he's out of sight, I slide his untouched lettuce and tomato onto my plate. A burst of nervous energy surges through me. Maybe it's the rush of nourishment and caffeine. More likely it's the mention of Paul. If I'd run into him instead of Doug, what would I have done? Strangled him? Shot him? Just screamed at him?

I rummage in my shoulder bag for the clipping I tore from a newspaper I found on a counter in a café south of San Francisco in early January. I was on my third refill of coffee by the time I turned to the tattered remains of the *Chronicle*'s business section. Below the fold, my eyes latched onto a double column about the Los Angeles City Council passing a ridgeline ordinance. Accompanying it was a photograph of a canyon construction site, with the caption: PROPERTY OF FUGITIVE DEVELOPER PAUL C. STEPHENS CITED IN CLAIMS OF GRADING ABUSES.

It was a shock to see Paul's name in print again, even more so finding him designated a fugitive. For once, my name wasn't mentioned in connection with his, a good omen. *Not* a good omen was spotting my waitress, slack-jawed and heavyset, her hand cupped over her mouth, talking with a woman at the far end of the lunch counter. Both were staring at me. I jammed the clipping into my bag, yanked my last few dollars from my wallet, and got up to leave.

I drove as far as Half Moon Bay, considering my options. My tires were practically bald, my wallet thin. Why was I on the run? Paul was the fugitive, not me. He was off somewhere living on other people's millions, while I was scraping bottom. I should have listened to Pat, my tough-as-nails agent, when I'd called her at the height of the media clamor.

"Pat, I'm going nuts here. I need to work. A location job would be great."

"Yeah, I hear you," she said in her husky rasp. "But I'm not having lotsa luck. There's a lotta resistance."

"Really? Because I've got media parked on my lawn that can't wait to get me on camera."

"I know, kiddo. So, what can I say? Maybe you need PR that specializes in crisis control."

But I hadn't gone that route. Instead I hit the road. Maybe I'd reached the end of it. I pulled into a lay-by and punched up Pat's direct line on my cell phone. I took a deep breath and said, "Hey, Pat, it's me."

She let out a long, low sigh that sounded like a year's worth of waiting and wondering. Then, "What's up, kiddo? How ya doing?"

"Good. I'm fine. Doing okay. I'm coming back and just wondered if you could get me some auditions."

The weather and pilot season are only two of the reasons I made my way back to L.A. after coming across that newspaper clipping about Paul. The third is that I need my life back.

I push aside my tray and settle in with the script. Still thinking of Paul, I try to project myself into the role of a murderess. If I had the chance, would I hire a hit man to kill him?

Chapter Two

As I cross the studio lot, a passing stagehand flashes me that unmistakable look that means I've been recognized as Jinx. Whatever other roles I've played in my career, Jinx is the character everyone remembers.

Then again, maybe the double take is the result of the stock photo of Paul and me that ran with every story about the scandal. One headline read: JINX COSTARS IN REAL-LIFE CAPER. How many people now automatically cross-reference "Meg Barnes" with "con-man husband"?

I take the elevator back up to the third floor of the production office. At the end of the corridor, half a dozen actresses sit on folding metal chairs, waiting to audition. I recognize most of the faces that look up with smiles a little too bright. How many of them are dredging up last year's headlines as they watch me make my way toward the producer's office?

Jenna, a tall, athletic blonde who once guest-starred with me in an episode on a medical series, leans against a doorjamb, script in hand. She looks up and taps my arm with her script. "Hey, you. I haven't seen you in ages. How's it going?"

"Great. How's it with you?"

"Fine. They're running behind, of course."

"Of course. What else is new?" I reach for the sign-in sheet. "I see they've rounded up the usual suspects."

Jenna laughs. "Just so we know when the last plane to Paris leaves."

We both laugh, though I'm not sure either of us knows what the joke is. *Why did I have to say "suspects"? Stop fixating! These women have nothing more on their minds than getting the damn job.*

The truth is any of us "callbacks" could play this guest star role. Only one brave soul has let her hair go more salt than pepper. Another has packed on a bulging midriff. I barely recognize a former supermodel-turned-actress whose face looks Saran Wrapped, evidence of a few too many trips to a plastic surgeon. Otherwise, we all look reasonably well preserved.

I take a seat next to a water cooler and tune in to the general conversation. For some, acting has become a sideline. Two women have become real estate agents; one is working toward her marriage and family counseling license; another is a landscape designer. The erstwhile model with the taut skin and trout lips owns a Pilates studio. Jenna runs a dog kennel with her actor-husband. Three are divorced (one still in the throes), and several are grandmothers. Business cards are exchanged and lunch dates promised while we wait for Todd-with-the-goopy-hair to escort each of us in. *How many of these gals had to pre-audition?*

At last it's my turn, and I follow Todd down the corridor to the producer's office.

"Hey, everyone," Todd says, before I've even crossed the threshold. "Meg Barnes, this is Lenny Bishop, our director. Melody Cohen, associate producer. Jake Ellsworth, writer. Take a seat, Meg."

I'm surprised that the young men and woman sprawled on the sofas are complete strangers to me. I feel like someone's dressed-up mom wandering into a dorm lounge. They half-rise as they repeat their names, each one lifting a hand in a kind of salute. The only name I catch is Lenny Bishop, the director, stick-thin with a stubbly beard. "Hey, glad you could come in," he says, sinking back into the couch.

As I'm taking a seat, a straight-back chair facing the window, the pretty brunette producer mentions she wrote a high school term paper (*last year, perhaps*?) on female empowerment, using the character I played in *Holiday* to illustrate a positive role model.

"You mean Jinx? I can't believe you watched the series. It was on ages ago."

"Oh, yeah, but I've seen reruns. My dad was a really big fan." She hauls up a weighty mass of curly hair, flops it over her head, and shakes it onto her other shoulder. "It's just so neat to meet you in person. For me, it was this really big epiphany when I got that it was Jinx, who was this *assistant person,* who really solved the crimes, not The Magician, right? I mean, there you have it!" she says triumphantly. "You portrayed this woman who was really hot and super smart—how bad is that?" She settles back on the sofa, pleased with her epiphany. "It really was this seminal thing, you know? You were just so ahead of your time."

Her colleagues nod, no doubt envisioning a seismic shift in gender relationships should her term paper circulate around Hollywood. Meanwhile, I wonder if her dad also had an old poster of me in the satin shorts and swallowtail jacket hanging over his bed. I was, indeed, hot stuff. But that was then. Today I just hope this producerette can see her way to casting her role model as a murderess.

"Well, thank you all very much. What can I say? Jinxed again!"

Everyone laughs and nods. Then the laughter fades into an awkward silence. Lenny leans toward me and clears his throat. "So, um, we're sorry to hear about your husband. Had to be awful."

Melody nods vigorously, her hair bouncing on her shoulders. "For the record, I don't think you had anything to do with it. I mean, the stolen money, or—well, everything."

My lips freeze, but all I can think of is that licking them will make me look guilty. I lick them anyway and say, "No, you're right. Of course."

I look to Todd, who looks at the ceiling, then says, "Okay, ready then? Let's do the scene when the detective tracks you down leaving the charity luncheon, and then segue into the meeting with your attorney, okay?"

I shift in my chair, taking a moment before I look up and find Todd staring at me intently, his foot jiggling impatiently.

JANE ELLIS

Sorry, Detective Farraday. You've missed the fashion show, but I can tell you this: Stripes are not in this season.

DET. FARRADAY

Oh, that's okay, Mrs. Ellis. We've switched to orange jumpsuits. We might just have one in your size.

JANE ELLIS

Sorry to disappoint you, but my wardrobe's complete. Now, if you'll excuse me—

DET. FARRADAY

Just one question, if you don't mind—

JANE ELLIS

I do mind. You're perfectly aware that I'm president of the auxiliary and that this is our biggest fund-raiser of the year. Accosting me in full view of everyone amounts to harassment. Would you like me to call my attorney?

DET. FARADAY

That's probably a good idea. You see, I've got orders to take you in. You're under arrest, Mrs. Ellis.

JANE ELLIS

You can't be serious. The district attorney's wife sits on the board with me.

DET. FARADAY

Sounds like you've got yourself a good character witness. But murder's murder.

I flip pages to the next scene, although the lines are so familiar I hardly need look at the script. Todd clears his throat and launches into the first speech, now playing the role of my attorney, Harry Walton.

Still haughty, but now frightened, I insist I had no knowledge of my husband's infidelity, that it's ludicrous to suggest I could possibly want to hire someone to shoot him. The scene reaches a climax at the Act One break. I demand that my attorney arrange bail, banging my script on the desk for emphasis.

The casting director blinks at me, then looks to Lenny Bishop as though waiting for him to call recess. Why do I half-expect young Todd to clap his hands like a two-year-old and burble, "All done, all done!"

The assemblage on the couch is a silent chorus of bobble-heads, their faces noncommittal. Lenny Bishop brushes his hand across his stubbly chin and says, "Yeah. Hey, okay. Great stuff. Thanks for coming in."

"Thank you." I rise quickly, smile, and beat it out of Dodge. No handshakes, no farewells, nothing that'll give them second thoughts. I close the door behind me. The hallway is empty. No additional actresses have arrived to read for the role. I scan the names on the list as I sign out. One of us will be getting a call from her agent within the next hour or so.

Great stuff? What does that mean?

I make my way across the steaming lot wondering whether the young Turks in their wrinkled shirts and blue jeans will settle on me, perhaps the only actress on their audition list who hasn't earned a license to do something else—or forked over the price of a midsize SUV for a facelift. I tell myself it's not just because I can't afford to spruce up or that I'm squeamish about cold knives on warm flesh. It's because I don't *need* one. And I sure as hell wouldn't inject poison between my eyes to immobilize a little crease or two. On the other hand, would that make the difference, give me a competitive edge? There's nothing like an audition to make an actress feel like she needs a complete overhaul with replacement parts. I take a deep breath and exhale slowly. The hardest part is the waiting.

It's not just the money, though that's key, after all. But with a job, everything in my day-to-day, godforsaken life goes on hold. I won't have to think about anything except acting. I'm handed a script, and I'm told when and where to appear for wardrobe. I'm fed, watered, made up, clothed, and led to the set, which is the most gratifying, pleasurable place on Earth as far as I'm concerned.

My shoulder bag begins to vibrate. I scramble for my cell phone, find it, and flip it open. *Please, God, let it be my agent.*

Instead it's Carol Baskin, her voice breathy and rushed, so I know she's on her treadmill. "Meg? Honestly, you're impossible to get hold of these days. Weren't we supposed to meet for lunch this week?"

"Carol, I'm so sorry. I meant to get back to you. I've just been busy. You know, pilot season." Lunch with Carol means an afternoon at Fred Segal's watching her buy shredded jeans at a price that would feed a family of six for a week.

"Well, good for you. I hope you get something. Now, listen. Forget lunch, can you fill out our table Friday night? The Hilton. Cocktails and silent auction at six thirty. Dinner at seven."

"What's the disease this time?"

"Hey, some of us give a damn." She laughs, her signature guffaw making me smile. "Be a sport, okay? Sid had to buy a table, and I have to fill it. I promise you'll be out before ten. We'll have fun."

"Business attire?"

"Suit yourself, pun intended. But I'm going a little dressier. You always look great. Want us to pick you up?"

"I'll meet you there."

"Perfect. Hey, it's been a while. Can't wait to see you again."

"Me, too." I jam the phone back in my bag, still amazed that people can reach me without knowing where I am or what I'm doing. So, what could be better to look forward to than a charity do at the Hilton, with drinks, dinner, and a goodie bag stuffed with the de rigueur T-shirt, CD, and shampoo—maybe even a gift certificate to a nail salon?

Besides, Carol, my former roommate and an old pal from my studio contract days, is the closest thing I have to a friend these days. She gave up acting years ago when she married Sid and took on the role of

Hollywood power wife. It was Sid Baskin, my longtime entertainment attorney, who got me through the worst of the mess with Paul. Unfortunately, the IRS saw my joint accounts with Paul, not to mention the press photos of me accompanying him to dinners and various other events where clients were present, as evidence that I was involved in his scam. In the end, I lost everything. Sid lost a lot, too, but his financial exposure wasn't anywhere near as devastating as mine.

In the bitter aftermath, when all I wanted to do was hide out, the Baskins invited me to stay in their pool house. I burrowed in like a slug, rarely venturing out. For days on end, curled in a wicker armchair, I napped to avoid thinking. I wasn't great company, and I'm sure I was a worry to them. But despite their insistence that I was welcome to stay, I moved out after a couple of weeks. Even though Carol and I had once roomed together, I couldn't handle living within sight of their bedroom window. They meant well, but I began to feel like I was on suicide watch. Either Sid or Carol, sometimes both, would drop by on the hour to ask, "You doin' okay, sweetie?"

No, I was not doing okay. Not with bankruptcy and foreclosure hearings pending. Not with even close friends wondering: *What did she know? When did she know it?* Instead, I'd packed up and hit the road, abandoning the few options I had left to salvage anything of my former life. Leaving town wasn't the smartest move I could have made, but neither could I bear living in a goldfish bowl with piranha circling.

Of course, if I hadn't set out on what became an extended road trip, I would never have discovered the Ritz-Volvo could be so accommodating. Not since Girl Scouts, sleeping in a pup tent with my gear in a duffel bag, had I felt so carefree and adventurous. Living simply, frugally, became a game. I reveled in my resourcefulness. I rediscovered myself to be an enjoyable, easy-going companion, willing to venture down side roads and indulge in unhurried reflection. I like to think of that time as a sabbatical, rather than my year on the lam.

I find my car where I parked it on the third level of the high-security parking structure. I double-click the remote control on my car key (how often have I used it to actually *find* my car?) and climb into my pre owned sedan, bought largely because it had tinted windows and a big trunk and cost a whole lot less to run than my vintage Jag convertible.

Once inside the steamy Volvo, I unbutton my suit jacket and wriggle out of my skirt. A wardrobe change is in order. With cold, clammy sweat drying in salt licks on my face and neck, I kick off my shoes and peel off my hose.

My suit goes on a padded hanger, joining my other dress clothes hanging on a pole wedged above the backseat windows. My good shoes go into a flannel bag under the passenger seat. Jeans and a T-shirt are neatly stacked with other folding clothes on one side of the rear seat. My sandals are in a box on the floor with my running shoes. Tidiness makes all the difference. I try to keep my little nest clean and well dusted. Windex and paper towels are wedged between the front passenger seats. As always, I slide my hand under the folded blankets and feel the smooth surface of my laptop, safely tucked out of sight.

I don't know whether the Baskins are aware of my current itinerant circumstances, but I'd like to think they have no idea I've taken up residence in my Volvo rather than return to their pool house.

Not all that long ago one of their invitations to a charity function would have sent me scurrying to Neiman Marcus and the second-floor designer dresses. Not that I ever wantonly threw money around or lived beyond my means. I saved against the rainy days forecast in any actor's career, investing even when all I could see down the road was more sunshine and fair weather. Who could have predicted I would open my life to a dam-busting monsoon—then drown in the deluge?

I peel out of the parking ramp, tires squealing on the tight turns. I should've traded in for a fuel-efficient hybrid when I had the chance. I could have been both homeless and green. But then, who knew gas prices would go through the roof? My trip to the Valley and back will cost me at least a buck, a hefty investment that'd better pay off with a job.

I unlock my jaw and loosen my grip on the steering wheel. I can't afford to have a stroke any more than I can afford a trip to Needless Markup. I delve into my storehouse of happy recollections that see me through bouts of anxiety—and, to call it what it is, self-pity. I'd loathe anyone else's pity, but I feel entirely justified in a private wallow of my own now and again. When I'm really feeling down, I picture my Spanish bungalow in Coldwater Canyon, with its swimming pool, herb garden, sweet-smelling bed linens, and the housekeeper who came three days a week—and imagine having it all back again. What wouldn't I give for a dip in my pool right now? Tossing a steak on my grill while I sip a Cabernet would be heaven.

With that thought in mind, I could go for a drink. How long has it been since I treated myself to a frosty glass of white wine at my favorite watering hole? I pull off Ventura Boulevard and swing into the parking lot behind the Valley Grill, a '60s holdover that hasn't sacrificed its banquette seating, checkered tablecloths, or generous happy hour spread. Easing into a shaded slot near the rear entrance by the kitchen, I check my watch. Ten minutes past happy hour. Dinnertime.

I mount the cracked cement steps at the rear of the restaurant and tug at the old screen door. It comes unstuck and grates noisily at the intrusion. The steamy kitchen socks me with its moist smell of hot grease and fruity disinfectant. Eddie, the fry cook, turns his head and shoots me a gap-toothed grin. "There ya are, sugar. I was hopin' you'd be stoppin' in soon. Saw you on *Rockford Files* the other night."

"The gift that keeps on giving, Eddie." A rerun means a residual check will soon find its way to my post office box. "You must've been up mighty late."

"Watched the whole thing when I saw your mug. You don't age a day. How you do it?"

"A steady diet of your chili." He laughs. I watch him lift a hefty pot onto the cooker, marveling that his stringy arms can hoist more than a spoon. "How're you doing, Eddie?"

"Can't complain." He dips a ladle into the pot. "Want a taste?"

"How about some to go on the way out?"

He nods. "Sure thing. Don't forget now. I'll have it packed up."

I salute him with a slice of warm corn bread I help myself to from a basket on the counter. I've been a sucker for Eddie's corn bread and chili since the days when he was working a catering truck on location. I'm only too happy to have scored a late-night snack.

Jimmy, the bartender, peers at me as I enter the twilight gloom of the taproom. The former UCLA quarterback, who was Winston Sykes's stuntman on *Holiday,* is now paunchy and balding, his hands arthritic. He pulls a bottle of wine out of the cooler and struggles to uncork it. "You barely come around anymore. You tired of the neighborhood?" He slides a glass onto the bar and pours to the brim.

"It's a long haul, Jimmy. A special trip, but I do it just to see you."

I climb onto the bar stool and sip the house white. There's no need to mention to Jimmy that my drop-ins are infrequent because I have to figure in gas money besides the bar bill and tip. He usually pours me a second glass on the house, but even with the free buffet, the margin on grazing to out-of-pocket expense is tight.

"You classy broads are too good for us, that's what." He slumps against the bar and folds his arms across his belly, glowering. "Don't come around at all if you're not going to come around, know what I mean?"

"Sure, Jimmy." His hearing's shot so I make sure not to turn my head when I'm talking to him. Most of the regulars know to do the same.

I bide my time, waiting for the joint to fill up before chowing down. The trick to this— and there *is* a trick—is to nibble while loitering at one end of the steam table. I eat a meatball, my eyes glued to some hockey game playing on the TV screen. My toothpick spears another gravy-soaked chunk before I move on to the guacamole and potato skins. High-fat, high-carb, but it's not like I do this every day. I feed when I can, like a jungle cat. I settle back on my bar stool with a saucer of chicken wings. My glass has been refilled.

That's when the call comes. As soon as I feel my shoulder bag vibrate, I know it's Pat, my agent.

"Good girl, you bagged it," she rasps. "I just had a feeling about this one. Here's the dope—ready?"

I wave down Jimmy. He hands me a pen. I pin a napkin under my elbow and scribble notes as fast as Pat spits out the deal: money (yeeeeeah!), billing, start date, wardrobe call, and— "They're messengering a script, so—"

"Wait, have 'em deliver it to your office, and I'll pick it up tonight from the security guard. Can you do that?"

"Sure, but—"

"I won't be home to sign for it. Besides, I'll be going right by your office. It's less of a hassle, okay?"

"Well, you're the boss. Congrats, Meg. This is a good one. You deserve it."

Pat, short, squat, and tough as an old boot, has represented me since my studio contract days. I even followed her when she and two other agents left to set up their own agency. Two mergers later, it's now one of the top agencies in town. I know I have only to ask and she'd advance me some cash, but I can't make myself do it. Word gets around, no matter what. I don't want to be anyone's lunchtime gossip.

I snap the lid on my cell phone and take a sip of wine. Jimmy sets his meaty forearms on the bar and leans close. "Hey, congratulations, kid. Lemme buy you a drink."

"Hell, let me buy *you* a drink!"

He gives me that look. Where is it writ that all bartenders are now in the Program? "You staying for dinner?"

"No, I'd better get back over the hill. Just the check."

"Your money's no good here, kid." He winks. Why is it that now, with a job and money coming my way, the drinks are on the house? I pull my billfold out of my bag to leave a tip. Jimmy smacks my hand. "Forget it. Just dress up the bar here a little more often, okay? It makes life sweeter."

I hoist my knees onto the bar stool, lean in, and plant a wet one on his kisser. "There's a place in heaven for you, buddy. But not anytime soon." I climb back down, not at all sure what I meant, but Jimmy's eyes mist over, so I couldn't have gone too wrong. I make my way through the kitchen, pick up my chili, and leave another smacker on Eddie's cheek.

"Take it easy," he says, his lips settling into a pucker around missing front teeth. "You get yourself back here more often, you hear?"

"You bet, Eddie." I suspect there's probably a slice or two of corn bread in the brown sack with the container of chili. I stow the bag next to me on the front seat and pull out of the parking lot, heading toward the canyon.

Things could be worse. I have a job and a full belly. My tires are holding up. Moths haven't got at my good suit. Unlike legions of casualties of my hippy-dippy–turned–yuppie generation, I don't crave drugs or booze. I don't have to attend twelve-step meetings or visit a probation officer. I don't even have to face a vengeful former husband: The first one is a vague memory, and the second is dead . . . *I hope.*

Chapter Three

I crest Mulholland just as the sun blazing low on the horizon shows Hollywood what Technicolor means, a riotous Looney Tunes rainbow that's missing nothing more than "Th-th-that's all, folks!"

I pull into my favorite lay-by at the top of the canyon, my sense of well-being expanding. I don't owe anybody anything, and I have all the time in the world. I bound out of the car, my eyes traveling across the mauve-shadowed hillside to the far reaches of misty coastline where *twenty-six miles across the sea, Santa Catalina is a-waitin' for me . . .*

I hum a few bars, rocking on my heels, picturing the island coming into view as I tack hard to the right, sails billowing in the strong breeze. Abalone for dinner, a dry white chilling in an ice bucket, and the sea glittering with fresh-tossed diamonds—who *wouldn't* feel like a rich lady?

A chill breeze sweeps down the hillside. I close my eyes against the dust swirling across the road, and turn away. The euphoria I felt moments ago vanishes, along with my view of the faraway coastline. Harder to block out is my mental image of the thirty-two-foot *WindStar,* now docked in some stranger's boat slip.

I poke the toe of my sandal in the gravel, kick hard, and send a dusty spray into the weeds. A rustling erupts in a scrubby patch of sage. I've disturbed some small creature's peaceful sanctuary, and I feel even worse. Live and let live, or at least do no harm.

I look to the right, taking in the scarred hillside and flattened ridgelines ringed by massive walls of concrete. Bulldozed mounds of earth, scraped up from a cavernous pit in the hilltop that's now half-filled with briny sludge, stand lumped along a rutted pathway. Tattered yellow flags, staked into raw earth, delineate six foundation pads at staggered elevations in a vast, graded expanse. Now an abandoned construction site, it was once meant to be my dream house, with views stretching from the mountains to the sea.

But first it was to be a model home, custom designed to lure the fabulously rich to the other villas Paul would build atop the canyon. He dreamed of turning that steep and unstable slope, best suited to mountain goats, into a gated, terraced community of luxurious mansions. He told me so on our second date, when he parked his four-wheel drive where the asphalt ended and the rock-strewn path began.

Before I had a chance to unbuckle my seat belt, Paul was already standing on the hillside, pocketing his car key. For a big man, he was surprisingly agile. Every motion easy, stoked with power. He rolled up his sleeves and looked back at me, the sun glancing off the bronzed slope of his forehead. "C'mon, sugar. What're you waiting for?"

My heart lurched. I reached for the door, breathless to keep up. He slung a blanket under his arm and binoculars around his neck, and we were off. The two of us hiked, his hand reaching back for mine, as we climbed up the slippery hillside to the topmost point of the ridge.

"Where you're standing right now, sugar, God help ya, that's what you'll see every mornin' when you wake up," he'd said, swamping me with his bluegrass charm. "And the stars at night, you'll want to hold out your hand and let 'em tickle your fingertips, that's how close they'll feel." He put his arm around me, a burly mass of muscle that tugged me close and made my knees go weak.

"Everyone tells me it's impossible, but they're wrong. I know I can build up here. We've got the means, the technology. We can actually move mountains, if we have the will to do so." His voice in my ear spoke to my soul.

"What'll it take to make it happen?" I breathed.

"I just need someone to believe in me," he whispered.

That was the sucker punch, the Ayn Rand call to arms. By then my soul had conveyed a message to a moistening, always receptive organ in my nether regions that took it from there. At the other end of the circuit, my brain received an urgent S.O.S.—*he needs me!*—then promptly shut down. I'd like to be able to say that Paul didn't take me then and there, but that would not be true. The blanket came in handy; the binoculars did not.

Like a hound dog marking his territory, Paul laid claim to me in the rugged terrain he promised we'd inhabit one day. Meanwhile, looking up at wide, blue sky, my back pressed into the warm earth, I laid claim to ecstasy in CinemaScope. Afterward, Paul and I made our way back to his four-wheel drive and sped away to my own house in another canyon. For more of the same.

I shiver, not just from the night air. Below me, smoky shadows obliterate the modest bungalows and tract houses dwarfed by the concrete retaining walls Paul built to hold his dreams. The folks below awaken each morning in the shade cast by the Great Wall. At night, they can no longer see the stars. Wildlife that once flourished here has moved on to more-open territory.

I climb back into the Volvo and join the last of the rush hour traffic heading toward the Westside from the Valley. By now, a messenger will have delivered my script, and there will be free parking available on a side street near my agent's office. I punch up a Diana Krall CD, good downhill listening, and practically coast straight to my destination, traffic lights favoring me all the way.

A note attached to the script I pick up gives me pause: Location shooting is in Pasadena. That means gas money and early makeup calls. Adjustments in my living arrangements will be necessary if I'm to be on the road, bathed and well rested, before six every morning.

I'm still considering my options when I pull into a parking spot at my health club, the best bargain outside of happy hour. At the particular time I was contemplating my bleak, bankrupt future, Carol mentioned that she was joining a new health club and wondered if I wanted to be her "buddy."

"It's that dangerous?" I asked.

"Spare me. It's just this special bring-a-buddy offer for the opening. It's a twofer, so if I join, you get in free, but you'll have to pay a portion of the co-monthly. You want to go for a 'complimentary' and check it out?"

We did, and I jumped at it, especially since I was allowed to take an extended leave of absence. Even now, I can't believe my luck. It makes my life possible. Validated parking. Opens at five a.m., closes at eleven p.m. Everything's laid on: showers, shampoo, towels, deodorant, hair dryers, hand lotion, and lockers. There are even bowls of cotton balls and safety razors. The place is big enough to be anonymous, and no one cares how often I come, how long I stay. Behind the sauna and steam room there are lounge chairs that no one else seems to have discovered. I can work out, hang out, a cell phone connecting me to the outside world. There's also a wall outlet I can use to recharge the battery.

Of course, I never see my "buddy" Carol at the club. She uses her gym at home and books a trainer three times a week.

I take an eight o'clock Zen Stretch class, then curl up on a lounge chair with my script. Eating at me is how I can make it into the club for a shower and still beat early-morning traffic for a makeup call when I film in Pasadena next week. Every move requires careful planning these days.

Shortly before eleven o'clock closing, I retrieve my car and head for my old neighborhood. The 1930s-era Spanish bungalow I once called home has been transformed into something resembling a massive pink Taco Bell without the neon sign—or perhaps one is on order. The first time I passed it, soon after moving in with Sid and Carol, demolition was already in progress. I somehow stopped myself from scaling the chain-link fence to beat off the workmen tearing away at her. Instead, I slumped down in my car and watched as they stripped flesh from her bones, leaving her exposed to the midday sun. I'd bought the house at a bargain price—with earnings from my first network series—from the estate of an early-talkies screenwriter. Being stripped of the first and only home I'd ever owned was more than I could bear. I left town a few days later, feeling as though my heart and soul had been torn from my body.

I park up the street in a cul-de-sac off the main road. Then, my overnight bag slung on my shoulder, I slip through a break in a boxwood hedge. In the shadow of a sycamore tree, I pause, listening to the sounds of the night. The lights are off in Marjorie Singleton's house. I don't know Marjorie well, though her garage was our customary neighborhood polling station. Whenever I voted, it was in that clean, spacious garage, her Bentley parked on the street to make way for a bank of polling booths. I'm sure Marjorie, if she knew, would be only too happy to extend a neighborly welcome to me.

It's Wednesday: Marjorie's son, who lives in Encino, is home with his family and won't stop by again until Friday afternoon, when he'll bring her Chinese takeaway. I know the rituals; I've watched Jake Singleton come and go. This is a safe night, and all is quiet.

I follow the flagstone walkway around the swimming pool, past the rose bed, and turn the knob on the side door to the garage. Inside, I slip quietly along the west wall to the workbench Marjorie's long-dead husband built, and set down my carryall. I plug my laptop and cell phone into an outlet to top up, then move through the darkness to Marjorie's Bentley. She rarely drives it anymore.

I toss my sleeping bag into the backseat, then strip off my jeans and sandals. I always sleep in a T-shirt and underwear, my shoes and pants handy in case of an intruder. Tonight I can pack in a good six hours and be gone before the gardeners arrive. On those nights when I've had to spend the night in my own car, I remain fully clothed, doors locked, windows open no more than a fingertip wide.

Usually I find a spot on the street around Holmby Park, the gates to the late Aaron Spelling's former mansion within spitting distance. Should his ghostly presence be hovering above his former abode, I can imagine his bemusement at seeing me camping out a stone's throw from his old bedroom window. I still get residuals from his shows, blessed checks from repeats of mindless fluff that pay my car insurance and buy me another month at the health club. But those nights parked on the street, hiding under spread newspapers, even with the tinted windows, are the tough ones, the only time it really hits me that I'm homeless.

More accurately, I am without a home. I am not actually a homeless person. I always manage to have a roof over my head, even if it comes with four wheels and a dashboard. I'm not a bag lady, a bum. I'm not a thief, though I suppose I've stolen a few pennies' worth of kilowatt juice from Marjorie. But the backseat of an old lady's car is only temporary accommodation, not home, sweet home. I awaken too often in the night, dozing more than sleeping.

I slide my legs deeper into my sleeping bag and hug my arms for warmth, trying to stop the rat-wheel of worry in my head. I am far from complacent about the fix I'm in. When I bump my head against the car ryall, a whiff of chili hits my nostrils. Would a slice of Eddie's corn bread put me to sleep? I drift off, savoring the thought while my mind roils in a stew of anxiety.

Little wonder I'm propelled into one of my agonizing furniture dreams. Like any actor, I'm plagued with the usual panic dreams, such as: I arrive on the set and don't know my lines because a) I wasn't sent a script, b) I was sent the wrong script, c) I forgot I had the job. I've had flying dreams, falling dreams, climbing dreams, naked dreams, and losing my purse/ticket/keys dreams like everyone else, but I hate owning up to having furniture dreams. I've never known anyone to say, "Boy, I sure had some furniture dream last night!"

Essentially, in this takeoff on a chase dream, I'm forced to jump from end table to dining table to sofa to the tops of various appliances, packing boxes, assorted chairs, and coffee tables. I used to think clutter was the problem, so I worked at being ever more organized and tidy. I still had the dreams. Then came a revelation: It turned out *furniture* was the basic problem.

I discovered it by accident. My first husband, Dirck, a self-described pack rat, and I were separated for several months early in my career when I was hired for a role in a miniseries shooting in Los Angeles. He remained in our New York rent-controlled apartment to do an Off-Broadway play. I moved into an unfurnished two-bedroom maisonette in West Hollywood and bought only bare necessities: a mattress, pillow, two sheets, a blanket, and some strictly utilitarian household goods. I lived that Spartan style for six months, blissfully happy.

No furniture, no furniture dreams. No husband, either. But I wasn't willing at the time to think Dirck might be the problem, even though the man never entered the apartment without bringing in something newly bought and never, ever discarded a single thing, including expired grocery coupons, empty coffee tins, egg cartons, broken appliances, and, indeed, *furniture* that was no longer of any use whatsoever. He'd saved every birthday card given him since childhood, each year's bounty in separate, neatly labeled packets. The space under the bed in our cramped New York apartment took on aspects of a landfill. My first husband's hoarding knew no bounds.

After my second marriage, when Paul moved into my Coldwater Canyon house, he brought with him only a laptop, a garment bag, and a small suitcase. He bought vast amounts of goods and services, but mostly as business-related gifts. His closet was spare. He was not the sort to accumulate stuff in drawers and cupboards. Who says you marry the same man twice?

A variation on the dream started up again after Paul vanished. *Furniture,* as it turned out, was not the problem this time. Indeed, *belongings,* and the *lack* of them, became a problem. For weeks after he disappeared I searched the house hoping to find among Paul's few possessions some clue to the man I apparently had not gotten to know at all well through courtship and almost two years of marriage. He left nothing of consequence behind, and I came to realize there'd been nothing in the first place.

Tonight—whether it's Doug's mention of Paul or fumes from Eddie's chili—my furniture dream attacks with a vengeance. I jump from place to place, urgently searching for something just beyond my reach. I hurtle through the maze of furniture, topple off a file cabinet, and feel myself falling, arms outstretched, my stomach churning in panic.

Moments later—or is it hours?—I'm fully awake and alert, every fiber of my being a listening device. What is it? What did I hear? My heart bangs in my ears as I strain to sort out the sounds. The irrigation system kicking in? A squirrel on the roof?

I slide free of my sleeping bag and reach for my jeans, sure now that what I'm hearing are footsteps falling softly on the flagstone walk. Who's coming for me? Who in hell knows I'm here?

I zip my jeans and pull sandals on my feet. I daren't open the door: The Bentley's interior lights will turn on. My heart flutters as the doorknob turns. I fumble inside my carryall, my fingers closing around a small can of pepper spray. I don't even know that the aerosol works. The container is old, and I've never had occasion to test it.

The garage door scrapes open. A beam of light arcs across the windshield. A male voice booms, "C'mon out. Now!"

I peer above the leather seat, directly into the beam of a flashlight, and raise my hands, my thumb curled around the small can of pepper spray. "It's okay. It's just me. I'm coming out."

"Whatever's in your hand, drop it. Just step out slowly."

I drop the can. It clatters on the cement floor. "I'm sorry. Is that you, Mr. Singleton? Please, I don't mean any harm."

"Just who the hell are you?"

"Uh, Margaret. From the neighborhood. Just down the street. Look, I had a fight with my husband, and—"

"Don't bullshit me. My mother's seen you sneaking in here before. I told her to call me if she saw you again. What the hell's going on?"

"I'll leave right now. I won't be back, I promise." My voice is barely a whisper. In the flare of the flashlight beam I see my laptop and cell phone plugged into the wall socket a good three feet away. I can't leave them behind. My mind races, plotting escape scenarios as I slowly hoist my carryall on my shoulder.

"Where do I know you from? You look like—"

"The neighborhood, that's all. I just needed a place for the night." A gate squawks noisily, followed by the fall of heavy feet. "The *police*? You didn't call them, did you?"

"It's the patrol guys, what do you think? Of course we'll call the police."

The information flashes through my brain. It's only the security bozos, not the police—yet. The flashlight beam plays across the floor of the garage. My eyes adjust. I see him now, a sandy-haired man in a windbreaker. I slide my foot closer to the workbench.

"Where do you get off thinking you can just break in here? What're you, crazy?" His voice sounds plaintive. Not angry. He glances over his shoulder and edges toward the door. Outside, plodding closer, shoes scrape and slap the flagstone walk.

"Mr. Singleton, I'm very sorry." I drop my voice, aiming for a register that sounds calm, in control. "Please give me a chance. I can explain everything. Please don't call the police. Please don't file a complaint. Trust me. Please."

"You know what you're asking? This is breaking and entering. You know that, right?"

"I know. I promise I won't do this again. Please."

He gives me a hard look, then turns the knob on the door. "In here," he calls out. My stomach turns over. Suddenly the flashlight arcs across the ceiling, leaving me in darkness. The door scrapes. Jake steps outside, holding on to the doorknob behind his back. "Looks like everything's okay."

"You sure, Mr. Singleton? We better check it out." The voice is hoarse, gruff with importance.

"Nah, I looked around."

I lunge for my laptop and cell phone, unplugging both and jamming them in my carryall. I swing around, yanking the sleeping bag out of the backseat and rolling it in my arms.

"Any problem, you gotta let us know." It's another voice, this one softer, lower pitched. "You want us to look around the bushes?"

"No, whoever it was is long gone. I heard someone running off earlier."

"Okeydokey. We'll be on the lookout. G'night, sir."

"Thanks a lot. Take it easy."

Why did Jake Singleton do that? I watch him turn back into the garage, his flashlight flicking around, sizing me up. I freeze, my heart thumping, wondering what I'm in for now.

"You said something about your husband? He's been giving you trouble? You don't look banged up. Are you hurt?"

"No, I'm not, it's just that—" I pull the sleeping roll directly in front of me and hug my carryall under my arm. "Look, it was wrong to sneak in here, but—honestly, I didn't have anywhere else to go."

"There are shelters, you know. There's no shame in going to one. If you're getting battered, they'll take you in. My wife and I give to one of those outfits downtown somewhere. If you need me to make a call—" He flips open his cell phone. "You got kids?"

"No. I really appreciate this. I can go now, really."

"Sure, whatever. It's up to you. It's just—I can't let you hide out in here, you know? Not with my mother on her own. If your husband's looking for you, you got to find some safe place. Anyone you can call?"

"Yeah, I'm fine. My car's just down the street."

"You want me to walk you?"

"Really, I'm fine. I can't thank you enough." I edge past him and step onto the damp grass. "You've been very kind."

"Just take care of yourself, okay?"

I make myself walk at a steady pace up the flagstone walk, skirting the swimming pool, knowing his eyes are on me. I slip through the break in the hedge, just before the garden gate, and hurry down the slope, keeping to the shadows. I stop abruptly, spotting the two security guards circling my Volvo like road kill. One of them kicks at the front fender; the other peers into the passenger window, then spits into the bushes.

A minute passes. I have to pee, but I don't dare move. My Margot Kidder nightmare isn't over yet. I could still end up with a "caught in the headlights" shot of myself disheveled, my arms clutching a sleeping bag, splashed on the cover of a supermarket tabloid: "ALL IN A DAY'S WORK! FORMER 'HOLIDAY' STAR DOWN AND OUT IN BEVERLY HILLS!"

Tears sting my cheeks. Wouldn't the paparazzi love this shot? Jinx, face puffy, mascara smudged, lurking in someone's hedge. I press my forehead into my sleeping bag, recalling poor Margot, missing her front teeth and in need of meds, cowering in someone's backyard. What's my excuse? If I'm busted now, it's the end of my job next week, the end of pulling myself out of this confounding mess I'm in.

I watch the two guards, Laurel and Hardy in size and shape, amble slowly toward their patrol car. I wait for Stan to pour Oliver coffee from a red thermos. I can taste it, smell it, but I'm hours away from getting a cup myself from the coffee urn at my Meals–on-Wheels gig. I help out in their kitchen once or twice a week—it's a free breakfast and a place to go, filling my stomach and making me feel useful. Besides, my wardrobe fitting isn't until tomorrow afternoon, leaving me plenty of time to shower at the health club.

Finally the patrol car pulls away from the curb. The moment they turn the corner, I sprint to my car. I know how they operate. They'll circle the block and drive by again. There's no choice but to spend the rest of the night parked in the shadows of Aaron's Holmby Hills estate.

The Playboy Mansion is just a short hike up the road from the Spelling place, and I've wondered now and again what it might be like to camp out for the night at Hef's Tudor-style mansion. It's been years since I was last invited to a Playboy party, but how tough could it be to slip through the shrubbery, mingle among a thousand guests, and lose oneself back in the north forty, somewhere behind the Woo Grotto and the nesting peacocks? It must happen all the time that some reveler, having missed the last van to the parking lot, is found sunbathing by the pool the day after a big bash, waiting for the next party to begin. Hef seems like a nice enough guy, the sort who might offer you a cookie and a cold Pepsi while you hung out.

But I'm truly fascinated by the Spelling mansion. Now owned by Petra Ecclestone, daughter of the Formula One racing magnate Bernie Ecclestone, the estate is a gazillion-square-foot pile bordering the southeast end of Holmby Park. Tonight, sitting in my car, lulling myself to sleep, I once again imagine myself discovering the electric gate ajar and strolling up the driveway to find the front door wide open. I indulge in a fantasy raid, my mind taking me on a virtual tour of the house, not as it is, because I've never actually been inside, but as I would want it to be, smelling of Rigaud candles and lavish floral arrangements.

My simulated tour is a comforting, mind-numbing relief during those long hours when, alone at the edge of Holmby Park, I feel like I'm clinging by my fingertips to the edge of the planet. I long for sleep, but the drowsier I become the more afraid I am of dropping off, leaving myself prey to whatever bogeyman might be out there. While I fantasize about Candy's famous gift-wrap room and Aaron's bowling alley, curling up in a big armchair in front of a crackling fire, a glass of fine Montrachet in my hand, my eye is on the long shadows cast by trees in the light of the street lamps, vigilantly watching for any stray movement, any sinister approach.

Tonight I scrap my fantasy when my eyes fix on a gunmetal-gray, unsafe-at-any-speed rattletrap that trundles up to the curb some twenty feet beyond my Volvo. It's not the first time I've seen this rusting road warrior, a convertible with a peeling roof, parked at the south end of the park, but I've never laid eyes on its owner. I crane my neck as the door opens. A dim interior light illuminates a broad-shouldered figure behind the wheel. A man slowly climbs out, throws his shoulders back, and stretches before closing the door again. He steps up on the curb, rocks back and forth, swinging his arms.

Then, with the stealthy grace of a coyote, he lopes across the grass toward the men's restroom. It's locked for the night. If he's a regular here, he should know that. He does. Without bothering to try the door, he stops at the edge of a pool of lamplight, fumbles for a moment, then thrusts his pelvis forward and pisses into a border of white azaleas.

The stream sparks against the wall, glinting in the light. Having marked his territory, he shakes, tucks, and zips. There's no figuring men. Under threat of death, I couldn't pee on flowers. Nor would I seek out a well-lit, public place to relieve myself. This is hardly a time to be house-proud, either, but my Volvo doesn't look like the only jalopy to survive the apocalypse.

A light rain begins to fall, leaving starburst specks on my windshield. I shift to get a better view of the hunky guy with the dark, curly hair. Is he homeless, checking in for the night? He tips his head back, his face pale in the lamplight. He's too steady on his feet to be drunk. Probably a druggy, or just crazy. Why else would he stand out there soaking up the drizzle? He leans back even further, his hands stuffed into the pockets of his blue jeans, his leather jacket glistening.

Abruptly his face turns in my direction. I hold my breath, not moving, praying he can't see me through the dark, rain-streaked window. I catch a last blurry glimpse of him running toward his car as a downpour cascades in sheets over my windshield. I breathe again, feeling snug and safe with the torrent drumming on my rooftop. Who would want to get drenched molesting me? Do rapists take weather into account?

Such abstract considerations aside, I know I shouldn't be alone in my car in the middle of the night. I should be in my own home, the one I no longer have. If I weren't so stubborn, I could throw myself on the mercy of any number of people who would take me in. Carol and Sid.

Even Dougie. Possibly Pat, my agent, who shares her Santa Monica bungalow with only her cat, Mimsy, for company. What stops me?

Here's the deal: In return for the helping hand, people want answers to questions I don't even ask myself. So I sit in a cramped Volvo, my body screaming for sleep, punishing myself for having been stupid, for having wrecked my life. Maybe this is what Dougie was talking about, not wanting to know and therefore not being able to move on.

My toe flips open the glove compartment. I reach in for a packet of snapshots. In the gloomy light of the street lamp, I riffle through dog-eared photos, stopping at one Paul and I had used for a Christmas card. Tanned and grinning, both of us in shirts and shorts, we're wrapped in each other's arms aboard the *WindStar*. As familiar as I am with this picture, I look at it now and again to test myself. Am I still susceptible to the man's undeniable attributes?

Once again, I fail the test. My eyes fall on Paul's laughing face, the curls of sandy hair glinting in the setting sun, and I feel the tug, knowing my heart would swell if I were to hear his voice on my cell phone. What will it take to wipe out the longing? I stare at the picture for long minutes before drifting asleep.

My eyes pop open again as the first dirty streaks of light filter through early-morning cloud cover. The rusting convertible is no longer parked at the curb. There's no sign of its soggy, hunky occupant. I stretch my arms, then look up through the trees on the hill, catching a glimpse of the mansard roof, pearly gray in the dawn light.

I check my watch. The health club will be open shortly. I'll have my choice of classes—Cardio Sculpt or Tai Chi—before taking a hot shower. If only the club served free coffee. I can grab a bite to eat at my Meals-on-Wheels gig, then go back to the club to freshen up before my wardrobe appointment this afternoon. Not a bad agenda for someone down and out in Tinseltown.

Petra Ecclestone is probably still tucked in bed, while staff get coffee percolating and set a basket of fresh pastry on a linen-covered silver tray.

I stretch some more, smelling the coffee, tasting the warm croissants. I ache for a bowl of oatmeal with milk and a dusting of brown sugar. At moments like this I wonder if I'm not slipping past Margot Kidder and heading into Frances Farmer territory. How nuts do you have to be to go from scrounging leftovers to imaginary dining?

Chapter Four

A harsh male voice sounds in my ear. "Is the Coop there?"

"What?" The cell phone almost slips from my fingers, and not just because of the clumsy baggy covering my hand. I glance around the Meals on Wheels kitchen. Cell phones are forbidden, but nobody appears to be watching me. "Coop? I don't know—"

"Don't gimme that. Your husband. C'mon, is he there?"

"My husband? No. Who is this?"

The caller hangs up. I yank the baggy off my hand and hit the button for recent calls. UNKNOWN. *Coop? My husband?* It had to be a wrong number. Fingers shaking, I hook the phone back on my waistband.

"You okay, Meg?"

Donna peers up at me, her springy gray hair smothered in mesh. She's the only volunteer willing to wear the required hairnet. Mine is tucked in the pocket of my regulation pistachio-green smock.

I look down into Donna's doe-like eyes and want to scream: *Okay? Sure! My eyes feel like grit. I haven't slept. I don't know when I'll ever see a bed again—and someone might have just called about my fugitive husband!*

Instead, I say, "I'm fine. Too much coffee."

"It's so bad for you," she says disapprovingly. "It got so I was shaking. I had to switch to decaf."

I let Donna talk, which she will do at length, her busy-woman's voice set on automatic. "Better get another tray of chicken out of the oven, Meg," she says. I set the tray on the counter, already knowing what she's going to say next.

"Just put the tray right here on the counter, dear. That's right." I want to slug her.

Why would someone call me asking for Coop?

I slide my hand into a fresh "sanitary" baggy and begin heaping individual plastic containers with chicken and a side of broccoli. Donna barely comes up to my shoulder, but she stands on an overturned crate inspecting each container of food I assemble. She hums nonstop. Not any recognizable tune, just a grating soundtrack in a minor key. I suspect we're about the same age, a sobering thought.

Donna, who clearly has more time on her hands than even I, volunteers several days a week. Fortunately, I've never been assigned to deliver meals with her. But today of all days, when I'm sleepless and edgy, I draw to an inside straight: Donna and I are teamed for one of the routes. She snaps the lids of the containers closed and piles the boxes next to a thermal carry bag.

Meanwhile, the phone call rattles through my brain on an endless loop.

Coop? Another of Paul's aliases? I can't remember *Coop* among all the monikers the FBI told me he used. It probably isn't that much of a stretch. The sourness in my gut tells me I'm either on to something, or I'd better lay off coffee.

"All righty-right, let's load up the car," Donna trills. I head toward the parking lot juggling two insulated carryalls, with Donna trotting behind me.

For obvious reasons we take Donna's car instead of my closet-on-wheels. With Donna behind the wheel of her aging Mercedes, and me riding shotgun balancing a carryall in my lap, we head into the leafy environs of Beverly Hills flats, not noted for its poor and indigent, delivering poached chicken breast Florentine to the elderly housebound. It's happened more than once that a startled old-age pensioner has gotten up from watching me in a television rerun to find me, in person, standing at his door. I'm sure I've brought on bouts of acid reflux, but no heart attacks that I'm aware of.

I scan the route for our first delivery, gratified to see that none of the regular names have been scratched from the list. That means no one's been moved into a nursing home, or a place more permanent, since my last visit.

"Okay, Donna, hang a right on Elm and we'll do Inez first."

I look up just in time to see the Mercedes on the verge of sideswiping a looming Dumpster. "Watch out!" I scream. The car lurches to the left, and I exhale.

"Don't worry, I saw it," Donna reassures me. "Listen, I just want to say I think it's great that a movie star like you would do this kind of thing."

"I'm not a movie star, Donna." I grip the carryall tightly as the Mercedes drifts toward the line of parked cars. "Donna, the cars—"

"I see 'em. So, are you in anything coming up? Really, I can't believe I'm driving around with you like this."

First and last time. "I've got a wardrobe fitting this afternoon for a TV pilot. I start filming next week."

"How exciting! Well, I've always been a big fan of yours."

We pull up in front of Inez Berger's bungalow, the only house on the street still in its original prewar state. Once Inez goes, it'll be torn down and replaced by another Persian palace with Doric columns and a three-story front door. Inez, her eyes bright, head bobbling with age, peers at me through the rusty screen door as I double-time it up the walkway carrying her meal.

"There you are," she says, thumping her walker against the door frame while she fumbles with the catch on the door. "I was hoping it would be you today."

"How're you doing?" I say, entering the small living room, pin-neat and smelling of floral deodorizer.

"Oh, you know—my fingers just won't hold a darned thing anymore." I look past her and see fragments of a porcelain vase littering the floor. "I had no business trying to dust this morning."

"Inez, I'm so sorry. Let me help clean that up for you."

I make my way through the dining room to the sunny chrome-and-tile kitchen of a bygone era. Inez follows, slowly pushing her walker. Her legs, spindly sticks swaddled in Ace bandages, may be giving out, but Inez does a nice job of keeping up appearances. Despite fingers wracked with arthritis, her hair is neatly combed, her lipstick and rouge carefully applied.

"All you have to do is call me, you know. You should have."

I quickly arrange the chicken on a plate and pour a glass of juice. Inez bumps her walker across the linoleum floor and waits for me to finish setting up lunch.

In a weak moment, I once gave Inez my cell phone number. Two days later I got a late-night call. I rushed over to find her stranded in her rocker, her walker toppled on its side out of reach. She'd spent hours trying to figure out how to retrieve it. After I'd set the walker upright, we played a few hands of blackjack and had hot cocoa—and I spent the night in her spare room.

I recall the comforts of the small second bedroom now and choose my words carefully while rooting around under the sink for a whisk broom and dustpan.

"Inez, I wonder if you should be on your own here at night. I could stay with you. You might feel a bit more secure."

"That's so nice of you to offer, my dear. But I finally bit the bullet this morning and called an agency. They're sending someone over later today." *Too late! Damn!*

She settles down at the table for her midday feast. "I don't really like the idea, but I don't see what else to do."

By the time I've swept the porcelain fragments into the dustpan and returned to the kitchen, she's nibbled half her chicken Florentine. I give her shoulder a gentle squeeze. "Well, if the agency doesn't work out, call me. Promise?"

"I promise," she says. "You know, I like it when you deliver. Everyone else is in such a hurry."

Including Donna, who looks at me anxiously when I return to the car. "Everything okay in there?"

"I had to give Inez a hand with something."

"You have to watch it with these people," Donna says, peeling away from the curb. "Some of them would have you dusting and vacuuming before you know it. Okay, where to next?"

By the time we complete our circuit, I've delivered a dozen reasonably hot meals and been forced by Donna to reveal the entire plot of my television pilot. I just want to pee and take two aspirin. My throat now feels raw, and my nose is running. I yank another tissue from the box Donna has stuffed between the seats.

"Are you coming down with something?"

"I just didn't sleep well last night."

"Too much caffeine?"

I grit my teeth. "No, it's—just my house. I'm a bit unsettled at the moment. That's all."

"Redecorating? Oh, God, that's the worst. Nothing where you can find it. Plaster dust and paint fumes. No wonder you're on edge. Are you having the whole house redone?"

"Pretty much." My brain turns over, gaining traction on a hideous thought that suddenly seems inevitable. "It is terribly stressful, especially now with filming about to start."

"Of course. Can't you stay with anyone?"

"I don't know. I hate to ask." *Just how obvious can I be?*

"Well, it might be worth it to stay in a hotel for a while."

"I could, I suppose. Anything to get away from the paint fumes." I look out the side window, waiting for the words I hope to hear.

"You certainly don't want to get sick. A hotel is the answer. That's what I would do." Donna swings around a corner into the parking lot of the Meals–on-Wheels kitchen complex. "Are you working with a decorator?"

"No. I'm doing it on my own. Even more stressful."

"You probably want to be around as much as you can to keep an eye on the workmen. I remember when I redid my sunroom."

Donna squeals into the parking lot, nearly sideswiping a green sedan parked near my Volvo. I suck in my breath and grip the door handle. Seemingly oblivious to the near miss, Donna pulls into a parking space and turns off the ignition, all the while prattling on about chintz slipcovers. I don't budge. I'm not unhooking my seat belt until I've scored a bed for the night. Nothing is going to stand between me and a decent night's sleep and—*please, God*—a free meal.

Biding my time, my eyes travel to the interior of the green sedan. A henna-haired woman in a chartreuse jacket glares at me over the rims of her oversized dark glasses. I shrug my shoulders, absolving myself of any responsibility for Donna's reckless driving. The woman turns abruptly to her companion seated in shadow behind the steering wheel and says something, her hands gesturing wildly. I brace myself, wondering how often Donna gets shouted at by irate motorists. But instead of an angry encounter, the driver starts his engine and heads out of the parking lot. The woman glances my way again. She looks vaguely familiar. I'm trying to recall the name of the country singer with the flaming hair whom she reminds me of, when my ears prick up.

"You know, Meg, I don't want to be too forward, but I was thinking—"

"Yes, Donna?" I turn to look her square in the eye, my inflection unmistakably encouraging. "What were you thinking?"

"It's really too presumptuous of me, but I'm on my own, you know, just rattling around in this big house, so—"

"Yes—?" *Spit it out, for God's sake!*

"Oh, never mind. It was just a thought."

"Wait. Were you going to suggest that maybe I—"

"If you'd like—"

"Are you sure I wouldn't be imposing?"

"You? Omigod, I'd love it. I'd just be thrilled to have your company. You'd have a bedroom and bath all to yourself overlooking the garden. You can just come and go as you like. Are you allergic to feathers?"

"Feathers?"

"Well, I am, so I always ask. I've got this very nice down comforter and pillows in the guest room. You can stay as long as you like."

Careful what you say, Donna.

"That's really kind of you. Maybe tonight? I could swing by around, say, seven?"

"Wonderful. I'll have supper waiting. Just let me jot down my address."

I hold my breath as she fumbles in her handbag. If I play it right, I can probably use her washer, dryer, and iron. And it wouldn't hurt to hang a few things in a closet for a change. Chances are, Donna's even a good cook.

"Here we go," she says, tearing a deposit slip out of her checkbook. I look at the address: Holmby Hills, where even a teardown goes on the market for five million.

"Thanks, Donna. You're a lifesaver." I open the car door and reach for the empty insulated bags in the backseat.

"Are you kidding? We'll have a great time." She taps my arm. "We'd better get these bags back to the kitchen. Atta girl."

After signing out on the daily roster, I almost skip across the parking lot to my Volvo. For the first time in weeks, I won't dread nightfall. I pull onto the street and smile at the sight of the green sedan idling at the corner. The driver has probably returned to vent his anger at Donna. She must deal with road rage on a daily basis.

The sun is high, the sky clear. A real bed for the night! I roll down the windows and play Édith Piaf at max while roaring up the canyon on my way to the wardrobe fitting in the Valley. Joining in a loud, untidy duet of "Je Ne Regrette Rien," I barely hear the *bing-bing* melody emanating from my cell phone. Bluetooth ignites on my dashboard. The name Sid Baskin flashes on the illuminated screen. Édith's voice cuts out abruptly, replaced by Sid's.

"Hey there, Sid. How're you doing? Carol called me about the charity dinner. I told her I can make it."

"So she said. Glad you can join us. And what's this I hear about an audition?"

"I got the job, believe it or not. Tell Carol, would you? I start next week."

"That's great! Congratulations, Meggie. We'll celebrate Friday night. Now listen, I thought I better give you a little heads-up here. I just got off the phone with Jack Mitchell. Remember him?"

My heart pounds at the sound of the name. "Good God, Sid. You think I'm going to forget? What does he want now?" The last thing I need is an FBI agent, especially this one, calling my attorney.

"Nothing to worry about, okay? Settle down."

"But if he's calling you—"

I detect a faint sound, a brief exhalation, then, "Meg, he's an old friend. We talk, okay? Believe me, he was on your side—"

"Like hell he was!"

"As much as he could be. Things could've gone a lot worse."

"Don't tell me he didn't suspect me, Sid. Instead of pulling out the stops to find Paul, he seemed to think I was in on something. How much worse could it get?"

"That's long ago, Megs. Nobody suspects you of anything, okay?"

"So he didn't call you about me? And this has nothing to do with Paul?"

"It has to do with how about meeting me for a cappuccino? I need to talk to you."

"Can't you just tell me?"

He laughs, a smooth lawyer-sounding chuckle that's meant to convey "no big deal." I'm not reassured when he says, "Just call my secretary when you get here, and I'll meet you downstairs in the coffee shop."

"I can't. I'm on my way to a wardrobe fitting. Just give me a hint."

"It's nothing. But something's come up I think you should know about. Can you make it around three?"

"I guess so. Listen, do you know anyone called—"

But he's already hung up. Maybe it's just as well. It might not be a good idea to mention "Coop." There's no point in volunteering information—especially if it might be passed along to Agent Mitchell. My chest tightens as I recall the husky-voiced caller. It wasn't a wrong number. Somehow I know there's a connection to Paul.

I knew my husband only by the name embossed on his business card: PAUL C. STEPHENS, PRESIDENT, STEPHENS PROPERTY DEVELOPMENT. Among other people, in other places, according to the FBI, he was also known as Paul Copely, Paul C. Findlay, and Pete Copley. *Coop*?

Who knows what his mother called him. I never met any of his family. Paul's parents had both passed away, or so he told me one afternoon not long after we met. He also mentioned having an older sister who lived in New Zealand. *Far enough away?*

"I'm pretty much on my own, too," I'd responded, feeling even closer to him as we sat side-by-side on his sailboat bobbing in the waters off Catalina. "My mother lives back in Nebraska near the farm where I grew up. I have a younger brother with a wife and grown kids. I try to visit maybe once a year, but we stay in touch."

"No kids yourself?" he'd asked, his sky-blue eyes locking on mine.

"None that I know of." I laughed. "You?"

He laughed, too, and put his arm around me. "Nope. Me neither."

I shivered, smiling in the face of a stiff breeze, and snuggled close, nestling in his warmth. "It doesn't get better than this," he whispered. "Just you and me. Sun and sea. Maybe someday I'll just run a little charter boat service, do some sportfishing. That suit you?"

"Mmm." I breathed a happy sigh, imagining a contented Hemingway-style existence with Paul in some quaint fishing village. *Yup, just two corks bobbing on the sea of life. Could anything be more perfect?*

But within minutes, the sky darkened. Winds battered our sails. I hunkered down, my face wet from sea spray and rain, never taking my eyes off Paul as he brought the *WindStar* safely into harbor. Then, both of us soaked, we'd raced the length of the dock and waited out the worst of the storm sheltered in a tackle shop, rain sluicing off its awning and splatting at our feet.

"There, there," Paul said, kissing my wet hair, nuzzling my ear with his nose.

Wrapped in Paul's arms, I recalled another time, when I was ten years old and waited with my father and mother under the eaves of the onion shed, safe from pounding hailstones ricocheting off the tar-paper roof. Out of nowhere, a storm had roiled up, purple-green, and descended over the fields where my mother and I had been sitting on the cabbage planter, a rig pulled by Dad's old Allis-Chalmers tractor.

Back and forth, through row after row of rich, black earth, my mother and I had worked in a steady, alternating rhythm, plucking cabbage seedlings from a wooden tray, tucking them into the furrow made by the plough, then pulling back quickly so our fingers wouldn't be caught by the wedge folding soil over the roots.

My dad, sitting sideways on the tractor, steered with one hand, his eyes scanning the field ahead for rocks, holding a steady course, keeping the rows aligned. We were so intent on our work that no one noticed the ominous musty smell and darkening stillness of the sky until the storm was upon us. My father grabbed us, and we ran like hell. An open field is no place to be in an electrical storm.

Winds blew cabbage crates across the fields and slapped at the loose windowpanes on the shed. We waited out the storm, silently counting the beats between the flashes of lightning and shuddering waves of thunder that followed. Then for a heart-jumping moment there was no beat, only crackling light and noise, a rumbling in my feet, and a lingering acrid smell that reminded me of fresh laundry.

"Whoa," my father breathed, "that was close." I pressed against him. He cupped his hands on my shoulders, giving them a squeeze. "There, there, now," he said, and laughed. I was trembling, but I laughed, too, and felt better.

The storm passed, and sun sparkled on the raindrops falling from the roof. My mother went to check the washing she'd left on the line. My father told me to go play. It was too wet to plant any more.

I climbed the elm tree next to the house and looked out across the rain-drenched meadow, like molten chocolate left in the sun. We'd lost a morning's work, and a full hotbed of seedlings, but not the whole summer's crop. My dad, sitting on the front steps with a cup of coffee, looked unperturbed—and as sturdy and dependable as the tree I clung to, my face pressed against the ageing bark.

I clung to Paul, too, his arms curling around me, holding me close, his voice whispering, "There, there." Even then I didn't want to let go of the moment, knowing how good it was and fearful that the hubris dragon would find me. Or did I have a feeling that things would go wrong? I replay the moment with Paul, realizing now that even as he held me close, his voice reassuring, clouds I had yet to see were already gathering.

As Piaf digs her heels in for the last bars of "Je Ne Regrette Rien," the sound of the threatening voice comes back to me. *Coop.* Could Paul reappear in my life as someone called Coop? With Paul, I've learned, anything is possible. Why not reincarnation?

Chapter Five

The possibility that Agent Jack Mitchell could intrude on my life again is as unnerving as the prospect of finding my Volvo with four flat tires and a dead battery. My coping mechanism would short-circuit. What could possibly "come up" now that concerns him?

While great gulps of time were swallowed whole in the year that followed, there are singular moments in those nightmare days after Paul vanished that are seared in memory. Much of what I'd like to forget involves Jack Mitchell.

Hour after hour, I drank coffee and waited. Eventually, when no one called to tell me where or when Paul would be released, I rang Sid. He was on full-bore alert from the moment he answered. Lawyers must surmise a predawn call means trouble. Mine proved the rule. I told him Paul had been abducted in Mexico.

"Fill me in," he barked. "How long's it been?"

"Tuesday night, after I got back from North Carolina."

"Damn, it's already Friday morning! Why didn't you let me know?"

"I'm sorry, Sid. I didn't dare—"

"Take it easy, Meg. Don't do anything. I'm on my way."

He showed up within minutes. He smelled of sweat, his face pale. He wasn't the Sid I knew, always freshly pressed and polished. But then, I didn't look like my normal self, either. He stared at me, his eyes pinched, nervous. I held the door wide, but Sid made no move to step inside.

"You should've called me right away," he said.

"I'm sorry, but I was warned not to, or—"

"My God, three days!" I needed Sid to be strong, take charge.

Instead, his eyes sagged deeper into his face. "You actually talked to Paul?"

"For just a second. Sid, please. You've got to do something. I'm scared—"

"I know. I've already made some calls." He brushed past me and slumped onto a stool at the kitchen counter. "I have an old classmate who's with the FBI. They'll find him, Megs."

I made a pot of coffee and watched Sid, still pale, his face tight, jabbing at his BlackBerry. He asked a question or two, glowering at my responses. I wished he looked more assured. In any case, it was a relief to let somebody take over, even if it was someone who looked as scared as I felt.

"Okay, he says he's on his way over." With his eyes still glued to his BlackBerry, Sid lifted his cup for a refill. "Jack Mitchell and I were in law school together. He moved back from San Francisco a while back, and we reconnected. So don't worry, okay? You can trust him. I just wish to hell you'd called sooner, Megs."

He shook his head and looked like he was going to say more, but thought better of it. I turned away to pour myself coffee. When I looked back, Sid had left the room. Just as well—I didn't need more scolding.

I pushed open the kitchen door and stepped outside. Shivering in the morning chill, I yawned and stretched, breathing in freshly brewed coffee and tangy, dew-soaked lawn. Feeling invigorated, hugging my sloshing mug in my hands, I flopped onto a chaise. Burrowing into the cushions, I didn't mind that splats of coffee stained my sweatpants and T-shirt, that the damp pillows smelled sour. The chaise reminded me of the narrow bunk on the *WindStar*. And Paul. I set the mug aside and closed my eyes. Sinking deeper into the divan, I hugged a cushion to my chest and recalled the feel and smell of Paul, hair tousled, skin salty, curling up next to me.

I slept for the first time in almost three days. Then, with the *sqrawk* of the garden gate, my eyes flew open. "He's here!" I shouted, still half-asleep. I catapulted from the chaise, tripping over cushions. "He's here, Sid! Paul's here!"

I raced to the bottom of the garden. Paul must have escaped. He'd made his way home. "There, there," he'd say as I flew into his arms.

I barely saw the man squatting near the gate before I stumbled over the roots of a tree trunk, went airborne, and landed on top of him. We knocked heads, my cheek grazing the stubble on his chin.

Panting, my body sprawled across his charcoal suit, I came nose-to-nose with a stranger who smelled of apricot. My eyes locked on his just as it registered that my bare foot was wedged in his crotch. I blinked. So did he.

"Who the hell are you?" The words slipped out even as I realized that the wreck beneath me had to be Sid's friend, the FBI agent.

"Jack Mitchell. I'm with—"

"Right, Sid said you were on your way. Why were you checking the garden gate?"

"I wasn't." He struggled to raise himself onto his elbow. "I dropped something."

Maneuvering to free my foot, I bumped against his thigh, my hand digging into his stomach muscles. I heard a sharp intake of breath as I slid onto the grass. "Sorry. Didn't mean to hurt you."

"You didn't." He rolled onto his side. "How's your head?"

"Fine." No need to mention the spiked marbles crashing around inside my skull. As Agent Mitchell sat up, I saw a half-filled bag of dried apricots mashed into the lawn where his shoulder had been. I handed him the crinkly bag. "Yours? I'm really sorry."

"It's okay." He hesitated a moment, then stuffed the bag in the pocket of his jacket.

I rocked back on my knees, looking down at my grass-stained, coffee-drenched sweats. Maybe they could pass for camouflage gear. I probably smelled bad, too. I hadn't bathed in days.

Jack Mitchell, back on his feet, brushed grass and apricot bits from his suit jacket, somehow still looking like a Brooks Brothers ad. Brows furrowed, he gave me a long look. Perhaps out of concern for his personal safety, he was keeping his distance. Or maybe he'd never come across a walking, talking toxic dump before. But then, I wasn't used to tripping over FBI agents in my garden, certainly not a specimen as camera-ready as this one. I took in the closely cropped hair, the even features, and recalled the smell of apricot on his breath.

Still watching me, he gripped the gate, rocking it slightly. "You're Mrs. Stephens?"

I nodded, gritting my teeth at the *sqrawk-sqrawk* sound. I laid a hand on the gate, stopping it from sawing back and forth.

"You said he's here?"

"Sid?"

"Is that who you meant? I thought I heard you say—" He cocked his head, as though having trouble hearing me. Wasn't I making sense?

"You mean—Mr. Stephens?" Panicked, I struggled to remember my husband's first name. *How could I forget his first name?* "No, I mean—of course he's not here. Don't be stupid! He's— Sorry, I didn't mean that."

"Mrs. Stephens?" His voice, crisp and cool, reached me through a muffled roar pounding in my ears. Three days of fear and frustration boiled inside me. "Mrs. Stephens? Are you all right?"

Stephens, of course. But what's his first name? Was I concussed, about to black out?

"Sorry. I'm okay," I mumbled. His spanking white shirt hurt my eyes, made them water. He pressed a handkerchief into my hand, one so soft, clean, and neatly folded that I couldn't bear to use it. But neither did I want to give it back. Why was he mixing me up?

I ached to rest my head on his sober gray shoulder, to be forgiven for not remembering my husband's name. But if Jack Mitchell could read my mind, he wasn't letting on.

Sid appeared at my side, still rumpled and sweaty. "Jack, thanks for getting here so fast. Meg says Paul, himself, called Tuesday night."

The mention of Paul's name brought me back to the real world. "I'm going inside. The phone could ring—"

I hurried into the kitchen, Jack and Sid on my heels. Within minutes, two other FBI agents arrived. I was introduced to Andrea Olsen, a pale blonde wearing wire-rimmed glasses, and Leroy Chen, broad-shouldered and compact, each carrying metal suitcases. They quickly took over the dining room, setting up laptops and monitoring equipment.

I started losing my grip again when Jack Mitchell took my elbow and steered me into the den. His sleeve brushed my bare arm. I leaned into him, feeling light-headed.

"Are you all right, Mrs. Stephens?"

"Sure. Just glad you're here." Did that sound like a come-on? I glanced at him anxiously.

"We're setting up a trap-and-trace, but it's a waiting game until we get a lead. Is there anything you might know that could help us?" He squeezed my shoulder. Or was he just guiding me to the couch?

"Ask me anything, whatever—" I glanced at Sid, who'd stationed himself at the door, his arms crossed like a sentry. He looked angry. *With me?* What had I done wrong?

Jack pulled up a straight-back chair, positioning himself directly in front of me, his arms resting on his knees. His eyes were warm, a dark caramel with flecks of gold.

"Mrs. Stephens?"

"Sorry, what?"

"I was saying that maybe you could tell me what happened, starting from the beginning." He leaned forward. I leaned back, wishing I could sprint to the bathroom to brush my teeth and change my clothes before being interviewed by these strangers. "When did you hear that your husband had been kidnapped?"

"Tuesday night. The phone rang just as I got home from the airport." I took heart that my voice sounded normal, that crazy thoughts weren't spilling from my mouth. "Actually I hadn't seen Paul in three weeks. I'd been filming in Wilmington, North Carolina. He was in Mexico on business. I'd barely opened the door when I got his call."

"What did he say?"

"His first words were 'Baby, listen to me. I'm okay, but I've been kidnapped.' "

"Did you get the feeling he was making the call on his own?"

"I guess so. I didn't think about it. He sounded scared, his voice sort of muffled, like he was cupping his hand around the phone. He said bandits ran him off the road. He thought they'd take his money and the car and leave him stranded. Instead they shoved him into the backseat and—"

"Did he know where they were taking him?"

I was so tired. If only I could slide down on the couch and close my eyes. I glanced at Sid, his hands still tucked into his armpits, his face glowering.

"Do you remember anything else?" Jack's voice was softer now, barely a whisper. "Think back—"

"I am thinking—you know that part about the bandits and the backseat? I think I made that up. I'm sorry, but I've been trying to picture what happened, and—"

"That's okay. Go on—" "We didn't talk long. Paul said not to call the police. Or get in touch with Sid."

"Sid? He specifically mentioned Sid?"

I nodded. I heard Sid grunt, but didn't dare look at him.

"Paul said he knew someone else I should call who could help me put together the money to meet the ransom. I would find the man's name and number on a scrap of paper in the desk drawer. This man would accept jewelry, whatever. Sounded like some sort of pawnbroker with a foreign name."

"Anything else?"

I began to fade. My head ached. I knew I'd made the call, but was I now mixing up Paul's kidnapping with the kidnapping of Winston Sykes, which Jinx wrapped up quite nicely? Wasn't there a pawnbroker involved? Wait, what was the question? Whose turn was it to answer?

"Mrs. Stephens?"

"Paul said I could trust this man."

"That's all?"

I nodded, my eyes watering again. I wasn't going to tell him about Paul's voice breaking. *Please, baby. I'm counting on you. I love you—* "The telephone went dead. It was the last time I talked to him."

"So you called this guy, the one Paul told you to call?" Sid interrupted, his voice sounding strangled.

"Of course. I'm sorry, Sid, but—"

"Sure was thoughtful of him. How many people leave contingency plans in case they get kidnapped?" His eyes were hard. I'd never seen Sid so angry. He exchanged a look with Jack, then turned away.

"I'm sorry. Maybe it was a mistake, but Paul knew the guy—"

"Mrs. Stephens, would you happen to have that scrap of paper?" Jack asked, his voice low, unhurried.

"Yes." I reached into the pocket of my sweatpants and produced the piece of lined notepaper I'd found in the drawer. Jack barely glanced at the note before passing it on to Agent Chen.

"What did this man look like?"

"Like I said, I never saw him. I called and mentioned Paul's name. The guy told me to put jewelry and all the cash that was in the safe into a grocery bag and leave it on the front step. He'd take care of the rest."

Sid turned and gaped at me. "The front step? Meg, for chrissake, he robbed you!"

A terrible thought hit me. "If it never even got to the kidnappers, maybe that's why I haven't heard—"

"Oh, no," Sid cut in, his voice rising again. "I'm positive the loot got to the kidnappers."

"Then they'll let Paul go, right?" I asked, pleading for assurance.

"Unless he knows them," Sid said, "and it was a setup. Chances are, your bank accounts are already cleaned out. Have you checked?"

"Sid, this isn't helpful. I need to hear about the abduction from Mrs. Stephens."

"She's my client. We need to know what we're dealing with here, Jack. You really think there was a kidnapping? C'mon—"

I looked to Jack, an even more terrible thought springing to mind. "No! Is that what you're thinking?"

"We know very little, Mrs. Stephens. We're looking into everything."

My breath stopped. "You're wrong! Paul wouldn't do that to me!"

"Do what? Tell me what you know—"

"Damn it, find him! Bring him back!" I screamed, jumping up. "You're not doing anything! Find him!"

Blinded by tears, I stumbled out of the den. Agent Olsen came to my rescue, guiding me to the bathroom. I knew I was out of control. I stood over the toilet, my stomach an empty, sour pit, convulsing in dry heaves. Agent Olsen handed me a towel.

Looking up into the mirror, I saw an old lady's face, hollow-eyed and sagging. Salty tracks creased my cheeks. My hair was dirty, stringy. Slowly I peeled off the stained T-shirt and baggy sweatpants.

Agent Olsen turned on the shower, then left me alone in the bathroom. Steam clouded the mirror, obscuring my face. If only I could completely evaporate, as though I'd never existed.

Before stepping into the shower, I reached to push the bathroom window open wider, then stopped when I heard noises in the garden. First a sharp thud, like someone kicking the door frame, then Sid's voice.

"You could've warned me. How was anyone to know, damn it! You have any idea what it took for me to find out?"

"That's how it works. I couldn't pull him in, Sid. We needed more to go on first."

"You're telling me he gets away with this? Not on your life! I'll blow this wide open. Believe me, I'm not keeping quiet on this."

"Keep your voice down. I never said he was getting away with anything. But you have to keep what you know to yourself, understand?"

"So now what do I do?"

"Just work with us, Sid. Come on, I want to check out the garage."

Keep what you know to yourself. A chill settled over me, shaking me to the core. *Just work with us, Sid.* Now who could I trust?

Chapter Six

I arrive early at the coffee shop and settle in at a corner table. The lunch crowd has vanished, and I have Le Petit Ferme virtually to myself. I call Sid's secretary, who tells me he's finishing up a conference call. The server, a lithe young woman barely out of her teens, comes by to take my order: *tarte aux pommes* and a large café au lait.

Not for the first time I wonder why a coffee shop in a sleek, towering office block would dress itself up as a *trés rustique boulangerie*. Pine trestle tables, artfully rough-hewn, rest on wide plank flooring, with shabby-chic cushions strewn on wooden benches. Belle Epoque posters advertising *pain* and *chocolat* line the creamy yellow walls. The décor contrasts sharply with the traffic-clogged, palm tree–lined boulevard visible through sheer café curtains.

Observing people is second nature to an actor. But these days, when I fantasize about being inside other people's skins, I find myself wondering if I could hold down their jobs, too. How long would it take me to master an espresso machine and make thick, foamy milk? When I order coffee from a waitress in down-market Du-par's (if I'm paying, Starbucks is way beyond my means), I mentally try on her starchy uniform, imagining myself scurrying around with a Silex pot.

I watch a saleswoman working behind a handbag counter and wonder how much she earns. At my age, with no experience, could I even get a job as a checker in a supermarket? Do I have the stamina for an eight-hour shift? I'm lucky to have a job lined up; roles get a little thin after a certain age—just ask Melanie Griffith. I'm not complaining. It's a fact of life. If I were a champion pole-vaulter or a Victoria's Secret runway model, I would have hit the wall a whole lot sooner.

But I find myself unexpectedly caught without a nest egg in that awkward, in-between stage—post-livelihood/pre-death. Too young to collect a pension, too old to count on steady employment. I'm back to looking for a bread-and-butter job just to keep myself warm, dry, and fed. Luxuries such as dental floss and skin cream aren't even on the priority list.

I'm already sipping my coffee and working my way through the *tarte* before Sid, immaculate in a dark pinstripe suit, breezes through the door, a newspaper rolled under his arm. His cheeks look freshly buffed, his hair slicked in place. I catch the familiar scent of vetiver before he's halfway to my table.

He flashes his best smile at the young woman behind the counter. "Just the house regular for me, Gina, and put everything on my tab." Then he points his finger at me, his voice booming in the empty restaurant. "Megsie, my girl, congratulations. Way to go!"

"Thanks, Sid." I stand and give him a kiss on both cheeks. "It's just a guest star in the pilot, but a terrific bad-guy role."

"Hey, you're back. You're on your way again, that's what counts." He settles himself on the bench across from me and unbuttons his suit coat. Gina delivers his coffee and hovers at the table. "Meg, you want anything else?"

I shake my head. "I'm fine."

"I don't know how you can put away the sweets and stay so trim," he says.

"Thanks to Carol, I get to work out every day." I wait until Gina is at a safe distance before I lean in to Sid and whisper, "Okay, don't leave me hanging. What's up?"

He laughs. "Probably nothing, but you never know. A coincidence, maybe."

"This has to do with Paul?"

"Maybe. I was talking to Jack this morning. He told me they're checking a burned-out hull beached on the far side of Catalina. There was a body, pretty decomposed, washed up on the rocks, and—Hey, you okay?"

"Hang on—" I put my cup down, my stomach churning. "Paul? Not Paul, is it?"

"No, no, Meg. Not Paul. But the thing is, this sailboat was once registered to P. C. Findlay. How about that?"

"When? How long ago?"

"The transfer dates back nearly five years." He shrugs and takes a sip of coffee. "It was just funny, the name surfacing like that. Sounds like one of the names Paul went by, you know? It makes you wonder."

"Five years, Sid. That's before I even knew him. It doesn't mean a thing."

"Like I said—"

"And Jack mentioned this to you? Why not me?"

"I happened to be talking to him, and it came up. Thought I'd pass it along. Look, if you hear anything—"

"Like what? Sounds like you and Jack still think I'm hiding something."

"Easy, Meg. The guy's a fugitive. Dead or alive, Paul's going to turn up one day." He folds his hand over mine. "Not so hard on Jack, okay? It's a question of making connections. You never know where the leads are. I'd like to see the son of a bitch caught. Wouldn't you?"

I nod. "If he turns up on my doorstep, I'll give a holler."

Sid slides his coffee cup away and rests his elbows on the table. "You know, if Paul does surface, you'll probably hear from him first."

"Why? What for? He's already taken all there is to take."

"Then maybe it'll be someone else who thinks you know where he is." He gives my hand a squeeze and says softly, "Trust me, Meg. You always want to go it alone, but you can't play around with this, okay? Don't do the Jinx thing, know what I mean?"

"What?" My shock must be obvious, because Sid's face reddens.

"Sorry, Megs. When you went off, disappearing for months without saying anything, I figured you were trying to track him down on your own. I can't say I'd blame you, but—just keep me in the loop, okay? I have a vested interest, too."

"Of course, Sid." I try to wriggle free of his grip, but he hangs on. I smile, relax my hands, and manage to slide my fingers from his grasp. "I told you I'd give you a holler."

"That's my girl." He takes the newspaper from his lap and lays it on the table. "Anyway, there was an item this morning. I didn't want you to get upset seeing the Findlay name."

"I appreciate it, Sid. And thanks for the *tarte* and coffee."

"Anytime." He stands up and buttons his suit jacket, his face glossy with goodwill. "Look, you want anything else, put it on the tab. I gotta get back to the office. See you Friday night, huh?"

"Looking forward to it." Then, because I owe it to him, because I sense he feels he hasn't yet closed the deal, I stand up and give him a hug. "You've been great, Sid. I really appreciate it. I promise you, anything comes up, I'll let you know."

"That's all I need to hear." He pats my shoulders and gives me a kiss that grazes my ear, then leaves by the side door.

I settle back in my chair and pick up the paper, folded to an inner page with a two-column story under a photograph of the beached hull. I scan the caption, fixing on the name of the boat. *The Coop II.*

I freeze, hearing the husky voice again: *Where's the Coop?*

My eyes drop down the text to a two-inch, one-column photo, a shot of a dark-haired man in an open-neck shirt. I stare at the picture, then at the name in the caption: Ricardo Aquino. I'm sure I've seen him before. Where? When?

For long minutes, I gaze at the charred remains of *The Coop II.* I can't get past my surprise at the reaction I had when Sid told me a body washed ashore—and thinking it was Paul's. But does anything connect Paul to the victim?

Then it comes to me, a glint of diamond. I glance back at the picture of Ricardo Aquino, recalling an evening in Catalina shortly before Paul and I married. A swarthy man with hair slicked back in a ponytail, wearing a leather jacket and an abundance of jewelry, appeared on the dock while we were having drinks aboard the *WindStar.* Paul brought him aboard, introducing him as Rick. The man took off his wrap-around shades and smiled, the late-afternoon sun glancing off a diamond stud earring. I offered him a margarita and was relieved that he declined. He was affable, but clearly in business mode. We exchanged a few words, then he and Paul strolled down the dock to talk privately.

At some point, two other men joined them. I watched for a few minutes, uneasy about the unexpected visit. By the time Paul returned to the *WindStar,* alone and unusually subdued, the sun had gone down and I'd put on a sweater. The following week, Paul made the first of many trips to Mexico.

For a moment, I consider calling Sid, but then decide I haven't much to report. I have no idea what they talked about, nor did I see Rick again. But I do remember the flash of apprehension I felt late that night when I awoke to find Paul on deck preparing to cast off before dawn—and offering no explanation for the early departure. I roll up the paper and stuff it into my shoulder bag.

Back out on Wilshire Boulevard, I head toward Saks Fifth Avenue, where I've parked my car. Once inside the store, I look around for the nearest salesperson to validate my parking ticket. But then, with time on my hands, I step onto the escalator. I have no business browsing in Saks, but it's too early to show up at Donna's house. I check out the cocktail dresses and evening wear, pretending that I'm actually in the market for a new ensemble for Carol's charity function.

An elegant slip of a dress in smoky mauve falls from its hanger, its silky softness floating onto my hand. I turn to a mirror, dancing the dress in front of me by its angel-hair straps. Without spoiling my pleasure by looking at the price tag, I head for the dressing room.

"Meg? Meggie?" The voice stops me dead in my tracks. I turn slightly and come face-to-face with my husband-before-last.

"Dirck? What a surprise!"

"Yeah. Do you believe this? You look great."

"So do you." And he does. Leaner. A little less hair, more of it gray, but the same gravelly voice, same craggy features. "I thought you were still in New York. What're you doing out here?"

"Oh, I'm up for a couple of things. You know, pilot season." He shrugs, that careless New Yorker's shrug I remember so well. "I'm still keeping busy with voice-overs. You know how it is."

I do know, so I nod and smile.

"What about you? Working?" he asks.

"Yeah, as a matter of fact, I'm shooting a pilot next week." I don't mention I'm just a guest lead.

"Wow, good for you. Still raking it in while everyone else is scraping bottom. I gotta hand it to you, Meg. No one bounces back like you do." He narrows his eyes, cocks his head. "Everything else work out okay? You had sort of a bad patch there after—what was his name? Paul something?"

"Yeah, well . . . that's over."

"Sorry to bring it up, but I saw it in the papers. As soon as I heard what went down, I said, 'She'll look out for herself. No guy gets the best of Meg.' He sounded like a real shit, though. You managed to hang on to everything, right? The house and all?"

"Pretty much."

"Yeah? Good for you. Just between us, did you manage to squirrel any of those millions offshore?"

"The stolen loot? No, I sort of missed my chance."

"Hey, just kidding, you know?" He laughs.

"Sure, I know." My jaws begin to ache. Am I really smiling? I don't dare ask if Dirck's still living in our former rent-controlled New York apartment. With nothing short of exquisite timing, my beloved two-bedroom prewar went co-op only a year before our divorce. My earnings had paid for it, but he managed to win it in the divorce settlement. Unfortunately, what we divvied up represented some of my best earning years. At least I didn't get stuck paying him support when I got tired of playing Wendy to his Peter Pan. "Everything good with you?"

"Couldn't be better. Pru and I are expecting. Can you believe it?"

I look at him in some confusion. "Pru?"

"C'mon, you didn't know Pru and I finally got married?" I follow his gaze. A pretty blonde, heavily pregnant, stands by the cash register smiling at us. "Yeah. She's due next month."

"Well, congratulations, Dirck. That's great." *Prudence?* Of course. She was a young student in the acting class he was teaching before the divorce.

"About time, eh?" He laughs. "She's turned my life around. I always wanted kids." He nods toward the dressing room. "Hey, I'm not holding you up, am I? Go ahead and try that on while I get Pru. She's just picking up something for her sister's birthday. You two gotta say hello."

"Sure. Why not?"

Why not? I close the door and sink onto the bench in the cubicle. The really bad thing about California earthquakes is that they never happen when you want them to. As I see it, an earthquake (anything above a 4.2 tremor) is the only remedy for this hugely hideous encounter.

"I always wanted kids"? I swallow hard, remembering the last occasion my doctor, a fan who appreciated my flirty pleading, reluctantly agreed to give Dirck and me another chance at in vitro.

At the time, I had a recurring role in a popular television series, a show about doctors in an inner-city hospital. I played a hospital administrator having an affair with the chief surgeon, but the storyline was steaming to its conclusion. Charting my fertility course against the story arc, I felt confident about starting the drug regimen necessary to produce a premium harvest of eggs. But at eight o'clock the evening before the follow-up procedure to introduce the fertilized eggs from some high-tech Petri dish back into my uterus, I got an unexpected makeup call for the next morning. The schedule had been changed. With a sinking heart, I called my doctor and said, "Trust me. Somehow I will make it."

By mid-morning I knew I was in trouble. But the director was Dougie Haliburton, and I decided to confide in him. He came through for me, shifting two scenes, grabbing my close-ups first and finessing the reverse shots. I wrapped in time to get to the clinic for the procedure.

But the toll was costly nonetheless. I wasn't in a physical, mental, or emotional state to become pregnant. Dirck, who'd insisted on taking me to the clinic, had neglected to fill his gas tank, and that essentially ended the union of two people who should never have mated in the first place. We'd been brilliant together in a national tour of *Barefoot in the Park*. But was *that* any reason to marry? I sat in the car fuming as Dirck tanked up, a Movieola replaying endless clips in my mind of every last humiliating act we'd ever submitted to in the fertility arena. Pumped up on hormones and adrenaline, I could have walked to the hospital carrying his goddamn car on my head.

When the in vitro procedure inevitably failed, Dirck tried to cheer me up, saying, "Hey, at least we're free to go cycling in Tuscany next summer."

I'm replaying this exact moment as I peek through the louvered doors of the cubicle and spot Dirck, looking impatient, poking his head around the entrance to the dressing rooms. I toss the dress across my arm and push open the door.

"Hey, okaaaay," Dirck says. "Meg, Pru. Pru, Meg. How about this?"

The bountiful blonde and I greet each other warmly, each of us signaling to the other that we're in a rush, no time for a long chat neither of us actually wants to have. No hugs or kisses on the cheek, either, because, thankfully, our hands and arms are full, and her belly's in the way.

"Pru's a big fan of yours. Tell her, Pru."

"A really big fan, Meg. I used to beg my mom to let me stay up to watch you on *Holiday*. You were just great."

"Thanks, Pru. And congratulations, you two," I say, slipping away. "Great to see you, Dirck."

"Ciao, kid. You're lookin' great."

I hurl myself onto the escalator, realizing almost immediately that the mauve silk dress is still draped on my arm. I spin around in a futile attempt to clamber back up the moving steps. All I need now is to pull a Winona Ryder, with some beady-eyed store detective body-tackling me for shoplifting. Dirck comes into view, steering Pru toward the escalator. I whip around and ride to the bottom, retracting my prayer for an earthquake. I've no desire to be trapped in rubble with Dirck, Pru, and their bun in the oven.

Holding the dress at arm's length, I step off at the next floor and swiftly head toward the nearest saleswoman. "Doesn't work for you?" She takes the dress, barely glancing at me.

"Afraid not, but I'll look around some more." I smile, satisfied our brief exchange sounded perfectly normal. She turns to another customer while I circle the Armani collection. I pause in front of a three-way mirror, holding a jacket on a hanger, examining my reflection. I look pretty normal, too, which is no small feat given my circumstances.

But while I may look normal holding a two-thousand-dollar Armani jacket, I know I have a zero bank balance and could be only a misstep away from pushing a bent grocery cart loaded with plastic bags and corrugated cardboard down the street. After all, I've watched a homeless woman getting hustled out of a drugstore while I stood three feet away from her, just as homeless. Keeping one's teeth and not wearing a grungy knit watch cap to cover matted hair is pretty much essential to keeping one's tenuous standing in the community.

The saleswoman, wearing a black suit and sensible shoes, appears behind me in the mirror. Has she seen through my guise? Am I about to be shunted into the street? *Here, you! Hand over that Armani before I call security!*

Instead, she says, "That jacket is made for you, trust me. You really ought to try it on."

"No, thanks." I smile and then give her the hanger. "I don't really need it."

I'm about to turn away when I notice a third figure reflected in the mirror, a red-haired woman browsing through a nearby rack. She looks familiar. In a flash I realize she's the woman I glimpsed in the sedan Donna nearly sideswiped. She's no longer wearing the chartreuse jacket or the oversized sunglasses, but it's definitely her. She glances up, and I anticipate a look of recognition, but she turns away, showing no sign she's even seen me.

I head for the escalator, reasonably sure my former husband and his pregnant missus are long gone. What if Paul had emerged from behind a rack of Calvin Kleins instead of Dirck? My heart bobbles at the thought. It occurs to me that wherever I turn I half-expect to see Paul. I've no idea what I'd do if he did appear. I'm pretty sure my first impulse would *not* be to call Sid. Or Jack Mitchell.

I stand outside Saks, waiting in the long shadows of late-afternoon sun for the parking attendant to deliver my car. There's nothing like complimentary valet service to make me feel privileged again. Only a year ago I used to take such things for granted, like a casual lunch with a friend. These days I dine alone. Any sort of get-together generally requires splitting a check and adding a tip. With a surge of giddiness I realize I'm actually looking forward to seeing Donna this evening. Am I that starved for companionship?

As I walk down the steps to my car, the redhead passes me, heading toward a familiar green sedan pulling up at the curb. I'm relieved that neither the woman nor the driver appear to recognize me.

The parking attendant opens my car door and steps aside, smirking as he gives me the once-over. I hand him my parking stub, looking him in the eye. What business is it of his if I choose to drive around in a car packed with several changes of clothing, a small library of reading material, and sundry items—toiletries, cleaning supplies, and a basket of small electronic heating and lighting devices that plug into the cigarette lighter? How does he know I'm not moving from house to house, a carload at a time? Homeless people don't have their cars valet parked—*do they?* One of life's small pleasures these days is free valet parking at selected fine stores.

Somehow I'll have to conceal the extent of my stowed belongings from Donna. Unloading will require multiple trips, perhaps under cover of night. I'm still mulling strategy as I reach the turnoff to her place. A road bordered by eucalyptus leads into a stone-paved forecourt encircling a fountain banked with azaleas. The elaborate entranceway is my first clue that any assumptions I've made about Donna require major revision. Inez Berger's bungalow would fit comfortably in Donna's driveway.

I pull up under the portico and park, staring agape at the stately two-story, half-timbered stone structure Donna calls home. Clearly a new game plan is called for. I pocket my car keys and leave everything else behind in the Volvo.

Rosebushes thick with white blooms line the walkway. I pause to breathe in their heady fragrance and take another look around. For all its baronial splendor, the house has a storybook charm. Wisteria clings to the gables, and flower-laden vines drape mullioned windows. Rust-colored ivy entwines a fieldstone chimney. Wide stone steps lead up to a heavy wooden front door fitted with a gated, wrought-iron peephole.

Before pressing the doorbell, I look back across the portico to the eucalyptus, native oak, and olive trees that conceal the property from the street. So content am I to stand in the portico, savoring the sweet scents of jasmine and rose, that I'm startled when the door swings open behind me. I turn, almost expecting to see a servant girl in mob cap and pinny.

Instead it's Donna, wearing a floral print shift and sandals, looking years younger than the woman I spent the morning with caroming around Beverly Hills.

"You're here," she says, with a sunny smile. "C'mon in."

"Thank you, Donna. Listen, I hope this is okay with you. I really appreciate it."

"Oh, please! I couldn't be happier. I'd hate thinking about you trying to sleep through plaster dust and paint fumes."

"Right," I say, thankful for the reminder. "It was pretty bad the last couple of nights."

I step inside, my eyes sweeping from the massive stone fireplace up to the balcony overlooking a two-story living room. The densely furnished interior, with its eclectic mix of Craftsman and Art Deco, has the feel of a '30s film set. I sense Donna enjoying my amazement.

"Tell me, did I just enter a time machine? Or is this where the rest of the MGM props ended up? And does Debbie Reynolds know?

"Feels like a museum, doesn't it?" Donna laughs. "My grandfather built this place back in the late twenties. I grew up here, actually. I've never really lived anywhere else. How about a glass of wine while I show you around?"

"Perfect." I follow her down three steps to a sunken living room, my eyes falling on a side table with stacks of vintage *Photoplay* magazines. "Your grandfather was in the movie business?"

"You'd think so. He would've loved it. You see that hat with all the ribbons on the piano over there? It belonged to Mary Pickford. The spectacles on the coffee table were worn by Harold Lloyd. This ice bucket was Charlie Chaplin's." She lifts a bottle of white wine from a silver urn on the coffee table. "My grandparents knew a lot of film people, but most of this stuff came from estate sales."

I pick a gray fedora off a hat stand near the stairway. "Let me guess. Fred Astaire?"

"William Powell." She pours wine into an etched goblet and hands it to me. "The crystal was a wedding gift to Joan Crawford and Douglas Fairbanks Jr. And those silver tap shoes on the bookcase belonged to Crawford, too."

"You're kidding!" I take a sip of wine, then hold the glass up to the last rays of sun splaying through the leaded windows. "I can't believe you actually use these."

"I've lived with this stuff my whole life. After a while—" She shrugs and sips her wine. "Anyway, I'm not a collector. I just dust the stuff everyone else in the family collected."

"So what did your grandfather do?"

"Remember the Savoir beauty bar? He started making soap in Belgium, then here. He sold the company shortly before he died. But he loved the movies. My mom ran Deanna Durbin's fan club for a while."

I shake my head, taking in the vintage lobby cards and posters on the walls, the bust of John Barrymore atop a credenza. "This place really is a museum."

"I'm afraid so," Donna says. "C'mon, let me show you your room." She heads up the stairs, and I follow, wondering what screen legend's bed I'll be sleeping in tonight. Garbo's, I hope.

As it turns out, the guest room at the end of the hall has been dubbed the Deanna Durbin Suite, but the only sign of tribute is an oil painting of the teenage star hanging over the bed. Donna assures me that the queen-size bed itself is relatively new.

"You'll be the most famous person who's slept in it so far," she says. "It was a bit of a shrine in here, but I cleared out most of Deanna's things this afternoon and stored them in the attic. By the way, that little chintz-covered armchair was in her studio dressing room. I hope you'll be comfortable."

"Oh, yes." I glance out the dormer window and see my Volvo safely tucked under the portico for the night. "I love it."

"Good. I'm glad. And the bathroom's through that door. The closet and drawers are empty, so you can just make yourself at home."

"Well, I won't be moving in." I laugh, even as that very thought takes hold. "But I'm tempted."

"Stay as long as you want. I hope you brought some things with you. Why don't you settle in while I get supper on the table?"

"Great." I look at Donna, wondering if she has any idea how easily she could end up with a permanent houseguest. Perhaps I could tell her I've decided to gut my house and do a complete renovation that will take, oh, six months or so. "Thanks, Donna. I'll just wash up a bit and then give you a hand."

I check out the closet, breathing in the scent of lavender sachets. Deanna Durbin herself would have been thrilled with the pink-and-white tile bathroom, its vanity shelves stocked with every sort of amenity one could need. This sure beats rooming with Inez Berger, or skulking into Marion Singleton's Bentley. I wash my hands with a bar of French milled soap, wondering how soon I'll have to call the Volvo home again.

I glance out the dormer window, trying to decide how much I should clear out of my car before dark. I can't wait to see what my underwear looks like folded in a drawer again. I'm about to turn away when I catch sight of a green sedan cruising slowly down the road, half-hidden in the shadows.

There's no mistaking the face in the passenger window. It's the red-haired woman, craning her neck to look up at Donna's house.

I step back, although I doubt she can see me in the darkened window. The car pulls slowly out of sight behind the eucalyptus. My legs cave, and I sink onto the bed. Who is she? What in the world does she want from me?

Chapter Seven

"Well, you're doing all right for yourself. Aren't you going to bid on the weekend for two in Paris?"

The voice is casual, the words mocking. I turn to look into the sultry eyes of Erica Wiggens, a former beauty queen and the widow of Nat, a studio executive. Poor Nat, one of Paul's early investors, was killed in a carjacking outside their Brentwood home. Erica and I go way back. She once guest-starred on *Holiday*, playing—what else?—a former beauty queen.

Her lips curl in a half-smile. "Go on. Wouldn't a little getaway be nice?"

"Sounds very romantic, Erica, but at the moment—"

"That's right. You're on your own these days, too. Do I have that right?"

"Erica, I'm so sorry about Nat. He was a great guy." I edge away, only to find myself blocked by a display of travel posters.

"Yeah, he was, until he met your husband. We need to talk, Meg. I think you know more than you let on."

"Please, Erica. This isn't the place for this."

My face burns. I glance around the silent-auction room to see who's within earshot. Carol, shimmering in a turquoise silk pants suit, is one table away, bidding on a digital camera.

"No? One hears so many things," Erica says, fingering the diamond pendant hovering above the abyss of her cleavage. "And then you were away for a while—"

"Not long—"

"Well, of course, we all wondered." She laughs shrilly, her voice rising. "I mean, it could've been like one of those caper movies, you know, where you two meet up in Brazil, or on some tropical island afterward, right?"

"After what, Erica?"

"Did I hear *tropical island*?" Carol sidles up next to me and slips her arm through mine. Her thick blonde mane swings onto her shoulder as she turns to face Erica. "Not Paris?"

"Whatever. I was just telling Meg she ought to bid on the trip, a little getaway." Erica's voice drops its edge, for Carol's benefit.

"Good idea. What a blast." Carol picks up the pen attached to a clipboard that holds a bidding sheet. "You can bid on Botox over there, Erica. Did you see it?"

"I'll leave it to those who need it." Erica smiles blandly and moves away. "Good luck. Hope you win that trip. And the Botox, Carol."

Carol swings me around, and we weave our way through the crowd. "C'mon, I'll buy you a drink. It's too early to go in to the tables yet." As tall as I am, Carol towers over me. With her linebacker shoulders and the agility of a seasoned quarterback, she steers us toward the bar area.

"She thinks I'm in cahoots, Carol. She seems to think I sneaked off to join Paul in Rio."

"Is *that* where he is?"

"Damn it, Carol!"

"Sorry, I was trying to be funny. You can't let her get to you. If Nat hadn't died, she'd have divorced him. The only problem is, he died broke, and she needs to blame someone. That's you."

"But how could anyone think I was a part of it? I got taken as much as anyone. I hadn't a clue what he was doing."

"They only see you at a party looking good. They don't know what you went through. Meanwhile, when they see you having a good time, they think of the bundle they lost. You give 'em a place to put the anger."

Carol holds up her hand before I can respond, and dives into the scrum around the bar to order drinks. I look around, wondering how many people in this room are whispering about me each time I turn my back.

She was married to that guy who ran the real estate scam. Claims she knew nothing about it.

Yeah, right—

Carol hands me a glass of wine. "Thanks," I say. "I may need a steady flow of this stuff. Tell me, do people ask you about me? You know what I mean."

"Well, they know we're friends. They know Sid lost money, too—hey, you sure you're all right?"

"I'm fine. It's just galling that people think I could've known about this and done nothing."

"Well, put it out of your mind. You look great, kid. Keep smiling. I'm really glad you wore that outfit. It always works. By the way, Sid did the seating, so don't blame me. And it's not a fix-up, okay?"

"Wait, you fixed me up? Who? What does he know about me?"

"It's not a fix-up, okay? It was Sid's idea. You know you can trust Sid, right?"

She's been through a lot, poor kid. Husband was a con man, bilked half the town, but don't bring it up, okay?

I catch a glimpse of myself in the mirrored panels on our way into the banquet room, looking just fine in the "outfit that always works." How can one go wrong with a well-cut black silk wraparound and decent earrings? *Tip: When packing for an extended stay in one's automobile, always bring along basic black and a pair of strappy high heels.*

Our table is nearly full, a mixed bag of people whom I suspect are mostly Sid's clients. The noise level in the room is already just short of a Lakers game at Staples Center, so there'll be little opportunity to talk with anyone. I circle the table, repeating my name, smiling and shaking hands with each of Sid's guests, none of whom I've met before. Obviously I was invited as a dress-extra. I don't mind in the least.

I spot Sid, looking freshly waxed, his balding pate gleaming in the candlelight. Next to him, his back to me, is a slim man of medium height in a charcoal suit. My heart stops. It's Jack Mitchell, and he's the last person I feel up to seeing. I turn on my heel, but I'm not quick enough.

"Hiya, toots." Sid catches my hand and reels me in. I breathe in a lungful of vetiver as he busses me on the cheek. "Meg, you remember Jack? He's been out of town for quite a while, just got back. Jack, Meg here's been doing some traveling, too." *Why didn't he tell me yesterday that he was going to pull this?* Sid smiles and claps us both on the shoulders. *Damn it, Sid, I could've used some warning!*

He catches the look in my eye and says, "Hey, it's been a long time. I thought you two would like to catch up."

Sid holds up his hands, as though giving us benediction, and sidles off to greet another newcomer. I glance at Jack, my mouth parched.

He smiles and shakes his head. "Well, this is quite a surprise. Certainly a nice one. How have you been?"

"Fine." *All the better for not seeing you,* I could add, though that's not really true. I take in the suntanned face, the warm brown eyes, and return his smile. *So Sid sprang this on Jack, too.* "You're looking well. Where've you been off to?" I ask, striving to sound casual.

He holds the chair for me as I sit down. "I've been running a case out of San Francisco for a while, overseeing a task force up there. It took longer than expected." He pulls his chair in and gives me an appraising look. "How about you?"

"Just traveling around. Here and there." I return his gaze, taking in the specks of caramel lighting up his eyes. Heat scorches my cheeks, but at least I'm not in the throes of the sort of meltdown I experienced the first time we met. "Just here and there," I repeat. "I wanted to get away for a bit. Let things calm down."

"That's what I heard. I don't blame you." He looks at me steadily, his voice even. "Did you stay in any particular place for long?"

My pulse settles, but my guard is still up. "I was in Mendocino for a while, then Seattle. I spent some time in Oregon, you know—then the Midwest to visit my mother. Obviously she was concerned about me."

"I'm sure she was." He gazes at me, looking expectant, as though it's now my turn to respond. I wait it out until he asks, "Did your travels take you anywhere else?"

"Here and there."

"Here and there." He smiles. "Got it. You don't give much away, do you?"

I shake my head. *I've given enough away.* "I didn't even send postcards."

Taking a sip of wine, he eases back in his chair. "I wondered what was happening with you. I thought I might catch you on television or in the movies. Are you doing any acting?"

"I am. I start work next week on a TV pilot. A mystery series. I play a woman who thought she got away with murdering her husband."

"Great. Sounds like my kind of show."

"Then you may not want to know the ending."

"If this is network, I'm guessing she goes down for it."

"You got it—but not without a fight."

"Good for you." He laughs. "I'll watch to see if I can pick up some tips."

"You should. It's a case everyone figured was dead, except for this one investigator who perceives I'm somehow involved. He grills me mercilessly. At least I'm the bad guy, so I deserve it. If I were innocent, it'd be hard to take."

"I see." The warmth fades from his eyes. There's an edge in my voice, and he's picked up on it. He takes another sip of wine and says, "Sounds entertaining."

"I hope so. It's good to be working again." I smile, but it's not enough to restore the firelight in Jack's eyes. I reach for water, the moisture on the glass slippery in my fingers. Droplets trickle down my bare arm onto my thigh. Enough silly banter. Why don't I just ask him about *The Coop II*? The dead body?

But even as the words form on my lips, the woman on Jack's right taps his arm and introduces herself. My heart races, the crowded room closing in. The stage is set for me to have a wide-awake furniture dream. I can already feel myself leapfrogging across tables and chairs to the nearest exit. I glance across our table and catch Carol sizing me up. I look away, avoiding eye contact. *This is some fix-up. I could end up having a stroke before the salad is served.*

I gulp more water, trying to breathe normally, hoping I won't have to ask the waiter for a paper bag to ventilate into. I cast a sidelong glance at Jack, still engaged in conversation. My eyes travel along the curves and hollows of his ear to his close-cropped hair feathering above his shirt collar. As though sensing my gaze, his hand reaches up, coming to rest on the back of his neck. His fingers are tanned. Unadorned. No ring. My heart bolts into a gallop. I pick up my purse and mumble to no one in particular, "Back in a minute."

As I steam toward the ladies' room, I try to sort out this turn of events. What is it about Jack that turns me into a cat in heat? Maybe post-traumatic shock takes strange forms, like craving sex with the nearest FBI man. Maybe it's just the heady effects of a night out, dressed up. It's been a long time since I've dined by candlelight, looking into the warm brown eyes of— *Stop!*

Is Sid out of his mind? Is this supposed to be a date? If so, aren't we breaking some sort of law enforcement code by socializing? It's been a good nine months since I last saw Jack. Maybe the FBI officially decided I'm no longer a suspect in my husband's disappearance. Or maybe this is a setup. *Wine and dine her, and maybe she'll spill what she knows.* I may be ripe for seduction, but this isn't going anywhere. I could hardly have my date, an FBI agent, pick me up at my Volvo for a night on the town. Besides, resentment lingers.

That morning a year ago, after overhearing Sid and Jack talking in my garden, I, too, became pretty much convinced that Paul had faked his kidnapping. But I was just as upset to know they'd concealed knowledge about my husband. I wanted to die, but pulling off suicide with a houseful of FBI agents watching me didn't look like a possibility. With nowhere else to turn, I stepped into the shower. But I'd barely soaped up when Agent Olsen banged on the door.

"The phone is ringing," she said, her voice taut. She threw a towel over my sudsy hair while I struggled into a robe. "Quick, take it in the bedroom."

I raced to my bedside table and snatched the receiver. A voice, harsh and accented, began speaking the moment I lifted the receiver. I made out "bus" and "La Paz," but before I could say a word, the voice cut off. The line went dead. I looked up to see Sid and Jack in the doorway.

I shook the receiver, crowing, "Did you hear that? He's alive! You see! He really was kidnapped!"

Sid took the receiver and put his arms around me. I sobbed into his shoulder, shaking with relief. Maybe Paul had been injured during his ordeal, but at least he'd be back, alive.

"I had to do what they told me, Sid. Thank God, I did. He's safe!"

"Okay, Meg, okay," he'd said. "Let's wait and see."

Jack raked his hand through his hair and said nothing. He offered no encouragement, no words of comfort. I kept to myself, refusing to leave the bedroom, sitting by the telephone. Running through my mind was the exchange I'd overheard between Jack and Sid. What didn't Sid want Paul to get away with? What did Jack want to keep to himself? Mostly, though, I tried to come to terms with my own willingness to believe Paul had betrayed me.

In the end, there was no sign of Paul at the bus stop on the stretch of road north of La Paz, Mexico, where the kidnapper had said he could be found. But a search team did come across a battered airline bag in a drainage ditch near where Paul was supposed to have been dropped off.

Inside was a damaged, scratchy cassette recording stuck in a cheap answering machine. I thought the cassette was a clue, proving that Paul had been kidnapped and was still alive. I was the only one who saw it that way. I begged to hear the tape, then cried when it was played for me over the telephone.

Recorded on the tape was an almost comical exchange. A gruff voice, perhaps the same one that made the ransom call to me, asked, "Where the hell is he? Stephens. Where'd you take him?"

An even more heavily accented voice responds in broken English: "He feenish. *Si, señor. Muerto.* You no say to feenish?"

"But isn't there more?" I insisted. "There *has* to be more. What did they do with him? I have to know!"

Jack shook his head, his voice cool. "I'm afraid that's it, Mrs. Stephens. That's all they could get off the tape. The thing is, I'm surprised we found it."

"What do you mean that's all? I know that voice. Isn't he the one who called me?"

"But why would this recording exist? Why would they do that?"

"It happens. Someone answers a telephone after the machine picks up, and the conversation gets recorded. Thank God it picked up, or we wouldn't know. I mean, why do I have to tell you this? It's obvious."

"Is it?" Jack folded his arms across his bone-white shirt and leaned against my bedroom door. "The thing is, the airline bag with the tape was found near the bus stop, right where we were told we'd find your husband. That tape could be a plant. We're supposed to think your husband is dead. Why?"

I stared at him, infuriated that I had to explain something so simple, so fundamental, to an FBI agent. "You can't just give up!" I shouted. "That tape will have clues to where he is! Don't you get it? You can do voice enhancement. Analyze background sounds. Maybe the guy lied and Paul is—"

"I didn't say we were giving up."

I took my cue, dropping to a vocal register as unemotional as his. I fell into the role of Jinx, the voice of reason, will of iron, telling Winston Sykes we had to try harder.

"Look, I know it can be done. I know you've got the technology. Send it to a lab. Just go over it. It's all we have. We've got to do everything we can."

"Mrs. Stephens, we're following every lead. If your husband is alive, we will find him."

"Good. I want to stay with you on this. Don't leave me out. I want to help, okay?"

"Okay. That's good to hear. There are a few things I'd like to review with you. You up to it?"

"Absolutely."

"Tell us once again, what was he doing in Mexico?"

"Like I said, he's in property development. He was trying to put together some deal for a coastal resort and hotel complex. I never knew any of the particulars."

"What can you tell us about the development he was working on here?"

"Construction was stalled, awaiting permits. He needed some land-use variances, so he was focusing on this deal in Mexico. Look, could I ask you a question?"

"Sure."

"Why are you so suspicious of that tape?"

"Doesn't it sound like playacting to you?"

I replayed the tape in my head: *You no tell me to feenish?* The voices suddenly reminded me of Pancho and the Cisco Kid in an old serial. *Hey, Cisco, I weesh.* Or maybe Cheech and Chong. *Feenish? Uh-ohhhhhh.* I felt sick to my stomach. It must have showed.

Jack leaned against the doorjamb, his eyes never leaving mine. "I think we were supposed to find that tape. I don't believe there ever was a kidnapping." His voice was cool, uninflected, perfectly calibrated to set me off.

"Damn it, you believed that from the beginning! Why?"

The flicker in Jack Mitchell's eyes was the only indication I might have caught him off guard.

"We've been looking into some property transactions your husband was involved in. Mr. Baskin has been cooperating with our investigation. We had hoped Mr. Stephens would, too. Instead he's disappeared."

"But why didn't you tell me? Why did you hide the investigation from me?"

"I'm sorry, Mrs. Stephens. We did what we had to do."

"Sorry? Nowhere near as sorry as I am."

If someone had given me a heads-up, maybe I could've ducked. Sometime later, when I was mired in debt, bankruptcy, and PR fallout, I met briefly with Jack again. He suggested I "drop by the Federal Building," which entailed showing ID, negotiating a metal detector, and wearing a visitor's badge to our rendezvous in a glass-enclosed conference room.

"Thanks for stopping in," Jack said, shaking my hand. "You look great. How're you doing?"

"You met me at my worst. Anything's an improvement. Any news?"

"The case is in the hands of the U.S. Attorney's Office, White Collar Crime Section. That's WCC-4."

"And Paul?"

"The judge signed the arrest warrant. No new leads. Sorry, Meg."

Sorry? Meanwhile, I was left to deal with a quagmire of lawsuits, bankruptcy filings, and endless media speculation. If I'd stayed to do battle and taken advantage of options available to me rather than abandoning everything, I wouldn't be in quite the fix I'm in today. I might even still have a roof over my head. But no matter what Jinx might have done, I saw no way to triumph. I left town.

Now, I'm back, and—for whatever reason—Jack Mitchell is back in my life. Sickened by memories still too fresh, too mortifying, I can barely look at myself in the ladies' room mirror. I have no desire to return to the banquet and make small talk with Jack. I've pretty much decided to forgo my free meal and abandon my goody bag at the table, when Carol enters.

"What're you doing in here?" she asks, tossing her sparkly Judith Leiber clutch onto the vanity. "You're missing the salad course. I was afraid you were skipping out on us."

"C'mon, I wouldn't do that."

"The hell you wouldn't." She gives me a beady look before disappearing into the first stall. I catch her reflection in the mirror, squatting over the toilet, one hand tugging her silk trousers. Her other hand holds the door open, not necessarily to keep an eye on me because she fears I'm going to make a run for it. Carol *never* closes a bathroom door. I shift out of her eye line just to irritate her.

"So, is there a problem with Jack?" she asks.

"It's not as though he and I don't have a history, in case you've forgotten."

"Just put it behind you, Meg. You had a little breakdown. Who could blame you? The best therapy is to deal squarely with the past. Put it in a little box and throw it over your shoulder." The toilet flushes. "You gotta just moooooove on."

"So that's what tonight's all about? Some sort of public therapy session? Look, Jack is not the problem—"

"Thank you, thank you. I am so glad to hear you say that." Carol wriggles her hips as she fastens her waistband. "Maybe we're turning a corner here. Besides, Sid thinks the world of him. Don't you think he's kind of cute?"

"Cute? So this is just a fix-up? Give me a break, Carol. I appreciate the effort, but your pool guy is cute, too. Why not him?"

"He's gay. Maybe the only gay pool guy in town." She shrugs dramatically. "Sorry."

I smile. "Leave it to you."

"So, could we please go back to the table and finish dinner? C'mon—you don't need any more lipstick."

We head back to the table, Carol riding herd as though I'd hotfoot it out of the ballroom if she wasn't directly behind me. I'm still tempted, but I'm also hungry. Besides, Carol's got the advantage on me in height and muscle. She'd think nothing of tackling me.

"There you are," Jack says, standing and pulling out my chair for me. "Let me pour you some wine. Where were we?"

"When?"

"You were telling me about your new role. Are you all right?"

"Couldn't be better." I look at the plate of healthy-choice salmon and asparagus that the waiter sets before me. "But only if we get something chocolate for dessert."

"If not, I'll take you out for a sundae," he says, clinking his glass against mine. He smiles, the warmth back in his eyes. The waiter serves him his dinner. Jack surveys the plate before picking up his knife and fork—obviously not a man who plunges into anything. Or maybe he just doesn't like fish.

"Your dinner okay?" he asks. He's caught me watching him again.

"Fine," I say. I try to gain traction on thoughts racing out of control. "So, where did you pick up the tan? Not San Francisco."

"Actually, I was in Catalina for a few days last week." His voice is easy, casual. "Ever been there?"

"Of course. Paul and I used to sail there. I think you know that."

"Right. The *WindStar.*" Jack lowers his voice, though in this din it's unlikely we'd be overheard. "I think Sid might've mentioned something to you about this business that came up."

"Yes, I saw it in the paper. *The Coop II,* right?"

He nods curtly, but makes no comment. Nor am I inclined to mention the phone call asking for Coop.

"You're still on the case, then?" I ask, as offhandedly as I can manage. "I read that the body on the beach was identified as the owner of the boat?"

"Aquino, right. His brother was gunned down a couple of months ago. Both were mixed up in a money-laundering racket. Drugs, of course.

We're checking out anything that might turn up a lead. That's as much as I can tell you right now."

"Thanks. I appreciate it. You can get in touch with me directly, you know. Just call my cell phone." The words slide out, too late to retrieve. "I mean, you don't have to go through Sid."

"I'll do that. Same number?"

"Right." I busy myself cutting perfect bitefuls of salmon and asparagus, debating whether it's a good time to mention that I once offered Rick Aquino a margarita aboard the *WindStar.* There's a chance the Aquino brothers are the Pancho and Cisco Kid team who were in on Paul's abduction, but why suggest that to Jack? He never believed Paul was kidnapped in the first place.

The entrée is followed by chocolate mousse hunkered in a puddle of raspberry purée. Neither of us mention the promise of a sundae. The program, complete with a current TV sitcom star doing bad standup, a singer on the rebound from rehab, and the inevitable charity pitch followed by honorees accepting awards, is none too short. Carol wins both the camera and the weekend in Paris, not surprising considering her hefty bids. Sid looks pleased enough, knowing much of the evening is a write-off. But through it all, my mind is fixated elsewhere. Why has Sid considered it so important to maneuver me back in touch with the man charged with tracking down Paul? Why now?

The screening of a three-minute wrap-up video lauding medical advances since last year's fund-raiser is a signal for everyone to paw around in the dark for their goody bags (containing a T-shirt, shampoo, and CD) and beat a hasty retreat to the valet parkers. I bound over to Sid and lean in close.

"You have some 'splainin' to do, Lucy. Give me a ring, okay?"

"Sure thing." He winks. "You have a good time?"

"Of course. Nothing beats an inquisition with dinner. Darn it, Sid, I'd still like to know what you're up to. As for Carol, maybe I can get her to take me with her to Paris."

"Why not?" He grins. "Love ya, kid."

"I heard that," Carol says, wrapping her arms around me. "Don't be such a stranger. Come for dinner one night, will you?"

"I'd love it, but weekdays won't be good until I finish filming."

"Fine, maybe next weekend. I'll call."

I make the rounds of our tablemates, with whom I've barely conversed, then turn back to Jack. "It was good to see you again."

"Same here." He takes my arm as I start to wend my way through the crush. "When will your show be on? I'd like to watch it."

"I have no idea. The pilot may not even be picked up. You'll have to check your local listings, as they say."

"I'll look for it."

"Take care, Jack," I say, with as much finality as I can muster. I veer off down a deserted hallway, hoping to slip through a side door and make my way to the dark, tree-lined street where I parked my car. I sense Jack has made a move to follow, but I walk swiftly, cutting around knots of stragglers bidding farewells.

I'm steps away from a clean getaway when a hand clutches my elbow. It's Erica, steering me into a recess behind a giant potted ficus, her bony shoulder butting against mine. She swings me around with some force, her eyes glittering even in the shadows.

"You better know where he is, because they think you do," she says, her face close, her fingernails biting into my flesh.

"Who?"

"F' chrissake," she hisses, "they burned the wrong people. I don't wanna end up like Nat. You gotta come up with something, because I told 'em—" She exhales in a rush, her breath hot. "They want their money back, and Nat sure as hell didn't leave any behind!"

"Erica, what're you talking about?"

"C'mon, just lead 'em to Paul. They know he's not dead."

"I have no idea where he is."

"So where'd you go, then? The heat's been on me, like I'm s'posed to know. Nat was killed because Paul told them he was holding the money. They want it back—"

"They? Paul conned a lot of people—"

"Right, big time—like Russian mafia types." She exhales again, her fingers pressing into my elbow. "Look, I got them to believe me. That doesn't mean I get to stay alive." She lets go of my arm and backs away. "Same goes for you."

She turns and hurries toward the exit, slamming her hands against the metal bar to open the door. I watch her head toward the end of the long parking queue. The thought occurs to me that she can't be that broke if she can afford valet parking.

Russian mafia? Carol's got it right. Erica has to put blame some where—but now I'm supposed to be in cahoots with the Russian mafia? *What next?*

I look around. The lobby has cleared. I slip out the side door and walk to the corner. It was twilight when I arrived for the banquet. Now, once I cross Wilshire Boulevard, the side streets are pitch black. Few of the stately houses, positioned well back on their lots, have lights in their windows. I hurry across an intersection and turn right, spotting my car among only three parked on the deserted residential avenue. Out of habit, my car key is in hand, my thumb hovering above the red panic button. If I pressed it, would anyone in this neighborhood even bother to respond?

I quicken my pace, irritated when I see a slip of white paper visible on the driver's side of my windshield. A parking ticket? I checked the signs carefully. Just as I unlock the door and reach for the paper tucked under the wiper, the headlights of a dark van parked diagonally from mine flash on. I yank the car door open and climb in, locking the doors at once. The interior lights stay on just long enough for me to read the note: TELL COOP HE CAN'T HIDE.

The van pulls away from the curb and passes by, its broad-shouldered driver hunched over the wheel. He doesn't look my way. At least it's not the green sedan with the redhead that's been dogging me. I jam the note in my handbag and, with shaking fingers, turn the key in the ignition.

I make a wide U-turn and swing toward Sunset Boulevard, passing familiar streets that look sinister shrouded in darkness. I scan each intersection and check my rearview mirror before moving on. Minutes later I pull into Donna's driveway and park under the portico. I grab my purse and goody bag and race along the walkway to the front door. Before I can push my key in the lock, the door swings open. Donna, in a flowered caftan, smiles and steps aside.

"I hope you don't mind that I waited up for you. Did you have a good time? I thought maybe we could have a cup of tea together."

I slip inside, shivering and out of breath. It takes a moment to connect Donna's greeting with the silver tray gleaming on a low table in front of the fire. The living room, with its eccentric furnishings, looks cozy and inviting. Glimmering votive candles dot the table. I huddle on the landing, still feeling anxious.

"It's chilly out," Donna says. "Come inside. I want to hear all about your evening. Did you see Alex Trebek?"

I shake my head. "I'm sorry, no. Is he a friend of yours?"

"Heavens, no, but I hear he always goes to these charity events. Now he's someone I'd really like to meet someday. Such a nice man. I have my supper in there with him almost every evening."

She nods toward the sunroom, a glass enclosure just off the living room, given over to vast pots of cymbidium orchids and wicker furniture with faded chintz cushions. I picture Donna curled up on the chaise longue, a tray in her lap, watching *Jeopardy* as the sun sets.

"I used to watch him with my mother, until she passed away. We'd play against each other. Come in, come in."

I move to the sofa and sink into the plush cushions, feeling the warmth from the fire.

"Here, let me—" Donna takes my evening purse and goody bag and places them on the coffee table. "That's better. Do you take milk and sugar?"

I nod. But the cauldron in my head finally boils over. Hot tears flood down my cheeks. *What's getting to me? Erica? Mafia? The Coop?*

Donna slips a napkin in my hand, a square of sheer batiste with *broderie anglaise.* It lies in my palm even as tears drip off my chin. *Maybe it's just seeing Jack again.*

"Nothing like a good cry," she says, mopping my face with her own napkin. She dabs my nose. "Feel better?"

I nod. "Thank you for being so nice."

"Not at all. Let's have some tea now."

"I'm sorry about this. I'm just tired."

"Of course you are. Sleep in tomorrow. Get all the rest you need."

I sip the strong English tea, listening to the crackle of the fire in the grate. *Did this tea service once belong to Dame Mae Whitty?* Donna, tiny and bright-eyed, perches on the fender of the fireplace, looking at me with concern. I manage a smile.

"Thank you, my dear. The tea has restored me," I say, in my best drawing-room diction. "But seriously. I don't usually react this way after charity events."

She shakes her head, uncertain if I'm joking. "I should hope not." She takes the cup from my hand and sets it back on the tray. In soothing tones, she says, "Off to bed now. Go on. You need some rest."

I give Donna a hug. "Thank you so much. I'll see you in the morning."

I mount the stairs and head to my room like a sleepy child sent to bed. I flip the light switch, and the room is bathed in a peachy glow. The coverlet is already turned down, the ruffled pillows plumped up. The memory of lying in the folds of the soft, sweet-smelling linens makes me so drowsy I can barely keep my eyes open. I slip out of my dress and wash my face, too tired to do more. The warm water and plush towel remind me that only days ago I made do with cold water and brown paper towels in a public toilet.

How can I repay Donna's hospitality? What treat, what kindness, would fit the bill? As my head sinks into the downy pillow, a solution comes to mind, one so perfect that I sit up in bed, fully awake. I pull on the robe Donna has provided and make my way barefoot down the hall toward the pool of light streaming from the open door of the master bedroom.

I stop on the threshold, about to call her name, when I hear a sound like the mewling of a hungry kitten. I peer inside and catch my breath. Donna, standing on tiptoe, lifts an antique doll from a glass shelf in a cabinet. Once again I hear the mewling sound as she lays the baby doll on its back.

"Shhhhush, now. Nighty-night," Donna coos. She brushes her fingertips across the doll's eyes, as though flicking out the lights for the night. "Sleep tight." Then, catching sight of me in the reflection of the glass cabinet, she gasps and turns abruptly.

"Sorry, Donna! I didn't mean to startle you."

"That's all right. I was going to show you, but I thought you were too tired." She smiles. "Meet my granny's pride and joy."

I look around at an astonishing display of antique dolls, each dressed in ruffled and beribboned finery, complete with hats, boots, and lacy parasols. "They're beautiful, Donna."

"Granny collected dolls all her life, and so did my mother." She shrugs. "Sorry. Couldn't you sleep?"

"I was just about to drop off when I had a thought. You know, maybe I could arrange for you to meet Alex Trebek. Do you want me to try?"

"Really?" She blinks. "You know him?"

"No, actually I don't, but Jinx was once a category. Maybe I could call and see if we could watch his show being taped."

"Now that would be fun," she says, pulling her robe closer and hugging herself. "I'd like that, but I'm afraid I'd be just too nervous to meet him in person. I'm sure he's tired of women gushing over him."

"No, no, I'm sure he's very nice. Let me see what I can do. 'Night, Donna."

"Nighty-night, dear. Sleep tight."

"Tell me, do you close the eyes on all those dolls every night?"

"Good heavens, no," Donna says wearily. "Only the big baby dolls. Otherwise I'd be up until dawn."

I pad down the hallway to my room, knowing Donna has gone back to making her rounds. How long does it take to tuck in the baby dolls every night, and flick their eyes open every morning? I may be a little crazy, but Donna is completely nuts. The thought comforts me.

Chapter Eight

Is there an actor alive who hasn't awakened in a bone-chilling panic, terrified that the alarm hasn't gone off? That the sun is already up and somewhere a makeup chair sits empty?

Eventually my brain unscrambles, and I realize it's Sunday morning. Despite the reprieve, my day will not be quite the same. Monday looms, the first day of the shoot. I'm prepared, but am I prepared *enough*? I obsess, my role constantly on my mind. I pick up the script to read through yet again, pondering my choices, wondering what I might be overlooking. I want nothing more than to be there, on the set, in front of the camera, fully made up, *now*. It's the only cure for first-day jitters.

To distract myself, after breakfast with Donna, I drive up into the canyon, checking my rearview mirror frequently. I see no sign of the green sedan. Maybe *they*—surely the man on my cell phone asking about Coop is connected to the redhead and the green sedan—have taken the weekend off?

I park at the top of Mulholland, open my trunk, and burrow in the recesses for a folder of clippings and documents I haven't looked at in six months. I settle back in the Volvo to dig into the court filings and newspaper articles, hoping to find clues to the Coop question, if not respite from my preoccupation with filming tomorrow.

One clipping, already crisp and yellowing, falls into my lap.

Legal Battle over Mortgage Deals

Major Real Estate Scam Alleged

Paul C. Stephens, President, Stephens Property

> Development, has been indicted on 26 charges of securing loans based on false and fraudulently inflated property appraisals to buy homes, using the excess funds to develop other properties. In a "flipping" scheme using straw buyers, loan application packages were made to appear legitimate, according to investigators, but in fact contained false appraisals, which overvalued the real property, as well as doctored verifications of employment and credit statements. It is further alleged that significant sums of illegally obtained investment scheme funds were used to finance Stephens' extravagant lifestyle, including lavish travel and dining, expensive automobiles, and a 32-foot sailboat. Stephens, 54, whose assets were frozen and whose Beverly Hills home was seized, is believed to have fled the country, his whereabouts unknown. Stephens' wife, the actress Meg Barnes, was unavailable for comment.

By the time that article appeared, I'd discovered my house had been mortgaged at almost twice its value and was no longer in my name. Since Paul was the property expert, I had been happy to take his advice and willingly signed whatever he put in front of me.

After Dirck, who left me to pay bills and balance our joint bank accounts, it was a relief to have a husband so skilled in financial management. But Paul was already in "whereabouts unknown" (in the company of Mexican bandits? Goons from a drug cartel?) when credit card bills, for accounts in my name that I knew nothing about, poured in, each maxed to the limit with airline tickets, limos, clothing, jewelry, and dining charges, to say nothing of substantial cash withdrawals.

The sailboat mentioned in the clipping was Paul's, confiscated along with his leased automobiles, a Land Rover and a Porsche. I'd closed my eyes to excesses that should have sent up red flags. Whenever I gently pointed out to Paul that he didn't have to pick up *every* dinner check, he'd say, "It's the cost of doing business, baby." That was also his excuse to lavish acquaintances with spectacular flower arrangements, cases of vintage wine, and expensive trinkets from Tiffany's. Despite having two luxury cars, he'd hire a limo to attend a midtown business meeting, or charter a helicopter to show property.

"You got to make people think big! The sky's the limit when you're sellin' dreams," he'd say, slipping into the backwoods drawl that disarmed everyone. "It's just dirt out there, baby. That's all they're gonna see if I just putt-putt them up to the site in some ol' jalopy."

I'd laugh in agreement, happy enough to have him wrap his arm around my shoulders and squeeze me close. Sitting in the jalopy I now call home, I cringe at the thought of that embrace. I roll down the window for more air.

After Paul's mortgage scheme became front-page news and his property seized, I hid out in the Baskins' pool house, "unavailable for comment." I brought with me only the clothing and personal belongings Carol and I could hastily box up. I managed to dump cartons of files and papers in Dougie's garage, but neglected to pack up possessions of greater value—my grandmother's rocking chair, a small writing desk, a watercolor, among many other significant items—that are now lost to me forever. It would not have occurred to me to tuck a painting under my arm on my way out the door. But at the time, I didn't fully realize how serious my situation was.

I stow the clippings in the trunk and pull back onto Mulholland. Either Paul's dead, killed by cartoon banditos, or he faked his disappearance, making off with all the cash and loot I could stuff into a grocery bag for his accomplice to pick up. Who knows how much more he salted away somewhere in embezzled funds? Is he really still alive? Enough people are trying to find him to make me think so.

All I need to play a murderess tomorrow is to think about Paul robbing me blind even as I thought I was saving his life. But then, I'd give anything to have back the man I thought I married. I'm struck once again by parallels between my own life and that of the character I'm playing, both of us deceived by husbands we loved. The difference, of course, is that my character is haunted by remorse for killing her husband and his mistress because they duped her, while I suffer regret for having played the willing fool. How differently would I have reacted if I'd discovered the deception *before* Paul disappeared?

I'm halfway back to Donna's house when my cell phone rings. I pull to the side of the road and rummage in my handbag. The melody becomes louder, more insistent. I seize the little monster, flip its lid, and shout, "Yes? Hello?"

"Sorry, did I catch you at a bad time? It's Jack Mitchell."

"Hi. Sorry, I just couldn't find my phone."

"I hope you don't mind my calling."

"No, unless I'm being indicted or something." *Easy, Meg, why so hostile?* "Sorry, joking."

"I don't think you need to worry. I'm out at the beach, and I was just wondering if you might join me for dinner at Chez Jay? That place on Ocean Avenue."

"Not tonight, I'm afraid. I start shooting tomorrow."

"Right, I remember. Well, maybe we could make it an early dinner."

"Thanks, Jack. Maybe another time."

"Promise?"

"Absolutely. Another time, okay? After I get this behind me."

I flip the lid on the phone and pull back on the road, wondering exactly what I meant by needing to get "this" behind me. The pilot? Or the whole business with Paul that's beginning to haunt every waking moment? It's being stuck in limbo, waiting for the next growly voice on my cell phone, the next scary note on my windshield. Why couldn't they have found his damn body so everyone could get on with their lives?

I reach the fork in the road at Mulholland and Coldwater Canyon and on impulse pull into the TreePeople nature preserve. Minutes later I'm hiking along a shady path, my footfalls silenced by a thick cushion of chipped bark and pine needles. I try to empty my mind and think of nothing, which has the effect of opening a floodgate of unwelcome thoughts.

For starters, I face the fact that my decision not to join Jack at the beach had a lot to do with the cost of the gas to get there. My half-tank will have to see me to Pasadena and back tomorrow. What fresh hell is this—weighing fuel consumption against a meal at a favorite restaurant with a man I find more than a little attractive?

Would I have met Jack at a restaurant that was only two minutes away? I consider calling him back, but I can't make myself do it. Even with the outside chance that over a bottle of decent Cab Jack might reveal more about *The Coop II*—or, more enticingly, himself—conserving fuel wins out.

Chapter Nine

Wearing jeans and an old flannel jacket, my hair still damp from the shower, I tiptoe down the stairs, careful not to wake up Donna and her six dozen baby dolls. I sip a few mouthfuls of coffee, sling my bag over my shoulder, and head out into the cold night air.

I'm stoked and ready for the day, my anticipation revving up as I turn on the ignition. Before releasing the brake, I run my wipers over the silvery dew on the windshield.

"Hey, fella," I murmur as my headlights pick up the brush of a tail, then the slinky gray body of a coyote loping across the road toward the eucalyptus. He turns his head, as though curious to know what mortal would venture out at this time of the morning. Just me, a lucky actor with an early call.

Less than a mile up the road I crest Mulholland. Across the valley floor, the San Joaquin mountains rise majestically, crowned with dawn's golden glimmer. In a rush, the night sky fades from starlit indigo to velvety purple, then bursts into shimmering lavender. I travel along the ridge, then turn down the Valley side of the canyon, no other car in sight. By the time I reach Ventura Boulevard, morning has bloomed, revealing a world of strip malls, fast-food joints, and gas stations.

Within minutes, the road is teeming, the freeway ramps jammed. Who are all these people, and where are they going at this hour? Surely they don't all have makeup calls. I glance at the page of location directions in the passenger seat, then at my watch. If I don't get lost or stuck in a major pileup en route, I should make it on time—but if I do run into trouble, at least I can make a call.

I shudder, thinking back on a career full of pre–cell phone, early-morning searches for remote location shoots, usually in rugged desert locales where Westerns, sci-fi, and action adventures are filmed. More than once, hopelessly lost in a dusty moonscape of parched earth and jagged rocks, I'd tear my eyes from the narrowing road and try to decipher scribbled directions in the half-light of dawn.

Invariably some vital piece of information had been withheld from the hurried instructions given by a third assistant director mumbling through the static of a field phone. On one occasion, "Bear left at the gas station on the other side of the hill" had left me in no-man's-land miles from the destination and only minutes away from my call-time. There is no greater relief than coming across the temporary encampment of behemoth production trailers and knots of crew members standing around a breakfast truck.

Somehow I've managed never to be late for a call, but I've come close, and it's always a sickening fear. If you're late, eighty-five people wearing shorts and Nikes are left standing idle in the early-morning frost. While you're zooming up one canyon road and down another, battling the forces of panic and doom in Location Hell, you can hear the growling spreading through the makeup trailer:

"Drugs," they're saying. "She just doesn't give a damn."

This morning, with plenty of time to spare, I pull up alongside a wall of location trucks parked on a leafy residential street in Pasadena. A wiry young production assistant, walkie-talkie in hand, sprints up to me.

"Miss Barnes, morning. I'm Sean. Your dressing room's over here," he says in a rush, pointing toward a trailer. "We'd like to get you into hair and makeup first thing. Can I get you some breakfast?"

"Just orange juice, thank you. I'll get something later."

"You bet. Let's get you over to the makeup trailer pronto, okay?"

His face is anxious. I smile. "Sure. Fine with me."

How many times, to how many far-flung locations all over the world, have I arrived just after dawn, bare-faced with damp hair, to climb steps to a cozily cluttered trailer where I hand myself over to a hairdresser and makeup artist? It's never an easy surrender, particularly on the first day of a shoot, despite casual introductions and bright smiles all around. Early-morning coffee has soured my stomach. Every fiber of my being resists being touched by unfamiliar hands, relinquishing control to strangers. Many times I've sat in a makeup chair, kicking and screaming inside, longing to slap on my own paint in my own good time. But however wary and ill at ease I feel, I'm always amazed when my face in the makeup mirror appears relaxed, trusting—my first acting of the day, and perhaps my best.

Smiling at Silvia, the makeup woman assigned to me, I settle into a vinyl-covered chair, my fingers gripping the armrests.

"You have gorgeous skin," she says, stroking a creamy liquid on my temples and cheeks. "Let me know if you're allergic to something."

"Thanks, but I can't think of anything."

I'd certainly know by now if there was, considering the variety of war paint applied to my face over the years. I've even survived unblemished from four-hour makeup sessions for *Star Trek*, complete with green skin, pointy ears, and a protruding forehead, painstakingly applied so as not to incur the wrath of the steely-eyed production staff, who keep the covenant with platoons of eagle-eyed Trekkies the world over. If my face can handle that, anything else is a piece of cake.

Silvia's cool fingertips flutter across my eyes. I melt into my chair, already succumbing to the drowsy warmth of the makeup lights. She strokes, blends, and dabs, earning my trust. It's not easy. I've experienced my share of calamities.

Early in my career, I was seated in the chair of a member of a legendary family of Hollywood makeup artists. That crusty old peacock, still vain despite liver-spotted hands, had a reputation for having bedded starlets who later became screen legends. I was in awe of him . . . until he finished applying his Pancake No. 3, cake mascara, and tangerine lipstick.

"Um, my eyes," I ventured, on the verge of sobbing. "Maybe we could, um . . ."

"Something wrong?" he asked gruffly. "You know how long I've been in this business? Hedy Lamarr never complained. Ann Sheridan never complained."

"Oh, no, I'm not complaining," I assured him, looking at the beaded, waxy clumps of mascara on my eyelashes. I was playing an innocent young schoolmarm in a television Western. I left his makeup chair looking like Mae West.

"I hope you're not going to sneak off and make a mess of things," he warned. "Gloria DeHaven always pulled that, and I don't like to be called on the set to fix things. I know lights. I know the director, and I know what he likes. Know what I mean?"

"Absolutely," I assured him, cowed and anxious that, as a contract player, I could be replaced before my first close-up was in the can. I resisted every urge to touch my face. That makeup man is long dead, but I still have to watch vintage reruns of myself with a face that looks like two prunes stuck in a bowl of orange Jell-O.

"Are you always this happy?" I open my eyes and see Silvia's twenty-something face peering at me in the mirror. "You've been smiling for twenty minutes," she says.

"Sorry, am I making things difficult?"

"No, not at all. I've just never seen anyone in my makeup chair so relaxed and cheerful this time of the morning."

Shortly before eight I'm led into the first setup, the living room of a threadbare Pasadena mansion. I'm dressed in a classic Courrèges suit, complete with tissue protecting the white collar until we're ready to shoot. A Jackie Kennedy–style pillbox hat is perched on my pouffed-up hair.

The authentic period set is like an attic full of youthful memories. I thumb through old copies of *Life* magazine and revisit my childhood world of rotary phones, a console radio, and an old stereo set similar to one on which we played Beatles and Dinah Washington LPs.

"Wow, no remote. Can you believe it?" I turn to see our director, Lenny Bishop, gazing at a Philco television set. "Only black-and-white," he says, shaking his head.

"Only three channels," I say with a smile. "And no DVD."

Lenny frowns. "Man, forget TiVo. How cruel is that?"

We spend most of the morning filming the flashback scenes when my husband's body is discovered and the police are called. The vignettes are dramatic but brief, with little dialogue. By early afternoon, we're rehearsing my biggest scene of the day, the one in which I confront my husband about his mistress. The two have resumed their affair, which he'd led me to believe was over. I discover the deception when a bank manager questions an overdraft, and I realize my husband has been supporting the other woman by siphoning money from the business we've built up together. When my husband arrives home late, I'm waiting for him, knowing he's spent the evening with her.

The young actor playing my husband appears on the set dressed in a business suit. He's good-looking and cocky, with an easy manner. My stand in, a young woman of my height and coloring, has taken note of him. She rarely strays out of his line of sight, a tactic that seems to be working. They lunched together, and she's given him a neck massage. As the day wears on, she sheds one layer of clothing after another. By the time we're set up for the confrontation scene, she's down to a low-cut tank top.

While Silvia and Lori do final touchups for the first take of the master shot, my eyes are on my stand-in, who is whispering to my husband. The distraction is grating, particularly as the actor and I are already in place on the set. The edge I need for the scene has been handily provided.

By five o'clock, I'm wrapped for the day. I head for my car, feeling as carefree as a kid waking up to Saturday. The sun lowers behind a cloud bank, and the air chills. A cool breeze flutters the collar of my shirt, but my hair, lacquered into a bouffant helmet, remains rigidly in place. I hurry toward the Volvo, key in hand. But even at a distance of twenty feet, I see that the doors are unlocked. I double-click UNLOCK, just to be certain. The buttons don't move. Was I that distracted this morning? I'm certain that I pressed LOCK and saw the buttons on the doors drop.

Fear laps at my throat. I consider racing back to ask one of the off-duty cops on the set to walk me to my car. At least my Volvo no longer looks like a homeless person's flophouse, crammed tight with odd belongings, thanks to the roomy closet in Donna's house. Still, what would the police think if I requested an escort? This is Pasadena, hardly the mean streets of downtown's skid row.

I glance into the backseat before pulling the front door open, then slide behind the wheel, noticing at once that the seat is too far back. The glove compartment hangs open. Someone's been in my car. I lock the doors, my heart racing. The redhead and her companion in the green sedan must have been here—and one of them knows how to disengage an alarm system.

I turn the key in the ignition, exhaling with relief when I'm not blown to smithereens. I pull away from the curb. *Why would anyone want to blow me up anyway? Am I coming unhinged?*

A few blocks from the freeway ramp, just as my stomach begins to calm down, I see in the rearview mirror that the lid of my trunk is bouncing up and down. I pull into a gas station and park near the convenience store. I should have realized that anyone checking out my car would also take a look in the trunk. I lift the lid and peer into the cluttered interior packed with boxes I'd decided not to unload at Donna's house. Someone has rifled through the folder of clippings about Paul. Papers lay scattered, not even the slightest attempt made to return the folder intact to the file box. Whoever was rummaging around in my trunk doesn't care that I know it.

I ease the file box out of the trunk and immediately regret it. An avalanche of boxes and bags slide into the empty space. Rather than struggle to repack in the hot, crowded parking lot, I transfer the box to the backseat, slam the lid on the trunk, and get back behind the wheel. My hands are filthy, my head throbbing. Damn!

I pull into rush hour traffic, molars grinding. What the hell do people think I'm hiding? What information could I possibly have that anyone would want? If Paul is Coop, and he's still out in the world, alive and well— Wait! If anger focuses the mind, the thought blasting through my brain is riveting. Could Paul himself be stalking me? If so, why? I grip the steering wheel, forcing myself to breathe deeply.

I head down the freeway, functioning on autopilot. What could Paul want? Or need? Nothing that I can think of; still, the idea sticks. Miles later, I realize with a jolt that I have four lanes of traffic between me and my exit ramp. I clamp my foot on the accelerator, trusting my turn signal to give fair warning to everyone in close proximity.

Before heading up the canyon, I swing by the post office, making it through the door with only minutes to spare before the entrance for box holders is closed for the day. I stuff the mail into my carryall and sprint for the exit, scanning the street before I unlock my car.

Donna is watching *Jeopardy* when I arrive home. *Must remember to call about Alex Trebek.* She waves me into the sunroom and pats the wicker chair next to hers. I sink down and kick off my shoes.

"Dinner's in the oven. Roast chicken," Donna says, her eyes on the TV screen. "What is a bloomer girl?" she shouts, clapping her hands like a schoolgirl who knows she's got it right. She gets the next two answers correct, too.

"You should be a contestant," I tell her during the commercial break.

"Me? Oh, no, I'd be so nervous I wouldn't remember my own name."

"But you should try out. I'll bet you could do it."

"With all those people looking at me?" She shudders. "I just think someone like you is so amazing. How do you remember all those words?"

"It's what I do, just part of the job. But I don't think I'd be any good on *Jeopardy*."

"You would if you watched it every night and got the hang of it. After a while the answers just pop in your head. Wait—Who is Sammy Sosa?" she shouts. Donna gets it right; the contestant doesn't. She throws up her hands, shakes her head. "How could anyone get that wrong?"

"You need to get out more, Donna."

She laughs. "Don't I know it. I wouldn't mind a little glamour and excitement in my life. But it just doesn't come my way, if you know what I mean. You want a glass of wine?"

"Sure, but let me get it."

"No, no. Won't be a sec." She pulls herself up from the depths of her armchair and heads for the kitchen, her slippers clip-clopping on the parquet.

I slide my mail out of my carryall and shuffle through the envelopes. No checks. No personal letters. Just junk mail, most of it offering special introductory rates on pre-approved credit cards. *Don't they know?*

I'm about to rip up another special offer when I notice an envelope addressed to MARGARET H. STEPHENS, forwarded from my old address. I open the envelope and discover it's not a special offer but a credit card bill in the amount of $7,218.63. I stare at the figure, numbed. The charges are not mine, and I certainly don't recognize the account number.

"Here you go," Donna says, handing me a glass of white wine. "Dinner's ready. Shall we have it on trays in here?"

"Sorry, I'm just not very hungry tonight." I stuff the bill in my pocket.

"Well, have something to keep me company. How did it go today? You must be tired."

I nod. "Very tired." So tired I just want to crawl into bed and pull the covers over my head. Instead, I eat a portion of chicken breast and sip my wine while Donna shouts answers to Alex Trebek.

Before heading upstairs, I retrieve the battered old file box from the backseat of my car and haul it to my room. I trudge up the steps, barely making it over the threshold before the bottom of the box gives way, dumping files and papers all over the bedroom floor. I groan and drop to my knees, scooping documents back into file folders. The box itself is beyond repair. I set about flattening it, salvaging only the lid to hold some of the loose papers.

As I do so, I find an old envelope stuck to the underside of one of the bottom flaps of the box. The glue on the envelope crackles as I tug it. I peel it loose more gently when I see the 1969 postmark on the pale green six-cent stamp. The address, penciled in childish script, reads: Mrs. Elvira Cooper, 212 Front Street, Lennox, West Virginia. No return address.

Inside is a square of paper with a gummed edge, the name of a plumbing company printed on top, folded over a black-and-white school photo. The hairs on my neck bunch as I gaze at the picture. Even with the crew cut, skinny shoulders, and rabbity front teeth, I see a resemblance to Paul. I recognize his eyes, his smile, on this kid with the jug ears and freckles.

My eyes go back to the box, trapped flat under my knee. It was Paul's file box. I found it empty in the garage. I grabbed it to use when I packed up the contents of my filing cabinet shortly before I moved out. This envelope must have been stuck inside the bottom flap, left behind by Paul.

I turn the picture over. My heart sinks. The name penciled on the back is Frankie Cooper. *Coop?* I take another look at the penciled numbers on the scrap of paper: 5/22/55. A birth date? It's not Paul's. Besides, Paul said he grew up in Kentucky. If one could believe anything he said. Could Frankie be a cousin?

I lean back against the bed, stretching my legs across papers strewn on the carpet. I turn the picture over again, staring into those solemn child's eyes, and fall asleep that way.

Chapter Ten

I spend most of Friday morning in court, or what passes for it on prime-time TV. My estranged son, Danny, who fingered me for the decades-old crime and caused the case to be reopened, has taken the stand. His testimony, revealing my association with the hit man, spells curtains for me.

Shelby Stuart, playing my defense counsel, is an old buddy from a long-ago acting class in New York and once played my husband in a TV film. I hadn't run into him in years until he showed up on the set. He's paunchy now, with thinning hair. I remember when he was a lean leading man never out of work. I watch him being powdered down for a close-up and wonder why he didn't have a major film career. Not enough edge for the big screen, perhaps. Low danger quotient. While his cohorts went on to careers in features, he went from series to series. Not bad, but not what he wanted. He's good, though, and the scene crackles. I'm scripted to go down for life, but if this were the real thing, I'm not sure he wouldn't get me acquitted.

The judge is an old friend, too. We've vied for many roles over the years. Only a few of us know she has MS, and that a recurring role as a judge in this series will keep her Screen Actors Guild health benefits going. That's good enough reason to pray this pilot gets picked up. That, of course, largely hinges on the young actors carrying this show, most of whom play attitude and wardrobe.

The kid with the crooked smile playing the prosecutor is pretty good but shows all the signs of turning into a monster if the show goes to series. He already has a retinue, and they'll soon be telling him that what he really wants to do is features. He'll take a fling in the movies the first chance he gets, and then it's anybody's guess. For now, the director indulges him with an extra take, and the kid gets another opportunity to flash his killer smile. If he has any sense, he'll ration that lopsided grin to one per episode.

We set up for the reverse shots. I'm on deck first for my close-up. Lori and Silvia finish touching up my hair and makeup as the actor playing my son takes his place tight against the camera.

On "Action," he shouts, "She knew my old man was seeing Patty on the side! She knew, and had them killed to make it look like a murder-suicide—"

I half-rise, tears welling: "No, Danny, no!"

The judge pounds her gavel. Shelby shouts, "Objection, Your Honor!" and the scene concludes with me sobbing and sinking into my chair, face in hands. Cut.

As we break for the next setup, Shelby wraps his arm around my shoulders and whispers, "Damn, you're good, baby."

"Thanks, Shel." I run my arm around him, giving him a squeeze. His hand slides to the small of my back, his fingers brushing the bare skin under my jacket. "But then, you always were," he says, his breath warm in my ear. I freeze. *My God, did we sleep together?* Possibly. Probably, but for the life of me, when? Back in our days in acting class? Good God, my past is catching up with me, and I can't even remember it.

"Wait! Am I—?" I grab the back of my skirt before remembering that the battery microphone I'd worn in a previous setup has already been removed.

"Gotcha," he says, laughing. "I love it, Meg. Still gullible after all these years. But seriously, kid, that was great stuff."

I smile, still not sure. I suppose it doesn't really matter anymore, but how could I forget lying naked in someone's arms?

"Listen," he says, wrapping his arm around me again, "how'd you like to have dinner some night? You know, catch up. I heard you were—I mean, you're not with anyone now, right?"

"Well, I've sort of been seeing someone." I laugh, desperate for some excuse. "An attorney, actually, would you believe—"

"Hey, that's great. Can't say I'm surprised. Someone like you doesn't stay on the loose for long—but hey, if you're ever free—"

"Absolutely, Shel. Dinner."

He gives my shoulders a squeeze and whispers, "You're still hot stuff, babe." He clicks his tongue and winks. *We* must've *slept together.* I'd just as soon be spared total recall, but I'd like to think I can still remember whether I shared a bed with someone.

Shelby pushes open the heavy door to the soundstage, and we head out into the bright sunlight to our separate dressing rooms. I turn on my cell phone as I mount the steps to my trailer. A call comes in before I have a chance to check voice mail.

"Meg, there you are. Did you get any of my messages?"

"No, Carol. I've been on the set all morning. What's up?"

"Sid told me Jack said you turned down dinner with him. What's that all about?"

"I was shooting the next day. I never go out the night before."

"God, you're such a stickler. So how's the big comeback going?"

"Okay. I'm hitting my marks. Improving the script when I can." I catch sight of my reflection in the mirror and pull myself up out of a slouch. "Actually, it just feels damn good to be in front of a camera again."

"You are just so Debbie Reynolds. Gotta dance, gotta sing—"

"Gotta laugh, gotta cry. So, Sid's taking a big interest in my love life, huh? He wonders why I'm not going out with Jack? I have to tell you, I didn't think guys got into that kind of stuff."

"Hey, look. He cares, okay? We both do. And Sid thinks Jack's a really great guy. It's time you started seeing someone again. Especially someone a cut above the last jerk in your life. You know, Sid and I worry about you. He asked me last night if I knew where you were living these days. I had to tell him I don't know. Now, what's that all about? Where *are* you living these days?"

"Same place. Up in Holmby Hills."

"*What* same place? Does it have an address?"

"Carol, I have to get back on the set. Can I call you later? Better yet, let's have lunch over the weekend."

"Fine. How about dinner here Friday night instead? I've left several messages for you, and I've already invited Jack. Okay with you? I mean, you can't be a complete hermit."

"Okay, sure. That's great. Gotta run, Carol. Talk to you later."

Damn. I snap the lid on my phone and flop into a chair. My life is now as small as I can make it, and the world still closes in. I force myself to unclamp my molars. Slumping deeper in my chair, I close my eyes and relax my shoulders. I try to empty my mind, but my brain stubbornly dwells on Carol's call. Unless she's sending me a floral arrangement, she doesn't need my address. And I don't need to dine with an FBI agent.

Do Sid and Carol have some inkling I spend nights in the Volvo? I doubt it. If they knew, they would have strong-armed me back to their pool house in no time. I'd hate that more than a night spent in a packing crate. I couldn't bear for anyone to know about the mess I've got myself into. Or worse, try to help.

I flick on my cell phone to check voice mail. Two calls from Carol regarding dinner, and one return call from a credit card company. It's an 800 number, which means a customer service representative in any time zone in the world could answer. When I first called to report the charges I didn't make on an account I never opened, a female voice, responding in a suspiciously singsongy, plummy accent, said, "Not to worry, Mrs. Stephens. We'll make inquiries, and a representative will get back to you."

"Excuse me. You're not really in Nevada?"

"Oh, dear, no, ma'am. I'm situated in Mumbai."

"Seriously? I'm glad I'm not paying for the call. What's the weather like?"

"Quite pleasant, but I've not been outside since dinner. It's 3:18 in the morning."

"Really? It's afternoon here. Quite hot for February. The Santa Anas are kicking in."

"You must be near Hollywood. Do you see Brad Pitt?"

"Regrettably, no. With all the kids, he keeps pretty much to himself. Well, I'll let you get back to work. Nice talking to you. Cheers!"

I may be bankrupt, but apparently my credit rating is still good enough for someone to rack up more than $7,000 in charges. I head back to the set without returning the call. I much prefer a make-believe confrontation with an enraged son accusing me of murder than dealing with the reality of my miserable financial situation.

After the reverse shots, I'm wrapped for the day. But before I leave the stage, I stop by the crafts services table and stock up on bottles of fruit juice and various other snacks to stow in my shoulder bag. With the rest of the afternoon to myself, I drive over the canyon, intending to go to the health club.

Approaching the summit and turning on to Mulholland, I'm startled by a spokesman on the radio asking, "Are you tired of paying high monthly insurance rates?" I immediately recognize Dirck's husky burr. "Look no further," he says. "I've got the answer, a trusted name you can rely on—"

I wouldn't count on Dirck to choose kitty litter, much less pick a reliable insurance carrier, but thanks to his folksy delivery, he can sell almost anything he can manage to pronounce.

"Just call this toll-free number. You'll be glad you did—"

"What the hell," I say with a laugh. "Glad you're getting work, buddy."

Then, as I hear Dirck's "Call now" tagline, it occurs to me to give him a ring, congratulate him. The urge subsides before I've even picked up my cell phone. Thank God I don't have his number. I have no desire to rekindle any sort of relationship with Dirck—or Pru. What was I thinking?

Whatever synapse the impulse to call Dirck has formed in my brain, Mumbai springs to mind, and with it, Coop. On impulse, I pull into a lay-by near Benedict Canyon. With the motor still running, I flip open my phone and call information. What are the chances there's a party named Cooper on Front Street in Lennox, West Virginia?

I hold my breath waiting to find out, then exhale in a rush when the operator says, "Hold for the number, please."

Heart banging, I wait for the automatic connection. Seven rings later, a quavering female voice drawls, "Hallow?"

"Hello. Could I speak to Frank, please?"

A sharp intake, then, "Come again? You want Frankie?"

"Yes, please. Is he there?"

I hear a clatter as the receiver is put down, then a harsh whisper. "Dorrie, come quick. Someone askin' for Frankie."

I press the phone tight against my ear, straining to make out the muffled exchange.

A hoarse female voice mumbles, "F' chrissake, Ma—"

"Talk to her, Dorrie. Maybe she knows sump'in—"

There's another clatter, then an irritable voice asks, "You lookin' for Frankie? Who the hell's this?"

"Dorrie? Hiya—" The phone throbs in my hand as I plunge into some semblance of her harsh twang. "Jis' wonderin' if Frankie's aroun'. You prob'ly don' even remember me—"

"Prob'ly not." She grunts. "Sorry, but it gets kinda hard keepin' track of y'all. So what d'ya want with Frankie?"

"Jis' hopin' to talk to 'im. Know where I could find him?"

"He ha'int been through here in years, an' he don't get in touch less'n he's behind bars, y'know?"

"Sorry to hear that, Dorrie. Where was he, last ya heard?"

"How come ya need to know? Who is this, anyway?"

"I was jis' thinkin' 'bout 'im. The Coop and I go way back—"

"I'll bet. You got a lotta company." Her laugh is bitter, ugly. "Nobody's seen Frankie in years. Dropped off the face of the Earth, and good riddance. Maybe you wanna save yourself some trouble. Frankie don't give a damn 'bout nobody. Never did. And while you're at it, don't bother callin' back and gettin' Ma all rattled again, okay?"

The receiver slams down with a bang. I snap my phone closed. Then wait. If Dorrie has second thoughts about hanging up, can she call me back? I check the call roster. I have Dorrie's number. If she has caller I.D., she has mine, too—just one more electronic innovation Jinx never had to deal with.

I pull back on Mulholland, running over our exchange. Dorrie didn't seem surprised when I mentioned the name Coop, and she volunteered that Frankie had been in prison. But since she claims not to be in touch with her brother, there's not much chance she'll pass my number on to him.

I maneuver through the canyon's twists and turns, random thoughts careening through my head. Given my circumstances, a cell phone makes my present life possible, especially with my generous usage deal. I take it for granted that people can reach me anytime, anywhere—but only if I've provided my number. How did the man who called about Coop know how to reach me? I'm not listed. If I know the person who called about Coop, why can't I recognize the voice? By the time I reach the flats of Beverly Hills, paranoia is burning a hole in my brain.

I turn onto Wilshire Boulevard and spot a familiar figure entering Neiman Marcus. I decide to forgo the health club and catch up with Adriana, the one female I can count on to fully appreciate a suspicious state of mind when it comes to troublesome spouses.

I veer into the left turn lane, then swing up the self-parking ramp. Once inside Neiman's, I head straight for the perfume counters, one of Adriana's favorite haunts. She's a woman of unique style, and not hard to find. I see her signature gray felt hat with the spray of feathers bobbing down the aisle ahead of me.

"Adriana, is that you?"

The woman turns, fixes me with hooded hawk eyes, and slowly blinks twice. "Meg, my dear, of course it's me." *If it's Tuesday, it must be Neiman's.* She arches a perfectly shaped brow. "You're looking very well, I must say."

"So are you, Adriana. As always."

She shifts effortlessly into a languid pose, her tailored gray suit skimming her body just so. Her face, with deep-socket eyes and sculpted cheekbones, is artfully made up and powdered to a smooth matte finish.

"Thank you, darling. I'm desperate for a decent hand cream. Walk with me, won't you?"

"Of course. I could use some moisturizer myself."

A pretty clerk beckons, her smile sweet, her eyes predatory. "We've got a special on our three-step cleansing, exfoliating, moisturizing treatment. Would you like to give it a try?" Adriana and I step closer, both of us lured by the possibility of a special offer with a free gift. The clerk squeezes a drop of cream on my wrist and smoothes it in little swirls with her middle finger. "See how quickly it absorbs? Feel how soft that is."

I nod and brush my fingers across my glistening wrist. "Lovely," I murmur, "but my skin tends to be sensitive. Would you have a sample I could try at home for a few days?"

The clerk eyes us both, her lids drooping to half-mast. "Samples? I'm afraid not. But if there's a problem, you can return the product for a full refund."

I smile. "Thanks anyway." I slide my parking ticket onto the counter for validation before Adriana and I move on down the aisle. Not quite out of earshot, I hear the young woman whisper to another clerk, "Did you hear that? It's always the rich who want something for nothing."

I catch sight of myself in a wall mirror, dressed in jeans and a T-shirt, my face in full camera makeup. Beside me, Adriana appears serene and aloof, her alligator handbag dangling on her arm. She glides toward another counter, pumps lotion from a demonstrator bottle onto her hands, and falls back into step beside me.

Adriana would have me believe she's in her forties. I know she's well over seventy because she and Jean Shrimpton were both top models in the '60s. Adriana went off to Italy for a few years of *la dolce vita,* appearing in several sandal-and-toga epics and spaghetti Westerns, until an ill-advised marriage sidelined her. A role in an '80s horror cult-classic rescued her from total obscurity. But these days few people, aside from Robert Osborne, would recognize her on the street.

We amble down another aisle, each of us spritzing fragrance from display atomizers, before heading for the rear exit. Once outside, we stroll toward a bench near the valet parking station. Adriana settles on one end, her shapely legs neatly crossed at the ankles, her handbag in her lap. She gazes into the middle distance, ready for her close-up.

"So, what's new, Adriana?" I reach into my shoulder bag for the bottles of fruit juice I filched from the studio. She selects mango, leaving the passion fruit for me. I rip open a small bag of M&M's and set it on the bench between us.

She sighs and brushes a hand across her brow. "I'm a time bomb ticking, ticking," she says, her voice uninflected. "A walking beacon, transmitting signals. Here, feel this." She turns her head, holding a lock of hair away from her ear. "You can see it throbbing. My former husband had the transmitter implanted. He controls my every movement, my every thought. His finger is on the remote. Flicking. Flicking. Always flicking."

She's invited me to inspect her neck before, but I've never detected any sort of device. I look again now and all I see is gray scum on her collar, unwashed skin, and strands of white hair beneath her wig. Up close, the cuff of her sleeve is frayed, her skirt stained. "I'm so sorry. That's terrible, Adriana."

"Diabolical," she says, slowly blinking twice.

Her expression is steely, her beady eyes hard. Adriana is completely batty, but she showed me great kindness the first time I parked my Volvo behind her vintage Chevrolet in Holmby Park for the night. Without her, I would never have known how to gain access to the public toilets once the park custodian locked the doors at six p.m. Adriana even showed me a gadget she could plug into her car's cigarette lighter to heat water for morning tea. She shared her cup with me.

I hand her the rest of the bags of pretzels and M&M's stashed in my carryall. "See you in the movies, Adriana. Take care."

"I will, my dear. Sorry I haven't been in touch lately, but everything's been so frantic. Beastly wardrobe fittings, you know. There's a role for you in my next picture, of course. You'll be getting a call shortly."

"Wonderful. Look forward to it."

I leave Adriana sitting on the bench, no doubt fantasizing about the gowns Edith Head is whipping up for her. I stroll back into Neiman Marcus, selecting a route that skirts the cosmetics counters, and head out the front doors to Wilshire.

I worry about Adriana. She's canny, but frailer than ever. How has she managed to survive at all, her smoker's lungs weathering cold, damp nights in her Chevrolet? Adriana is my cautionary tale, the perfect model of a mentally unstable woman, homeless too long. I don't believe her husband planted a radio transmitter behind her ear, but who am I to say? When I begin to fear that I really may be going crazy, I have only to spend time with Adriana to feel completely sane.

Before I know it, I'm strolling past the building where Sid has his offices. I glance through the windows of Le Petit Ferme on the chance he might be there, knowing he wouldn't mind if I joined him. Sure enough, I spot him at a corner table and push open the plate-glass door, buoyed at the prospect of apple tart and café au lait. With one foot on the threshold, I jolt to a stop. Sid's tablemate, half-concealed by the serving counter, is the woman I saw in the green sedan. I back away from the door, my brain scrambling to make a connection between her and Sid. Staff? Client? Friend? Private eye? Maybe he's hired her to keep track of me.

I continue down Wilshire, trying to find my way through the apprehension clouding my brain. The woman doesn't look like office help or a friend of Sid's. Why tail me? Besides, what professional P.I. would go out in flaming red hair and a lime green jacket to spy on someone? Whenever Jinx did surveillance work, I was issued the standard movie garb: dark glasses, wig, and trench coat.

This woman must be conferring with Sid as a client, someone who can afford to be billed several hundred dollars an hour. But who? Why? For one reckless moment it occurs to me to just barge up to their table and see what happens. I have absolutely no reason to be suspicious of Sid, so why not?

Instead, I cross at the intersection and slip into a corner shop, still trying to decide what to do. I stand next to a rack of clothing near the window, feeling completely idiotic. Out of the corner of my eye, I spot a young salesclerk advancing on me.

"Just looking," I sing out, hoping to waylay her.

She continues unfazed. "Anything special?"

My eyes take in the rack of age-inappropriate, navel-baring T-shirts and flippy miniskirts. "Just a gift. Something for my niece."

"How old?"

"Young." My eyes shift back to the windows. "Eleven."

"Great. What size?"

"Uh, this looks about right." I brush my hand across a minuscule orange top dangling on a hanger, trying to keep my eyes glued on the entrance to Le Petit Ferme. "Just give me a minute to look around, okay?"

I glance at the rangy brunette with a navel ring and a belly tattoo, who stands, arms crossed, looking miffed. What were the chances of actually encountering gung-ho sales help?

She nods and moves a few feet behind me. "We have some things on sale in the back."

"Thanks." I shift to another rack to get a better view of the café. "I'll just look around." I hold up one hanger after the other without even glancing at the garments.

I flash back on the note left on my windshield: TELL COOP HE CAN'T HIDE. Obviously the redhead and her companion must be the suspects who broke into my car. Is she one of Frankie's old girlfriends? If so, how does Sid figure in?

The salesgirl works her way back over to me. "Those knit boleros are really hot."

"Sorry. It's hard to decide."

She smiles. "Take your time. Let me know if you need help." She backs off again, but I feel her watching me.

Maybe Sid thinks that having me followed will lead him to Paul. Even as the thought occurs to me, I push it aside. Why doubt Sid, of all people? No one has done more than Sid to help me through this whole ordeal.

The door to Le Petit Ferme opens. The redhead steps out, her hair glinting orange in the sunlight. She pauses for a moment and checks her watch before heading down the street. I glance back at the restaurant, but there's no sign of Sid. He's probably used the interior side entrance to the lobby and taken the elevator back up to his office.

"Sorry, nothing that's quite right," I say, hurrying toward the door. "Thanks anyway."

"Sure, anytime."

I move quickly down the street in the direction the woman was heading. At the corner, I stand in the shadow of a canopy, looking up and down the street. There's no sign of her. I wait a moment, weighing my options, wondering if, in fact, she might be hiding somewhere watching me. I give it another minute, then walk back toward Neiman Marcus to retrieve my Volvo from the self-park structure.

I hurry through a side lot, moving against the flow of shoppers streaming out the back entrance as the store closes for the day. Long shadows have settled on the forecourt, but I see that Adriana has not relinquished her seat on the bench. She's as inviolable as a bird of prey, her gaze implacable amid the crush of people flocking around her, valet parking stubs in hand. Despite her composure, though, she has to be feeling the late-afternoon chill.

I cut through the crowd and drop my hand on her shoulder. "Adriana, can I give you a lift somewhere?"

"That would be divine, darling. How terribly kind." If there was a flicker of relief in her unflinching gaze, I missed it. Yet I know her Chevy must be parked blocks away, beyond the streets designated Permit Holders Only. She certainly hasn't left her car in the parking structure for the day.

"Not at all. Maybe you'd like to wait here and I'll pick you up."

"Whatever suits you, my dear. Oh, look." Her icy fingers prod my elbow. "It's Rhonda Fleming."

I turn my head in time to see my flame-haired hanger-on tripping across the sidewalk toward the green sedan pulling up at the curb.

"Looking like a fruit salad, I might add," Adriana says witheringly. "Poor Rhonda does herself no favors dressing in last year's salsa colors."

Adriana, of course, would know. She herself is wearing vintage Mainbocher, a Salvation Army find. But with days spent trolling Beverly Hills, she's as au courant as any trendy fashion editor. It's a shame she's got it wrong about Rhonda Fleming, though. If only Adriana could put the real name to the redhead who throws me a hasty look before slamming the car door.

"She recognizes me," Adriana says, assuming a haughty tone. "You saw the look Rhonda threw? Errol Flynn always preferred me, and it got her goat."

I watch the sedan turn the corner. How long was I being watched—and why?

"Wait here, Adriana. I won't be long."

I race to my car, relieved to see no messages under the wiper.

Perhaps their shift is over for the day. Maybe Holmby Hills Man in his junkyard heap takes over when the Green Sedan Driver and the Redhead go off duty. Am I completely paranoid? I adjust the rearview mirror, and in the dim light of the parking garage I catch a glimpse of my face, strained-looking even under the studio makeup.

"All in a day's work," I mutter, wishing I had the platoon of writers Jinx could count on to send her in the right direction. I pull out of the garage and turn the corner into rush hour traffic. I hang a right at the next corner and pull up to the curb in front of Adriana. She buckles herself in with a studied air of indifference. *Oh, to be mad and only have to feign sanity.*

"Where to, kiddo?"

"I don't want to put you out. Just drop me on Elevado near Doheny."

You're sure?" For a fleeting moment I imagine the look on Donna's face if I were to bring Adriana home with me. It's tempting. Adriana could use a hot meal, a warm bath, and a clean bed for the night.

"Absolutely, darling. This is too, too kind."

I shift my eyes from the halting flow of vehicles clogging Beverly Drive to the palm trees silhouetted against the setting sun.

"Tell me, Adriana. Do you actually know where your former husband is?"

"Of course," she says, without hesitation. "So do you."

"My husband? No, I've no idea."

"Darling, you only think you don't know. It's elemental, really." She sighs and passes her fingers across her forehead. "So ruthless, so fickle. We're pawns in their terrible game of domination. Creatures to be toyed with, passed around, then dumped by the roadside with nothing. They watch and gloat. Believe me, one knows—"

"What?" I laugh uneasily, then glance over. She sounds like Dr. Phil channeling Bette Davis. But Adriana looks straight ahead, her expression immutable.

"Seriously, Adriana. I don't know where my husband is. Maybe I should be able to figure it out, but—no, I don't know where he is. And if I did—"

"Trust me. You know," she says, cutting me off, her eyes unblinking, "pain gets you through the night. Anger gets you up in the morning. In between, *you know*."

"Right. I know pain. I know anger. But I don't know where he is. Believe me."

But do I?

I turn onto Elevado and glance in my rearview mirror, half-expecting to see a flotilla of surveillance vehicles in my wake, the green sedan with Rhonda Fleming in the lead. *Is that any crazier than having a metaphysical discussion with a deranged woman?*

"So where do you want me to drop you, Adriana?"

"A little farther. I'll tell you when," she says cagily.

I know what this is about. Adriana's found a hassle-free place to park, and while it lasts she's not going to share the location with anyone. I don't blame her. Two blocks farther on, she signals me to stop. I pull over, feeling the cold draft as she opens the door and climbs out. I watch her disappear into the shadows, wishing I could send her off with a plate of warm food, an extra blanket.

But in the time I wait at the curb watching her drift into darkness, it occurs to me that while I don't actually know where Paul is, I *am* convinced he's still alive. With access to my Social Security number and my mother's maiden name, he'd managed to return to the well one more time. My bankruptcy was still fresh on the books; he would have had to sign me up at an exorbitant interest rate for that credit card, but why would he care? Did anyone care? Somehow I had to put a stop to this, or I would end up as crazy as Adriana bleating about her brain being jammed with a radio transmitter.

Chapter Eleven

The value of a warm bath and a soft bed really can't be overestimated. Neither can Donna's stuffed smoked pork chops with homemade applesauce. The thought has occurred to me, while turning down my coverlet at night or tucking into the dinner always awaiting me when I walk in the door in the evening, that Donna might be open to adopting me. Or maybe she'll get so used to having me around, she'll forget I'm the houseguest who never left.

A week under Donna's roof and I still wake up in awe of my good luck. I don't want to spoil it. With some trepidation, I mention to her that I have dinner plans Friday evening. It will mark our first supper apart since last weekend. Has she already planned a menu, laid in food? She's not what you'd call a slapdash cook.

"Oh, what a relief," she says when I finally screw up the courage to tell her. "I was going to leave something in the oven for you. I'm dining with my golf partners at the club and hated to let you down."

I'm touched, but taken aback, too. "Thanks, Donna, but you shouldn't ever feel you have to go out of your way for me. Really, no need to fuss," I finish lamely. "I'm fine on my own."

The exchange has left me a bit unnerved. Adoption would actually be a terrible idea. Later, as I'm about to set off for the Baskins', it occurs to me that Donna might wait up for me if she returns home and doesn't see my car in the driveway. I quickly write a note and leave it on the kitchen table where she's sure to see it: BE BACK LATE, SO DON'T WAIT UP. SEE YOU IN THE MORNING. THANKS! MEG. *Must remember to call about Alex Trebek.*

Carol and Sid Baskin reside in a two-story mock Tudor on three lush acres within a gated development off Mulholland, not far from the site where Paul dreamed of building his luxury estates. The architecture in the neighborhood runs the gamut from Doric Revival and Roman villa to Versailles and Monticello (think plantation-chic). One house appears to be an almost exact replica of the New York City Public Library, with Bryant Park for a backyard. These newly minted relics boast all the features a modern-day Hadrian couldn't live without: screening room, tennis court, swimming pool, waterfall, koi pond, serenity pavilion, and twelve-car garage.

The sun is setting as I pull up in front of the vine-covered entrance to what the Baskins like to refer to as their *Howards End* home. Through the rose-covered arch leading to the back garden, I glimpse the pool house, disguised as Anne Hathaway's cottage. I once called it home. Shakespeare himself would have loved its fully equipped exercise room and sauna beneath a faux thatched roof. I did.

I ring the bell. A dark-haired woman with a shy smile opens the door. I realize at once that the Baskins have changed "couples" again. During my month-long stay, I'd grown fond of Grete, an Austrian who made amazing apple pancakes. Sadly, she and her husband, handyman/gardener Oskar, appear to have been replaced.

"Hi, I'm Meg Barnes."

The woman bobs her head and steps aside. "Please," she says, her voice barely a whisper. She closes the door and scuttles down the hall toward the kitchen. I peer into the hushed twilight of the vast living room. A chill hangs in the air despite dozens of flickering candles and a fire blazing on a raised hearth. *Hello, Hollywood—the roaring inferno competes with frigid blasts from an air conditioner.*

"There you are," Carol says, sweeping in through the patio doors. She's wearing silk print evening pajamas with regulation Manolo Blahniks. "I thought I heard your car. Did Olinda let you in? She's the most darling Portuguese. I just got them. Her husband, Guillermo, is pouring drinks."

"I thought you said casual." We brush cheeks with kisses.

"I meant no tiaras."

"I'm in blue jeans."

"I see that. Well, never mind. It's just the four of us. Do you want to freshen up a bit?"

"I'm feeling pretty fresh. Do I look bad?"

Carol laughs. "Don't get so touchy. I just thought we could have a minute to ourselves. You want to come upstairs?"

"Sure. Jack's not here yet?"

"He just arrived a couple of minutes ago. Sid's showing him his new hybrid SUV. Honestly, such a savings in fuel. C'mon up."

I follow Carol up the dark-oak stairway and along the balcony with its lavishly carved minstrels' gallery overlooking the living room. For larger gatherings, Carol usually hires musicians. She likes gypsy violinists. Sometimes she has harp or flute music to entertain her guests during cocktails. We continue down a long passageway to the master bedroom, actually a suite of rooms that occupies an entire wing of the house. Carol's sitting room, in an alcove next to her dressing room, has a tiny Juliette balcony with a view of her rose garden. It's my favorite corner of the house. But it's a long trek, and I wish I'd asked for a glass of wine before we'd set out on our journey.

Carol plumps herself down on a velvet settee. She curls her legs under her and shakes her blonde hair onto her shoulders. "It's been ages since we've had a good natter," she says, her voice cozy. I realize immediately that I'm in for a heart-to-heart. Whenever Carol's anxieties get the better of her, I'm the lucky recipient of the overflow. Sorting me out calms her.

"Ages," I agree, wondering what perceived inadequacies in herself she's about to transfer to me. I perch on the window seat, making myself as comfortable as possible. Below me, I watch Guillermo in the thatched-roof bar pouring martinis and carrying the tray toward the garage. I'm not really a martini person, but facing one of Carol's tête-à-têtes has made me suddenly thirsty.

"Water?" Carol reaches into a faux-painted bamboo cabinet stocked with miniature bottles of Evian. "You can't drink too much water." She smiles again and hands me a bottle.

"Thanks. But won't the guys wonder where we are?"

"No rush. We've got the whole evening together. Besides, I think Sid wants to talk some business with Jack. So, what do you think of him?"

"Since the last time you asked me? Frankly, I know nothing about him, except that he knows damn near everything about me. Otherwise, he seems nice enough."

"Meg, he's more than just nice. He's a widower, for God's sake. No alimony, nothing. I mean, how many available guys do you think are out there, anyway?"

"Well, figuring your pool guy is a no-go, let's see—"

"Oh, boy. You know, this is what I want to talk to you about." She smiles, her voice seeking a soothing register. "You just seem sort of edgy lately. I know you went through some hard times last year, but that's behind you now. Things are looking up. You've got a job, for heaven's sake. You should be on top of the world. Instead, I get the feeling you're still carrying around a chip on your shoulder. Sometimes bad things happen to good people. You have to move on, Meg. Get out more. Socialize."

I nod, keeping my mouth shut so I won't scream.

Carol nods and smiles. "Sometimes these things just need to be said. I mean, how long have we known each other?"

Too long? "A long time, Carol." I look around the room, hoping this is the end of the sermon before supper. I need a drink. Now. If this were my little sitting room, I would have installed a wet bar long ago.

"A long time." She mouths the words slowly, her head nodding. I nod, too, wondering where this is leading.

"It's not easy to bring these things up," she says, "but I don't know anyone who knows you better than I do. We're friends, and I hope you feel you can say anything to me. Anything at all."

Should I risk it? "I could really go for a glass of wine, Carol."

"I know you could," she says. "That's another thing. Do you think you might be drinking just a bit too much these days?"

"No. I don't. I'm not drinking nearly enough." A firm tone is required here, because I can already see where this is going. Carol has decided she is drinking too much, which means I'm to be penalized. At least she's not vegan this week, which bodes well for tonight's menu.

"Hey, you don't need to get pissy with me, okay? I'm just trying to help. I would more than appreciate a little suggestion like that from you, if you thought I needed it. That's what good friends do for each other."

"Sorry, but I don't need an intervention, Carol. I'd just like a glass of wine."

"Fine. We'll get you one. All in good time. You know, I think all of us drink too much. I don't have a single girlfriend who doesn't think she drinks too much. We should all cut down." She waves a hand, and I detect an unsteadiness that indicates she's already hit the Chardonnay. "Anyway, that's not what I wanted to get into."

She picks up a sheaf of papers laying facedown on a side table and turns them over. I see a zodiac pie, and my heart sinks.

"Believe me, this is far more important. I've updated your chart, and I'm telling you, I have never witnessed such an amazing convergence. Uranus has changed direction and is sitting right on your Seventh House, along with the Sun and Venus. On top of that, your moon has just entered Libra, and whenever the moon enters a new sign it stays there for a couple of years. This places a lot of emphasis on relationships. Your Venus has progressed to the top of your chart, and that portends love, maybe marriage. With all this power, this could be a critical time for you. I see big changes in store for you."

Carol's eyes glitter and her voice is hushed, so this must be good news, but I have no idea what she's talking about.

"I could use big changes, but do we have to go into this now?"

"Yes! Absolutely!" she says, her face fierce. "I see a huge relationship break in which you sever ties with the past. Get this, Pluto is even more powerful in your chart right now. Pluto represents the phoenix bird, reborn from its ashes. Something has to die for new growth, right? But you have to play your cards right. I can only think that this somehow involves Jack. I mean, who else? I think he's really, really key here."

I see only one way out of this, and that's sincerity. If I can fake that, as they say, I'll get my drink. "You're right, Carol. With Pluto in the picture, I get it."

"Well, it's just so logical. Sid says Jack turned up at this crucial time when Paul got himself kidnapped—"

"Sid called him. He turned up because Sid called him."

"Is that what he said? That's strange." She blinks, and time stops. "Well, I suppose that's the case. I knew they'd been in touch. But, whatever, right? I mean, it speaks to me of more than just chance. Sid was the means, you see?"

"The means for what?"

"For getting the two of you together."

"Right. Kismet. I understand totally. I mean, out of all the FBI men out there, Sid's got a buddy—"

She nods vigorously. "This could really turn things around for you. And just between us, who knows how long he'll be with the FBI, you know?" She winks and covers her lips with her fingertips as though smothering a burp. I long to ignore the bait but can't resist.

"So, how long?"

"I can't really say. Sid told me it was confidential, so don't say anything, okay? Anyway, just remember your critical dates, the twenty-second and twenty-third of this month. Focus, okay? It's there for you if you let it happen."

"Okay, got it. Thanks, Carol. I really, really appreciate this."

"I know you do. And I really, really care about you."

She smiles, and I smile. The truth is, she really does care, and I feel bad not fully confiding in her, but I just can't. Carol would want to do something to help, and I'd want to strangle her. So we smile at each other, conveying care and understanding. Maybe even love, but certainly not truth. What a blessing we can't read each other's minds.

"The thing is," she says, her voice distant, "I sometimes wonder if you aren't still carrying the torch for Paul."

"What!" My laugh is stopped short by her frozen look. "Sorry, but that's such a funny expression."

"You think it's funny?" she asks, ice clinging to her words. "Because sometimes I think you do, and that would be a mistake. I'm saying this for your own good."

"I can assure you—"

"Excellent. Because life's short. We're heading into our September years, my friend. You've got to grab your chance when it comes along." Carol sighs, and I know she feels better now. She unfolds her legs and stands up. "Here, I've written it all down for you. Tuck it in your bag."

I dutifully stuff the pages in my shoulder bag as I move, with some speed, toward the door. I have no intention of looking at this horoscope and haven't a clue what I would do any differently on those critical days. Wash my car? Refold my sweaters?

I stop at the door while Carol tops up her lip gloss. "So when did Jack lose his wife?"

She smacks her lips together and gives me a sidelong look. "See, you *are* interested."

"You brought it up. If it's recent, I just don't want to say something thoughtless. Forget I asked."

"God, you are *so* touchy. Anyway, from what I understand, she passed away a couple of years ago. Long enough that there's not a big grief thing going on. And forget what I said about leaving the FBI. Sid would kill me if he knew I told you." We head down the stairs into the living room. The air is still chilled, the fire blazing in the hearth. "But what do guys know, anyway? They just go for the bottom line without appreciating any of the intricacies of getting there."

Perhaps my masculine side is asserting itself, but I could go for more bottom line and fewer intricacies. Should I just strip away the niceties and ask Sid straight out: "Hey, who was that redhead in the lime green jacket I saw you having coffee with?" Is that intricate enough?

I can't make myself do it. I'm probably not going to ask Jack how his wife died or when he's leaving the FBI, either. But Carol, who loves to roil things up, must smell blood in the water; shark-like, she glides onto the patio.

I breathe in the sweet-smelling jasmine clinging to ye olde arches. Paul and Jack are sitting at a candlelit table stationed in front of the little rough-hewn Elizabethan pub, a neighbor's palm tree rising incongruously above its thatched roof. My eyes focus on Jack, leaning back in his chair, wearing a white open-neck oxford shirt with a suede jacket and jeans. A small thump in my chest tells me I'm glad to see him, despite all my protests.

As we approach, Jack stands, smiling. I note a look of relief on his face. Maybe he thought I wouldn't show up. Or maybe Sid's been feeding him the same kind of buildup I've been getting from Carol. The Baskins have perfected the tag team to an art. This evening smacks of being well plotted. I sail up to the table, the wind in my face.

"Sorry. Just girl talk," Carol says. Sid, martini in hand, stands and wraps his arms around me.

"Hey, kitten. Glad you could make time for us."

I give him a hug. "I always have time for you, Sid."

"What'll you have?"

"Oh, I don't know. Maybe just some white wine."

I turn to Jack, aware that both Sid and Carol are watching us.

"Hey there. Good to see you again, Jack."

"Hi, Meg."

Instead of shaking my hand, he grasps it between his. It's an unexpected gesture, and I'm not inclined to pull away. His eyes crinkle, and in their warmth, I see that he's also picked up on the Baskins' attention.

"How's the filming going?" he asks.

"Great. I'm still hoping to beat the rap. I think the government's got a shaky case." Everyone laughs, a cue to sit. Carol busies herself with a plate of hors d'oeuvres, while Guillermo serves my wine. "Thanks. Cheers, everyone."

"Cheers yourself," Jack says. "If anyone can pull it off, I'm sure that would be you."

"You can never tell about a jury, though," Sid says. "They'll fool you."

"I know. I'm afraid I'm being painted as the black widow. The women may side with my husband."

"He was an absolute son of a bitch," Carol says blithely, biting into a canapé. "He fooled everyone—including Sid." Startled by her own comment, she freezes, endive slathered with blue cheese protruding from her lips like a lumpy green tongue. She blinks, and shoves the rest in her mouth. "Oh, sorry," she says, her eyes big. "What were we talking about?"

"Leave it to you, Carol," Sid says.

I smile. "The eight-hundred-pound gorilla has joined us." Under the circumstances, I feel justified in swilling my wine. I take a big gulp. "Don't worry about it. It's not a secret—certainly not from Jack."

"I know, but—" She turns to Jack. "I'm telling you, if he ever showed his face around here again, he'd be lynched. I would personally string him up after what he did to us—I mean, Meg. But we all felt it." She dabs a napkin on her lips, regaining her composure. "How could he get away with it, that's what I'd like to know?"

"So would everyone else," Sid says. "Let's stop talking about him, okay?" He slaps his hands on the table and shrugs. "Jack, another drink? I could use a refill." He nods to Guillermo.

"Fine. But just let me say, as bad as things got for Meg—and let's face it, this town can be incredibly cruel, as if some people, and I won't mention names, don't have their own scandals to live down. I mean, the stuff Sid tells me that never even gets in the papers, like—"

"Carol, is there a point to this?" Sid holds up his hand and looks toward Guillermo, who arrives at the table with fresh martinis and wine. "Thank you, Guillermo."

His warning clear, Sid waits until the drinks are served and Guillermo has retreated before saying, "There's a reason some things don't get in the papers, Carol. You don't talk in front of help."

"He barely speaks English, Sid. I'm only saying that poor Meg had to endure all of this publicly, when even more salacious, truly unbelievable, not to say criminal, things go on, like—what's that case you got a call about today?"

"You're pushing it, Carol. When's dinner?"

I glance at Jack, wondering if he's enjoying the Sid and Carol Show, a novelty act they've worked up over the course of their marriage. Jack's mouth is curled in a smile, but his eyes are alert. Does he really think anything significant will be revealed? I'll be disappointed in him if he does. Carol revels in elevating the danger quotient with provocative teasers, hoping to loosen tongues. I take another swallow of wine. No one is ever safe with Carol, whose agenda is never quite clear.

"Whenever you're ready, Sid, we can go to the table." She takes a large sip of wine, then turns to Jack. "Seriously, I just wanted to say, I really admired Meg's courage through all that."

"Carol, please!" I say, throwing her a look she purposely doesn't catch. "I didn't take a bullet. Just some bad PR."

"Sorry, this has gotta be said." Undeterred, she looks Jack in the eye, dropping her fingertips lightly on the back of his hand. "Look, Miss

Grace Under Fire here could have parlayed this thing into a book deal, maybe a TV movie, and done her career some good. All the biggies wanted one-on-ones, right, Meg?"

"Right. Lots of fruit baskets. Floral displays."

"She was a 'get' for almost a week. Katie, Diane, Meredith, Greta, whoever—they wanted her. Sid fielded a lot of calls."

"Carol, you forget, Jack was around during all of that—"

"And you handled yourself very well, Meg," Jack says.

"With the FBI or *Access Hollywood*?" I quip.

"Both." Jack's eyes barely flicker. His voice is light despite my dig. "We were the ones without the fruit and flower budget."

"It's the thought that counts." I smile. "Believe me, whatever I knew was never worth the price of a fruit basket, right, Sid?"

"Right, kid. But when the celebrity thing kicks in, all bets are off. Everyone wants to see a public face get smeared. You did well to hightail it out of town and let it blow over. The guy's dead, as far as I'm concerned. Forget him."

"Right, forget him. He's dead," Carol says, her voice slurring a bit. "Dead, dead, dead."

"That's not exactly what I said," Sid mutters. "But never mind . . ."

The terrain has turned bumpy for everyone, not least Carol and Sid, who eye each other in stony silence. I glance at Jack. His eyes are guarded. I long to see them crinkle again. In an effort to lift the pall hanging over the table, I laugh and raise my glass.

"So, that's it? Well, so much for the movie-of-the-week deal and my fifteen minutes with the Sob Sisters. Maybe I should just make up a story and cash in. Who'd doubt me?"

His eyes don't crinkle. "No bouquet is worth it."

I haul in a deep breath and change course. "So, how was your day, Jack? Were you in court, too?"

"Me?" He looks confused, then smiles. "No, nothing as exciting as your day. Let's hope you beat the rap."

"I won't, you know. I'm scripted to go down for life." Still feeling like a dancing bear with a stubbed toe, I try again, dipping into my standby Barbara Walters grab bag. "Okay, here's the question," I say. "If you were to choose your last meal before going to jail, what would it be?"

Sid bites. "Easy, pastrami on rye. Cheesecake, what the hell."

"Oh, God, a smorgasbord," Carol says. "Do they let you send out? French fries, sundaes, pecan pancakes, chocolate, the works. What about you, Jack?"

"I'm a meat–and-potatoes kind of guy. I'd go for a pepper steak from Chez Jay."

"Me, too," I say. "With the banana home fries, right?"

"Right. There's nothing better." His eyes crinkle, and my heart leaps.

We go in to dinner then, served at a small round table in the library, candlelit and fragrant with logs burning in the fireplace. On the menu is roast lamb with wine from the renowned Baskin cellar.

Sid and Jack share an interest in music, jazz in particular. Much of the evening is given over to playing selections from Sid's collection of vintage LPs. We move out onto the patio, where the two men swap jazz lore over coffee and cigars. I settle back, breathing in the night-blooming jasmine, feeling more content than I have in a long time.

Jack, too, looks relaxed, his legs stretched out, his head tilted back as he puffs on a cigar. We both hear the distant chime of the mantel clock. He turns to me, putting his hand on mine. "I'm about ready to call it an evening. How about you?"

I nod. "Me, too." We linger a few minutes at the door, thanking Carol and Sid. Jack walks me to my car, newly washed and no longer bearing signs of residency. Even though I'm parked behind electronic gates, I automatically scan the windshield, looking for unwelcome calling cards.

"Well, that was fun," I say, opening the door and slinging my bag onto the passenger seat. "Did you enjoy yourself?"

"Of course. But I'm sorry you were put on the grill for a while."

"It happens. But they're good friends, and Carol means well. It was all for your benefit, if you hadn't guessed. She figures the business with Paul is over, so I should be able to put it behind me. It's not as easy as it sounds."

"I know." Jack looks as though he's about to say more. His hand rests on the open car door, his face close. Heat rises to my cheeks. If he leaned closer, I'd meet him halfway. His hand drops to my shoulder, releasing a swarm of butterflies in my stomach.

"Look," he says, his grip on my shoulder tightening, "it's not all over and done with. You know that, don't you?" I nod, butterflies dropping like ball bearings. "This business is not finished. If there's anything you know, anything that's worrying you, call me. Will you do that?"

I flash on the green sedan. The note left on my car. Hell, I could even mention my call to West Virginia. Does he know about Frank Cooper? If he does, he hasn't shared it with me. I'll be damned if I'll let him lead me along again. Does he still think of me as a suspect? Is that what all these dinners are about?

He raises his other hand. There's a business card in it, which he slides into the pocket of my jacket. I nod again, my cheeks burning. *What was I thinking?* "Of course, I'll call. Promise."

He steps back and smiles. "Anytime, okay? And maybe after the verdict is in, I can buy you steak at Chez Jay."

"Verdict?"

"You're still shooting, right?"

"Sorry, of course. Sounds good."

I slide behind the wheel, my knees weak, and pull the door closed. Jack steps a few feet away. I fumble to get the car started, then back up to turn around in the driveway. I hate that he's watching me. It would be just my luck to ram my fender into a planter or to barrel through the fountain. I manage some sort of wave as I squeal over the pavers and head for the security gates. *Please God, let them open!*

Chapter Twelve

Jack.

He's got access to a whole bulging file on me, while the little dope I have on him comes via inference and deduction based on few facts. He and Sid met in law school. The two worked together in the same firm until Jack joined the Bureau and Sid opened his own office. Jack's wife died. Children? Who knows? He may or may not be into a career change. His business card still has him working out of the Federal Building. He looks good in white shirts, and he drives a late-model Beemer. He drinks martinis. I suspect his hair looks better than mine straight out of bed in the morning. With some annoyance I realize that a part of my brain I apparently have no control over is entirely libidinous, despite the fact that in my present circumstances dating is out of the question.

Jack's also into jazz. He and Sid played in some band while in law school. Between them, they managed to rattle off the names of every player in Benny Goodman's 1938 Carnegie Hall concert. Even Carol's eyes glazed, and she's used to Sid sounding like he's reading liner notes. What in the world do Jack and I have in common, aside from sharing a taste for Chez Jay's steak au poivre? Do I really want to see this guy again?

Yes.

I come to that conclusion after mulling the question since awakening at dawn. While morning sun bounds into my room in golden leaps, I loll in bed listening to Donna sweep the patio and water the pots below my window.

I turn over, my hand floating through a puddle of sunshine lapping at my pillow, my fingers soaking up the warmth. What luxury to lie in on a Saturday morning, breathing in the sweet smells of early spring. Thanks to Donna, there's no need to rouse myself from the backseat of Mrs. Singleton's Bentley, or hide from the curious stares of early-morning joggers in Holmby Park.

Eventually the garage door grinds open, and Donna leaves to play golf. I have the house to myself. If I wanted to, I could lie in bed all morning, doing nothing more than watching the dust motes dance in the sunlight. Or daydream about Jack, remembering the weight of his hand on my shoulder, the musky smell of his suede jacket.

Had he kissed me last night—what then? My lovely fantasy skids to a full stop.

Nothing. There isn't space in the narrow confines of my life these days to accommodate anyone else. I must be an idiot to imagine ever again lying naked in some man's arms, especially someone like Jack, with whom I share little other than a preoccupation with my fugitive, not-dead husband.

Maybe I should have confided in Jack last night, another question I've mulled since daybreak. If I'd mentioned the note and the threatening cell phone call to him, maybe I would've learned something about "Coop." Or confirmed a connection between Paul and Frank Cooper.

From the night table, I pick up the photo of the jug-eared kid and look at the name penciled on the back. How could I ask Jack about Frankie Cooper without telling him I've found this picture? I don't want to turn it over to him. Nor do I want to reveal what I know about Cooper's family if it will somehow lead me to Paul. I want the satisfaction of meeting him face-to-face again, but on my own terms, not the FBI's.

A snatch of the edgy exchange between Sid and Carol comes to mind. I'd have done well to ignore Carol's probing, especially concerning Jack. Even in jest, I can't afford to make comments that lead to personal questions such as "By the way, where are you living these days?" At least I know Carol's not the one having me followed, or she'd know by now that I'm squatting in the house of a relative stranger.

And that brings me to another sobering issue: I can't bunk in Donna's house forever. As it is, I feel like I'm only a step away from "Honey, I'm home. What's for dinner?" I barely crunch to the top of her gravel driveway before she swings the front door open, bouncing up and down on her Dearfoams like an exuberant spaniel. I know a frosty glass of white wine awaits me in her sunroom, and I've come to look forward to it.

There were decades of my life when I lived a *mi casa es su casa* lifestyle, too. I always had a spare room for any New York actor buddy making the annual pilgrimage for pilot season. On one occasion it came as something of a surprise to realize that a friend had remained in the guest quarters over my garage throughout one whole season of his TV series. He made great margaritas and always tended the grill, which counts for something. That the tables have now turned, and I'm the guest who doesn't want to leave, can perhaps be justified on some karmic level. I'm just grateful to be on the receiving end, as long as it lasts.

Early makeup calls have spared me from having breakfast with Donna, although she never fails to set Mr. Coffee's automatic timer for me. There are always fresh berries in a cling-wrapped bowl in the fridge, a pre-sliced bagel on a plate next to the toaster. We've had dinner together every evening but one, and I know Donna puts herself out. Women who live alone usually end up standing over the kitchen sink eating something out of a skillet, or forking salad out of a plastic container from the grocery store. I've certainly done it, but Donna seems not to have succumbed. I always find a linen napkin, bone china, and a bud vase on my wicker tray. I'll miss her home cooking, as well as her hospitality, when I decamp and am back to eating takeout with a plastic fork.

But I'll miss Donna, herself, most of all—even though she's now outed herself as a full-fledged *Holiday* fan. After gorging on her hand-churned prune Armagnac ice cream and recklessly telling her I would do anything for another scoop, Donna demanded, "Teach me how to throw the hat."

"*The* hat?" I said. "Sorry, but I'm afraid Jinx's top hat went to prop heaven years ago. I have no idea where it is."

"I do," Donna said, going to the mahogany credenza she claimed was a Garbo castoff. Reaching into the top drawer, she handed me a thin cardboard box that I recognized immediately.

"No, I don't believe it!" I gasped, flipping open the lid. Inside, wrapped carefully in tissue, was a hard, black satin disk. "My hat! Where'd you get it?"

"I won it in a church charity auction nearly twenty years ago," Donna said, her face beaming. "Go on—pop it!"

I snapped the brim with a well-practiced flourish, and Jinx's collapsible magician's hat popped open. With both of us peering into the hall mirror, I settled the top hat on my head, cocked to one side just as Jinx always wore it.

"It still fits," I joked. "Thank God they weren't auctioning off the satin shorts and jacket."

"You fishing for compliments?" Donna laughed. "Okay, show me how it works."

I took off the hat off and collapsed it, then sailed it to her over the bust of John Barrymore. Donna put her hands out to catch the whirling disc but got whacked in the shoulder. "Watch it—that thing is lethal!" she yelped.

"That's the whole idea. How do you think Jinx knocked out the bad guys?"

Donna tried to Frisbee it back to me, but the disc nosedived to the floor. "Damn, what's wrong with me?"

"It takes years at Actors Studio to learn this stuff, Donna. That's why we get paid the big bucks."

I showed off a few of Jinx's signature moves, even managing to twirl and do a fancy backhand. There was a time when I could sling the disc while managing a one-hand cartwheel, too. But that was then.

After a few more practice throws, I showed Donna how to place her fingers on the edge of the brim to get the right spin. Finally, both of us exhausted, I autographed the inside of the hat before Donna gave it the place of honor atop John Barrymore's head on the mahogany credenza. It was hard work, but worth it for the extra scoop of prune Armagnac ice cream.

Over the past week, I've acquired quite a head for trivia and luxury goods, thanks to a steady diet of *Jeopardy* and *The Price Is Right*. Occasionally, when I've arrived home a bit late, we've dined with one or another team of Barbie and Ken look-alikes hosting Hollywood celebrity shows. Who are these squealing, plastic-faced, terminally adolescent people? Since taking up enforced outdoor encampment I've watched little television. To my astonishment, the young actor with the killer grin playing the prosecuting attorney in the pilot I'm shooting appeared in a red-carpet segment.

"Donna, that actor there—I know him. We did a scene together yesterday."

"He's in your pilot? Lucky you—"

"Well, more like I'm in *his* pilot. You like him?"

"Not bad," Donna said airily. "A sort of young Brad Pitt meets Colin Farrell. Cute, but a bad boy. He was in a series that got picked up mid-season. Didn't catch on. Terrible time period. How come you never show up at these things? You should, you know."

"Because I'm not invited."

"You'd better get your PR person on it," she said, with raised eyebrow. "You need this kind of exposure to let people know you're still around. You need to get on the list."

"What *list*? I don't have a PR person."

"You should. If this pilot gets picked up, there'll be a ton of press. Have you ever considered doing one of those infomercials? Or a game show? Maybe you could write a diet book. That would get you on the morning shows."

"You're scaring me, Donna. How do you know all this stuff?"

"Are you kidding?" She waved at the television set. "They feed you all the inside news. Who's hot, who's not. You have to stay relevant. You should have your own series again. You're a star. You can't let yourself slide off the radar."

"I've slid, Donna. Believe me, I'm not on anyone's radar anymore. I'm lucky to be working." I picked up my tray and stacked her empty Villeroy & Boch plate on mine. "Anything I can get you in the kitchen?"

She looked at me, lips pursed, eyes in lockdown. "I just hate to see you give up."

"I'm working, Donna! I've hardly given up."

It was as good an exit line as I could muster, and it carried me safely into the kitchen without further comment from Donna. The exchange had gotten under my skin, though. Industry jargon is loathsome enough without having to hear it spew from the mouth of a civilian. My God, is nothing sacred anymore? Would I volunteer career advice to a doctor, a schoolteacher—or Donna herself, for that matter? Have I told her that sleeping in a doll museum can't be good for her psyche? Or nagged her about staying "relevant"? What red carpet is she walking down? What disease has she cured? I dumped the tray on the counter and ran water in the sink. Why would anyone think I'd given up? And what business is it of Donna's, or anyone else? Even if I could afford it, the last thing I'd do is hire a PR person to drum up publicity for me. I've had a belly full of it!

I washed our dinner plates and returned to the sunroom, bearing a bowl of grapes and feeling calmer. There's no reason to bite the hand feeding me. I already feel like a moocher, having contributed nothing more than a quart of milk and a box of plain-wrap oatmeal to her larder, while she's supplied me with room and board for more than a week. I even have my own key to her house. How long can I keep up the pretense that my house is still being repainted without Donna suggesting I sue the contractor?

"Sorry, Donna. I didn't mean to overreact." I offered her some grapes and put the bowl on the side table. "I'm just a little touchy these days. You know, work."

"And your house is torn apart. I completely understand. I didn't mean to upset you."

"It's not you, really." I stood in the doorway, feeling awkward. Donna means well, just as Carol does. Neither one could possibly guess my circumstances, unless I'm wearing a subliminal sign flashing on my forehead: ON THE SKIDS. PLEASE RESCUE. "I think I'll just go up and study my lines. Good night."

"Sure, good night. If there's ever anything you want to talk about, I'm here. Okay?"

"Okay, thanks."

How could I ever confide in Donna? What would she think if I told her I didn't have a house, that I'd been lying to her? Once shooting wraps and I no longer have early calls, I'm going to have to clear out. Which brings me back to the issue of the day: a room of my own. Also, unless I'm out of the house soon, I will be running into Donna returning from golf. With that prospect in mind, I hurl myself out of bed.

Just as I've done every morning, I peek out the dormer window to see if a green sedan, a white van, or a fried-looking convertible might be idling behind the eucalyptus. All clear. Will whoever it is follow me to a cheap motel, too? Maybe it's time I take the lead. The idea takes hold as I head for the shower.

Even with the clock ticking, I linger, appreciating Donna's taste in French milled lavender soap and high-end hardware. I wrap myself in a thick bath sheet, aware that I'm only days away from skimpy towels and wrapped soap patties.

I pull on blue jeans and a T-shirt, then hurriedly jot a note to Donna and leave it on the kitchen counter: "CHECKING ON MY HOUSE. SEE YOU LATER. CHEERS, MEG."

The sun is high and hot—not a cloud in the sky. I turn onto Avenue of the Stars and whiz through Century City's canyon of high-rise office buildings. I'm reminded of my earliest days in Hollywood, and picture the old 20th Century Fox studios with the *Hello, Dolly!* sets fronting the production offices. Now, yet another gleaming tower is under construction on what used to be the back lot where I filmed episodes of a hospital series.

I round the corner onto Pico Boulevard, passing the studio's front gate, then swing into the far left-turn lane. I have something even more pressing on my mind than checking out cheap motels. I turn off Motor Avenue and cruise through Cheviot Hills on my way to see Dougie Haliburton. I glide down a dip in the road that curves onto a picture-book street of prewar bungalows, then pull up in front of a gray-shingled Cape Cod, two houses from the corner.

The question of whether it's okay to drop in on Dougie and Evie unannounced is answered almost immediately. I barely turn off the ignition when I spot Doug rounding the corner, dragging a leash collared to his golden Lab, now slump-backed and moving even more slowly than his master. I watch the two shuffle up the street. When Doug is alongside my car, I open the door and climb out.

"Hey, Dougie. I *thought* that was you I passed. Good morning!"

"G'morning yourself." He pushes his cap back on his head. "What are you doing around here? Did you get that job you were up for?"

"Sure did. We wrap the end of next week." I give him a hug. His safari jacket seems to hang more loosely on him than it did when I saw him in the studio commissary. The skin behind his ears has hollowed. "Hope you don't mind, but when I saw you I had to stop."

"Glad you did. You know, I figured you'd get hired. You're looking great, kid. You must be paying the devil his price. Remember Ridley?" The Lab eases slowly back on his haunches, his head drooping. "He's a bit arthritic these days, but who isn't?"

I bend down and ruffle Ridley's ears. "How're you doing, Doug? How's Edie?"

"No complaints. Can you spare time for a cup of coffee? I'd like to show you something I've been working on."

"You bet." Ridley scuttles to his feet, and we slowly amble toward a ramp leading to the back door of the house.

"Maybe you can see Edie later. She's lying down, having a nap."

I pull the screen door open, and we enter the big, sunny kitchen. Doug reaches into the cupboard for a mug and sets it on the counter next to the coffeemaker. "Make yourself at home while I look in on Edie. Back in a minute."

While I pour coffee, Ridley laps water from a tin pan, then collapses in a shaggy heap near the back door. Taking my coffee mug with me, I find the cozy den that opens onto the back garden. The long coffee table in front of the fireplace is cluttered with books and scripts, and the pine-paneled walls are hung with framed photos and posters. My eyes fall on a framed old *TV Guide* cover for the *Holiday* Christmas episode, featuring Winston Sykes and me in red Santa hats. Christmas-tree balls dangle over our heads, containing our famous catchphrases: "Awfully good of you, my dear" and "All in a day's work."

Below the framed cover is Dougie's director's chair with his name stenciled on the back. I feel nostalgic recalling my days on the set with Winnie and Doug. I was given my chair, too, when the series went off the air. I have no idea where it is now. It was auctioned with my other furniture. With that thought, I'm reminded of the packing boxes Dougie stored for me nearly a year ago.

I push open the door to the garden and head down the walkway, hoping the key to the garage is still hanging on a hook under the eaves. It is. The lock sticks, and I have to slam my hip against the warped door before it swings open. I turn on the dim overhead light and wait for my eyes to adjust to the gloomy interior. The space behind Doug's Chrysler is cramped, but I manage to squeeze through to a recessed area in the far corner.

On a dusty pallet wedged against the wall next to a tool cabinet, Doug's IRS records are stored in neatly labeled file boxes. Six of my own file boxes are lined up next to his. Behind them is a sagging stack of grocery-store cartons that I also recognize as mine.

I reach back and pull open the overlapping flaps on one of the cartons, startled to find a plastic bag containing the mildewed remnants of the latex ears I wore in *Star Trek*. Did I throw *nothing* away? With a mixture of dread and wonder, I riffle through a batch of publicity stills from half-remembered MOWs and miniseries produced in the days when there were still few VCRs but plenty of shoulder pads and false eyelashes.

I dump everything back in the carton and heave it on top of the stack of file boxes. The second grocery carton, newer and sturdier, contains photographs and the few mementos I have from my marriage to Paul. I come across a manila envelope stuffed with snapshots and flip through them. A few are from our wedding at an Arizona resort, just the two of us with a justice of the peace. Most are photos taken while sailing on the *WindStar*. I stop at one of me, smiling and carefree, eating an ice cream cone on the Catalina pier.

Shuffling through the stack, I come across a digital printout of 25 thumbnails—shots I don't remember taking. More than half are landscapes, stunning panoramas of ocean and beach that I don't recognize. However, the steep, scrubby terrain pictured in several group shots is familiar—the Mulholland building site, newly graded, before the retaining walls were constructed. I pick out Paul easily and recognize Rick Aquino on his left, both laughing. I can't place the third man, heavyset and rumpled, wearing a light-colored suit and straw hat.

Paul's right arm is slung across the shoulders of the fourth man, slight and fair with a toothy grin. It's Nat Wiggens, Erica's film-producer husband, who was shot during an early-morning carjacking outside their home. These photos were taken only months after I met Paul. I riffle through the box but can't find prints to match the thumbnails.

"A heap of old memories, huh?" I turn to find Doug at the door, slippers on his feet.

I jam the printout and a packet of photos into my shoulder bag. "Afraid so. Sorry, but I dumped more stuff on you than I thought."

"Don't worry about it. Take what you want, and leave the rest."

"Thanks. One of these days I'm going to pitch the whole lot in a Dumpster. Don't know why I hang on to all this junk." I restack the cartons, then follow Dougie to his editing room above the pool house.

"You know, it's a good thing you came by," he says as we climb the outside stairs. "I was figuring on calling you one of these days. I've got to ask a big favor of you, Megs. I don't think you'll let me down."

I stand back as he unlocks the door and scrapes it open. As the lights flicker on, I look around at the vintage equipment that Dougie has kept in this workroom, a reminder he started out as a film editor. It's not the first time I've been up here. Ever since I've known him, he's spliced together reels of hilarious outtakes to show at wrap parties and Sunday get-togethers.

"It's a little something I've been working on for the kids, a sort of family history. My mother was a chorus girl when she met my dad, a stunt rider on the old Republic lot. They did a Western together back in the thirties. She played a dance-hall girl. Anyway, I've been collecting bits of film on both of 'em, along with some home movies I came across. How would you feel about laying down a voice track for me? You'd sure be better at it than I would. What do you say?"

"I'm hooked. Let's do it." I settle onto a stool next to Doug's well-worn swivel chair.

He hands me a yellow legal pad with a handwritten script. "I didn't get a chance to type it up yet."

"No problem. And I've got a favor to ask, too. You told me you thought you saw Paul down near San Diego a while back, remember?"

"I'm sure of it. I know faces."

"Could you tell me where you ran into him?"

"Sure. I passed him as Edie and I were going into a restaurant and he was walking out. I was pushing Edie in the wheelchair, and he held the door for us. I recognized him right away."

"Did you talk to him?"

"No. Something about him kept me from saying anything. Maybe the way he seemed to turn his head away, as if trying not to be recognized. He was with a woman. A bottle-blonde. Sort of hard-looking. I just said 'thanks,' and he nodded. That was it. I'm not sure he knew I recognized him."

"Did you see him get into a car?"

"No. No car." Dougie busies himself turning on equipment. After a moment, he says quietly, "He didn't have a car. I happened to look out the café window as I helped Edie to the table. He and the blonde walked to the end of the street, then crossed over to a little stucco house sitting off on its own."

"A little stucco house? That doesn't sound like Paul."

"No, guess not. The house was a mustardy color, not much to look at. Not a great end of town, either, but Edie needed to stop. She can't stay cooped up in a car too long."

"Where exactly was this?"

"If I tell you, you'll go there, won't you?"

I nod. "But first I'll voice the track for you."

He smiles. "Fair enough. I'll write out the directions. But I'm not so sure I want to see you heading down there on your own."

I smile back, anxious to get my hands on the directions before Dougie thinks better of it. "Just jot down the route, and let's get busy. I want to see your film."

It's no surprise that Dougie, a master craftsman with a lifetime of experience, has put together a film that's far more than just a "family thing." He knows it, too. I narrate *The Cowboy and the Chorine*, Doug's short about two Hollywood unknowns starring in the story of their lives together, with everyone from Joan Crawford and Fred Astaire to Hoot Gibson and Johnny Mack Brown playing bit roles.

The hours roll by. Now and again, Doug goes in to check on Edie. I take a break to make some peanut butter sandwiches. By the time we settle back to watch the film with the soundtrack, the sun is going down.

Doug walks me back to my car when we're finished. "I got to thinking it wasn't such a good idea giving you those directions, you know? I think you're well rid of that sucker, if you don't mind my saying so."

"I'll be careful. Besides, you were right. I am curious. I do need to get to the bottom of things." I climb into my car and turn on the ignition. The headlights splay across the darkened street. "Thanks for everything, Doug. It's a wonderful film. I'm honored you asked me to narrate it."

"Well, it was awfully good of you, my dear."

"All in a day's work. Good night, Dougie."

I pull away from the curb and make a U-turn. Doug steps back on the sidewalk and waves. I wave back. A shiver races up my spine, not just because of the evening chill. With Dougie's directions stuffed in my pocket, I know now that I never doubted it was Paul he'd spotted in that café. That makes Adriana, who's nuttier than a jar of Skippy, absolutely right. I do know where he is, or at least was—even if it took me a while to admit it.

Furthermore, the digital printout I found in Dougie's garage is evidence of the connection between Paul and the owner of *The Coop II* beached on Catalina. Was Paul responsible for Rick Aquino's death—or that of poor Nat Wiggens? I shiver again, and glance in my rearview mirror.

Forgoing my plan to check out motels on Pico, I take a more direct route back to Donna's. With any luck, I'll make it back in time for supper. But shortly after the canyon turnoff, the Volvo begins to sputter and knock. I check the gauges. The gas tank is half-full. I grip the steering wheel, urging the car on. Finally, just down the hill from Donna's driveway, I manage to pull to the curb before the Volvo cruises to a complete halt.

Damn! There's not a chance I can get the car repaired on a Sunday. Instead of telling Donna I'm moving out soon, I'll have to get her to drive me to work. Worse, I have to figure out how I can afford to get my car fixed. I grab a flashlight, climb out, and slam the door. With my bag slung on my shoulder, I lock up and set out on foot.

As I round the curve, not twenty feet from Donna's driveway, I stop abruptly. Parked at the curb is a green Pontiac. I click off my flashlight and move slowly, crouching as I approach the passenger side. The interior is dark, with no one inside.

I glance up the driveway. There's light in the kitchen window, but nowhere else downstairs. If Donna is home, she would be watching television in the sunroom at the rear of the house. I walk on the grassy verge to avoid the crunch of gravel. Creeping around the side of the house, I see pale light in the upstairs hallway and in Donna's bedroom. I peer into the garage window and see the Mercedes. I try the kitchen door, but it's locked. Easing my key into the lock, I quietly let myself in.

I pause for a long moment, listening to the loud tick of the kitchen clock, smelling the pungent marinara bubbling on the stove. Overhead, there's a faint creak. Maybe Donna is putting her baby dolls down for the night. Maybe not.

I creep slowly down the carpeted hallway to the living room. My fingers brush across the mahogany credenza to the bust of John Barrymore. As I reach up and grab Jinx's top hat off Barrymore's head, I hear the scrape of a foot against a floorboard.

A dark form emerges from the dining room and moves toward the landing below the stairs. I hear a sharp intake, then the bulky shape stops abruptly about fifteen feet from where I'm standing. I snap the brim to collapse the top hat, then whirl the disc toward the figure hovering in the archway.

There's a scream of pain, then a male voice yelps, "Hey, lady! Watch it!"

Chapter Thirteen

I flip on the lights and look around. Cowering near the staircase is the brawny young driver of the green sedan, his hand cupped over his bleeding nose.

"What'd you hit me for? You could've knocked my eye out!"

"Who are you? What are you doing here?"

He looks at me with injured eyes, blood oozing through his fingers and running down his face. He glances at his hand, then glances down at the red splotches staining his fawn-colored jacket.

"Man, look what you did! Fourteen hundred bucks, lady. This is an Ermenegildo Zegna, okay? You don't go swinging at people, you know?"

"Then you shouldn't be wearing a fancy jacket for breaking and entering, you idiot. You think insurance is going to cover it? Who the hell are you?"

"None of your damn business. What'd you hit me with?"

"Who said I hit you with anything?" Out of the corner of my eye I spot Jinx's top hat, which popped open on impact, tottering on the Victrola where it landed. "Maybe you just walked into a door."

"You kidding me?"

"Does it look like it?" My anger mounting, I grab Donna's letter opener—a dagger said to have been a *Gunga Din* prop—off the coffee table, and wave it. "Where's Donna? Is she hurt?"

"Ma," the man bellows. "Ma? Help!"

A door slams. A voice calls out, "Denny, are you all right?" The red-haired woman rushes onto the landing at the top of the stairs, her eyes fixing on the dagger I'm brandishing.

"Stop!" she shrieks. "What do you think you're doing?"

"Who the hell are you? Or do you want to wait and tell the police?"

"My God, Denny! You're bleeding!" she screams. "Leave him alone!" she demands, pointing a finger at me. "Denny, get back—she's crazy!"

"She wrecked my jacket, Ma. I didn't even touch her!"

"Where's Donna?" I raise the dagger higher. The woman shrieks again.

"You gotta do something, Ma!" Denny cowers against the banister, moisture glistening on his pale forehead.

"I said, where's Donna?"

"I'll get her, I'll get her. Just leave him alone!" The woman flutters her hands, then hurries off toward Donna's room, slingback mules slap slapping against her heels.

"Ma!" Denny bellows. "Get me a towel!"

"Denny, you want to tell me what's going on here? Just what are you and your mother after, anyway? Why'd you break in here?"

"We just wanted to talk, okay? We didn't know your friend was here. We weren't trying to rob the place." He glances at the top hat on the Victrola with disdain. "Who'd want this junk, anyways?"

"You've been following me. What's this all about?"

"My mother just wants to get her money back, that's all. Your husband swindled her out of almost everything she won in an insurance settlement. Losing her investment's bad enough, but what your husband did to her—"

"Look, I don't know any Coop, okay? You've got the wrong person."

"Who's Coop?" He flaps his arms, looking exasperated. "Gimme a break, lady. Who's Coop?"

I stop cold. "You broke into my car, right? Left notes for me?"

"Like hell I did! What're you trying to accuse me of?" I raise the dagger again, and Denny backs up, his palms raised. "Okay, okay, I left a note. Big deal."

"Why did you do it?"

"To get Ma's money back! Look, in case you don't know it, he was going to dump you. He's a liar. A cheat. A shit. How come you're sticking with him? Just tell me where he is. I'll take him on with my bare hands—"

"Denny, give it a break." The woman reappears at the top of the stairs, tosses a wet hand towel to her son, and disappears again. Denny grabs the sodden towel with his bloodied hands and presses it to his face.

"Where's Donna?" I shout. "What have you done with her?"

The woman reappears gripping Donna's elbow. "Okay, happy now? Here's your friend, safe and sound. Just tell us where Paul is."

Barefoot and wearing yet another of her loose-fitting smocks, Donna looks even more diminutive next to the overbearing redhead.

"Meg, what's going on?"

"I don't know. Are you all right?"

She nods, her eyes wide. "I was out in the garden. The next thing I know, he's grabbing me and pulling me into the house—"

"Whoa! Hey, I didn't hurt her, okay?" Denny flaps his arms again, his exasperation mounting. "We just put her in the closet. Man, everyone wants to accuse me."

"Don't you get it? You broke into her house. You scared the hell out of her. You can't do that!"

"Listen to you!" the woman shouts. "Okay, my son got carried away. You want to know what we've been through?" She stomps down the stairs, her breasts jostling like puppies inside her tight leopard-print jersey.

"I don't even know you."

"My name's Lorraine Munson." She stops midway down the stairs, hand on hip. "Of course you don't know me. That's how Paul wanted it. But I know all about you, the big TV star. You don't impress me, okay? Paul wasn't impressed, either. If everything hadn't got all screwed up, Paul and I would be together now. I think you got wind of that and pulled a fast one."

"Me? I haven't a clue what you're talking about. You and Paul were running off together? Sorry, I think you missed the boat."

"Don't play dumb. Paul got my son into real estate, buying up houses. That's how I met Paul. And he fell for me, if you want to know. Then he takes me up to those million-dollar homes he was building, right? Well, I know a deal when I see it. So I jump in and invest. Now my money is gone. So's Paul."

"And you want both back, of course."

"You're damn right. Plus my son's good name back. My boy was promised good money for putting his name on those loans, then they crash—"

"How much, Denny?"

Denny shoots his mother a look. "I got nothing to say."

"Thousands?"

"You kidding me? Yeah. Thousands."

"On mortgages, right? For houses valued double their worth?"

"I don't know any of the particulars on the loan amounts. I was just doing what I was told—"

"So you never figured it out? Who's being dumb now? It was in the newspapers."

"Allegations, that's all. I've been hauled in and grilled over and over, but I had nothing to do with all that. You know what I had to pay to my son-of-a-bitch lawyer? I'm handling things on my own now. Your husband could tell them what went down, that I was only doing my job."

"Denny, pipe down a sec." Lorraine shifts her weight, sighing deeply. "Could we just calm down here?" She lays her hand on my shoulder. I shrug her off. "Let's cut the hostility, okay? I think what happened is you found out about Paul and me and blew the whistle on him. Now he's having to lay low somewhere, hoping to clear his name. I think you know where he is."

"Ma, it doesn't add up—"

"Shut up, Denny." She eyes me shrewdly. "You disappear, like, for months. Then my son spots you in the health club. Where've you been all this time? With Paul?"

There's a squeal of brakes, then headlights fan across the windows.

"What the hell—" Denny backs into the living room. "Cops?"

"Open the door, Meg. It's the security patrol," Donna says, her voice triumphant. "I tripped the silent alarm upstairs."

"Damn you, when?" Lorraine shouts. "You had no business doing that. This is a complete misunderstanding."

Donna darts around Lorraine and hurries down the stairs to the entryway. I swing the door open and spot Laurel and Hardy, my two favorite security guards from Marge Singleton's garage, climbing out of their car. I ease away from the doorway. Denny and Lorraine race past me toward the kitchen entrance.

"Hurry, they're going out the back," Donna yells to the guards.

"Don't worry. We got it covered."

I peek out the dining room window to see Hardy strut up the driveway. "The police are on the way. You okay, ma'am?"

"Yeah," Donna says. "Just don't let 'em get to their car—"

"Right, the Volvo down the street. Recognized it right away. Someone's lurking around here living out of it. Seems pretty harmless, but you never know."

Donna turns, her eyes fixing on mine. "Actually, there are two people. A man and a woman, and they're not harmless," she says.

The police siren grows louder, then abruptly shuts off with a burp. Pulsing red and blue lights flash in the dining room windows.

Donna looks pointedly at the dagger in my hand. "Douglas Fairbanks Jr. would've been proud of you," she says quietly. "Why don't you put my letter opener back on the coffee table and make us some tea?"

"They'll want to talk to me, too, you know." A sick feeling claws at my stomach. How long will it take me to vacate the Deanna Durbin Suite?

"Of course. You're my houseguest," she says briskly, moving back to the doorway. "In the meantime, you'd better turn the heat down on the marinara sauce. I'm afraid it's fried by now."

A reprieve hangs in the balance. I take another look out the window. Two squad cars are parked askew in the driveway, doors open. Lorraine and Denny Munson are in the custody of police officers. Hardy, looking important, approaches one of the policemen and gestures toward the road beyond the eucalyptus. If they check out the Volvo, at least they won't find it crammed like Fibber McGee's closet.

I retreat to the dimly lit kitchen, replacing the *Gunga Din* dagger on my way. As I fill the teakettle, I hear footfalls and a murmur of voices in the front hall, but I'm unable to make out what's being said. I slide the pot of marinara onto a back burner and turn up the flame under the teakettle. As I move about the kitchen, setting up the tea tray, I expect any moment to see police officers appear in the doorway.

I'm about to pull the cork on a bottle of red wine when the teakettle begins to whistle. Before the shriek of a full boil takes hold, I swing around, grabbing the handle with my bare hand. Stifling a cry of pain, I manage to set the kettle onto a cold hob without a clatter. I blow on my throbbing fingers, then press them around the cool glass of the wine bottle, my heart pounding.

How long before I have to face the police? They'll probably talk to Lorraine Munson first. *Paul and I would be together now. In case you don't know, he was dumping you.* Was I completely unconscious? In my wildest nightmare, I couldn't imagine Paul leaving me for Lorraine—or her big-bucks investment!

Feet thud up the stairs. Donna must be showing the police the closet where she was held. What will the officers make of all those dolls? I pour myself a glass of wine and tiptoe into the dining room. Red and blue lights streak through the French windows. Police stand guard over Denny, seated in the back of a squad car, the towel pressed to his face. Lorraine sits alone in the back of another car. Did they have time to concoct some plausible story for dropping in on a stranger and shoving her into a closet? Maybe it's begun to dawn on them how serious the charges will be.

How could I have brought this down on Donna? There's no question of my staying on here now. But where do I go? The Volvo won't get me anywhere anytime soon.

I hear the faint chiming ring of my cell phone and hurry back into the kitchen, where I've left my bag. Before I can answer, the caller has hung up. I check the call records. Sid's rung three times. I'm about to call back when Donna and a police officer enter the kitchen.

"Meg, thank you so much for making tea," she says brightly. "I was just showing Officer Rodriguez and his partner around upstairs. Officer Denham is having a look in the backyard. It doesn't seem like anything was taken. Officer, would you care for some tea? Anything?

The ruddy-faced young policeman stands just inside the doorway, his feet planted a foot apart, looking at me, not Donna. "No, ma'am, nothing at all. I just need to ask your houseguest here a few questions. You're Mrs. Stephens, ma'am?"

"Meg Barnes. I don't know what Donna has already told you—"

"Just that these people broke in hoping to find your husband," Donna says, pouring herself tea. "Not that I've ever met him—"

"No," I say, picking up on her breeziness, "and I haven't seen my husband in more than a year. I have no idea where he is. This woman and her son seemed to have some business dealings with him that I knew nothing about."

"They're obviously both screwy," Donna says. "Bonkers. Just lock 'em up. Is it okay if I finish making dinner?"

"Sure. Go ahead. I just need to get a statement from you, Mrs. Barnes."

"*Ms.* Barnes. She has nothing to do with her former husband." Donna shoots me a look. "Why don't you and Officer Rodriguez just settle down at the table there. You can tell him how you walked in and this guy you've never seen before jumped you, right?"

"Right. It was dark—"

"He was a complete madman. Who knows what would've happened if you guys hadn't shown up so quickly," Donna says, filling a pot with water for pasta. "Anyway, don't mind me. Just ask your questions."

"Ms. Barnes, maybe you could just fill me in here. You don't know either of these people?"

"She never met them before, right, Meg?"

"Never."

"There was no warning at all," Donna says. Her eyes are bright, her face flushed. "They just barged in here. Unbelievable!"

I'm grateful for Donna's intrusiveness. Officer Rodriguez is not. He eyes Donna, then flips his notebook closed. "Ms. Barnes, maybe you could walk me out to the door and just show me what happened."

"Be happy to, sure." I lead Officer Rodriguez along the route I took from the kitchen to the stairway, carefully averting my eyes from the dagger glinting on the coffee table. I show him where Denny Munson accosted me, parsing my answers carefully. Once they interview Denny, I'm bound to be asked about the dagger.

"By the way, that's your Volvo parked in the street?"

I nod. "It is."

"Just checking," he says, making a tick in his notebook.

Officer Rodriguez surveys the living room. I follow his eyes.

"Those are Fred Astaire's tap shoes over there," I tell him, as I set Jinx's top hat back on Barrymore's head.

"You don't say," he says, rocking on his heels.

If anything, Donna's eccentric hodgepodge is a conversation stopper. Donna herself bustles in from the kitchen, wiping her hands on a towel.

"Is that about it?" she asks cheerfully. "I just wondered if I should cook the pasta."

Officer Rodriguez straightens his shoulders and looks down at Donna's beaming face. "Sure, go ahead. That should wrap it up for now.

You've got my card if you think of anything else. The excitement should be over for the night."

We both stand on the steps watching Officer Rodriguez confer with another policeman. As the squad car carrying Lorraine Munson backs up and swings around, I catch a glimpse of her in the backseat, head down, brushing away tears. Did Paul wipe out her savings and leave her destitute, too? *Wait, am I feeling sorry for a woman who might have had an affair with my husband?*

"Are you all right?" Donna asks, pushing the door closed. "You look pale. C'mon, let's get some food."

"I'm fine." I follow her down the hallway. "But you're the one who got knocked around. Are you okay?"

"Just hungry. Why don't we eat in the kitchen tonight? It might be nice for a change."

"Fine. I'll set the table as soon as I put a note on my car."

"Something wrong with your car?" she asks, sliding pasta into the pot of boiling water.

"It broke down. I just want to make sure it's safe until I can get it towed somewhere." I pick up the pad and pencil near the telephone and head for the kitchen door.

"Nobody's going to be able to fix it on a Sunday. What time's your call on Monday? I'll give you a lift to the studio."

"You're sure? It's a lot to ask, Donna."

"You're not asking. I offered." She stirs the marinara and looks at me. "How else would you get to work?"

"A rental, I guess." I stand with the note in my hand, my feet pointing toward the back door. "I can't tell you how sorry I am, Donna. This all had to do with me, and I can't apologize enough. You're sure they didn't hurt you?"

"No. But it was scary to turn around and find two strangers in my garden. And that guy, Denny, practically carried me up the stairs. It makes me so mad when people think they can just pick me up and haul me around like that."

I refrain from asking how often that sort of thing happens to her. "Believe me, on Monday, as soon as I finish work, I'll move out. I promise."

"Where do you think you'll go? Back to your car?"

My heart thumps to a stop. "What?"

She reaches for the bottle of wine and pours herself a glass. "I've known all along that you've been living out of your car, you know." She tops up my glass on the counter and hands it to me.

Feeling less than steady, I reach for the glass, holding it in both my hands. "How? How in the world could you know that?"

"I looked in the windows of your car in the Meals-on-Wheels parking lot. It wasn't hard to figure out. Nice setup, but pretty obvious. I could tell you weren't just picking up your dry cleaning."

Platoons of ants scuttle under my skin. If Donna figured it out, how many other people know? "C'mon, Donna, you could've said something. Why let me go on like that about getting my house painted? It's embarrassing."

"Yeah?" She leans back against the counter and sips her wine. "Why are *you* getting irritated with *me*?"

The pasta boils over, foam sizzling onto the burner. I watch her deftly mop up with one hand, the other still holding the stem of her wineglass. What band of etiquette elves brought her up? "You don't really plan to move out, do you?" she asks, her voice unnervingly calm.

"Don't you think I should? Life with me here could get a little hairy. I'm carrying around a lot more baggage than what's in my car."

"Well, if this is up to me, and I guess it is, I think you should stay. At least until something better comes along."

I swallow hard. "It doesn't get much better than this, Donna. Do you mean it? Because I would be very grateful if I could stay a bit longer."

"Good. It's settled. I'll get Triple-A to tow your car tomorrow. My mechanic can fix whatever's wrong with it."

"Seriously? Why are you doing all this? I don't deserve it."

"Maybe not, but life's a heck of a lot more interesting with you around." She flashes me a smile, enjoying her moment. "Besides, you're useful. Could you hand me that pasta bowl up on the shelf? I hate having to pull out the stepladder every time I need something."

I almost cry. Instead I hand her the bowl, then reach for the colander hanging on an overhead rack. "You could just rearrange your kitchen, you know. Put everything within reach."

"Thanks, but that would be giving in." She stirs the pasta, checking it again. "Anyway, I've lived this way a long time, and it suits me. Not that it doesn't occur to me I could use a bit of a shakeup in my life."

"Careful what you wish for."

She throws me a look. Inevitably, I've opened the door to questions I'd rather avoid. I lay placemats on the kitchen table, feeling her eyes on my back.

"You know, I just don't understand how you could lose everything. You had this big career, big house—the works. How could it happen?"

"I turned a blind eye. By the time I realized—"

"But everything? Even your house?"

"As it happened, yes. For the most part, I didn't have a choice. Then, when I saw the way things were going, it was easier to let it all go than scramble for what was left." It's the answer I give myself, and it ought to be good enough for Donna, but she's not buying it.

"Okaaaay—" Her unspoken "but" lingers over the steaming pot on the stove.

"C'mon, you don't think I miss my old life? I'd grab it back in a flash." I reach for the Portuguese bowls, their colors vibrant on the pine plate rack, and feel a pang remembering my own vintage Fiesta ware, bought at a flea market when I first arrived in Hollywood. Will I ever stop missing stuff?

"Frankly, I think you should have scrambled harder. There's no reward for giving in, but that's my opinion."

"Believe me, Donna, it's no picnic watching everything you've worked for itemized and hauled off. Maybe heading up Highway One was the easy way out, but that's what I did."

"I'm sorry. I really am." She stands at the stove, ladle in hand. "It must be awful."

"Let's forget it." Tears begin to clog the back of my throat. "It's the bargain I struck. There's no point in looking back."

"I think I'm going to cry." She looks at me helplessly, her eyes welling.

"Don't! Just stop it! Drain the pasta before it's overcooked."

I grab the colander and slide it into the sink. I'm about to reach for the pot, but Donna's already lifting it off the stove. I stand back as she tips the heavy lid, sending a cascade of foaming water and rigatoni into the colander.

"Right," she says, shaking the pasta into a bowl. "No need to spoil dinner. But I have to know. Where did you go? How did you manage?"

"I just pointed my car north. My gas tank was full. I still had some money at the time. I kept driving until my joints ached. If I got hungry, I stopped."

"Nobody knew where you were?"

"I didn't exactly fall off the map. I kept in touch with a few people. I didn't want to risk adding *missing person* to my résumé. Besides, Anne Heche had had her alien encounter somewhere outside Modesto. I was afraid some reporter up there with too much time on his hands might try to run me to ground. I could see the headline: ESTRANGED WIFE OF FUGITIVE, TRACKED DOWN EATING MCNUGGETS IN A MOTEL 6."

Donna laughs. "So you just kept on the move the whole time?"

"Pretty much. Sometimes I'd stay somewhere for a couple of weeks, working off the books in a bed-and-breakfast, waiting tables, doing laundry. In Mendocino, I spent a couple of weeks helping a woman make

Christmas wreaths from twigs and pinecones. We sold them at a roadside stand. I slept in her spare room. Over Christmas, I visited family. I really just knocked around, played hooky."

In fact, for the first time in memory, I woke up to each new day without plans or appointments. No auditions, no wardrobe fittings. I threw my cell phone in the glove compartment, occasionally taking it out to make a call or two. Somehow I expected Paul would get in touch, and I wondered what would I do if he asked me to meet him somewhere. The call never came, so I didn't have a chance to find out.

Donna tosses the salad and sets it on the table. "Well, I'm glad you came back."

"Where else would I go? Actors are migrant labor. We return to familiar fields. At least I still have an agent. It's dangerous to be away from the business too long."

I fold napkins and lay silverware beside our plates, breathing in the smell of marinara sauce and bread warming in the oven. I couldn't bear to move back into my car, or feed on happy hour scraps again. Who in their right mind would give up deluxe accommodations in swanky Holmby Hills? I let out a sigh, the words "not me" falling from my lips.

"What?" Donna asks. "Did you say something?"

"Just telling myself how lucky I am."

"Some luck," Donna mutters. She sets the bowl of pasta on the table and hands me the serving tongs. "I don't mean to pry, but just how much of what that woman was saying do you think is true?"

"I'm sure Paul did what he had to do to get his hands on her money. Sounds like he used her son, too."

"So you didn't know there was another woman?"

I shake my head. "It never crossed my mind." Infidelity might seem like a minor blow compared to everything else, but my stomach tumbles over at the thought of it.

"Sorry to have to ask this, Meg." Donna twirls her fork in her pasta. "You don't think Paul would show up here, do you?"

"Why? I'm the last person he wants to have know his whereabouts."

"Just a thought," she says, not sounding convinced. "But if he did, what would you do?"

"Are you kidding? I'd call the police!"

Donna smiles and shakes her fork at me. "Okay, but just in case he does, I'll show you how to trip the silent alarm. Sometimes, like tonight, it can come in handy."

I smile back. If Donna's truth detector is functioning at all, I've swung way off her meter. I am not at all sure that Paul, or whatever he's calling himself these days, won't track me down. And to come clean on the biggest whopper of all, would I really trip the silent alarm and sic Laurel and Hardy on him?

Rattling through my brain at the oddest times is his voice, sounding frightened and desperate: *Please, baby. I'm counting on you. I love you, baby.*

I wash up the dinner dishes while Donna goes to the sunroom to watch the last hour of a sudsy drama about a woman stalked by her former husband. I hope the plot doesn't give her further cause for alarm.

I pour myself the last of the Pinot Noir and walk out into the back garden. A flagstone path, lit with wrought-iron lanterns, winds through an herbaceous border to a grassy knoll with a white frame pavilion. I settle down on a wooden step and sip my wine, looking back across the lawn to Donna's stone-and-timber house. Bathed in the glow of artful lighting, the house looks like a fairy-tale cottage, secure enough to fend off big bad wolves and wicked stepmothers.

I know I'm deceiving Donna, but I'm doing a good job of denying the truth to myself, too. What I should be doing is calling Jack, letting him know that someone has been stalking me in search of the mysterious Coop. Denny and Lorraine were reckless, but I can't believe either of them is actually dangerous. But even though it's a professional matter, I can't make myself retrieve Jack's card and call him. Beyond dealing with questions about my present circumstances, there's residual anger I still can't confront.

I sip wine, running it over my tongue, resolving not to call Jack—yet. With that, I'm suddenly reminded of Sid's calls—why was he meeting with Lorraine Munson?

Denny spotted me at the health club and left the note on my car. Has someone else seen me and followed me, too? Otherwise, how do you track someone down who has no fixed abode? I have only a cell phone, an e-mail address, and a post office box. How could anyone find me? I look around.

Darkness has swallowed up the lawn. Spires of cypress cast long, jagged shadows across the swimming pool. The back of my neck prickles, the silence making me even more aware of my solitude. Am I really alone? I rise quickly, the abrupt movement making me light-headed. I grab the railing, trying to regain my equilibrium. My glass accidentally smashes against the side of the pavilion, raining wine and shards of glass down my arm. I shriek, then gasp, frightened by the shrillness of my own voice in the quiet night.

I scramble up the steps, turning this way and that, blindly trying to make out the bulky, black shapes of bushes, pots—and what else? The wooden treads creak, and I snap around, crying out, "Who's there? Damn it, who?"

The rage I thought I'd smothered months ago grips me once again. Angry at being dumped, sick of feeling sorry for myself—do I really want to live like this? What the hell more do I have to forfeit to get my life back?

I edge into a wisp of moonlight, cold and gray, looking at my hand holding the stem of the broken glass. Wet, red droplets run down my arm, dripping onto my sandals. I'm ashamed of my weakness, my stupid longings. Why can't I move on?

"Damn it!" I scream. "What am I supposed to do, damn it?"

Tears flood my cheeks. *Lorraine frigging Munson!* How could that happen? I kick the railings, stubbing my toe, wailing with grief. "Damn, damn, damn!"

This has to stop! Hiding does not work. I can't run anymore. I'm tired of being alone and afraid. I've got to find Paul, face him down, and take my life back. "Damn it to hell!" I scream. "Damn it!"

"Meg? What're you doing?"

I look over the railing to see Donna peering up at me. Leave it to her in those damn Dearfoams to sneak up on me. She must think I've had an attack of Tourette's—or lost my mind.

"Nothing. Just running some lines."

"Are you all right?" She asks doubtfully, crossing her arms. "You didn't sound it."

"Of course I am. Actors are crazy. This is what we do when no one's looking." I hold up the broken glass. "Sorry. I got carried away. I hope this wasn't one of Charlie Chaplin's."

"You're in luck. It's from Ikea. By the way, I just heard on the news that Erica Wiggens was found dead. Did you know her?"

"Erica?" My stomach takes an elevator ride. "Killed? What happened?"

"Killed? No, apparently it was suicide. The housekeeper found her in the garage, asphyxiated. Carbon monoxide poisoning—just like Thelma Todd. Didn't you work with Erica?"

"Years ago, but I saw her again the other night. I can't believe it."

"You wonder why someone like that would kill herself. She was so beautiful." Donna hugs her arms, shivering. "You want to come inside? I'll run lines with you."

"Thanks, but I think I've got them down."

I follow her up the path toward the house, my brain turning over the news. *Mafia? Russians?* I replay Erica's last words to me: *That doesn't mean I get to stay alive. Same goes for you.*

What more do I have to do to reclaim my life? If it's on the line like Erica's, it's time I stopped playing the victim. *Thelma Todd's death was a doubtful suicide.*

"Donna, I was thinking maybe we could take a little Sunday drive tomorrow. You up for it?"

Donna looks around at me, blinking in surprise. "Great idea. Have you got some place in mind?"

Chapter Fourteen

The year Donna's baby blue Mercedes-Benz 450SE was born, Nixon was still president. It might be one of the few prize possessions Donna's grandfather didn't acquire used from a movie legend.

"Grandpa was told it would last a lifetime." Donna says, reaching to tune the Blaupunkt. "Well, it saw him through. I see no reason why it won't see me through."

Barreling down the 405, we're fast outdistancing the reach of Los Angeles airwaves. Donna twiddles the tuning knob again. With a hiss of static, Mozart morphs into mariachi.

"Hey, let me get that," I yelp, as the car swerves sharply to the right.

It's a terrific car, and it's delivered hundreds of Meals-on-Wheels. I only hope that with Donna driving, we'll make it to San Diego and back without injury or loss of life.

"Don't worry. I got it." Donna redoubles her efforts with the dial, her line of vision sinking even farther below the rim of the steering wheel. I keep my eyes glued to the road, ready to grab the wheel should we drift across the median again. To make matters worse, Donna has a lead foot. To her, an amber light is a cue to accelerate, not brake.

"I don't mind driving for a while. You want to pull into a rest stop?"

"If you need to go, just say so. I'll find a gas station up ahead."

"No, I'm fine. I just thought you might need a break."

I've offered to drive from the minute we left the house, but Donna won't hear of it. Her thrill of the day is that she has a passenger and is therefore eligible for the carpool lane. Her exultation in zooming past four lanes of clogged traffic dashes any hope I have of wresting control of the wheel.

"You know, I wouldn't mind some coffee, if you'll pour it." She flings her hand in a vague gesture toward the backseat.

I make a sorry attempt to reach for the thermos. The last thing we need is Donna careening down the 405 juggling a cup of hot decaf. "Let's wait a bit. We'll be there soon."

"You're the navigator. Just set the course."

I unfold the yellow lined paper with the directions. "Dougie said the restaurant was in a seedy, industrial neighborhood. Sorry it's not La Jolla or some other place near the water. That would certainly be more in keeping with Paul's lifestyle."

I glance up at an enclave of newly built luxury homes, replete with a private road and gatehouse, perched on the verdant bluffs above the freeway. It's the sort of development Paul dreamed of building. Why, with all the time he spent meeting with investors and working up plans and proposals, did he go for the con instead of a legitimate project?

Donna glances at the sprawling development, too, and gives me a look. "It would be pretty amazing if Paul's been living only hours from LA. What are the chances he's down here?"

"It's probably a wild goose chase, but I can't resist checking it out. Besides, have you ever been to San Diego?"

"Of course, many times. My grandparents loved driving down for a weekend. Tell you what, if this turns out to be a fizzle, I'll take you to lunch at the Hotel del Coronado. Why waste a beautiful day?"

"Suits me, but I can't let you buy me lunch, too. I'll pay you back for the gas and all, but—"

"Are you kidding? This is fun. I'm glad you suggested it. I certainly wouldn't be driving down here on my own."

"I know, but I should be treating you."

"Well, you don't have the money, do you? But I know how you can make some fast cash—"

"Sorry, I'm a little long in the tooth to stand on a street corner soliciting—"

"Shucks, too bad. Okay, I've got another idea."

"Better be good. And I'm not up for phone sex, either."

"This is getting really tough. Anything else you're too proud to do?"

"That about covers it."

"Good. Leave it to me. You'll have a few thou in your pocket by this time next week."

"What do I have to do?"

"Trust me. I'll set it up. All you have to do is be there."

"Donna, you are scaring me. Okay, get out of this lane. Our exit is coming up."

"Righty-ho," she says, and the Mercedes lurches out of the carpool lane. With death-defying speed, we jackrabbit diagonally toward the exit, leaving a trail of honking cars behind us.

"Easy, Donna! We've got another mile to go." I grip the armrest and press myself against the back of the seat. Glancing into the rearview mirror, I spot a beat-up Chevy several cars back maneuvering just as recklessly. "You've set a trend. We're going to cause a pileup back there."

"I've got my signal on." As she pulls into the path toward the exit ramp, my stomach muscles jump. I then realize it's my cell phone vibrating on my waistband. I flip the lid and see that Sid's on the line.

"Hi, Sid. Sorry I didn't get back to you. It was too late last night, and I didn't want to wake you on a Sunday morning."

"I've been up for hours, cookie." Sid sounds peeved. "I left a couple of messages, you know."

"I know. I'm really sorry. How's Carol?"

"Carol? She's fine. She's off to see her mother again for a couple of days. What about you?"

"Everything's great. I wrap the pilot next week. I've got only a handful of scenes left."

"Yeah, good for you. So, what gives? I hear you got yourself involved in some excitement last night." There's no mistaking the edge in his voice.

"What do you mean?" I tense, wondering how word reached Sid. "Are you talking about the commotion with the police? It was sort of weird. Some people tried to break into a friend's house. She called security, and they sent the police. That's all."

"That's all? So who's the friend? How did you get mixed up in this?"

"Hang on a second, will you?" I glance at Donna, whose eyes are on me, not on the road. We're hurtling down the exit ramp, and her foot is not on the brake. I stab my finger in the direction of the red light and signal her to move into the right-turn lane. "Sorry, Sid. I was at my friend Donna's house, and these people broke in. Actually, I think you might know them?"

"Yeah, as a matter of fact. The guy's screaming bloody murder that you bloodied his nose. What the hell were you doing?"

My scalp prickles. "C'mon, Sid, you're sticking up for him? What was he doing breaking into my friend's house? Do you represent these people?"

Donna abruptly pulls over to the side of the road, causing more honking horns. She turns to look at me, oblivious to the cars slowing down to pass us by. I avert my eyes from the drivers glaring at us.

"Listen, where are you? What's all that racket?"

"Just traffic, Sid. You didn't answer me. Are you this guy's lawyer?"

"No, a colleague of mine used to represent him. As of last night, he's representing him again. I'm just trying to get to the bottom of this. It's not looking good."

"For whom? I assume you mean the guy and his mother, right? Did they mention me?"

"Denny did, yeah. Said he thought you could lead him to Paul. Why would he think that?"

"You're asking me? I have no idea. Ask him." Why isn't Sid

mentioning Lorraine Munson? Why is this all about her son? "You know, he roughed up my friend and locked her in a closet. So that's assault and unlawful detainment on top of trespassing. And breaking and entering and—what else? You would know the charges."

"He messed up, no question. If charges are pressed, it could be serious."

"*If?* That's up to my friend, not me. But I don't see why you're so concerned about him. What else did he say?"

"Some cockamamie thing that you accused him of breaking into your car, leaving notes. Is that true? Somebody's been doing that?"

"He already copped to it, Sid. He's been following me around leaving threatening notes!"

"So just where are you living these days? I don't get it, Meg. Why are you staying with this friend when you can stay with us?"

Perfect. Just like Sid to answer a question with a question. "I appreciate the offer, Sid. You know I do. It's just that a friend asked me to stay with her. She's lonely and likes the company."

Donna makes a sad clown face, blinking her eyes at me. I smile. Meanwhile, I hear a deep sigh from Sid.

"Fine. Whatever suits you, but why the mystery? Carol doesn't even have an address for you. You want to meet me for brunch later? You can fill me in about last night."

"I've got other plans today, but thanks. Maybe you ought to spend a little more time talking to Denny. I believe you already know his mother, right?"

The pause is long enough for me to think we've lost the connection, but then I hear Sid's voice speaking softly, barely above a whisper. "Yeah, I've met Lorraine. You know that Denny used to work for Paul, right? I met him a time or two. He's a slick half-wit, but he's got it into his head that you know where Paul is. I'm telling you, Meg: If you *do* know, don't do anything dumb, okay? You've got to tell me what you know. Understand?"

"I understand, Sid."

"Okay. Not that Denny hasn't been questioned before, but who knows what he's picked up since. He's blabbing like crazy, and insists you must have some line on Paul's whereabouts. I think you should know I put in a call to Jack, too. You'll probably be hearing from him."

I freeze. It's not just Denny blabbing, but the specter of Jack hearing Lorraine Munson's diatribe that makes me cringe. *The big TV star doesn't impress me. Paul wasn't impressed, either.*

"Cookie? You still there? Listen, if there's anything at all—"

"I don't know where he is, Sid."

"Okay, kid. I'm always here for you. Just know that."

"Thanks, Sid. By the way, you heard about Erica?"

"Yeah, that's one helluva shame. I guess she just never got over losing Nat."

"So it's definitely suicide then?"

"What else? She was depressed."

"Too bad. Anyway, give my love to Carol when you talk to her."

"Okay, I want to know everything," Donna says when I flip the phone shut, her eyes laser bright. "Who was that?"

"My attorney. He thinks Denny is right, that I know where Paul is. I don't, you know."

"But aren't we going looking for him? Your friend Doug saw him down here. Maybe you should've told Sid that."

"It was just a sighting, Donna."

"Got it." Her lips curl in a lopsided grin, and she slowly nods. "If I've figured this right, you don't want anyone else to get to him first. Is that it?"

I nod, too, momentarily at a loss for words. "I'm sorry, but it's hard to explain. I don't even know what I'd say to him. You'd think he'd be the last person I'd ever want to see, but I need to do it. I just need—to know."

"Of course you do. I understand that." She gives me a reassuring smile, then slams the gear into drive. "Come on, let's track him down." She peels away from the curb without a glance in the mirror.

I hear the squeal of brakes behind us but can't bear to look. Instead I glance at the directions on the yellow lined paper. "Okay, hang a left at the corner. How about if I take the wheel for a while, Donna?"

"No, better that you navigate. I could drive this car in my sleep." I slump back in my seat, shutting my ears to a honking horn.

We go about a mile before making a right turn into a sleepy residential neighborhood with rows of boxy, postwar bungalows. Eight blocks farther, we make another right turn onto a shabby street lined with used auto parts, hardware, and restaurant supply outfits. Most of the storefronts are closed, their entrances shuttered with graffiti-covered corrugated gates. Few people are on the street.

Just as I'm wondering what in the world Doug and his wife were doing in this rundown area, I spot a sign painted on the side of a large brick building: CINEMA CITY—LIGHTS! CAMERAS! LARGE SELECTION USED/VINTAGE EQUIPMENT. Obviously Doug was down here doing more than just visiting his wife's niece.

At the next corner, across from another subdivision of single-family homes, a shopping strip comes into view, with a café that looks like the one Doug described.

"Donna, pull in here, but park down a ways from that coffee shop."

"You got it." The old Mercedes rocks to the left as Donna makes a sharp right into the narrow parking area and stops in front of a Laundromat. A run-down bar with a stucco-and-flagstone façade stands on the corner at the far end of the strip. A neon martini glass blinks sporadically on the weathered wall above a faded awning with the lettering: LUCK O' LUCY. A nail salon and a pet supply, both with CLOSED signs in their windows, fill out the stand of storefronts.

"What do you think? Should we get a cup of coffee?" Donna asks.

"In a minute. I want to get the lay of the land first." I swivel in my seat, my eyes fixing on a mustard-colored house on the corner across from the bar. Drapes are pulled across the front picture window. Shades are drawn on what appear to be kitchen windows. Blistered paint peels off the sagging gutters and trim. The house looks deserted, but I'm betting it's occupied. The lawn is patchy and brown but not overgrown with weeds. No dried leaves or freebie ad circulars have piled up at the front door. The windows aren't caked with dust, and the rusting air conditioner hanging out a side window is dripping water. Someone's home.

"Sure, let's have coffee. I'm not quite ready to knock on any doors yet." I reach into my shoulder bag for a pair of tinted eyeglasses, then tuck my hair into a cap, pulling the visor low on my forehead.

"No mustache?"

"This isn't a disguise, Donna."

"Really."

"Really. I just don't want to draw attention to myself."

"Works for me. Everyone'll think you're Madonna and leave you alone."

"Gimme a break, okay? If it takes Paul an extra minute or so to recognize me, it's worth it." I take another quick glance around before climbing out of the Mercedes. The street is empty, except for a boy on a bike. In the Laundromat, a Latina and her toddler look up as we pass by on our way to the coffee shop.

The Eat 'n' Run is everything you could ask of a neighborhood café. The air is heavy with the smoky smells of bacon and grilled onions. Well-worn red vinyl-covered stools ring the counter, with chipped chrome tables and chairs set against steamy walls. A plastic dome covers a platter of breakfast pastry. Slices of pie and cake glisten on plates inside a glass cabinet. It's Dougie's sort of place. I'm sure he and his wife stop here every time they're in the vicinity.

A scrawny waitress, who clearly doesn't sample the carbs on display, looks up as we enter. "Sit wherever," she says, her voice a dry bark. She pushes aside her newspaper and reaches for the Silex pot. "Coffee?"

"Two—make mine decaf," Donna says. "Thanks." She slides into a chair at a table in the front window. I drop my shoulder bag on the other chair, realizing this must be the same table Dougie and his wife occupied.

"Just coffee. Nothing else for me, thanks. I'll be back in a minute."

I head toward the rear of the café. Following the signs, I locate the black-and-white tiled ladies' room with its grimy chrome fixtures and cracked mirror. I wash my hands, then rub my cold, damp fingers across my taut neck muscles. The tension is only partly due to Donna's diabolical driving.

I glance at my image in the mirror, my face pale in the fluorescent light. My eyes are bright with the fever of too many adrenaline rushes on the road and too little sleep last night. This is the face Paul would see if I were to open the door right now and just happened to bump into him outside the men's room . . . *What if?*

I shake my head, smiling at the thought. What if Paul, the man who chartered helicopters and rode in limousines, was actually holed up in the teardown across the street and took his meals in this greasy spoon? The notion takes hold, no longer seeming preposterous. On impulse, I yank the ladies' room door open, half-expecting to see Paul looming before me in the cramped entryway.

Instead, I come face-to-face with startled kitchen help, a thickset, bearded Latino wearing a white apron and baseball cap. He turns abruptly and slips back through the swinging kitchen door.

I lean against a bulletin board tacked to the wall, surprised to feel so let down. My eyes travel through the hodgepodge of ads and leaflets: MOTORCYCLE FOR SALE. ROOM FOR LET. KARAOKE NITE AT LUCK O' LUCY. SPORTFISHING RENTALS. BABYSITTING "ALL HOURS"—with a telephone number printed on a fringe of pull-off tabs. FURNITURE MOVING—"CHEAP, FRIENDLY SERVICE." LOST DOG. What did I hope to find down here? I glance back into the restaurant and see Donna peering anxiously for me.

By the time I return to the table, the waitress has already poured Donna a refill. "What happened to you? Your coffee's cold by now. You want a fresh cup?"

I glance at the waitress, hand on hip. She clearly has no intention of making such an offer. "I'm fine."

"No sign of anyone over there," Donna whispers, nodding in the direction of the house on the corner. She reaches for the straps of her handbag and brushes past me. "Okay, back in a jiffy."

I stare at the house across the street, hoping someone will open the front door or pull the blinds open. It's hard to imagine Paul stepping onto the cracked sidewalk wearing one of his custom-tailored suits and French-cuff shirts. Would he see me in the café window? *Ridiculous! Get it together.* I pull my cap farther down on my forehead.

The waitress clears her throat. "You waitin' for someone?"

"No, that'll be all."

She nods gloomily and pulls her check pad from her waistband. I glance at the nameplate on her breast pocket and flash her a suck-up smile. "Jeri, I'm kind of sorry we're not stopping for lunch. A friend said the food's really good."

"Yeah?" The waitress looks around as though searching for the idiot who could have made such a claim. She shrugs, her eyes resting on the lone diner, an elderly man sitting at the far end of the counter. "We don't get much of a crowd on Sundays, but it's pretty lively during the week."

"Regulars, I'll bet. Neighborhood people."

"Some. Why?" She sniffs and shifts her gaze out the window. "It must be Lucinda over there you've been talking to. Your friend kept looking across the street. You know Lucy?"

"You mean the corner house? Actually, I think she's a friend of someone I know. She's in here a lot?"

"You kidding me?" The waitress shifts her weight and hooks her hand on her hip bone. "Sorry, thought you knew her."

"Not really, but I was going to look her up because of my friend. I hate to barge in on her, but I don't have a phone number. You think she's home today?"

"See for yourself." She nods toward the window. I look across the street. A tall woman with yellow hair, the same hot-dog-mustard color as the house, is locking the front door. "Lucy gets all her meals here. She's not much for cooking, I guess. 'Scuse me, I gotta get her lunch all packed up."

I stare at the woman with the yellow hair and try to imagine what connection she could possibly have to Paul. Dangling a cigarette between her fingers, she adjusts oversized sunglasses on her face without setting her hair ablaze. Somehow, even in high-heeled sandals, she manages to speed-walk across the scraggly lawn. Busty and broad-shouldered, she's wearing what looks like a stretchy velour top, studded with beads that glint in the sun, over a minuscule leather skirt. Her legs, long and bare, are showgirl-shapely.

And she knows it. Before stepping off the curb, she lifts her foot in a ballet turnout and places it on the pavement as though strutting onto a catwalk. She pauses, takes another long drag on her cigarette, then sprints across the street. At a guess, I'd peg her age in the mid-forties range.

I lose sight of her for a moment, and crane my head against the plate glass. Suddenly she pulls up in front of the restaurant window and stares straight at me, her gold earrings winking in the sunlight. I freeze, cursing my luck. She pulls her sunglasses down her nose with her right index finger. Her lips curl into a smile. She takes another drag on her cigarette, drops it on the sidewalk, and grinds it out with a flourish of her foot. She glances at me once again and continues on.

My eyes flick back to the house on the corner. She locked the door, which means no one else is home. Paul is not there. I take a deep breath when I hear the door of the restaurant *whoosh* open behind me.

"You!" the woman says in a girly voice somewhere behind me. I turn slightly, but she's already reached my table. "You. How do I know you?"

She whips her sunglasses off and smiles, as though all will now be revealed.

"I have no idea," I say, looking into her eyes, as blue and bright as the San Diego sky. Her skin is clear, lightly tanned. I immediately shave a couple of years off her age. "I don't think we've met before."

"I coulda sworn," she says. "Hmmmmm." She tips her head to one side, then the other, and bites her lip. "Oh, gosh, don't tell me . . . Wait a sec—Las Vegas? You weren't in the line at the Stardust with me, were you? Or maybe a cocktail waitress?"

I smile and shake my head, wondering what she's up to. "Sorry, no, but I'm flattered." Over the woman's shoulder, I spot Donna returning from the ladies' room.

The woman looks at me again, pursing her lips. "I know you from somewhere. The cruise ship? You worked the casino?"

I laugh. "Nope, I don't think so." Thankfully, Donna slips into her seat at the table. "This is my friend Donna. We just stopped for a cup of coffee."

The woman smiles at Donna. "Hi. Wow, okay, this is really weird because I never forget a face. Wait, it'll come to me—"

"She's Meg Barnes," Donna says. "You've probably seen her on TV. She's been in a ton of stuff. Remember *Holiday*?"

If I could have kicked Donna, I would have. But it's too late now.

The woman blinks, then stares at me. "Omigod, you're Meg Barnes!" She claps her hands around both of mine. "What an idiot I am. Sorry, I'm Lucy Delano. You know, Luck o' Lucy's on the corner. Pleased to meet you."

"Pleased to meet you, too. So that's your bar?"

"Yeah. I'm just about to open. Say, you wouldn't give me a signed picture of yourself for the wall, would you?"

"Be happy to, but I'll have to mail one to you."

"Great." She looks back toward the counter. "Hey, Jeri, you got my order ready? I gotta buzz."

"You bet." The waitress picks up a brown bag and hands it across the counter. "Here you go." She turns to me. "So you're Meg Barnes? I thought you looked familiar. Didn't you say you knew a friend of Lucy's?"

"Yeah?" Lucy looks at me expectantly.

I flash her a smile, marveling at her ability to keep up the game. "Paul. Aren't you a friend of Paul's?"

She blinks at me again. "You're kidding me? You know Paul?" She slaps her hand on mine again. "I don't believe this. How is he?"

"Great . . . I guess. Actually, I haven't seen him in ages." Out of the corner of my eye, I see Donna raise her eyes to the ceiling.

"Can you believe this?" Lucy says. "This is so amazing. Imagine you knowing Paul. He's such a character. Listen, I gotta open up. You want to come over? C'mon."

"Sure. Let me settle up here."

"I got it," Donna says, handing a couple of bills to the waitress. "Let's go."

Lucy pushes her sunglasses back on her face, and we follow her out the door, past the Laundromat, pet supply, and nail salon, to Luck o' Lucy's. With a ring of keys jingling in her manicured hand, Lucy unlocks the door and pushes it open. She reaches inside the gloomy entrance and flicks on a light switch.

Low wattage bulbs in '50s-era Atomic Age wall sconces dispel some of the murkiness. A metal mop tub on rollers leans against the triangular-shaped bar. The pervasive odor is a sickening meld of stale beer, cigarettes, and bubblegum-smelling disinfectant.

"You shoulda seen this place when I moved in," Lucy says with a sigh. "It was a real dump, you know? Hang on a sec." She grabs a pole next to the door and bangs it sharply on the floor several times. "Mice. God, I hate mice. I just like to let them know I'm coming in, you know?" She bangs the pole again. "Scram, you suckers!"

She reaches up with the pole to open the skylight and several windows along the top of the outer wall. Shafts of daylight splinter the darkness. Dust motes dance like jazzed confetti against the black matte walls.

"Air. A little air and this place'll be fine. The A/C packed in yesterday, and I can't get it fixed until tomorrow. The joys of ownership, you know?"

I laugh, but my eyes scan the pockmarked linoleum floor for scurrying mice. Donna is at my elbow, both of us still hanging back at the door. "How long have you had this place?" I ask.

"Just over a year. I always wanted my own joint, but I was thinking maybe Newport Beach or Laguna. I'd been saving up for years, and then this sort of fell in my lap. You gotta start somewhere. I know it doesn't look like much, but I put a lot into it. I got a band in on weekends," she says, waving her hand toward a black-draped dais in the back corner. "This whole area is turning around. I'm trying for a sleek, retro look to pull in a young crowd. Trouble is, people are really hard on a place. Things go missing. Stuff gets spilled. You want something to drink? A beer?"

"No, thanks," Donna and I chorus. I pick up a couple of leaflets from stacks on a shelf, one of them advertising karaoke, another the Shreak Wizards, which I assume is the band.

"C'mon, guys. On the house." She moves easily behind the bar, unlocking several cabinets and flipping on a switch that illuminates the glass shelving. "I'm telling you, everything I learned about running this place I picked up in Vegas working as a cocktail hostess. Look at this," she says, laying one glass ashtray on top of another, carrying them to a bin. "My bar staff always caps an ashtray. Keeps ash from flying in everyone's drink. And man, am I strict about the bar tabs. You gotta keep your eye on every damn thing."

"You can smoke in bars down here?" Donna asks.

"Gimme a break. Nobody's busted me yet." She laughs. "So, what's the deal, Meg? How do you know Paul?"

"I ran into him a couple of years ago up in L.A.," I say, climbing onto a black vinyl-covered bar stool. "We used to go sailing a lot. But I lost touch with him a while back. I heard he was down here somewhere."

"Really? So you thought you'd look him up." She flops a bar cloth on the counter and begins wiping. "Wish I knew myself. He's quite a guy"—she winks knowingly at me—"but you can't pin down someone like that. Last I saw him was five, six weeks ago. He came through here pulling a U-Haul, and I put him up for a couple of nights."

Five weeks ago? That would have been around the time Dougie and his wife bumped into Paul at the café. My tongue is suddenly thick as a sausage. I can barely get the question out. "How'd you meet him?"

"A little over a year ago, down in Ensenada. I was with a girlfriend, and we ran into him in Hussong's Cantina. You know how it goes. One margarita leads to another, and pretty soon, hey." She shrugs. "I mean, you know right away he's trouble, but what the hell? We shacked up on his boat for a while, who knows how long." She laughs. "He can con anyone, right? He had me believing he was this big shot, but it didn't take me long to see through his cover. I met his kind before—all show, no dough. How 'bout you?"

I nod. "Same. Didn't take long."

She nods. "But hey, I can't complain. He put me in touch with some people who knew about this place. So I figured I owed him. Then, a few months after we met, I get a call. Middle of the night, could I pick him up south of the border somewhere. 'You kidding me?' I say. But I owe him, you know? So I get in my car and race down there. Man, he was a mess."

"He was hurt?"

"Oh, yeah, real bad. Someone had kicked the shit out of him." She opens up the brown bag on the bar and unwraps a sandwich. A whiff of tuna fish fights its way through the smell of disinfectant. "Want some?" she mumbles through a mouthful of sandwich.

"No, thanks. So this was a year ago?"

She nods, biting into the sandwich again. "At least." She guns a spurt of soda water into a glass and drinks thirstily. "Gotta be a year. But I'll say this for him, the man cleans up nicely. A week later he looked good as new. All he wanted was to get back on his boat. That was the last I saw of him until a month ago. He rolls in here like he'd been gone a week. He just wanted to pick up some stuff he'd stashed in a closet."

"He took everything?"

She nods. "Everything." She pulls a chunk of tuna bulging from a corner of the bread and drops it into her mouth, watching me. "You gotta love a guy like that, don't you?"

"What do you mean?"

Her eyes flicker. I wait for the other shoe. She knows Paul. She has to know my relationship to him. How long can she keep this up?

She takes another swig of seltzer and looks at Donna, still standing at the door, before her eyes rake back to me. "So. You're Meg, huh?" she says, her voice dropping. "Yeah, I figured it out as soon as I heard your name. You look different from your picture in the paper. Anyway, I gotta ask. How'd you find me?"

"Sheer luck." I try for a smile, keeping my voice level. "Obviously my husband never mentioned you."

"Yeah, what can I say? Guys cheat. This surprises you?" She shakes her hair off her shoulders and juts her chin. "But I gotta know, okay? How did you find me?"

"Why would I be looking for you? I didn't even know about you." I shrug. "What are you worried about? Is someone trying to find you? Or Paul?"

"Don't get cute. You didn't just happen to be in the Eat 'n' Run. I don't think it's your kind of neighborhood."

"But you've been to my neighborhood, haven't you? Were you there with Paul? The only reason I ask is that you're wearing my earrings."

Lucy's hands fly to her earlobes. "Shit."

Donna gasps, but my eyes stay fixed on Lucy.

"The last time I saw those earrings, they were part of a ransom I put in a bag on my doorstep. Where's Paul?"

"Shit." She slides the earrings off her lobes and into the palm of her hand. "Here. Take 'em." She slaps them on the bar, her eyes never leaving mine. "You got me wrong. I was just trying to give him a hand. He helped me. I helped him. Same as you would. But I don't have any idea where he is."

"Why don't I believe you?"

"It's the truth. I'd tell you if I did." She leans against the back bar, arms across her chest. "He cleaned out my cash box before he left." She shrugs. "I told you I owed him, but I'm paid up now."

Suddenly I believe her. I pick up the earrings and drop them in my jacket pocket. "Thanks."

"Wait a minute. You wanna tell me how you found me? Seriously, I gotta know."

"Easy. A friend told me."

I head for the door, not taking a breath until I'm out on the pavement. I gulp in a lungful of air and hurry back toward the Eat 'n' Run, Donna trotting to keep up. "Could you start the car? I have to get something."

I break into a run, slowing only when I reach the door of the café. The waitress looks up from her newspaper, only mildly surprised to see me again. "Sorry, Jeri. Forgot something." I smile, moving quickly toward the ladies' room. I yank a brochure off the bulletin board, stuff it into my bag, and race back. "Thanks, found it." The waitress barely looks up as I whiz through the restaurant and out the door.

Donna has already backed the car out. I slide into the passenger seat, for once grateful for her bank-heist lead foot.

"You still up for lunch at the Del Coronado?" she asks.

"Why not?" I sigh. "And step on it!" I reach into my pocket for the earrings, pulling out a business card along with them.

Donna laughs. "Man, did you have any idea?"

"Not until I saw the earrings." I turn the card over in my fingers, realizing it's the one Jack gave me when I saw him at the Baskins' dinner. I pull out my phone and punch in his number.

Chapter Fifteen

The prosecutor's words cut like a knife.

"You knew your husband had a mistress! You knew, and you couldn't stand it. You saw your whole world collapsing, everything you'd dreamed of. Everything you'd worked so hard to achieve. So you took your revenge!"

The prosecutor, the kid with the killer grin, isn't smiling now. He jabs his finger in my direction, his glare steely. I sit at the defense table, wilting under the hot studio lights. But with my eyes on the young actor circling the courtroom, it is Jack's voice I hear, quiet and uninflected, cutting me to the quick. We finish the scene, but Lenny Bishop calls for another take. While camera adjustments are made, I remain in place, thinking about my call to Jack yesterday after leaving Luck o' Lucy's. I replay our conversation, once again feeling the heat of the exchange.

"Meg, if you had reason to believe Paul Stephens was in San Diego, you should have notified me immediately. We might have caught him. Chances are, he's fled the vicinity by now."

"I'm sorry, Jack, but what if Dougie had been mistaken? Besides, Paul wasn't there. Just the woman."

"You don't know that."

"I do know it! Look, I'm sorry I called you!" I took a deep breath, telling myself to calm down. Shouting at Jack only made Donna's driving more erratic. "Tell me something, Jack, why are you giving me a hard time? You asked me to call you if I had information. She's there now, at a place called Luck o' Lucy's. Maybe she can tell you more about Paul's whereabouts."

"We're on it. Listen to me. You can't take matters like this into your own hands. He's a fugitive. You could have been in danger."

"Fine. Got it."

What was he trying to say to me? That I was such a dim-wit I didn't know how to take care of myself? That I didn't really know my own husband?

"Patronizing bastard," I muttered when I hung up.

"Prick," Donna said, and I laughed. "You're not going to tell Jack about the rest of it? Your earrings that she had?"

"Hell, no. Let him find out whatever he can on his own."

"You might've mentioned to him that she lets people smoke in that place. He could probably have her arrested."

"I doubt the FBI follows up on stuff like that, Donna."

It was an interesting idea, though. What would I give to see Lucy, who'd been hanging out with Paul when I thought he was in the hands of kidnappers, behind bars? Her saloon shut down, her life ruined because she capped ashtrays instead of banning smoking—it was rough justice, but I was all for it.

I look up to see Lenny Bishop standing in front of the defense table. "You okay, Meg?"

"I'm fine."

"Great. I like that glint of defiance. It works. Keep it," he says, before turning away. "Okay, guys. Finish touch-ups, then let's clear the set and go for another take."

So all I have to do is think of Jack throwing Lucy in the slammer on a smoking violation, and I can ace the scene. Whatever works, use it. I turn my face to Silvia for a dusting of powder and fresh lip gloss.

I dare not imagine Lucy pawing through the paper bag to select a piece of my jewelry. My face would betray murderous inclinations. Why did it take me until the middle of the night to wake up wondering if it was really Paul himself who had retrieved the bag from my doorstep? Had

Lucy been with him? Maybe it was someone else entirely who had picked up the loot, but somehow Lucy ended up with my earrings, a favorite pair I bought at an estate auction years ago.

I smile at Silvia and take a look in the hand mirror she holds for me. I look a bit tired, and no wonder. I'd tossed for hours last night, imagining every sort of scenario. I pictured Paul dumping my jewelry on a bed and the two of them picking out the perfect keepsake for Lucy. Did they fence the rest? In a weird waking nightmare, I saw Dirck holding out the bag for Lucy to make a lucky draw. In an endless loop, first Paul, then Dirck, held the earrings behind his back while Lucy had to guess which hand held her bauble. Even a furniture dream was a breeze compared to one featuring two former husbands, a bag of jewelry, and another woman.

It wasn't until this morning, when I was pouring milk in my coffee, that what Alfred Hitchcock called "refrigerator logic" kicked in. That's when, hours after you've seen a movie, you open the fridge, the light goes on, and you start to rethink the plot. I'd barely placed my hand on the milk carton before I started to wonder why Lucy had bothered to talk to me at all. Why would she acknowledge she knew Paul? What game was she playing?

I regret my call to Jack. I have more questions to ask Lucy, and I wonder if Donna might be game for another trip south. On the other hand, once my Volvo is out of the shop, I can drive to San Diego alone.

The buzzer goes off to signal quiet on the set. True to form, the young star gets another take on his close-up. I suspect it's because he thinks he can dip his chin and do a better version of his lopsided leer. If this series goes, I predict the editor will pull together a Christmas blooper reel of killer-grin outtakes. As usual, Shelby Stuart, playing my defense attorney, races at the speed of light to clap the young actor on the back and schmooze with Lenny Bishop before the next setup. I leave him to it.

Halfway to my dressing room, I run into Donna, my cell phone in her hand. "Okay, it's the distributor cap. No problem. My mechanic can fix it. I told him to go ahead and do a complete tune-up. You need new brake pads, too. It'll be ready tomorrow."

"Not 'til then? Wait a minute, I can't afford all that work."

"When did you last have an oil change?" She shakes her head, her Brillo Pad hair vibrating with indignation. "You can't just run a car into the ground. What if I did that with the Mercedes? Where would we be now?"

"Donna, I won't have money until I finish the shoot. How am I supposed to get to work in the meantime?"

"Don't worry about it. I'll get you to work. I already called and got myself a replacement for Meals-on-Wheels tomorrow. Also, I think I got everything sorted out with your credit card."

"How'd you manage that?" I climb the steps to my trailer, Donna on my heels. "You talked to the lady in Mumbai?"

"Yes, hope you don't mind. Your cell phone rang, so I answered it. She thought I was you. Anyway, you shouldn't have any more problems with them." Donna perches on a corner of the dressing table, looking pleased with herself. "I gave the woman my fax number at home, and she's sending some information."

"Thanks, Donna. I really appreciate it." I glance around my coffin-sized space, not quite sure where to put myself. I'd like nothing better than a few minutes of solitude, but that doesn't loom as a possibility anytime soon.

"No problem. Oh, by the way," she says, handing me some goldenrod-color pages, "someone dropped off these rewrites for your scene tomorrow. You want me to run lines with you later?"

"Sure, later. That would be fine. Listen, you don't have to stick around here, you know."

"I know," she says, flashing me a smile. "But I'm getting a kick out of it. Everyone's so nice. Your stand-in is just great."

Alarm bells sound. "You've been talking to my stand-in? What did she want to know?"

"Nothing. Don't worry. She couldn't have been more sympathetic. She seemed to know all about everything you went through last year, stuff even I didn't know. She really felt sorry for you. Anyway, if you don't mind, she said I could stay with her and watch the rest of the filming this afternoon. Is that okay with you?"

My heart sinks. The last thing I need is Donna becoming pals with a snoopy stand-in who probably feeds stuff to the supermarket tabloids. "Sure, but go easy. I'd rather you didn't talk to anyone about me, okay? No one. Don't even nod in agreement. Please."

The sunshine fades out of Donna's face. She shakes her head, her mouth tight. "I'm probably getting on your nerves. I'm sorry. I was only trying to be helpful."

I feel bad, but not bad enough to recant. I try for a smile, but my lips are too stiff. "I really appreciate everything, Donna. It's just that when I'm working, I try to stay clear of that stuff. Seriously, some people have nothing better to do than gab and make trouble. Wait! I don't mean you—"

She gets up and moves to the door, her back rigid. "I should leave you alone."

"I didn't mean it like that. Please stay on the set and watch all you want. You're my guest. I've already cleared it."

"You mean it?" Her face scrunches. "You're sure?"

"Positive. Really." My heart swells when I see her smile again. "Hey, tomorrow, too, if you like." *Wait! Why overdo it?*

"Thanks, Meg. You're terrific." She leans in to me, wrapping her arms around my waist. I hug her back. "I have to tell you, being here is really a blast."

She leaves, the door clicking softly behind her. How could I be crappy to someone who's done so much for me? I still haven't made arrangements for her to meet Alex Trebek. I sink down on the narrow divan and swing my feet up, knees bent, to fit the space. I can think of no excuse for being so mean to Donna.

Then again, after managing to work decades in the business without a personal assistant, Donna has assumed the role unbidden, unpaid. I'm grateful for the help but appalled at the same time. How can I impose boundaries when I'm living in her house, eating her food, and being chauffeured in her car—to say nothing of risking her life? I can't accept her largesse, then exclude her. Can I?

I pick up the goldenrod pages, checking to see if I've been handed a reprieve, a "not guilty" by reason of some brilliant acting that's snookered the jury. Maybe I could win an appeal in another episode, and string this into a recurring role. Maybe some network hotshot will see dailies and cry, "Hosanna! She's *it*! Sign her to a series!" I can't imagine having steady employment and a place to call home once again.

A whirring sound, growing louder, catches my ear. It's my cell phone, throbbing on the dressing table like a small, agitated animal. Before it can burst into full cry, I snatch it up and flip the lid. "UNKNOWN" flashes on the tiny illuminated screen. I hesitate, my instinct warning me not to take the call, but I do anyway.

"Hello?"

"Meg? It's Jack Mitchell. Am I calling at a bad time?"

My heart pounds at the sound of his voice. I had to answer, didn't I? "Not exactly, but I have to be back on the set shortly. What's up?"

"I need to talk to you."

"Go ahead."

"In person."

"I can't. I'm shooting tomorrow."

"I'm not calling about dinner. This isn't a date."

"I realize that." I hadn't, of course. Now what? The last thing I need is another confrontation with Jack, especially when his voice is in FBI mode. "Do I need an attorney?"

"No, but I talked to Sid."

"Oh, great. So you've already talked to my attorney. Is this is about the Munsons? I'm sure you heard I gave Denny a bloody nose. Bad manners, but he was about to jump me."

"Actually, it was a broken nose. But the Munsons are a different matter. They posted bail. They've been released, pending a hearing. I doubt they'll be showing up on your friend's doorstep again."

"Good. I'll tell Donna."

I detect a faint sound, a brief exhalation that sounds a lot like exasperation. What does he want? I hold my breath. He remains silent. I've played this game before, filling in the silences and saying more than I should. I jump in anyway. "So this is about Lucy Delano? Did you talk with her?"

"I'm afraid not."

"You didn't? Why? She saw Paul only weeks ago. She can tell you more than I can."

"We tried. We couldn't find her."

"She's gone? Wait a minute. She'd just opened the bar when I saw her. Did you check the house across the street?"

There it is again, the soft exhalation. "What time do you finish work today?"

"I'm not sure. I'll have to call you." Then, because it would require too much explanation to ask Donna to drop me off at the Federal Building, I add, "Let's not meet at your office, okay? My car's being repaired, so I'll have to get a lift. Could we meet somewhere else?"

"No problem. Just give me a call later. I'm in San Diego, heading back shortly."

"Fine. Talk to you later, then." I shut the phone, conscious of my own exhalation. So that's what I was hearing, the sound of exertion as Jack walked around Lucy's stomping ground trying to find her. Of course she's not there—she's gone to meet Paul somewhere. It would have taken Jinx less than a commercial break to figure that one out.

What kind of idiot would assume Lucy would tell the truth? Besides me. Maybe Paul did clean out her cash box, but that doesn't mean Lucy doesn't know where he is—or doesn't care. Instead of racing off for lunch at the Del Coronado, I should have taken a page from Jinx's handbook and hung around to keep watch. Chances are Paul would have shown up, or she would have led me to him. I'd give anything to be on my way back down to the old Luck o' Lucy's bar after work. That's what Jinx would do. But Jinx had a car that worked.

I head back to the set, turning over yesterday's conversation with Lucy. What else did I miss? I wonder if Jack managed to talk to Jeri, the waitress. Something tells me she doesn't miss much, even with her face in a newspaper.

I hit my marks behind the defendant's table, remembering that I have to find some place to meet Jack. Somewhere public, but with some privacy. Not noisy, but a place where we won't be overheard. Not a bar, either, though a drink would be welcome. Not a restaurant, since dinner is not part of the bargain. Somewhere open, but indoors—and not a bench in a shopping mall. Where?

Chapter Sixteen

By midafternoon I'm wrapped for the day. In a stroke of inspiration, I call Jack to suggest meeting in the Farmers' Market. Donna is willing to drop me off at the corner of Fairfax and Third, but not without knowing why.

"It's an interview, that's all," I tell her, satisfied when she assumes I'm meeting a writer.

"Great! I knew you'd be asked to do some publicity. You want me to come along? I could pretend to be your press agent."

"Thanks, Donna, but I can handle this myself."

"How about getting home again? Just call, and I can swing by to pick you up later."

"No need. I'll ask him to drop me off."

"Okay, but if it's out of his way—"

"Don't worry. I'll call. Thanks a lot, Donna."

I step onto the curb at Fairfax and firmly close the door of the Mercedes. With a wave, I stride quickly toward the barn-like entrance to the market, knowing that Donna will still be idling at the curb watching me. If the Volvo isn't repaired by tomorrow, I'll shoot myself.

There's no sign of Jack near the entrance. I walk around the fruit and vegetable stalls, hoping that if I run into him we can just walk and talk. I don't want to sit at a table and feel like I'm being grilled again.

I make another circuit, then lean against the plate-glass counter in a fudge shop, transfixed by the huge mixer rotating in a copper vat of thick chocolate. Around and around the paddle goes, sluicing through the molten fudge while my mind runs through a checklist of don'ts: Don't get defensive. Don't be sarcastic. Don't offer information. Don't let him get you angry. Don't imagine your naked body, coated in fudge, pressing into his— *What's wrong with me?*

I turn back to the courtyard and spot Jack, fully clothed, standing not five feet away in the shadows of a souvenir shop. How many years of training does it take to hide in plain sight? Our eyes meet, and my cheeks burn. "What the hell? How long have you been standing there watching me?"

"I just got here."

"And decided to shop for postcards?"

"I swear." He grins. "Want some fudge?"

I knew he was watching. "Hate the stuff," I say.

"Well, I'm hungry. How about a hot dog?"

"Uncle Sam's buying?"

"Sure. He can almost afford it." He takes my elbow. "C'mon, you want the brat and sauerkraut, the foot-long, or the all-beef?"

"That's a tough choice. I'll go with the brat and a papaya juice. Lots of mustard, no kraut."

"Suits me, too. Wanna grab a table while I order?"

"You bet." I swivel around and lay claim to a green metal table and two chairs, scrapping my resolve to stay on my feet. I've also managed to get defensive, sarcastic, and angry within a breath of seeing him. What's left? Volunteering information? Standing naked, covered in fudge?

I watch Jack move up the line and order. Late-afternoon light filters through a red-and-green striped awning, spotlighting his face in gelled color. He tucks his wallet back in his pocket and waits, his stance that of a musician on a bandstand, alert but easy. With a start, I remember he actually is a musician.

Jack glances my way and catches me staring at him. I start to look away, then brazen it out. I hold his look until the counterman interrupts our chicken match to hand over two red plastic baskets. Jack pumps mustard on the bratwurst, then holds up a plastic container of chopped onions. I nod, and he heaps a spoonful on each bun. By the time he makes his way back to the table, my mouth is watering.

"A girl after my own heart," he says, sending mine into a brief flutter. "Lots of onions. I laid on some relish, too." The metal table wobbles precariously as he sets the tray down. I grab the lurching juice cups before they topple over.

"Here's to dinner on the Bureau." I hand him a cup and raise my own. "Cheers."

"Cheers yourself."

I hoist the bun to my mouth and tuck in, savoring the first pungent taste of warm, spicy sausage. I mop mustard off my chin and pause before taking another bite.

"So what instrument do you play? You probably mentioned it the other night, but I've forgotten."

"Me?" I've caught him with a second mouthful and take some pleasure in watching him struggle to chew and swallow before answering. "I'm a reed man. Mostly tenor sax."

"Really? Where do you play?"

"Nowhere these days. I used to play in San Francisco with a little mainstream jazz group. We had a regular Tuesday-night gig at a neighborhood spot, but not anymore."

"How come? Too busy?" I sip my papaya juice, enjoying the novelty of doing all the asking rather than the answering. "The Bureau sent you somewhere else, so you had to give it up?"

"That was part of it." He slowly mops up the fallen bits of relish and onion in the basket with the last of his bun. "Actually, my wife used to sing with the group, even during the years when she was battling leukemia. When she passed away, I asked the Bureau to reassign me. I felt like I needed a change of scene."

His voice is conversational, his gaze steady. I travel a mile or so behind his eyes, my breath caught short. I hear myself saying, "I'm sorry about your wife, Jack. Very sorry."

He nods and swipes his mouth with a napkin. "Well, it's more or less how I ended up down here a year or so ago. I still sit in with the guys whenever I'm in San Francisco, but that's not often."

"I'd like to hear you play some time."

"You may get a chance, if Sid has his way. We used to play in a little pickup group years ago, Sid on trombone. That's how we met. He wants to get something going again."

"So that's it. That's the business you're setting up with Sid?" My brat, laden with relish, crumbles in my fingers. I lick up the dribbling mustard and bun, but manage not to drop the conversational ball so firmly in my corner. "Sorry, I got the idea there was something else. Guess I'm wrong."

Jack settles back, wipes his fingers, and finishes off his papaya juice. "Actually, there is something else on the table. Nothing definite."

"But something you'd leave the FBI for? A business venture? Something with Sid?"

Jack's eyes crinkle. "You're pretty good at this. Yeah, I might be open to something along the lines of a P.I. division in Sid's law firm when I leave the Bureau."

"And that's why you looked up Sid after so many years? I've known him a long time, and he never mentioned you."

"I hadn't seen Sid since law school. I was the one who called him." Jack glances down at the screen of his cell phone, frowning slightly, but makes no comment. I remain silent, too, turning over in my mind some things that don't quite add up. Jack catches my eye and smiles. "You look like you could go for another sausage. How about it?"

I shake my head, managing to swallow the last mouthful before answering. "No, thanks. Please, even if I beg, don't indulge me. That was perfect." I slip my empty basket inside his and slide the tray to the side of the table. "So, what about Lucy Delano?"

"Not a sign of her. She seems to have vanished. The bar was locked up. She wasn't at home. We checked the neighborhood."

"Too bad. Despite what she said, I think she's in touch with Paul. She's quite a character, by the way. It would be fun to play someone like her. Ex-showgirl. Barkeep. Big hair, flashy wardrobe. A real babe. And pretty shrewd, too, it seems."

"Also, a former croupier on a cruise ship," Jack says. "Sales rep for a liquor distributor. Broker with an outfit catering to day traders in a mall setup. That was her last job. Drives a leased SUV registered to Lucinda Platt Delano. A single parking violation outstanding, but otherwise a clean record."

"Wow." I can't help but wonder how far back Jack's checked me out. "I see why Sid wants to hook up with you as a private investigator. What else have you got?"

"She doesn't own Luck o' Lucy's, though she holds the lease. The property was registered in the name P. C. Stephens Enterprises, but it's been flipped several times in the last six months."

"So Paul owned it? Why do I have this sick feeling it could be my money that bought the joint?"

"Could've been, but the title is now in Jerilyn Fenster's name."

"Wow again. Tips must be good at the Eat 'n' Run."

"Better be. But I doubt her credit ap mentions waitress." Jack leans in, his voice low. "I'd like to hear anything else Lucy said about Paul Stephens."

"She claims it was through Paul that she got the place. She took up with him a little over a year ago in Ensenada. About the same time he called to say he'd been abducted, he apparently also called Lucy to pick him up in Mexico. She said he was a mess, that someone had beat the hell out of him. At least some parts of his kidnapping story ring true, it's just that . . ."

"What?"

"What do you think?"

Jack looks at me with a blank expression. *Why is it these things just sail over guy's heads?*

"Look, he escaped and called *her* for help. Not *me,*" I explain impatiently. "All I got was a call to send money. Sorry if I sound pathetic, but it's no fun finding out about all this stuff."

"No, but—" Jack's eyes shift away. "Am I missing something here? He lied to you. He was stealing from you."

Being faced with male-pattern blindness only fuels some idiotic need I have to mortify myself further. "He was beaten up! I can't help it, okay? If Paul had called me I would have been behind the wheel, tearing down to Mexico the minute I hung up the phone. But I wasn't the one he called. Instead, he was with Lucy while I was—God, what was I thinking? Stuffing cash and jewelry in a grocery bag. It makes me sick."

He studies me, shaking his head slowly. Is that a shake of sympathy—or is it complete bewilderment?

"Okay, I sort of get it," Jack says. "I know this can't be pleasant for you to dredge up, but we have to talk. Tell me again, *how* did you happen to come across Lucy?"

"Out of the blue. An old director friend of mine, Dougie Haliburton, happened to see them together in the Eat 'n' Run. He recognized Paul. I went down to check it out. Lucy showed up, but without Paul. I wish now I'd stayed longer and pressed her more. Or hung around and kept an eye on where she went."

"Leave the detecting to us," Jack says, his voice sharp.

"Too late for that. I'm already in it up to my neck. C'mon, Jack, I need some answers, too."

Jack reaches across the table and cups my hand with his. It feels strong, comforting. "I'm sorry," he says. "I'm just trying to get to the bottom of this. I don't want to see anyone—" He pauses, struggling. "I don't want to see you get hurt. You need someone looking out for you. Trust me, Meg."

A thick silence falls between us. I hesitate, my resolve melting with the warmth of his hand on mine. "Anything else you remember?" he asks finally.

The table rocks gently as I pull away to reach into my shoulder bag. "Lucy may have been part of the scheme all along. When I saw her yesterday, she was wearing these earrings."

I open my hand, the antique clips turning over in my palm. "I'd put them in the bag as part of the ransom. Lucy gave them back to me. She knew they were mine."

Jack glances at the earrings, then at me. "I'm sorry, Meg. I wish I could make it easier." The words are like salve on a burn.

"Thanks, Jack. If she was in on this, I should have strangled her when I had the chance. I'm sure she knows more. Probably where Paul is now."

"I can't argue with that. How about some coffee? Or a cappuccino? Let's make sure we haven't forgotten something. I'd like to hear about the rest of your meeting with Ms. Delano."

"Great." I smile, taking note of the *we*. Fair enough. I don't mind spilling what I know as long as I'm not treated like a suspect. Or is this a new ploy?

"I'll be back in a minute," he says, getting up, his hand falling lightly on my shoulder.

I settle back, wondering if his touch was accidental, hoping it wasn't. I watch him moving through a knot of tourists on his way to the coffee bar. I smile, realizing I've just given Jack a reason to consider me a suspect in Lucy's disappearance. It's probably not smart to joke with an FBI man about strangling your husband's mistress.

I look around and notice a man leaning against a pillar near the entrance. When he sees me, he turns away, slouching with his back to me. I recognize the set of his shoulders, the bulk of his arms. A chill runs up my neck as he turns to glance my way again. He's the man I saw at Holmby Park—and I could swear I've seen him somewhere else. Driving the van?

In a flash I'm out of my chair, moving as fast as I can among the crowded tables. The man moves quickly, too. In three strides he's no longer visible. I stop at the entrance, scanning the parking lot. There's no sign of him.

I head back, but too late to reclaim our table. Jack returns with our coffees, surprised to find another couple settling into our chairs. I reach him as he's doing a one-eighty looking for me.

"Sorry, Jack." I brush his sleeve. He turns, his face registering relief, then confusion. "Thought I saw someone I knew."

He hands me a container of foaming coffee, and I take a sip. Racing through my mind is the question of who else, aside from Jack and Donna, knew I'd be here.

"I'm sorry I lost our table."

"It doesn't matter. There are some benches outside. How's the cappuccino?"

"Terrific, thanks." We head toward the side entrance, my eyes darting around the produce stands on either side. "Did you happen to mention to Sid we were meeting here?"

"Yes, why?"

"Just wondered." We settle on a bench, the smells from a nearby caramel-apple stand sweetening the air. "You know he introduced me to Paul?"

"I know," Jack says, his distraction apparent. He checks his phone again, then says, "If you don't mind, I'd like to go over everything that happened yesterday. I'd also like to hear a little more about Doug. How well did he know Paul?"

"Dougie? He wasn't one of Paul's investors. They barely knew each other." I take another sip of coffee, wondering if I should bring up Sid again. Meanwhile, with a little prodding from Jack, I tell him all about my trip to San Diego.

It's dark and growing cold by the time Jack and I walk to his car. I mention that I'm staying with a friend and give him Donna's address. Jack opens the door for me, his hand on my arm as I slide into the passenger seat.

As I watch him walk around the car and climb in, I consider the nagging question of how Jack and Sid met up again. Before putting the key in the ignition, Jack turns to me. "You look like you've got something on your mind."

I shake my head. "Just trying to put something together, that's all."

Jack touches my chin, turning my face toward his. I look into his eyes, at the charcoal rings encircling the caramel-flecked irises. He leans toward me, pulling me closer, his hand grazing my breast as his lips meet mine. We kiss, and I wrap my arms around his neck. His breath is a warm whisper in my ear. "Meg, I've wanted to kiss you for a long time—"

I open my eyes and touch his face. "Me, too." We kiss again. Then, his arm cradling my neck, we gaze at each other. "So that's what you wanted to see me about?"

"Not officially." He smiles and runs the back of his finger down my face. "But it was on my mind."

"The Baskins will be relieved. Carol was getting pretty anxious." I smile and make a face.

He laughs and leans back. "Well, I'm not going to hold it against them."

"Me neither." I shift in my seat, tucking my legs under me but keeping my eyes on Jack. "I wonder when it occurred to them."

Jack gives me a quizzical look and reaches for his seat belt. "I'm not following—"

I savor the lingering taste of him on my lips, knowing I'd be better off not saying more. Yet, the suspicion lurking in the back of my mind returns. "What I mean is, the first time we met was hardly a fix up, was it? Sid called you after I told him Paul had been kidnapped. That's how we met."

"I guess it was." Jack smiles and turns the key in the ignition. "Lucky we didn't both end up in the hospital. That was some fall you took."

"Sorry about that." I smile, too, recalling the morning we knocked heads in the garden. I hope Jack isn't reminded of how awful I looked—or that I jammed my foot in his crotch.

We back out of the stall and swing around to pull onto Third Street. I know I should keep my mouth shut, but I hear myself say, "You had suspicions about me before the so-called kidnapping, right?"

"What are you getting at?"

Great, freshly kissed and I'm already antagonizing him. *Why am I pursuing this?* "Even before we met, you figured that I was involved in Paul's scam, so you made Sid withhold information from me. Tell me, what wasn't I supposed to know? What is it my own lawyer couldn't let me in on?"

There's the briefest hesitation before Jack says, "Okay, you're right. There was an open investigation proceeding. Somebody must have tipped off Stephens, and that's when he disappeared."

"Stephens? So that really is his name, not an alias? Nice to know he cared enough to marry me in his own name. But while this investigation was going on, how come I was left in the dark? Nobody let me know what was going on."

"Sorry, Meg. There was a lot involved. We were nowhere near bringing him in at that point. He was tipped, and we got caught between the bases."

"Too bad for your team. Meanwhile, I was left hanging like a yo-yo on a dead string."

"Meg, it's more complex than you think. I can't go into it with you."

"I'm sure I wouldn't be able to grasp it anyway," I say sarcastically.

I press the button to lower the window, turning my face into the rush of cold air.

Jack stretches his hand toward the vicinity of my knee. I shift away. We ride in silence along the twists of Sunset Boulevard toward Holmby Hills. Still unable to hold back, I vent the thoughts leaping through my mind.

"Damn it, why didn't I figure this out sooner? When you arrived at my house that morning, you already knew Paul had a rap sheet. You knew there was no kidnapping. You strung me along. Now I'm supposed to trust you?"

My words hang in the fresh silence as we swing around the last bend before Donna's house. I'm already reaching for the door handle as Jack's BMW pulls into the driveway.

"Listen, you have to trust me." Jack leaves the car in gear so the doors remain locked, a neat trick. "At the very least, promise you won't go checking things out on your own again."

"Really? I'm his wife, remember? Someone should have told me about him a long time ago instead of watching me sink with the ship. I lost everything!"

"I'm sorry, Meg. I can't tell you more right now."

"So leave things to trained professionals? That does me a lot of good. I'm supposed to wait around to be the next person to wash up on a Catalina beach?"

I have the satisfaction of seeing surprise flicker in Jack's eyes. "What about Catalina? Tell me."

"Rick Aquino. I recognized his photo in the paper. I met him once aboard the *WindStar,* before Paul and I were married. Tell me, what kind of business would he have with Paul? Drugs? What, for God's sake?"

"What did they talk about?"

"I've volunteered enough. Your turn now. I want to know about Paul."

"He's not who you think he is. And Stephens isn't his birth name. We go back a long way with this guy, Meg. Stay clear of him."

"Yeah? Now you tell me? A little late, wouldn't you say? When do I get to hear the rest of it?"

I lift the side flap of my shoulder bag and hand the digital printout to Jack. "Maybe you can explain these pictures I came across."

Jack flips on the interior light and examines the images on the glossy printout. "Where did you find these?"

"In a box I'd stored with Dougie. I'm sure you recognize the man standing between Rick Aquino and Paul, right? He's Nat Wiggens, the film producer killed in a carjacking. Nat was one of Paul's investors, and we attended his memorial service. Now his widow is dead. Do you know who this man is—the one wearing the straw hat?"

There's the briefest pause before Jack mutters, "Vladimir Proznorov, head of a Russian syndicate that's moved into the Mexican drug trade."

A chill runs through me. *Erica was right!* If I'd believed her, given her some support, would she still be alive?

"So Paul's mixed up with Russian mafia—and drugs? I thought he was just an ordinary swindler."

"I told you, Meg—"

"What? You told me nothing! Most of it I've figured out for myself. Proznorov is the name of the guy Paul had me call about the ransom. I thought he was just some sort of pawnbroker. You couldn't tell me who he was when I gave you that piece of paper? And what about Sid? Is he involved with Proznorov, too?"

"Sid? No—"

"But Nat Wiggens was?"

"Wiggens brought Proznorov in—"

"Then got caught holding the bag when some money disappeared, right? "

"Something like that. I can't tell you more, Meg."

"Thanks. Keep the printout, if you want. Now, if I'm not under arrest, open the damn door and let me out."

Jack shifts into PARK. The door locks release. I get out.

"Good night, Jack. Thanks for the brat and cappuccino."

The last words I hear before I slam the door are, "Stay safe, Meg. Call if you . . ."

He may have said more, but by then I was already slamming the front door.

Chapter Seventeen

I hoped, even as the judge rapped her gavel and I rose to hear the verdict, that the jury would come in with a surprise "not guilty." It was not in the script, of course, but that glimmer of hope certainly aided my performance. I caught the look of triumph on my son's face and felt a surge of anguish that he would never understand I'd only wanted to protect him. I held my arm out to him, pleading for some sign of forgiveness, only to be pulled away, sobbing, as he turned his back.

Shelby Stuart delivered a rousing summation in my defense that would have swayed any jury other than ours, a panel of bored extras holed up on Stage 9 checking cell phones. With their "martini" shot glimmering on the horizon, their minds were focused on little else than securing their next gig. Not that anything would have made a difference. In prime time, the glove always fits. The guilty pay no matter how persuasive the attorney.

The real justice is the possibility that, if the pilot is picked up, Stuart will win himself a recurring role as a defense attorney. He certainly deserves the chance, not only for his terrific work in front of the camera but his arduous sucking up off camera. He makes a beeline to schmooze with the executive producer the moment Lenny Bishop says, "Cut. Check the gate."

The buzzer sounds, and I head for my dressing room. Despite Donna's best efforts, I've managed to retain custody of my cell phone. On the way to my trailer, I flip it open to check messages. Jack's number comes up three times, but he's left only one voice message: "Meg, call me. Please."

My knees go weak at the sound of his voice. I replay the message, my reaction shifting from relief to longing, with more than a twinge of irritation thrown in. It's about time I heard from him. Just because I slammed his car door the other night doesn't mean he can't stay in touch. My anger is genuine and thoroughly justified, but I regret that show of temper. Aside from coldcocking a romance before it had a chance to take hold, I effectively shut myself out of the loop regarding Lucy. Jinx would not have been so stupid.

Figuring Donna is ensconced in my dressing room, I detour around another soundstage while replaying the message. "Meg, call me. Please." I hover in the shade of an awning and punch in his number.

He answers almost immediately. "Meg? Where are you?"

"You first. Why haven't you called?" The words I hadn't intended to speak recoil like a blast from a shotgun.

"Sorry, I believe I did." His tone is even, but the irony is unmistakable.

"Sorry, I didn't mean to come off like that. How's it going?"

"I'm in San Diego. I'm afraid I've got bad news. Jerilyn Fenster's dead."

"What! How?"

"Her body was found in a Dumpster this morning."

"Killed?" As my brain grapples with the word, I see flashes of the skinny, sallow-faced woman bent over her newspaper. "Why in the world—? It doesn't make sense."

"When you saw her in the restaurant that day, she connected you with Paul, right?"

"Of course. Lucy showed up, and I mentioned I knew Paul. Oh—"

"What?"

"It dawned on me afterward. When Jeri recognized me as Meg Barnes, she probably remembered reading about Paul and me in the papers. She would've put it together."

"She probably did."

I wait, expecting a follow-up question. Instead, Jack says, "Thanks, Meg. Look, I don't know when I'll be back. I just want you to promise me again you'll call if anything comes up. Just call, okay?"

"I promise. Jack? Listen, about the other night—"

"I know. I don't blame you. I wish I could tell you more." His voice grows husky, and I hear the hesitation. "Now's not a good time, but we'll talk later. Just take care of yourself—and call."

"And call. Yeah, I will." I think about all the times in the past several days when I wanted to do just that. I'm about to ask Jack how Jeri was killed, when I realize we're disconnected. I also meant to ask if he'd found out where those panoramic shots of beach and mountains were taken—certainly not on Catalina Island. I consider calling back but decide to wait. I'll have many more questions once I've had a chance to think. I return my phone to my pocket and look around.

Donna emerges from my trailer, spotting me just as I see her. Two thoughts collide: *No need to tell Donna* and *What would Donna make of this?* I decide the news flash can wait. I head toward the trailer, meeting her halfway.

"Hey, Meg, they went ahead and picked up some other scenes, so you're wrapped for the day. I got your call sheet for tomorrow. We don't have to be here until eight tomorrow morning."

"Great. Thanks." Even though I finally have my Volvo back, Donna insists on driving me to the studio and spending the day on the set. I mount the steps, unbuttoning my suit jacket on the way. "Give me five minutes to change, okay?"

"You got it," she says cheerfully. I don't know which of us will miss the studio more when this pilot is wrapped. But I'd bet on Donna.

With a good chunk of the afternoon to myself, aching to be alone, I make no more than a pit stop at Donna's. After promising her I'll be back for dinner, I throw my gym bag in the Volvo and head down the canyon toward the health club.

Crossing the flats of Beverly Hills, approaching Santa Monica

Boulevard, I see a ragtag band of people in shabby, mismatched clothing streaming out of a church courtyard. I slow down and pull to the curb, looking for Adriana. According to her, the Episcopal church serves the best "homeless" meal of the week. It's her favorite place to dine. Food donations come from the best restaurants. The prayer service is optional.

She arrives early to get a good parking spot, and serves as a volunteer, usually dispensing beverages. Besides providing her with the pretense of feeling like staff, working as a volunteer permits her to eat her meal before the doors open to the unwashed masses lining up in the courtyard. She also gets first crack at rummaging through the reading bin for donated back issues of *Atlantic Monthly* and *The New Yorker.*

After Adriana gave me the whole rundown, she invited me to join her in serving beverages. My stomach turned at the thought of it. I never consider myself *that* kind of homeless. Of course, Adriana doesn't think *she's* that kind of homeless, either, which is why she serves as a volunteer. She has her Chevrolet, just as I have my Volvo. Besides, according to her, some of the diners who show up here aren't really homeless at all—they just run out of money before the end of the month, and enjoy the food and conviviality.

Volunteering for Meals–on-Wheels and having a bite to eat with the rest of the staff before hitting the delivery circuit is a far cry from joining a breadline in a church hall with people who spend their days pushing grocery carts containing all their earthly possessions.

Even Adriana seems to understand that, and knows she's crossed over. She calls it "the grip" and taps her forehead so I know what she means. "Can't lose the grip," she says in her saner moments, when she's not fretting about the homing device she claims her husband implanted in her skull.

I idle at the curb watching two hulking transvestites in filthy leatherette miniskirts and pink tank tops trudge toward Santa Monica Boulevard. They'll join other transients waiting in clots at bus stops on opposite sides of the street for either a trip east to Hollywood or west to Santa Monica. No one ventures across the boulevard toward the Gucci, Prada, and Cartier shops on Rodeo. Adriana herself usually stays on to help with cleanup, then packs up a little bag of leftovers to snack on later in Holmby Park.

I glance back up the street toward Adriana's parked car just as an elderly, shabbily dressed man crosses behind the Chevrolet and pulls at the door. I jump out of the Volvo and hurry down the sidewalk, intercepting the man just as he's settling himself behind the wheel.

"Hey, wait a minute!" I grab the door as he's about to close it. "What do you think you're up to? This is Adriana's car."

"I know." The man turns rheumy eyes on me, his voice belligerent. He's wearing a stained tweed jacket the color of his teeth. "I'm lookin' out for it. She asked me to." He tries to pull the door closed.

"Who are you?"

"Murray, if it's any of your business. The lady's a friend of mine." He juts his chin out. I try to place the accent. English? Australian?

"Then why don't we just wait until she gets here."

"Hah!" He squints up at me, shaking his head so vigorously that his comb over slides in a gray streak toward his ear. "That's all you know. They got her in St. John's. Ambulance took her a coupla days ago. She collapsed on the esplanade whilst taking in the sea air."

"What happened? How is she?"

"Not so good. They had to operate. Found a brain tumor, wouldn't ya know." He swipes a trembling hand up over his ear, pressing his hair back in place. "Ya mind lettin' go of the door? I'm goin' out to see her."

"You're driving there? You've got a license?"

"Who says I'm drivin'?" He slaps the steering wheel, agitated once again. "I gotta move this bucket once a day or it gets taken. Soon's you let me get it back behind the church here, I'm catchin' a bus. You're makin' me miss it."

I step back and close the door. It creaks shut and latches with a thump. Murray shakily inserts the key in the ignition and grinds the starter. Slowly, very slowly, the Chevy lumbers toward a space near the rear door of the church and lurches to a stop. Murray climbs out, hitching up his baggy trousers. He's short, almost gnome-like, with an oversized head and shoulders. Without giving me another look, he heads toward the bus stop, his rubber flip-flops slapping on the sidewalk.

"Hey, Murray. Wait up." I catch up to him just as we're passing my car. "No need to take the bus. I want to see her, too. You want to ride along with me?"

Without a word of acknowledgment, Murray shuffles toward the passenger side of the Volvo. Before I've climbed behind the wheel, Murray's plugged in his seat belt and rolled down the window.

"Stuffy in here, idn' it? You know the way?"

"Sure. Santa Monica, right?"

"Spot on." He pulls his jacket around himself and peers out the window. "Take whatever route you fancy. I'm having a kip."

"Where are you from? I hear an accent."

"I'm Tasmanian, if it's all the same to you. And I believe you're the one with the accent, dear."

I'm about to ask him more about himself—and Adriana—when I see that's he's snuggled against the door and closed his eyes. I suppose a nap after a big lunch is in order. I turn onto Santa Monica Boulevard, wondering if Adriana's homing device was misdiagnosed as a brain tumor—and if she'll get her grip back now that it's been surgically removed.

Shortly after Murray and I enter her draped cubicle, Adriana's eyes blink open. She looks elegant, even without makeup, her head swathed in a turban of white surgical bunting. One can't fake good bones, and Adriana has them. Moreover, her pale skin is scrubbed of its grayness, taut with slight swelling, making her look younger, fresher. She's as ready for a close-up now as she's ever been since I first met her, filling her water bottle at the drinking fountain in Holmby Park.

She blinks again. The hooded lids give her the look of a bird of prey sizing up her quarry. Her sharp eyes flick from Murray to me and settle back on Murray. A corner of her mouth lifts in a coquettish smile. The hardness melts from her eyes. "You found me," she whispers.

I glance at Murray and see a tear glistening on his ruddy cheek. "Been here every day, love. Held your hand in mine 'til they sent me on my way." He stretches his grimy hand to hers, locking her little finger around his, jostling it gently against the coverlet.

I edge back toward the door, feeling like a third wheel. My movement causes Adriana to shift her gaze, her piercing eyes clamping on mine with a startling suddenness.

"Hey, Adriana. It's me, Meg. How're you feeling?"

"Glorious, my dear. But the shoot was arduous. One must always refresh oneself at a good spa after finishing a picture."

"Right. So they're looking after you well here?"

"The baths are divine. The waters so soothing."

Murray's face is a mask of reverence as he strokes her hand. "Just what the doctor ordered, my dear," he says before turning to me. "You'll stay with her while I use the facilities? I shan't be long."

"Of course, Murray." I play along, desperate to find my role in this screwball comedy. In doing so, I manage to pick up Murray's "Tasmanian" accent. "Run along. I shan't budge 'til your return."

"Dear man, do tell them we'll take our tea service now," Adriana coos. Murray puckers his lips over his large beige teeth. Not a pretty sight, but it seems to delight Adriana. He runs his fingers across her hand before turning to leave.

"Dear, dear man," Adriana breathes as Murray slips out through the curtains encircling the bed.

"Well, you're looking pretty good, Adriana. How long do you think you'll be staying here?"

Her eyes harden. She blinks twice. "Until that villain sets me free. I'm under lock and key, you know. He's paid them off."

"Who? Murray?"

"Shhhh. He's my husband, of course. Cruel. Scheming. He's seen to it that a new transmitter has been implanted. Far more powerful. I'll never be free."

I whisper, too, the plot having taken a grim new turn. "Forgive me, Adriana. I thought Murray was your friend. You had me completely fooled."

Her eyes glint. "Of course, my dear. Nothing is ever what it appears to be. People fool you every chance they get. You must be very clever to stay ahead." She taps the surgical bunting covering her temple, her voice a hiss. "Stay sharp! You mustn't let on you know the truth. It will be the end of me."

"Of course. Your secret's safe."

"You would do well to learn from me, child. Hold your friends close, your enemies closer." Her eyelids waver and shutter closed. "That goes for husbands, too, of course. Always a different guise, but perpetually evil. Tiring. So tiring."

I watch her for a moment, her face growing slack with sleep. She ages with each shallow breath, her skin wilting like a lettuce leaf into a patchwork of soft, fine lines. Behind me, the curtain rings slide open. Murray holds a corner of the cloth, his shoulders sagging in his old tweed jacket.

"Sleeping. That's good," he says.

"I think I'll slip out, Murray. Do you need a lift anywhere?"

"Oh, no. I'll stay here as long as they let me."

"Listen, I hope you don't mind my asking, but—"

Murray presses a grubby finger to his lips, his eyes shooting me a warning. "No, we're not married," he whispers. "But I had to tell them we were in order to get in to see her. They're very particular here."

"I see. Okay. Well, I'll be on my way then. Nice to meet you."

"And you." He touches my arm, his voice still a whisper. "You mustn't mind what she says. She's completely mad, you know. But I love her. She was so splendid in her day."

"Sure, Murray. I know. Take care." There's no point, really, in asking him about the homing device. I slip through the drapes and hurry out the door into the hallway.

I walk along the neighborhood streets, praying each step of the way that my car hasn't been towed or ticketed because I parked in a "resident permit" zone. But I wasn't going to pay the extortionist fees charged by the lot—why are hospitals allowed to fleece everyone for parking?

Murray had been quite put out that he'd been made to walk so far, pointing out that the city bus would have dropped him off only steps from the hospital's entrance. But then he also grumbled about having to venture all the way into "congested" Beverly Hills to get a good meal when he preferred remaining in Santa Monica for the quality of the "bracing sea air." I suspect Murray resides on one of the park benches above Pacific Coast Highway. In any case, when I reach the Volvo, I'm relieved to find my windshield devoid of bad news.

While bucking rush hour on Santa Monica Boulevard, I mull over my crazy visit with Adriana. Of course, her paranoid obsession with a Moriarty is the product of out-of-whack brain chemicals, but still I can't help wondering if she might have a mean-minded husband lurking somewhere, homing device or not. And nuts or not, maybe she's right. People will fool you every chance they get.

I rush into the health club in time to take a cardio-ballet class, a strenuous paramilitary session that leaves me sweaty but revitalized. After a quick shower, I head back to Donna's, my brain churning.

It's not until I'm pulling into the driveway that my mind seizes on the underlying thought eating at me since I spoke with Jack. Once the waitress recognized me, she would have made the connection between Paul and me. Why the pretense? If she had her head stuck in a newspaper every day, how could she have missed the stories about Paul being a fugitive? She had to know, yet she said nothing.

Before I can push my key in the lock, the door swings open. Donna, dressed in her floral caftan, waves me in, her eyes bright. "I was hoping you'd get here soon. Come quick. You've got to see this."

I follow her into the den. Donna plops onto the chaise and points her hand toward the TV screen. Suddenly my face pops up in a grainy close-up, bleating, "Paw, I can *so* ride Blackie!"

"That's you!" Donna laughs. "That's you, isn't it?"

I nod, transfixed by my twenty-two-year-old self portraying an adolescent in pigtails and cowboy hat. An actor, long since dead, grips my shoulder and says, "Hush, now, child. A scrap of a thing like you can't handle a horse like Blackie."

"I can so, Paw. Watch me!"

Donna, sitting cross-legged on the chaise, grins and thumps her hand on the cushions. I perch next to her.

I watch myself race across a dusty corral and clamber aboard a stomping black stallion. The horse rears. I appear in close-up again, holding the reins in one hand, my hat in the other. Then there's a cut to a long shot as the horse bolts out of the corral and we gallop across the prairie.

"Wow, I'm impressed. You ride well."

"Of course I can ride. Actors can do anything. But actually, in that close-up where I'm waving my hat in the air, and that other part where I'm galloping—"

"A double?"

"What do you think?" My close-up, with freshly powdered nose, was shot hours later with me seated on a stool on an inclined platform, no horse in the vicinity. "Tricks of the trade. All make-believe."

Donna passes me her wineglass, and I take a sip. Meanwhile, on the screen, there's a quick cut to Paw and me pulling up in a buckboard at a country church. An impossibly handsome young man offers me his hand. I wave him away and climb down on my own.

"You're a spunky little devil," Donna says, "but I bet you kiss him."

"Of course. Although I seem to remember kissing girls wasn't something that particular actor liked doing—but then, actors can do anything. At least he didn't ask for a stunt double."

Donna laughs, and we settle back, sharing her glass of wine while watching the last few minutes of the serial. As soon as it's over, Donna hurries to the kitchen to check on dinner. I wait to watch the credits roll, catching my own name and the name of the little tomboy with pigtails and freckles that I played—Frankie.

Suddenly the image of Frankie Cooper, the schoolboy in the photograph, pops into my brain. I flip off the television and head to the kitchen, the solemn, gap-toothed face of Frankie Cooper hovering in my mind. As I near the breakfast nook, I smell tarragon and mustard. Donna has set the table with the French faience, which probably means she's preparing her chicken Dijon with braised radicchio. Above the din of clattering pans and splashing water, she calls out to me.

"Yes?" I pour myself a glass of wine from the bottle on the kitchen counter. "You were saying?"

"A fax from that credit card company finally arrived with the printout of the charges. It's there on the table. It doesn't matter much, since you won't be liable for anything. Pour yourself some wine."

"I have, thank you." I pick up the fax, grateful the matter has been settled. I've seen enough dunning letters from credit card companies to last a lifetime.

"And don't make any plans for Saturday, okay?"

It's Donna's tone that's a giveaway, a little too bright and way too emphatic. "Why? What's up?"

"Nothing," she says, pretending absorption in garnishing the chicken with bits of chopped tarragon. "I've just arranged something I think you'll get a kick out of. Anyway, dinner's almost ready."

"Lovely. I'll just use the facilities. Shan't be a moment," I respond, in what I think would pass for a Tasmanian accent.

I run up the stairs, looking at the fax from the credit card company as I hurry to my room. My eyes travel down the postings, most of them charged in Arizona, but two in California and one from Mexico: gasoline, U-Haul rental, computer equipment, office supplies, airline tickets, meals. *U-Haul?*

I toss the fax on my bed and fling open the cupboard where I stashed the school photo of Frankie Cooper. Stuck in my brain is Jack's comment that "Stephens" isn't Paul's birth name. I'm betting it's Cooper. *The Coop.* Forget the birth date—that school photo of little Frankie has to be Paul. That makes Dorrie Paul's sister, the one he claimed was in New Zealand.

Another thought springs to mind: If I married a man masquerading as someone named Paul Stephens, was I ever legally married? If not, a phantom husband managed to rob me of everything I possessed—and is still at it. Adriana's warning rings in my ears: *Always a different guise, but perpetually evil. Tiring, so tiring.*

I hear Donna's voice calling me to dinner. I drop the photograph on my bed next to the fax and hurry back downstairs. I retrieve my glass of wine from the kitchen and bump into Donna bustling in from the dining room. "Your cell phone went off in your handbag. Better check your voice mail."

I take note of the fact that Donna didn't rummage in my bag to take the call herself. Either we're establishing some boundaries, or she's off duty for the day as my P.A. This roommate thing isn't easy. Meanwhile, I listen to a message from my agent, Pat. "Hey, Meg. Expect a call from a guy named Steve Dorfman. Hope everything's going well."

Steve Dorfman? Now what? I sip my wine, wondering who he is—and what Donna has in store for me tomorrow. I don't like surprises.

Chapter Eighteen

Somehow I'm trapped in Luck o' Lucy's, clambering onto a jukebox that's lying atop a pool table blocking a door. I search frantically for a way out. Mice scramble underfoot, squealing and buzzing—buzzing? I roll over, my ears picking up a fuzzy but familiar sound. My eyes open and travel the length of the bed to my throbbing, blinking cell phone, its melody muffled in the folds of the bedspread. Steve Dorfman? Who would call me at this hour? I reach down and flip the lid: CAROL glows on the screen. I note the time.

"Meg? You there? Hi, sweetie. It's me."

"Who else?" I close my eyes again and sink back into the pillow.

"Sorry. Am I calling too early? I wanted to catch you before you went out."

"Where would I be going at 6:38 in the morning?"

"Just making sure. Today's a Focus Day, so I want you to make good use of it. What's up, anyway? I haven't heard from you in a week."

"I wrapped the pilot, that's about it. I'm just trying to catch up on some sleep. It's Saturday. I don't need to focus."

"You've forgotten! Honestly, Meg, didn't you look over those notes I gave you? This is your Pluto day. You've got a life-transforming event happening in the next twenty-four hours. There's a pretty good Jupiter aspect today, too . . . so come on, get out of bed. Your fortunes could change. On top of all that . . . Uranus is still hanging around, so . . . expect the unexpected."

She's begun speaking in small gulps. Her treadmill must have been programmed to move into Steep Incline.

"Thanks for the warning, Carol. Listen, can I call you back later? Maybe after I've had some coffee?"

"Sure, but swear to me . . . you've got your feet out of bed . . . on the floor . . . otherwise I'm not hanging up."

I slide my knees to the edge of the bed, my toes peeking out into the chill. "Thanks for your confidence. I could lie to you, you know."

"Don't. Honestly, Meg . . . I just know you're going to blow it. I mean, you've got to expect the unexpected and make it work for you. You plan to see Jack today?"

I mash a pillow behind my back and struggle to sit up, pulling my toes back under the covers. "Nope. Haven't heard from him. But a friend has something planned."

"Really? What're you doing?"

"I don't know. It's a surprise, but it's supposed to take up the whole day. I'll let you know when I know."

"Well, maybe that's it . . . the unexpected. Fine. Just be aware . . . this could be a really meaningful day . . . Like a total change of direction. Hang on a sec . . . gotta hydrate." I hear the snap of a twist-off cap, followed by gurgling sounds, then a deep breath. "You still there? Listen, I have to share this with you. I woke up this morning thinking . . . like, omigod, this is the September of our lives . . . I mean, think about it. I love autumn and all, but when you think of what it means in terms of—" Carol's voice grows breathier, and I don't think it's just exertion.

"Easy there, September girl. It means we're past the dog days of summer. September couldn't be anywhere near as crummy."

Carol sighs. "Leave it to you to take the piss out. You know what I'm saying. Autumn, for God's sake. You know what's coming next."

"I do, and it's not more sleep. Boy, am I glad you called. If you would just sleep a little later in the morning, you'd wake up to sunshine. Seriously, Carol. It makes all the difference."

"I'm talking about you! How can you lie in bed losing the day?

There's a world out there . . . waiting for you . . . don't let time slip away . . . Really, I worry about you . . ."

"About me?" Once again I'm the designated donkey on which Carol pins her anxieties. "I appreciate your concern, but I think I can handle whatever comes along. How are you doing?"

"Fine. I'm fine. It's you . . . Listen, I'd love to talk, but I have to jump in the shower. I'm off to visit my mother for the weekend. Gotta run. I'll call you later, sweetie. Stay alert!"

"Sure." I drop the phone onto the carpet and slide deeper into bed. I smell coffee brewing. Donna's up. For a moment I weigh the choice of catching more sleep or heading down to the kitchen. Coffee wins. I throw back the comforter and reach for my robe, my eyes falling on piles of snapshots scattered across the carpet.

I drop to my knees and take another look at the pictures that kept me awake until well after midnight, all of them from the packet I found in Dougie's garage. There are two snapshots from our wedding in Arizona, both taken with Paul's digital camera. He'd tossed the tiny camera to the justice of the peace, who obligingly took our picture after performing the brief spa-lite ceremony. Paul and I are wearing dark glasses and holding champagne flutes in the midday sun.

But the photos of real interest are those of the Mulholland development. One is of a heavyset man in a rumpled suit and straw hat with his arm around the shoulders of a young man I immediately recognize from Holmby Park, wearing a familiar-looking leather jacket and holding a guitar. The older man is Vladimir Proznorov, the Russian mobster Jack identified in the photos with Paul, Rick Aquino, and Nat Wiggens. The Holmby Hills hunk is likely Proznorov's son.

There are several more photographs of the *WindStar,* and another of a similar sailboat, but the flare of sunlight on the hull obscures its name.

I take another look at the school photo of Frankie Cooper, struck again by the boy's resemblance to Paul. I stare at the child's eyes, his smile, looking for some insight into the man he would become. There's a hint of mischief, a sense of self-possession in his gaze, the tilt of his head—but could anyone imagine this kid growing up to be a con man? A felon? I try to picture the face of the man I knew appearing in a mug shot with ID numbers printed across his chest, and I can't envision it.

I pack up the pictures and stuff the bulky packet into my shoulder bag. Minutes later, I'm brushing my teeth, wondering what Donna has in store for me. I consider the possibilities, none appealing. Wearing sweatpants and a T-shirt, I head downstairs.

"Morning!" I pad barefoot into the kitchen, startling Donna mid-pour. She sets a bottle of prune juice back on the counter, a smile vacating her face when she takes in my outfit. I, in turn, check out Donna's ensemble, one of her smart St. John pantsuits with shiny buttons.

"I take it we're not going rock climbing."

She laughs. "Let's have some breakfast. You've got plenty of time to fix yourself up." She pops bagels into the toaster. A bowl of fancy fruit and berries is still wearing its cling wrap. The breakfast set du jour is pink-flowered Minton on damask place mats.

"*How* fixed up?" I can only hope I haven't been set up for ladies' day at the country club. Or an antiques auction.

Donna laughs again, but her eyes are wary. "This'll be fun, I promise you. Coffee?"

I nod, and pass her a mug from the dish rack. A bone china cup in a saucer somehow makes morning coffee taste thin. "Then why aren't you telling me? You have your doubts, right?"

"Not really. I mean, not once you're there, if you know what I mean."

"And we can always leave."

Donna's smile tightens. "Trust me. You'll see."

I feel compelled to repeat, "And we can always *leave*?"

"Whatever you like." She spreads a thick layer of cream cheese and marmalade on a bagel for herself. She knows I like mine plain. "How about if I just pick out something for you to wear while you jump in the shower?"

"Will that give me a clue? This doesn't have anything to do with charity, does it? Or a fashion show?" A terrible thought occurs to me. "This isn't some sort of retro est seminar, where I'm going to be harangued all day and not be able to pee?"

"Nope. Or golf. Or shopping. Or even lunch, although we'll probably eat. Don't worry, okay? You'll take all the fun out of it."

"I hate surprises."

"Not this one. At least I don't think so."

The outfit Donna chooses from my scant wardrobe is not alarming. When I step out of the shower, I'm relieved to find my favorite black pants and a cobalt blue jersey laid out on the bed. Donna is nowhere in sight, so I'm apparently trusted to choose my own underwear and shoes. How odious could the excursion be if I can dress comfortably and leave when I choose?

We set out shortly before nine, Donna behind the wheel of her Mercedes, and head for the 405 freeway.

"Got it!" I sing out. "We're going to the Getty Museum. Why does that have to be such a big secret?"

"Not today," Donna says, as we sail up the entrance ramp and lurch into the far left lane. Another ten miles down the 405, just as I begin to think the surprise destination is another trip to San Diego, Donna pulls off at the La Tijera exit and heads for the airport.

"So where are you taking me? Paris? Las Vegas?"

"Hang on. You'll know soon enough."

We swing onto Century Boulevard and almost immediately swerve into a parking area—but not before my eyes have caught sight of my name on the hotel's marquee. My stomach contracts as I take in the words: MEET THE STARS!

"What the hell! Donna, what's my name doing up there?"

"Isn't that great!" Donna says gleefully, swinging the car door open. "It's an autograph signing. I know the organizers and help out sometimes. They were thrilled to get you, even at the last minute."

"No, wait!" My eyes fly back to the marquee and the other names sharing billing. What am I getting into? "Shelby Stuart's doing this?"

"He'll be sitting next to you. C'mon, give me a hand." She slides out and hands her keys to the valet parker. I jump out, too, panic lapping at my throat. I race back to the trunk, where Donna's already rummaging around.

"Donna, wait. This isn't something I do!"

"Why not? Everyone else does. Actors. Ballplayers. Astronauts. Here, take this." She hands me a box. "That's two hundred bucks worth of eight-by-ten glossies I had made up. So, do me a favor and give this a try, okay?"

My dread deepens as I picture that god-awful photograph of me with big hair and linebacker shoulder pads. "This is crazy. Who's going to want my photo?"

She nods toward the hotel entrance. "Most of the people over there. And they'll pay you twenty bucks to sign your name."

I see a ragged line of people, of every age and description, standing in a queue that winds around the side of the hotel. Many of the fans have their eyes trained on me. A few are waving. I lift a hand to wave back, realizing my fate is sealed.

Donna shoulders a big satchel and leads the way. Ten feet from the entrance, as if on cue, everyone with a camera begins snapping my picture. A few call out my name and wave autograph books.

"Miss Barnes will be happy to sign photos inside, everyone," Donna says briskly. "The doors open in half an hour."

She herds me through the revolving doors and into the relative quiet of the hotel foyer. Signs reading CELEBRITY AUTOGRAPHS direct us toward a large ballroom off the reception area, but Donna seems to know her way. Long banquet tables draped in hotel linen are set up end-to-end in long rows, each with a placard bearing an actor's name.

"My God, look at these names, Donna. Do you believe this?"

"Of course. I told you." She squeezes through a space between tables and drops her satchel in one of the chairs. I hand her the box of photos and stand back, feeling like a kid about to be dumped at the dentist's office. Throughout the room, other celebrity signers are claiming tables and setting up their wares. I spot two actresses who appeared in *The Poseidon Adventure* tacking posters to the wall at the far side of the room. Another actress, gray-haired and bent, slowly unfolds an easel on which she mounts a display of vintage photographs. I recognize her as the star of an adventure series I watched as a child, but the realization that I've forgotten her name stabs home.

"The early bird gets the worm," Donna says, busily stacking photos on the white linen. "I'll never understand celebrities who show up late at these things. Once those doors open, people just swarm the tables."

She sets a cash box on the table and spreads out a handful of pens. "I'll handle the money. All you have to do is sign. What do you think of the pictures?"

"Great." I'm relieved to see that two are *Holiday* publicity stills of Jinx in her top hat, and a third is a glamour shot from my studio contract days. "Where did you find these relics?"

"Actually, they're mine. I just had copies made." Donna glances at me, her face reddening. "C'mon. I told you I was a big fan."

"You want my autograph?" The moment the words spring from my lips, I regret them. "Sorry! Just kidding."

"Yeah, I would, actually, if you don't mind." Donna quickly slides a photo in front of me and uncorks a pen with silver ink. "Just put something like 'To Donna, friends forever.' Or whatever you'd like."

"Okay, but I'm not going to charge you full price." We both laugh, but I can feel myself tensing. This event is shaping up to be a colossal embarrassment.

"Look at you, already hard at work."

I look up to find Shelby Stuart wheeling a piece of luggage behind the table next to me. "Hi, Shel. You spending the night?"

He winks. "If you'll spend it with me, I'll get us a suite."

Donna explodes into reckless giggles, startling me. I introduce them. Shelby looks her over and extends his hand. "Hey, baby, didn't I see you on the set last week?"

"I was helping Meg out," she says, her face aglow as she shakes his hand. I'll have to make sure he signs a photograph for her before the end of the day. I once again remind myself to see about Alex Trebek.

"Why didn't you tell me you were going to be here?" Shelby asks. He unzips his roller bag and produces four binders of photos, a plastic tube with an assortment of pens, a money belt, and a bag of trail mix. He also lines up several cellophane-wrapped boxes of an action figure representing a lead character he portrayed in a sci-fi series back in the mid-seventies. I pick up one of the boxes to get a closer look.

"Don't bother turning it upside down," Shelby says. "It's not anatomically correct."

Donna breaks into convulsive giggles. I put the box down.

"I didn't know I'd be here until this morning, Shel. You're obviously an old hand."

"You kidding me? You do one cult series, and you can travel the world doing these shows. And it's all cash, too," he says, out of the side of his mouth. "If you're interested, I can hook you up for a bunch of these. Expenses paid. Guarantees. You name it." He leans closer, speaking just loudly enough for Donna to hear. "We could travel together. Have a little fun, you know?"

Donna makes a gasping sound that dissolves in a strangled giggle, but it's enough to satisfy Shelby. He winks. "Think about it, Megs."

The doors open to the public. Fans surge to my table, saving me from having to respond. Before I know it, there's a crowd three deep waiting to get Jinx's autograph. I sign. I smile for snapshots. Not one fan fails to address me as Miss Barnes. Several ask complex questions about plotlines for shows I barely remember doing. Almost everyone asks if Winston Sykes is still alive. Three people show up in black cardboard top hats they want me to sign.

Shelby leans over. "You gotta brand yourself, Meg. Buy up a bunch of those top hats wholesale and sell 'em to the fans. You'll make a mint."

"Great idea!" Donna says, nodding shrewdly. "I'll look into it."

This isn't what I do, I remind myself. But then I glance at the bills piling up in the cash box and have second thoughts. Two hours later, Donna closes down the line, and we make a break for the restrooms. On our way out of the banquet room, we pass Jenna and her actor husband seated side by side at one of the tables. I catch her eye and wiggle my fingers in greeting. Does everyone I know do these shows? Why have I never heard about them?

The main lobby is a carnival scene. Donna runs interference through mobs of fans, many dressed in what appear to be Halloween costumes. Ghouls and Trekkies mill about, but there are creature look-alikes of every description. We order tuna fish sandwiches from the coffee shop and wolf them down in a sunny patio near the swimming pool. Then it's back to work in the noisy, airless banquet room.

By four o'clock, my hand is cramped. My jaw muscles ache. Time for another break. Donna packs up the cash box and leads the way to the restrooms. I follow, squirming past a knot of space warriors checking out one another's garb.

Dead ahead, I spot a familiar figure. I stop abruptly, toe-to-toe with my former husband. Dirck is wearing a leather jacket, his hair artfully mussed, looking not unlike a character he once played in a motorcycle movie early in his career. If the stars had been aligned to advantage, and his biorhythm chart properly attuned, Dirck would like to think he'd be enjoying Robert De Niro's career today. Alas, there was a cockup in the firmament that summer, and Dirck scored nothing more than a modest paycheck and a leather jacket.

"Dirck? What are you doing here?"

He cracks a smile at my surprise. "Not much, as it turns out. An old buddy of mine is working the show. He thought he could get me a table if somebody backed out at the last minute. What the hell, it was worth a try. You want to grab a coffee?"

"Where's Pru?"

"At her sister's. C'mon, let's get some coffee."

Up ahead I see Donna peering around, looking for me. "Sorry, Dirck. I'm with a friend. I ought to get back."

"What, all those years together and you can't give me five minutes?" He serves up an elaborate New York shrug. "I gotta stand in line and buy a picture to talk with you? Gimme a break already."

"Why not?" I laugh, as much at the familiar gesture as Dirck's delivery. I raise my hand to snag Donna's attention. "Go ahead. I'll catch up with you in a minute."

She nods, craning to see who I'm with, but Dirck's already steering me into the throng. The moment we veer off together, I regret it. This can't be a good idea. He must sense my change of heart, because he squeezes my arm and says, "No reason we can't be friends, right? Bygones are bygones."

We skirt the cappuccino trolley with its long line of fans and head for the relative calm of a roped-off alcove that's been designated CELEBRITY HOSPITALITY. We bypass the snack table and find the coffee urns.

"I saw you with ol' Shelby in there. He's still trying to get into your pants? That guy never quits."

"You've got that right." My heart bangs an extra beat. I still can't recall if I ever slept with Shelby. I hope I don't remember. "We're close to wrapping the pilot we've been working on. He played my defense attorney."

"Yeah?" Dirck shakes his head, his eyes dull with envy. "No kidding. The bastard sure gets the breaks. Series regular?"

"Recurring, at best." I sip my coffee, knowing I'm about to slip into my give-Dirck-a-boost mode. "But so what? You're teaching. You've cornered the voice-over market. And you've got Pru."

"Yeah, yeah. And Pru." He touches his Styrofoam cup to mine and gives me a friendly squint. "I have to give you full credit, Meggie. I saw you sitting there, raking in the dough. Man, I wish I'd bagged a big series like you did. You're set for life. To tell you the truth, I wish we could've shared all that. But someone had to stay behind and hold down the fort, right? I guess you figured you needed to travel light."

"Hey, that's not what happened—and you know it." His words pick at scabbed flesh. Somehow I'm always to blame when things don't work out for Dirck.

"No? Maybe you've forgotten." He leans in, his fingers running across my wrist. Fans snapping pictures at a distance would think he was hitting on me. In a way, they'd be right. I edge away, but Dirck catches my arm. "We made quite a team, you and me. Too bad you felt you had to move on. You saw your chance and made a break for it. What do you think that did to me? I was left with nothing. I'm still trying to make a go of it."

"Look, maybe this isn't such a good time to talk. I'd better go back."

"Why? It's not like you need the money. What're you doing this for? I'm the one who could use a little cash. They won't even give me a table."

"You need money? Is that why you wanted to talk?"

"C'mon. I got bumped from a table because you'd be a bigger draw. I'm forced to go on a reserve list because you've got some manager who throws her weight around at the last minute. Man, that pisses me off."

"You're blaming me? I don't have a manager. Donna's just a friend. I had no idea I'd be coming to this thing. Are you really short on money?"

"What do you think? We got a kid on the way. I'm out here scrambling for work, and it's not happening. You think I want to worry Pru? You haven't a clue what it's like."

"Just stop, okay?" Shaking, I set my cup on the counter, squelching an impulse to toss coffee on his tough-guy jacket. "Look, I'm sorry. Stay here. I'll be back in a minute."

I slip past a knot of people standing at the ropes watching celebrities hobnob, and race back to the banquet room. Hordes of fans surround my table. Donna catches sight of me and flaps her hands. "Thank God! Where have you been?"

"Sorry! I'm really sorry," I say, nodding to everyone. I lean in to Donna, my back to the crowd, and whisper, "Give me a couple hundred, okay?"

Her face turns to stone. "What for?"

"A friend. Just a couple hundred. We can spare it."

"Are you nuts? You're giving money to your ex-husband? Why?"

"That's my business. How do you know who he is?"

She makes a face. "Because I recognize him. You're crazy. You know that, don't you?" Still, she fishes money out of the cash box and hands it to me.

I turn to the fans, several of whom look irritated. "Sorry to keep you waiting. I'll be right back."

Dirck is waiting for me at the door. I press the money into his hand. He unfolds the bills and glances down. I can tell by his look it's less than what he'd hoped for. I also see relief. "Thanks. I appreciate it. Hey, I'm sorry, all right?"

"That's okay. It's a baby gift. Take care, Dirck."

I'm about to return to the needy, impatient faces at my table, but instead I flee to the ladies' room. It's jammed. While I hesitate at the door, wondering if I should join the long line, everyone queuing up turns to look at me. A teenage goth in a fright wig shoves a scrap of paper in my hand. "Just make it to Sandi, with an *i*. Thanks."

I look at the white face with the maroon lips and realize that while I wait in line to pee I will be signing autographs until I can make it into one of the stalls. That is not something I want to do.

"Sorry, I don't have a pen." I manage to smile as I back out the door.

Making my way through the mobbed lobby, I feel like I'm in my worst ever furniture dream, except that I'm wide awake and these are people, not sofas and chiffoniers. By the time I squeeze behind my table and take in Donna's accusing look, I'm in full-blown panic. Still, I smile. I smile at everyone, even Donna, who is not smiling.

"Glad you could make it."

"Sorry, Donna." I pick up a pen, the din in the room crashing in my ears. "How soon can we wrap this up?"

"Are you kidding? Look at this line. We still have more than two hours to go."

"I'll make you a deal," I whisper. "Find the last person and cut off the line. I mean it."

Donna grasps that I'm serious, although it's probably hard for her to tell since I'm still smiling. But she gets it. Eleven fans and eighteen signed photos later, we're packed up and heading for the door.

"You're mad at me," she says when we reach the parking lot.

"I'm not mad. I'm just not cut out for this."

"What about tomorrow? We're signed up for two days."

"Sorry, but I'd prefer spending the day fasting in the hot sun, wrapped in barbed wire."

"You won't make as much money doing that."

"We've made more than enough, okay? Too much adulation can't be good for the soul. Deduct your expenses and we'll split fifty-fifty."

"Not a chance. This was for you. You need the money. I'll deduct the car repair and photographs. You keep the rest."

"Nothing doing." I sling my arm around Donna's shoulders and give her a hug. "Thanks, okay? I really mean it. Why don't you tell the organizers to give Dirck my table tomorrow?"

"Honestly, no wonder you're broke. You really are nuts—"

I hear Donna's protests, but I'm distracted by the sight of an all-too-familiar junk heap parked in the next aisle, its convertible top down. Out of the corner of my eye, I see its occupant slouched down behind the wheel.

The anger simmering since my encounter with Dirck boils over. I tighten my grip on Donna's shoulders. "Listen, something's up," I whisper as we turn toward her Mercedes. "Just open the trunk and stay quiet."

"What? Someone's following us?" She hugs the cash box to her chest.

"Sort of. Just stay behind the car, okay? No matter what—"

As soon as Donna flips the trunk open, I duck down and make my way between the cars. The rusting convertible's only occupant is asleep behind the wheel, his keys still in the ignition. Crouching low, I sneak up on the passenger side. With my heart banging, I reach over and snatch the keys.

"Hey!" The curly-haired hunk grabs for my arm.

I leap back. "Hey yourself. Who the hell are you?"

"Gimme my keys—" He climbs out of his car, looking more exasperated than menacing. He throws his shoulders back and tugs on his T-shirt, a gesture at once vain and insecure. His face has a Slavic cast, with dark, brooding eyes and full, pouting lips. "C'mon, lady, the keys!"

"I don't think so. What's your game anyway? Why have you been following me?"

"Keeping an eye out. That's all I'm supposed to do."

"For who? Sid Baskin?"

A smile cracks his face. "You kidding me?" He shakes his head and saunters around the front of the car. "Lady, you're gonna wreck everything. Just gimme the keys—"

"Get away from her!" Donna shouts. "Stalker! Leave her alone!" She clicks on her car alarm. At the sound of the raucous beeping, people in the next aisle turn to look.

"Hey, lady, gimme a break. I'm no stalker!"

"So why are you following me?"

"Protecting an investment, okay? For interested parties—"

The alarm attracts the attention of several fans who've bought signed photos from me. The young man looks uneasy as a small crowd gathers.

A warrior from some space tribe that wears spandex and shiny white plastic armor steps forward and removes his helmet. "You need help, Miss Barnes? This guy bothering you?"

"Back off, space monkey. This doesn't concern you—"

"Then leave her alone, mister—"

Taking advantage of the distraction, I reach into the passenger seat of his car to grab a packet of mail. I edge back toward the Mercedes, glancing at the address on one of the letters before stuffing them in my shoulder bag.

"Hey, Grigori. Is that your name? Who are these interested parties?"

The young man whips around, glowering. "Greg! My name's Greg, okay? Can we drop this? I'm just helping out my dad. Like part-time. I got a band, okay? I'm a musician, not some—"

"Really? A band? Like the Shreak Wizards, maybe?"

An inspired guess, as it turns out. Greg slaps his forehead like he's been dive-bombed by a hornet. "Oh, jeez, let's forget this, okay? My old man's gonna kill me if he hears about this—"

"So who's your dad? A guy named Vladimir Proznorov would be my guess—I'll bet he doesn't want to be called Bill, either. Tell me, what line of work is he in?"

"Oh, man." Greg shakes his head. "You don't want to know. Can we just move on? Gimme my keys and I'm outa here. Fair enough?"

"And you don't call me anymore asking about Coop, okay?"

Donna shuts off the alarm. The beeping stops mid-burp.

In the silence, the man stares at me, his jaw slack. His dark, sullen eyes give nothing away, but his Adam's apple bobs as he swallows hard a second time. "Look, with me you got it easy. All I have to do is keep track of you. Nothing rough. Nobody gets hurt. I'm not into that, okay?"

"But your old man is, and he thinks I'll lead him to Coop, right?"

I've already opened the door to the Mercedes by the time Greg says, "Who? I don't know anyone by that name."

"Sorry, Grigori. I don't believe you. And I don't want you following me anymore."

I fling the car keys to the space warrior, who catches them in his helmet. Greg lunges toward him, but not before the keys are lobbed to a Trekkie in maroon polyester, who tosses them skyward toward the hotel's maintenance facility. The keys arc high over a sign—DANGER! HIGH VOLTAGE—and disappear on the roof behind curling barbed wire.

"Shit!" Greg breaks away and runs toward the utility building. Meanwhile I jump in the Mercedes and slam the door. Donna turns on the ignition. I lean out the window. "Thanks, guys!"

The space warrior grins. "You take it easy, Miss Barnes. See you next time."

I wave as we pull out of the parking space and drive past Greg, who's looking up at the barbed wire. Appropriately enough, Donna makes the tires squeal as we skirt the crowd and pick up speed. I plug in my seat belt and grip the armrest.

As we approach the exit, a middle-aged woman, wearing sweats and a sun visor, pumps her arm and hollers, "Go, Jinx, go!"

Chapter Nineteen

Less than an hour after roaring out of the parking lot, Donna and I are once again barreling down the 405 toward San Diego. But this time, after considerable negotiation, I'm behind the wheel. Donna is riding shotgun, the cash box hugged to her chest, her expensive St. John cardigan buttoned around it.

The Mercedes is parked at the airport. I'm driving a rental blue compact with a lousy radio. Thank God the air conditioner is working, because I'm steamed. I would have preferred it if Donna had driven her tub back home and stayed there, but she is not a reasonable woman. She also remains in possession of the cash box, and no matter what, Donna isn't about to let go of it. She's steamed, too, and I don't care. She did not have to come along. She turns down the radio, which means I'm in for another earful.

"You can get mad at me all you want, but I can't help worrying about the way you just throw money around."

"So I have to travel with my banker? Half that money is mine."

"There's no reason we couldn't have driven my car. For that matter, it would've taken no time at all to go home and pack some things. We don't even have toothbrushes. I assume we're not making the drive back home tonight?"

"That Proznorov kid knows your car. He also knows where you live, and by now he's let someone know what happened. Chances are, he's also managed to hotwire his car. It's better to get a jump on them."

"This is crazy."

"So you've said. I didn't force you to come along."

"Just for the record, my credit card secured this vehicle. I should be the one driving." She sniffs, knowing there's little reason for me to respond, as it's a moot point. I'm the one behind the wheel, and I won't be giving up the keys. The silence lingers as long as Donna can stand it. "So what do you think you'll find there anyway?"

"I just want to check something out. If you can bear to pry your hands off the cash box, take a look at those letters in my shoulder bag. The only envelope without a postmark is that fat brown one. Several of the letters are addressed to Grigori Proznorov, but look at all the others with different names going to the same post office box. Do you see the name on the large white envelope? Ms. Jerilyn Fenster. That was our waitress in the Eat 'n' Run."

"The pickle face who served us coffee?"

"Right. Jeri was her name. Ms. Warmth. But maybe we shouldn't speak ill of the dead."

"You're kidding! How do you know she's dead?"

"Jack told me. Her body was found in a Dumpster yesterday morning."

"Somebody killed her?"

"I'm afraid so, unless she crawled in and committed suicide." I glance at Donna. Her lips are pursed, and she gives me a reproachful look. "Sorry. Yes, she was killed. I don't know how, because Jack didn't say. But here's the question: What is the Proznorov kid doing with Jeri Fenster's mail?"

"Isn't this something you should tell Jack about?"

"Is it? I'd kind of like to figure this one out on my own and see where it leads. Especially since he's not willing to let me in on anything. He had to have known about Paul and Lucy long before I told him, and he didn't bother to tell me."

Donna shifts sideways and turns the radio down even lower. "A woman was murdered—and you want to barge down to the crime scene?

What makes you think we'll get anywhere near the restaurant? There'll be police everywhere."

"Probably, but I need to check an address and see if I'm right."

"That's about all you'll have time to do. It'll be dark when we get there."

And cold. By the time we exit the freeway and head toward the vicinity of the strip mall, I've turned the heater on. We both fall silent as we pass through the bleak industrial backwater. We reach an intersection lit in the poisonous glare of a street lamp, and turn into the grim residential section. Truth to tell, I'm glad I have Donna for company. I've spent enough solitary nights sleeping in my car to be wary of dark, isolated streets.

But the strip mall, when we reach it, is anything but a lonely place this evening. We drive past the parade of shop fronts, checking them out. The Eat 'n' Run is bustling. How many of its occupants are police detectives? The Laundromat is brightly lit. At least three people are standing at washers. The nail salon and pet supply are both closed, but two people are leaning against the brick wall between the plate-glass windows. Only Luck o' Lucy's is entirely dark. Even the neon martini glass isn't blinking tonight.

I pull up at the stop sign on the corner, my eyes scanning the mustard-colored stucco house. It's dark, too, except for a low-wattage porch light that's probably on a timer. The illumination is faint, but sufficient to read the black numerals next to the front door.

I signal and turn left, driving slowly past the side of the house. There's no sign of occupancy. Window shades are pulled. Garage doors closed. I drive down another block and pull to the curb.

"What do you want to check out?"

"I've already done it. The house on the corner is number 3194, the same address as the one on those mortgage documents sent to Jeri Fenster."

"But the address on the envelope is that kid's post office box."

"Take a look inside at the address printed on the documents."

Quickly, before Donna can flick on the bright overhead light, I reach across her to open the glove compartment. We lean into the faint glow, and I show Donna the street address printed on the first page of the mortgage document.

"You mean that place actually belonged to the waitress, not Lucy?"

"According to this mortgage application, that's the way it appears. Maybe she did own the house and was only renting the place to Lucy. But even if that's the case, I think Jerilyn Fenster would have been shocked to learn how much her house is worth."

Donna's mouth hangs open as she stares at the figures. "Come on, there's no way that ugly little tear-down is worth that much. Not in this neighborhood."

"Look, all I know is that someone was running paper on that property. Maybe Jeri was in on the scam. If not, imagine her counting on tips to come up with the mortgage payments. By the time she knew what was going on, the house would be in foreclosure and her credit destroyed."

"That's what happened to you."

"More or less. Actually more, since I was married to the bastard who did it."

Donna's face looks fierce in the ghoulish light of the glove compartment. I laugh in spite of myself.

"Would you mind telling me what's so funny?" she demands. "You really are something else. Maybe you're just trying to find Paul so you can give him half the money you made today. You lined Dirck's pockets. Why not Paul's?"

The jibe stings, but I can't blame Donna for getting her licks in when she can. I flip the glove compartment closed and check the rearview mirror, then pull away from the curb and make a U-turn.

"Are you hungry yet?" I ask.

"Starving. But I don't think I care to dine at the Eat 'n' Run."

"No, but how about getting us some coffee to go?" I pull up at the curb next to Luck o' Lucy's.

"Sure. Aren't you coming with me?"

"There's one other thing I want to check out."

"No. Absolutely not, Meg. I'm not letting you out of my sight."

"I'm not going to drive off and leave you, for God's sake. You can take the cash box with you."

"That's not it!" She looks out at Luck o' Lucy's and groans. "I've got a creepy feeling you want to sneak in there for another look around. Am I right?"

"Wrong. But there's something in the Eat 'n' Run I want. I'd just as soon not take the chance someone in there will recognize me. Maybe you could just ask a few questions while you're at it."

"What about?" I'm relieved to see Donna look more intrigued than suspicious.

"Ask about Jeri. You might even mention Lucy's name. See what happens. But go back to the ladies' room and have a look at the bulletin board. If you see a brochure about sportfishing, take it."

"Sportfishing? Why in the world—"

"Just a thought. I'll be parked right here."

Donna unplugs her seat belt, then gives me a grudging look. "I'm going to trust you, okay?" She unbuttons her jacket and stuffs the cash box in a canvas holdall. "But I'm taking this with me."

"Whatever." I smile. "And make mine full strength. No decaf, please."

"You got it." Donna slides out and closes the car door. She hugs her arms and hurries across the parking lot in short, quick steps. I'm glad I didn't tell her to take her time in there. It would only have made her more suspicious. She stops before opening the door to the diner and looks back at me. I wave, then she steps inside and I lose sight of her. I open the car door, climb out, and quickly lock the door behind me.

The night air is cold. I duck across the side street, avoiding the pool of light spilling from the strip mall's lamppost. I hurry down the darkened sidewalk across the street from the mustard-colored house. Once

I'm directly opposite the garage at the rear of the property, I pause for a quick look around. The street is empty. I make a break for the shadows cast by the tall laburnum hedge.

I peer through a grimy garage window and see no vehicle inside. Inspecting the rear of the house near the hedge, I spot broken panes in a corner bedroom window. A plastic recycling bin has been overturned and placed in the weedy patch below it. How convenient. Someone else without keys has managed to find a way to get inside.

I stand on the bin and gingerly push aside the window shade. The touch is enough to release the spring. I cry out and leap off the box as the shade snaps halfway up the window with a loud clatter. Standing motionless in the damp grass, my heart pounding, I watch the bottom of the shade flap noisily against the window frame.

No one appears. No one calls out. If that blood-chilling racket didn't raise an alarm, I probably have the place to myself. I'm about to jump back up on the box when it occurs to me that whoever broke in through the window probably took the easy way out.

I run up the three steps to the back door and gingerly turn the knob. The door swings open almost too easily. I take my penlight from my shoulder bag and flash the narrow beam around the interior of the kitchen before stepping across the threshold.

The air is musty, the house itself cold and dank. I shiver, not necessarily because of the chill. The only sound is the burr of the fridge. I open the door, as much for the illumination as to check the contents. A carton of soy milk, a tomato with puckered skin, two raisin bagels tied in a plastic bag, a jar of instant coffee. No wonder Lucy took all her meals at the Eat 'n' Run.

The living room, a low-ceiling box with ratty shag carpet, is furnished with a Naugahyde recliner facing a TV set on a metal stand. A sagging couch is shoved against the wall. In this slumping housing market, this dump couldn't be worth a quarter of the mortgage appraisal.

The larger of the two bedrooms appears to be recently done up, with light-colored carpet and a matching suite of blond furnishings. The bed is unmade. The pink flowered sheets look none too fresh. I rummage through a chest of drawers heaped with lingerie, scarves, and T-shirts. The vanity overflows with lotions and cheap cosmetics.

A mound of soiled clothing is heaped into an overflowing laundry basket on the closet floor, along with a tangled pile of belts and bags. I back away from the stink of shoes and stale deodorant, having no stomach for a closer inspection. What would I hope to find, anyway? The jumble of clothing dangling off wire hangers belongs to Lucy, not Paul. He traveled light, and this hole-in-the-wall couldn't have been more than a stopover for him. I take a quick look in the bathroom, checking out the medicine cabinet, finding the usual unguents and cold remedies but no surprises.

The back bedroom is a deep freeze. A cold draft from the broken window flutters the window shade. I flick the penlight across a bed frame and bare mattress upended in a corner, then follow the beam as it lights up a telephone, its receiver hanging like a plumb line.

I jump. There's a cold draft, then eerie shadows sway across the floorboards to my left. My hand shaking, I dance the penlight across a string of dangling telephone receivers. Above them is a bank of maybe a dozen multiple-line wall phones. Index cards are thumbtacked alongside each telephone. I bend closer, trying to make out the names penciled on the first card: LINE ONE—EDUARDO VASQUEZ; LINE TWO—OZZIE BISHOP; and LINE THREE—LOLA DETROIT. Moving along the wall, I read several other names jotted on the cards, spotting JERILYN FENSTER—LINE TWO on the fourth telephone.

Moving backward, I brush up against a long folding table stacked with forms, file boxes, and metal trays piled high with manila folders. I flip open the top file marked BRUCE HARLEY. Inside are printouts of W-2s, paycheck stubs, employment records, and a credit statement. On another worktop, dusty computers, a fax machine, two printers, and a copier are crowded next to stacks of blank Social Security cards and credit applications. A grimy box contains pens, Wite-Out, and an assortment of rubber stamps, everything anyone would need to forge counterfeit employment and credit documents.

I stand in the L of two folding tables, focusing my penlight on a box of computer forms, trying to take it all in. Shaking off a flash of déjà vu, I realize why I feel like I've been here before. Jinx, in a St. Patrick's Day episode about conmen trying to score off the Irish Sweepstakes, broke into just such a boiler room. The *Holiday* series screened long before computers and fax machines, but the telephone setup is familiar.

Jinx, of course, busted up the boiler-room gang in the nick of time. No such luck here. This boiler room is stone cold. Whoever was involved in forging documents and flipping property is long gone, and Jeri Fenster is very dead. Did she even know she was a straw buyer? Or did she get too snoopy—or greedy?

Whatever happened, it's obvious the scammers cleared out quickly. I pivot toward the closet, its door standing slightly ajar. Copping a move I picked up playing Jinx, I press myself against the wall and kick back the flimsy door. With a bump of adrenaline, I shine my penlight around the interior. No dead body heaped on the floor. No clothes, either. Just empty wire hangers.

I flash the light into the dark corners, almost jumping at the sight of a pair of shoes with curling rawhide laces. I know without looking that the dusty, well-worn Top-Siders sitting there are size eleven.

The shelf above the hanging rack looks empty, but standing on my toes, I spot a brightly colored cigarillo tin. Next to it, just within reach, is a cloudy plastic box I also recognize. I pry the lid off the shallow Tupperware, Paul's customary traveling cigar container. Inside are three silver tubes of Romeo y Julieta Churchill Habanas and a crumpled cocktail napkin with COOP'S printed in jaunty red letters below the logo of a blue sailboat, in wavy blue lettering: BAJA.

I blink hard at this found treasure, then quickly stuff the booty into my shoulder bag and toss the Tupperware back on the grimy shelf.

The blood pounds in my ears as I hurry through the other bedroom. I glance once again at Lucy's closet, the doors open and sagging off their tracks. I can't leave without taking a closer look. I plunge my hand quickly in and out of all the jacket pockets, finding only odd change and crumpled Kleenex. The handbags yield the same sort of detritus. If she left all this behind, she must have had scant warning to clear out.

It's time for me to get out of here, too. I don't bother closing the back door on my way out. I sprint down the street, hugging my shoulder bag to my ribs. When I see Donna's head above the passenger seat, I run faster. I pull at the door handle, which is locked, then rap on the window. Donna releases the lock, her face livid in the sudden light as I open the door and jump in.

"I don't believe you! Where the hell have you been?"

"Sorry. Didn't mean to be gone so long."

"You weren't supposed to be gone at *all*! Do you know how long you left me sitting here?" She looks like a ferocious terrier, her short, wiry hair vibrating with fury.

"I'm sorry. How did you get in?"

"I opened the door. Whaddaya think?"

"Did you see anyone?"

"No, other than people leaving the restaurant. I looked around when I didn't see you in the car, but then I got in and waited. Hang on, you didn't go to Luck o' Lucy's, did you?"

"No. I went down the street." I realize this isn't the time to tell Donna I locked the car doors before I left. Nor is there any need to mention my search of the mustard-colored house. I toss my shoulder bag in the backseat and press the key into the ignition. "Let's go get something to eat."

"Fine. You want your coffee? It's cold."

I take the cup, but my hands are shaking too much to manage more than a sip. "Sorry. I'm freezing."

"Here's an idea. How about we get back on the freeway and stop at one of those discount stores? We can pick up whatever we need and find a room closer to San Diego. Frankly, I don't care where we eat. Let's just hit the road and get out of here."

I half-listen to Donna plot the rest of our evening and try not to think about the Top-Siders on the closet floor, or how the car doors got unlocked. I pull away from the curb and swing into the alley behind Luck o' Lucy's to turn around. As the car bumps up the slight incline and across a pothole, the headlights flick up and down on a Dumpster in front of us. It's wrapped in neon yellow tape. A squad car, unoccupied, is parked behind the bar, facing the Dumpster.

"Well, at least I feel better knowing there were cops nearby," Donna says, looking out the side window. "You know, you're crazy to leave a car unlocked, even for a minute. What were you thinking?"

"Sorry. Good thing the cops were around." I glance at the Dumpster again, knowing it's where Jeri Fenster's body was found yesterday morning. I hear Donna suddenly gasp. She's made the connection, too.

"My God, Meg! That's the—"

"I know." I cut into the parking lot and swing back onto the side street, heading toward the freeway onramp. "What about the restaurant?"

"Actually, it's touching. People really cared about her. There were a couple of little bouquets on the counter next to a framed picture of her, a sort of memorial. The waitress working Jeri's shift tonight kept breaking down. I talked to her for a minute. She told me everyone figured Jeri had been mugged on her way to her car. I doubt anyone knew about that house belonging to her, because there was a little straw basket for donations. According to the guy who runs the restaurant, she was having some financial troubles— a pending bankruptcy, he said. She had to hire a lawyer. She had no savings left, so they were trying to collect enough for her funeral."

"Were any police in there?"

"Not that I could tell. But they'd been around yesterday and today interviewing people. The waitress said they didn't have a clue who might've done it. She figured some junkie killed her."

Or one of Proznorov's mob. Lucy's probably a target, too, if she knows where Paul is.

"By the way, there was no brochure about sportfishing on that bulletin board. Why did you want that?"

"Not important. I grabbed one the other day, and I'm pretty sure I remember what it says. Donna, are you still okay with a trip to Mexico?"

"I figured that was the plan. But not tonight, okay? Let's get a fresh start tomorrow."

"Suits me."

Once on the freeway, we pass a mile or so of car dealerships. Balloons, banners, and American flags flutter in the beams of searchlights fanning the night sky. We also pass warehouse-sized superstores and fast-food outlets. I let Donna navigate and wait for her tell me when to pull into one of the endless parking lots.

We put off dinner in favor of stocking up on jackets, sweaters, pants, shoes, socks, and a change of underwear. Donna tosses a tube of purse-sized toothpaste and a plain-wrap deodorant into the basket, but passes on shampoo and any other toiletries.

"They'll have all this stuff free in the motel room," she says, as though I would have no knowledge of that little cost-saver. I'm in Donna's hands now, and she controls the cash box.

"The one thing about chain restaurants is that you know what you're going to get," she says a little later, as we cruise down a brightly lit boulevard.

"Unfortunately," I say. "You choose."

"I'm easy. Anything except a pancake house or sports bar. And no fluorescent lights or video arcade. Not a place with high chairs and strollers stacked at the entrance. Or anything that says Seniors Welcome. Also, I'd like some decent wine."

"You call that easy?"

Amid a jumble of neon logos, we spot a squat, brick-fronted building with coachman lamps and a red awning. It's possibly the only non-chain restaurant in the entire county, certainly the only one dating back to the days when this area was nothing but a vast bean field. I park in a space near the door, and we stroll into the comfort of low lights, red leather banquettes, and the promise of decent steaks.

Even before our wine arrives, I've pulled out the rest of the mail I lifted off Grigori Proznorov. All of the envelopes are open. Greg was probably sorting through the mail while waiting for us to return to the parking lot. Aside from the documents pertaining to the Fenster mortgage, there are also letters to several other parties regarding appraisals and bank loans. But it's the fat, brown envelope without a postmark that contains the most compelling material: a CD and a computer printout with hundreds of names, addresses and Social Security and bank account numbers. The name printed in marker pen on the CD is Vladimir Ivanovich Proznorov—Grigori's old man.

Donna and I have barely grasped the significance of these columns of names and numbers before I see the waiter approaching with our drinks. I slide the CD and printout back into the brown envelope and fold down the metal clasps. Not until we've placed our orders and watched the waiter retreat to the kitchen do we allow ourselves to refer to our find, and then only in whispers.

"It looks like Greg handles a little part-time computer hacking for his dad. Or he's a go-between."

"This is serious, Meg. They know you have this stuff now. We're way beyond knowing how to handle this. A woman's been murdered. Your former husband is probably involved. Let someone else track him down."

"And miss all the excitement?" Just to be annoying, I tap my wineglass to hers. "Unless I find him first, I'm never going to have my time with him. That's all I want."

"But he's dangerous!"

"Could be." *Particularly now that I've stolen his cache of Habanas.* The thought makes me smile, even as I recall the boiler-room setup. Somehow I can't picture Paul working the push-button phones with flashing red lights. It's not his sort of operation.

"What's so damn funny now?"

"Nothing. It's just that I don't see him murdering anyone. He's a con man, not a killer."

"Right. Like you've never been wrong about him before."

Chapter Twenty

I stay in the car while Donna uses her credit card to get us a room for the night. It's not hard to persuade her once I point out that two women with luggage consisting of nothing more than Discount Mart shopping bags, paying cash to register for a room together at well past 10 p.m., might draw some unwelcome speculation.

"Besides," I add, "if you use your credit card, you'll earn double mileage."

"Good idea. But I want you to park right in front where I can see you. And don't go wandering off again."

She gives me a look that means business, then trots inside to the brightly lighted front desk to sign for a room. She stands sideways so she has me in her peripheral vision at all times, glancing frequently my way to let me know she's watching. It doesn't matter, because I've got what I wanted—time to examine the car to see if anything has been taken, or left, by whoever unlocked the door.

I try the glove compartment first, and find only the envelope with the car rental documents. I flip through them, my eyes lighting on the $25 extra insurance charge we signed up for in case we drove the car south of the border. It had been my idea. Donna, after a slight hesitation, agreed to initial the surcharge. I wonder if whoever broke into the car took time to peruse the rental agreement. If so, they know where we're heading.

The space between and under the seats is clear. I wedge my fingers behind the seats and find nothing. I slide my seat forward and check out the back. Nothing. Maybe the intruder also looked around and found nothing. After all, I had my shoulder bag with me. Donna had her handbag and the cash box. We left the photographs, pens, and other signing paraphernalia in the trunk of the Mercedes. What was there to find? Or perhaps whoever broke in and left the door unlocked did so just to let me know he could.

"Lose something?" Donna opens the door and, always the perfect lady, perches on the seat and swings her legs in as though she's just stepped off a red carpet.

"I got us a nice room with single beds. Second floor. Parking in back next to the stairs. Continental breakfast from 6:30 a.m. in the lounge. Probably just orange juice, coffee, and doughnuts, but it's free." She hands me an apple. "These were in a bowl on the counter. Free."

For a fleeting moment, I imagine what it might be like to take a cross-country road trip with Donna. I dismiss the thought immediately. "Sounds good. I wouldn't mind getting an early start."

I pull the car around the back of the motel and park. As I turn the key in the lock, I take another look at the car door, inspecting it for signs of jimmying, all the clues Jinx would've looked for. The only difference is that Jinx would have actually found something. There'd also be a tight close-up of it.

I unlock the trunk. Donna and I gather up our shopping bags.

"So, did you find what you were looking for?"

"Nope. But it doesn't matter."

She peers through the back window. "What'd you do with my envelope? The one with your picture in it?"

"Excuse me?" I take a deep breath, my chest tightening. "I didn't see it. Are you sure you didn't leave it in your Mercedes with the rest of the stuff?"

"I meant to. But I could swear I had it in my hand when we were driving away from the rental place. I thought I put it on the backseat, but I guess not."

As Donna heads up the stairs to the room, I relock the trunk, wondering why I'm bothering. Why didn't someone just steal the whole damn car instead of a signed photograph of Jinx in a top hat?

I'm still pondering these questions at two a.m. as I lie in bed listening to Donna's even breathing. She's a sound sleeper, even with the cash box tucked under her pillow. Without awakening her, I've made several trips to the window to check on our parked car. I made two visits to the bathroom, with side stops at the door to the room to make sure it's still double-locked and the chain is in place. I'm skittish as a cat at the slightest sound. Every whir, bump, and creak sends my heart racing.

I roll over, wondering if I should have another look out the window. But who would know we were here? From the time we left Lucy's, I checked the rearview mirror constantly and saw no sign of anyone following us. Even if Greg managed to retrieve his keys or hotwire his car, I'd recognize that rattletrap instantly. Besides, how would he know where I was going? What am I missing?

Back in my crime-solving days with Winston Sykes, we dealt with our share of international jewel thieves, political assassins, drug traffickers, and spy rings. But identity theft and computer hacking hadn't yet been invented. Otherwise I could at least draw on a rudimentary experience cracking high-tech crimes. Instead, I've been caught on the wrong side of this new technology. I don't understand the mechanics of it, only the empty, stomach-churning aftermath of being robbed without even knowing it.

I roll onto my belly and look down at my cell phone plugged into its charger, the rhythmic blinking a beacon in the dark. When I was playing Jinx, even cell phones didn't exist. Drowsiness overtakes me, and I close my eyes, lulled by Donna's steady breaths. Yet I fight sinking into sleep, a nagging thought I'm unable to pin down still eating at me. I somehow feel as though I'm being led as much as followed.

I shift as quietly as possible and roll over, careful not to awaken Donna. A thought has occurred to me, something I need to act on as soon as possible. My mind drifts as I try to hang on to that fleeting thought . . .

"Hey, sleepyhead. You're the one who wanted an early start."

I open my eyes to streams of sunshine and the sight of Donna in her bubble-gum-pink polyester nightie. My own is mint green, both rescued from a 99-cent closeout bin. I sit up in bed, realizing I must have slept for hours.

"They're not gonna let us back into Beverly Hills with these nighties, Donna. They'll confiscate them on the outskirts of town."

"You're showing your true colors, you know. For a homeless person, you're actually quite a snob."

"Just down and out, not trashy. You slept well?"

"Fine, and I know you did. You were dead to the world. I'll shower first if you want to loll some more."

"Sounds good to me."

The moment Donna closes the bathroom door, I leap out of bed, throw on the new fleece jacket, pants, and sneakers, grab my shoulder bag and run out the door. I take the stairs two at a time, my eyes scanning the parking lot. I fish my penlight and powder compact out of my bag, drop to my knees, and scan the undercarriage of the car just as Jinx once searched the underbelly of a hijacked semitrailer in an episode about a ring of designer-label thieves.

I crawl around the back end of the car, my penlight in one hand, my compact mirror tilted in the other. Examining the wheel casings on the rear passenger side, I spot the little devil, two inches long and a bit grimy from its travels since Luck o' Lucy's. I pry the magnet loose from its mooring, drop the device in a trash bin, and race back to the motel lobby. Donna is already out of the shower, her head wrapped in a towel. Her glower vanishes when she sees I'm carrying two Styrofoam cups of steaming coffee.

"Is that where you went? How thoughtful. Thank you, thank you!"

"You're welcome, welcome. Wait—there's more."

I hand her a cup, then reach into my shoulder bag for the bran muffins. In doing so, I spot the grime on the underside of my sleeve. Fortunately Donna doesn't notice. As soon as I have the bathroom to myself, I wash the dirt off the jacket and dry it with a blast from the hair dryer. I feel like a hero. The day has barely begun, and I've already thwarted evildoers and won over Donna, at least for the time being.

I quickly shower. Then, fortified with more coffee, orange juice, and bran muffins, we check out of the motel, the pockets of our twin fleece jackets stuffed with apples. I've traveled light before, but even homeless, I carried more baggage than this. Donna and I set off for the Mexico border, the tracking device traveling in some other direction with whatever garbage truck picked it up.

Forty-five minutes later, after stopping to fill the tank, change money, and buy a map and guidebook, we approach the border entrance. We slow down to pass through the glass-and-metal archway spanning the five-lane highway, then loop through the outskirts of Tijuana in sparse Sunday morning traffic.

Mexican boys wearing plastic milk crates strapped across their shoulders stand near intersections selling dry cell batteries and Chiclets. Graffiti-scarred shacks in carnival colors line the dizzying jumble of streets and alleyways that meander up a hillside to the left. On the right, visible beyond a no-man's-land of green cement walls crowned with barbed wire, is a glimpse of pristine San Diego Bay and the verdant rolling hills we're leaving behind.

"Any idea where we're going?" Donna sounds apprehensive, which makes me grumpy. The truth is I don't exactly know, but I'm not willing to admit that to her.

"Just sit back and enjoy the ride. We'll dip into the cash box for some lobster and margaritas in Ensenada. Why don't you check out restaurants in that Triple-A guide?"

"We're taking the toll road, I assume?" She curls her legs underneath her and settles back with the guidebook, mollified for the time being. "We'll be coming up on Rosarito in a half-hour or so."

"Right. Just sing out if you see anything we should stop for."

I lower the sun visor and squint toward the brown hills to my left, pockmarked with sagging lean-tos and the carcasses of broken machinery. Souvenir stands, thick with terra-cotta pots, garishly painted urns, and wiry figurines, line the roadside, vying for space with weather-beaten food stalls. I see nothing that would inspire me to stop.

To my right, a vast new entrance gate, with LAS CASAS DEL SOL freshly painted above an ornate arch, leads to scrubland littered with bottles, cans, and loose debris. In the distance, forlorn shells of abandoned construction sit at odd angles along the rocky coastline. Nearer the road, concrete blocks, with rusted rebar poking in all directions, form half-finished walls crumbling in the salt air like broken promises. It's ugly beyond description, much like the gouged ridgelines ringed in concrete that Paul left behind when the bills for his Big Dream came due.

"It's criminal," I mutter.

"Well, the place could use a good cleanup. My gardener wouldn't stand for this," Donna says, closing the guidebook with a snap, "and he's Mexican. I don't understand why people can't just throw things away. Or finish what they start."

She tucks the book between the seats and busies herself counting money from the cash box. "I'm divvying up so I don't have to carry this thing around anymore. Half goes into my wallet for safekeeping, okay? Where do you want me to put the rest?"

I glance at the wad of bills she's clutching. "I feel like a bank robber. Did I remember to say thank you?"

"You did. We're still a couple thousand in the clear. You want an expense breakdown?"

"Nope. But the lobster's on me. So's the Day-Glo nightie and everything else. Just zip the cash into the side pocket of my shoulder bag."

I stare out to the magnificent expanse of cobalt waters shimmering below the rocky cliffs. I roll down the window and breathe in the biting sea air, taste the tang of the ocean. Once again I remind myself to check about Alex Trebek. Donna requires more than a lobster dinner and a glow-in-the-dark nightie as a thank you.

Traffic is light. The only stops are for toll booths. A little more than an hour later, past a sprawl of hotels, trailer parks, and a hulking fish cannery that fouls the air, the glittering Ensenada harbor comes into view. In the distance, beyond the rusting hulls of fishing trawlers and spanking white pleasure craft, huge cruise ships lie tethered to long docks.

I snag a parking spot near the harbor. Leaving our fleece jackets behind in the car, we step out into the blaze of midday sun. The streets are jammed with tourists and locals alike. Donna, guidebook in hand, leads the way. We stroll through a narrow corridor near the harbor, lined by a gauntlet of souvenir shops, fish stalls, and open-air restaurants with tables sporting red-and-white checkered cloths. The smell of deep-fried seafood reminds me I'm hungry. I'm about to slide onto a stool at one of the fish stands, but Donna grabs my arm.

"Margaritas at Hussong's first. It's been here since 1892. I'm dying to see it. Have we got time?"

"Sure." Why didn't I think of it? Hussong's is where Lucy supposedly first encountered Paul a year ago.

"One margarita," Donna says, patting her handbag. "Just to celebrate."

We head up another crowded street, stopping at a sidewalk cart to watch a woman squirt dough into hot fat to make sugary, caramel-filled churros. I can't pass it up, nor can Donna. We each get a pastry and eat them on our way down the sidewalk.

Hussong's Cantina is choked with teenaged gringos in shorts and tank tops, drinking and flirting beneath clouds of cigarette smoke. The long narrow barroom shakes with the shouts of cruise-ship tourists and the strains of the local mariachi band, moving from table to table. Donna and I squeeze through the door. The tables are filled. It's three-deep at the bar, but she manages to burrow her way through just as a green bar stool becomes vacant. Having established a beachhead, she orders drinks and beckons me to join her. By the time I reach her, a burly bartender has slopped margaritas into two salt-rimmed stemmed glasses and slid them across the tequila-soaked wood.

I wedge myself into a space next to her stool, and we clink glasses. "Cheers, Donna." I take a sip, the icy tartness of tequila and lime puckering my lips.

"Cheers yourself. I gotta say, life's a lot more interesting with you around."

"Wait, you're the one who surprised me with the autograph signing. It's my turn to surprise you. Let's hope I can deliver."

"Uh-oh." Donna makes a face. "Any clues?"

"Nope. Just expect the unexpected." I look around, taking in the ornate red bar and cracked mirror, the stained cream walls with giant photos of Marilyn Monroe next to framed snapshots of local fisherman. My eyes travel the length and breadth of the crowded saloon, but there's no sign of Paul. Or Lucy.

The mariachis reach us, strumming guitars. We listen to a sweet, if ear-splitting, rendition of "Mallaguena Salle Rosa." Donna drains her glass.

"Go ahead, have another. I'm driving."

She nods to the barman, and he gives her a refill. A quarter of an hour later, after yet another refill for Donna, we make our way back onto the street. We blink in the bright sunlight, trying to spot a place to eat. My head is buzzing after only one margarita, and Donna looks less than steady. She grips my arm. "Just a taco. Something easy. Fast."

"Coming right up. There's a place on the corner." We reel diagonally across the street toward a boisterous cantina. "It's lively. Gotta be good."

But the patio is filled, as is the ground-floor restaurant. We stumble toward a stairway to the second floor. A sign reads: 18 OR OLDER TO ENTER. We climb the steps, sucked forward by whooping cheers and screams of laughter.

There's another bar at the top of the stairway, even more crowded than the first, but I spot an empty table in an alcove on the far side. A waiter struggles past me, balancing a tray of tacos and margaritas high over his head. Above the din and crush of people, I catch his attention and point to the table. "Tacos. *Dos, por favor?*"

He holds up two fingers. I nod. I pull some money out of my shoulder bag as we edge toward the table.

Suddenly the crowd swells back, jostling us against the bar. A young woman wearing a blindfold and a short bridal veil over her ponytail is hoisted up over the heads of the crowd. She shrieks as she's flipped over and drops back out of sight.

Donna tugs at my arm and pushes forward. "What's that all about?"

Standing on tiptoe I glimpse a young blond guy, his arms bulging in a red T-shirt, hoist the woman in the bridal veil up over his shoulders again. He buries his head between her legs before tipping her back on the table and grinding his pelvis into her crotch.

The audience screams approval. Several young women sitting together at the table cheer, "Yeah! Go, Betsy, go!"

"You don't want to know, Donna." But she's already churning her way into the crowd for a better look.

One of the women, wearing a halter top that shows off a tattoo on her shoulder, waves money over the head of a buxom girl wearing a USC sweatshirt and shorts. The girl's eyes pop in horror as the hunk in the red T-shirt grabs her upper arms. She shrinks back, gripping the table, grinning even as she shakes her head.

"No? You're telling me *no*?" He pushes his face into hers. "Sure? Okay, then. Who else?"

A chorus of disappointment goes up as he turns away. He flexes his muscles, scanning the crowd. His eyes light on Donna, pushing her way to the front. He spots the money in my hand and grabs Donna by the waist, flinging her high over his head. He rips her handbag off her shoulder and tosses it to me. The crowd, mostly college kids and middle-aged cruise-ship tourists, whoops as Donna screams.

I glimpse her horrified eyes as he twirls her around, scoops his hand between her legs and flips her upside down, her legs straddling his neck. I reach out to stop him, but he snatches my money instead.

Then, as the crowd roars, he pulls Donna's T-shirt up over her face. He grabs a can of Reddi-wip, shakes it vigorously, and sprays a mound of foaming cream on her crotch. Lifting her by her hips, he swings her legs back onto his shoulders and laps up the cream.

Above screams of laughter, he yanks her T-shirt over his head, burying his face between her breasts. Donna, her face flushed, looks wild-eyed at the bulging head bobbing inside her shirt.

In a flash it's over. Donna's off the table, gripping my hands, her body trembling as I wrench her out of the crowd.

"He licked me," she whispers as we reach the stairway. "He licked my breasts!"

"That's not all. He went for the whipped cream, too. Are you okay?"

"Whipped cream? You're kidding me." She looks down at her khaki pants, caked with white sticky stuff like Elmer's Glue. "Omigod!"

"Good news. I didn't have a camera."

"How could you let him do that to me?" She turns Garfield eyes on me, a new horror dawning on her. "Please, God, tell me you have my handbag!"

"Right here." I swing the smart leather bag off my shoulder onto hers. She immediately snaps it open to check the contents. I decide now would not be the best time to mention the money the young guy took from me, obviously a tip he considered lavish enough to warrant the full

Monty. The waiter scurries up, two paper baskets with chicken tacos on his tray, plus cups of margaritas.

"We'll take it here," I say, dipping into the side pocket of my shoulder bag for more cash. "Just the tacos, please. No margaritas."

"Not so fast," Donna says, whipping the cups off the tray. "Never needed this more."

I pay the waiter, giving him a healthy tip just for locating us, and take the baskets of food. Hunched in a corner, balancing the baskets on our cups, we down the tacos.

Donna, her face still flushed and sweaty, sluices through both margaritas in record time. "Yowza!" she shouts as the blond guy flips the USC co-ed, stripped of both her sweatshirt and shorts, over his shoulder and spanks her.

Donna tilts her head, her mouth crooked, and gives me a bleary look. "He's cute. Gotta say . . . sh'cute, you know?" The words slur. She tries again: "Sh'cute."

"You ready for another go?"

"You betcha! Sh'cute," she slurs with a leer that sobers me right up. "He got me sorta turned on, y'know?"

I nod, wondering how much the girlfriends of the USC co-ed tipped the hunk. At least Donna was spared being stripped and spanked.

"Time to hit the trail, pardner." I grasp Donna firmly under the arm and half-walk, half-slide her against the handrail to the bottom of the steps. She's limp and rubber-legged. It's slow going to the car, but I manage to keep her sufficiently ambulatory even as her head lolls like a rag doll.

I ease her into the passenger seat and buckle her up, then roll down the windows. Her khaki pants and T-shirt are sticky and rumpled, smelling like booze and spit-up milk. But her face wears the smile of a child enjoying sweet dreams. *I wonder if this in any way makes up for Alex Trebek.* I shouldn't have let her get manhandled, or wasted on margaritas. She'll hate me when the hangover kicks in and she remembers her *Girls*

Gone Wild fling. Moreover, I don't know what lies ahead, and she's in no shape to fend for herself. I should have come down here on my own and not risked involving her.

I let Donna sleep it off while I spend some time with the map, the guidebook, and a cocktail napkin printed with the word *Coop's*.

Chapter Twenty-One

Two hours later, driving south on Highway One, I pass several shops, a gas station, a power plant substation, and a restaurant before slowing for a turnoff. I roll down the window and pull onto a gravelly shoulder. A rough-hewn sign with a faded red arrow reads: HARBOR QUEEN LANDING. SPORTFISHING. CHARTER SERVICE. Below it, a second sign dangles from chain hooks: COOP'S BAJA CANTEEN. CERVEZA. ALMEJA.

If the words blinked in neon they couldn't be more electrifying. I glance around, expecting—what? Sirens? Flashing lights? A loud hailer telling me to turn back? Instead I hear twittering birds and the rippling sigh of tall grass. I turn onto the unpaved service road, feeling queasy. I put it down to apprehension, the stage-fright variety that comes with an equal measure of jittery anticipation.

The tires rock into deep, hard-packed furrows, as though locking into sprockets. A grassy hump running down the middle of the narrow lane brushes against the undercarriage with a persistent whisper that sounds a lot like *foolish, foolish, foolish.*

Maybe. The road to the bay is more isolated than I expected. I glance at Donna curled against the passenger door, her fleece jacket balled up under her head. Her short gray hair curls damply on her forehead. A gentle whiffling escapes her slightly parted lips. I don't want to disturb her. Nor do I think I could. She's dead to the world.

I lean out the window and breathe in cool, briny air. The ocean can't be far ahead. I slow up, almost missing a narrow turnout cutting into the grassy verge. With a soft thump, I ease the tires out of the ruts and manage a tight U-turn. Glancing back through marshy reeds, I glimpse a curving expanse of water and a tile roof glittering in the sun. How close have I come to pulling up at Paul's doorstep, my inebriated passenger still out cold?

I glance at the guidebook open in my lap. Following directions, I turn right at the first road, go one mile, and bear left at the fork in the road. After driving past several small shacks along a strip of land separating the bay and the Pacific Ocean, I come across Ed's Land's End Motel. The pavement stops abruptly at a gray shingled building with a blue door marked OFFICE. Beyond a cluster of weathered cabins, gray with faded blue trim, a broad stretch of empty beach runs south from the mouth of the bay as far as the eye can see. I pull up and park.

Careful not to awaken Donna, I ease myself out of the car, leaving the door unlatched. I walk a few steps, my feet settling into the sand, and gaze out at the vast, unspoiled view of the bay. Silence, broken only by the distant lap of water, fills my ears. I breathe in the musky tang of salt water and lift my face to the sun. Slowly my stomach stops jumping, my shoulders relax.

I size up the Land's End, taking in a late-model station wagon and faded red sedan parked near two cabins at the far end. The place looks clean enough. There's a VACANCY sign on the office door. I see someone move behind one of the open windows, the ocean breeze whipping the gauze curtains like trailing veils.

I step carefully onto the rotting boardwalk and pull open the snap-spring screen door. Inside, the air is cool and musty. A young barrel-chested Mexican, warm-eyed and toothy, lifts his forearms off the counter as I enter. The door clatters behind me, shaking the timber frame.

"Oops, sorry about that." I look into the kid's ruddy, smiling face. "Have you got a room available?"

He shrugs. I look at the Diet Coke on the counter, sweating in a damp puddle on a dog-eared copy of *Sports Illustrated.*

"*Se habla Inglés*?" He shakes his head. "Ed? Ed *aqui*?"

His smile dims. So does mine. Aside from *guacamole* and *hasta la vista,* I've pretty much exhausted my Spanish. I point out the window to a cabin, then to myself.

"*Si,*" he says, then hands me a plastic sheet encasing a page printed in English. Clearly I'm not the only gringo to pass this way. My eyes light on the words CASH ONLY. NO CREDIT CARDS. NO TV. NO TELEPHONE. NO ELECTRICITY AFTER 11 P.M. No mention of mints on the pillows.

I pay the twenty-five-dollar rate and fill out a registration card with Donna's name rather than my own. I smile and hand him the card. He smiles and gives me a key.

I head back to the car, shivering in a chill sea breeze, and drive down the narrow strip of cracked tarmac to the third cabin. Donna is still sound asleep when I open the trunk to get our luggage, the two Discount Mart shopping bags.

The salt air has corroded the lock, but the flimsy door shudders open when I lean into it. I flip a wall switch, and a light flutters on inside a tin shade dangling from the ceiling. The room, small and spare, comes equipped with twin beds, each with a white towel folded at the foot of a blue chenille coverlet.

A toilet is visible behind a partition, with a shower cubicle in the corner. There's no sign of complimentary toiletries on the washstand. A weathered orange crate serves as a night table between the beds. I push up the sash on the window, hoping Donna appreciates the beach shack simplicity.

I hear a groan and turn to find her standing on the threshold. She's slumped against the door frame, her face pale and puffy. "Where are we anyway?"

"A little south of Malibu. Nice, huh?" I smile brightly. "How're you feeling?"

As if in answer, Donna turns abruptly, cupping her hands over her mouth. She disappears around the corner of the cabin. There follows all the sounds associated with barfing up a taco and a pitcher or two of margaritas. I soak the corner of one of the bath towels in cold tap water. When Donna reappears slumped in the doorway, I hand her the towel.

"How about a shower?"

"How 'bout surgically removing my head?" she says, her voice thin. "I feel awful."

"You can shower later. You'll feel better."

Donna looks down at her trousers. "Promise me you'll burn these. I don't ever want to see them again." She glares at me. "And not a word, okay? If you ever bring it up—"

"Suits me. I'm sorry, Donna—"

She holds up a hand, palm toward me. " Not a word . . . ever."

I walk over to the plastic cubicle and turn on a faucet. It spins in my fingers. I turn the second knob. A thin stream, rusty and cold, spatters from the showerhead. "Maybe we should go for a quick swim before dinner, okay? I promised you lobster tonight—"

Clearly the wrong thing to say. Donna disappears, and I hear more retching. I fiddle with the faucets, praying for clear, warm water. By the time she reappears, the last of the rust has chugged out of the showerhead, and the water is marginally less frigid.

While Donna strips off her party-animal outfit, I busy myself emptying the shopping bags. I lay out her Pepto-Bismol pink nightie on the washstand and dispose of her khaki pants in a tin wastebasket, all the while sorting through my options. I can't abandon Donna, but I can't take her with me, either.

I look out the window, giving her as much privacy as a small room without a bathroom door can provide. The sun is still high, but the sky over the bay has taken on a milky cast. I catch sight of the swarthy young desk clerk ambling down the beach, then lose him from view as he disappears behind one of the other cabins. I rest my arms on the window ledge, my eyes scanning the water foaming on the shores of the bay. The young Mexican comes into sight again, farther down the beach, trailing three horses, one black and two roan, their halter ropes slack in his hand.

I straighten up with a jolt, banging my head on the window sash. I sprint for the door, grabbing my shoulder bag off the bed on the way.

"Be back in a minute. I'm just going to stretch my legs on the beach," I call back to Donna.

I hear a faint "okay" as I pull the door closed. I slog across the sand toward a shed and small corral about fifty yards behind the office. I have no idea what the Mexican word for horse is, but I'm determined to get one.

The desk clerk sees me and stops just inside the corral gate, waiting. I wave and quicken my slog.

"Hello, again," I begin brightly, then run my hand along the flanks of the black horse. Nodding, smiling, and pointing, we manage to work out a deal that sets me back twenty dollars for the use of a saddled horse until the sun sets. I spot an ice chest inside the shed and negotiate four Cokes for another five bucks.

Fifteen minutes later, I'm back in the cabin. Donna, wearing the fleece jacket over her nightie, lies on the bed, both pillows propped under her head. When she sees me walk in clutching four cans of Coca-Cola, her eyes light up. She reaches out, fingers wriggling.

"Sorry, but I could drink 'em all."

"Be my guest." I pop the tab and hand her a Coke. "Listen, I don't suppose you'd be up for a horseback ride, would you?"

"Are you nuts?" She gives me a look, then glugs half a can before coming up for air. "Where in the world would we go horseback riding? And why?"

"On the beach. They rent horses here. I thought it'd be fun, but I understand if you want to rest a bit. Why don't you take a nap while I go for a ride?"

Donna eyes the three cans of Coke I place on the orange crate next to her bed. "Maybe a nap's a good idea. But don't be gone too long. And be careful. You've got your cell phone?"

"I do. Have a good sleep."

I grab my fleece jacket and head back to the corral. By the time I reach the shed, Prieta is saddled, her reins tethered to the wooden gate. The desk clerk gives me a leg up. Like riding a bike, I assure myself, settling into the saddle. It's not, of course, despite a spate of lessons back in my contract player days. The last time I was on a horse was years ago while on location in Phoenix.

Prieta has already surmised that. She takes charge, bumping back and forth a few times, stomping and shaking her coarse, black mane. The desk clerk gives her a smack on the rump and leans into her. With a bit more of that sort of encouragement, Prieta and I eventually rock and roll out of the corral, heading toward the firmer wet sand along the shore.

My sense of direction isn't great, but I've studied the map carefully enough to have a sense of the inner bay. I slide the guidebook out of my shoulder bag and flip to the earmarked page that caught my eye back in Ensenada.

> *Touted as one of the largest protected waterways on the coast, the long, narrow strip of sandy beach extends several miles south along rugged coastline until opening up into the main bay. A bridge used to cross over to the other side of the bay, but washed out some twenty years ago. A natural access road runs west toward the ocean before entering the majestic Harbor Queen Landing, a locale affording miles of fantastic scenic views, solitude, and adventure from the mouth of the bay down to the marshes. Is there a new resort on the horizon for this area?*

If Paul has anything to do with it, I'm sure there will be.

I glance back over my shoulder. The Land's End cabins are now distant smudges on the sandy beach. Marshy shallows and an outcropping of jagged rock obscure my view of the corral. How long did the desk clerk keep his eyes on me, wondering if I was up to handling his horse? He appeared sublimely unconcerned, looking more confident in me than I was. Besides, he knows I have to make it back by sundown. I've left behind my car and a hostage with only Coca-Cola to sustain her.

Prieta settles into an easy pace, sudsy water lapping at her hooves. Sand, rock, and swaying marsh grass meet in pastel harmony with the milky wash along the horizon. Pristine nature. Ripe for development. A new resort? A housing tract?

I look up at the bluffs, imagining them ringed in concrete, with telephone poles and power lines piercing the sky. McMansions looming like giant pink Taco Bells with acid-green irrigated lawns. Ten-car garages. And Paul in charge of it all, throwing down a blanket, inviting me to share his dream of moving mountains, or at least rearranging them. *I just need someone to believe in me, cookie.* If a development here was Paul's latest scheme, surely it was shattered in the mortgage meltdown. Or has he found more willing dupes?

The fire in my belly is stoked. Prieta picks up on it. She twitches her mane and snorts, her pace quickening. I crane my neck, expecting any moment to see signs of the Harbor Queen Landing. Boats. A dock. A ramp. Instead, I see an inlet with a stand of eucalyptus trees.

I turn away from the shore, heading across dry sand toward outcroppings of grass and bleached logs set upright at regular intervals near the trees. As I pull closer, I realize that the eucalyptus trees ring the backside of the inlet. The landing must be just on the other side.

I've come far enough on horseback. I dismount and stroke Prieta's neck, guiding her toward the shady recess of grass between the logs and the trees. I tether her and reach into my shoulder bag for one of Donna's free apples, now a bribe to buy Prieta's patience.

I creep into the shadow of the trees, for the first time giving some thought to Jack. I'm doing precisely what he told me not to do, and I have no intention of turning back. I'm not afraid of confronting Paul. Nor do

I have any doubt I'll find him on the other side of these trees. Meanwhile, with dampness seeping into my athletic shoes, I'm more concerned about the spongy ground and dense undergrowth. Snakes, rats, and poisonous insects come to mind. So does a swampy sinkhole.

With some relief, I edge out of the woods and climb up an outcropping of rock. To my left I can see the rutted road I followed earlier across the marshy fields. Barely visible through the reeds, parked at the edge of the road, is a gray, mud-spattered SUV, one of its tires sinking in the marshy shoulder. From there, the access road winds around a terra-cotta hacienda with a turquoise door and tile roof. The windows are dark. There's no sign of anyone.

I squat low, scanning the terrain. The cell phone rings inside my shoulder bag. I scramble to find it beneath the jumble of keys, Kleenex, and Habana cigars.

"Where are you? I don't see you on the beach."

"You're supposed to be napping, Donna."

"I couldn't sleep. I got to thinking you were awfully anxious to race off. The guy pointed me in the direction you were going, but I don't see you anywhere."

"You're not following me, are you?"

"Just what I figured. Meg, you promised!"

"Go back to the cabin. I'll see you there."

"No, damn it!"

"I'm turning off my phone, Donna. I have to do this alone, so don't call me back. I mean it. Don't follow me."

I snap the lid and set the ringer to vibrate. I attach the phone clip to the inside of my waistband. Easing back to the far side of the outcropping, I begin climbing among the rocks, trying not to think of Donna slogging down the beach. Why couldn't she just stay put?

I scramble to the topmost boulder and lie flat, my cheek against the warm stone. After catching my breath, I look up to get my bearings and almost gasp. The milky-white veil has lifted, revealing a breathtaking panorama I instantly recognize from the photographs I found in Doug's garage.

Sparkling cobalt water shimmers against creamy sand and glittering stone cliffs. In the clear, rippling water, a dinghy rocks gently against a rough-hewn dock with a rope handrail. A wooden ramp, buttressed with fraying rubber tires, inclines from a rough cement track. Further out, a thirty-two-foot sailboat, canvas battened down, bobs in the water, its name gleaming gold against sparkling white lacquer: *Coop, Too.* It's an almost exact replica of the *WindStar.*

My stomach soaks up the warmth of the boulder as I watch the boat gently bob, recalling how it felt to lie on such a deck, the sun on my back, the sea rocking beneath me. Lulled by memory, I listen to the distant *caw* of gulls and the wash of the ocean against the ramp pilings. I hear something else, too, even closer. A swishing sound and someone humming.

I look to my left, to a flight of wooden steps leading down from the side of the rock face to a flagstone courtyard with tables and a bar area. Swinging on chain hooks, barely visible through a tangle of bougainvillea, is the mate to the sign near the highway: COOP'S FAJA CANTEEN. CERVEZA. ALMEJA. Beneath the sign is a kidney-shaped bamboo bar with wooden stools. Stemware and liquor bottles crowd the shelves behind it.

I lean farther over the edge of the boulder. A cubbyhole booth, with the words HARBOR QUEEN LANDING: BOOKING OFFICE stenciled above shuttered windows, is sandwiched into a corner of the courtyard. The patio in front of the thatched-roof bar is deserted, but I hear the splash of water. Just then a spray wets down the area just below my perch.

A woman in T-shirt and cutoffs comes into view, humming to herself while she hoses down the flagstones, her bare feet swishing through the foamy swirls. I hold my breath, my fingers digging into rock. As crazy as it seems, I know the voice. I recognize the loose blonde ponytail, the long slim legs. It is Carol Baskin.

I press myself hard against the rock, my body rigid with shock. Did I gasp? Could she have heard me over the splashing water? With horror,

I realize that the shadow of my own head is imprinted on a driftwood table directly below. I watch Carol's profile tilting toward the sun-bleached tabletop. Her toes stop wriggling. The hose falls from her hand and slithers across the flagstones. As she whips around, I spring to my feet.

She screams and sinks back against the table, staring up at me. "My God! You scared the hell out of me. What're you doing here?"

"Just thought I'd drop by." I watch her warily, my mind racing. "So your mom's down here? How's she doing?"

Her shoulders drop. "Oh, shit. Don't get cute. I can't stand that." She glares at me, shaking her head. "Man, I really don't need you here." She reaches in the pocket of her cutoffs and pulls out a pack of cigarettes, a red plastic lighter tucked inside the cellophane wrap.

"Smoking? You're kidding me."

"Well, I couldn't smoke at home. Sid hates it." Her hands shake as she puts a cigarette to her lips. She starts to light up, but her trembling hands knock both the cigarette and the lighter into a puddle at her feet.

"Shit. Just shit, shit, *shit!*" She fishes the lighter out of the water, shakes it, and then fumbles to get another cigarette. "Damn! Why do you have to spoil everything?" She makes another attempt, holding the lighter in both hands.

I watch her dip her head to the flame, my own shakiness ebbing. "Sorry, Carol. You don't seem happy to see me."

Carol sucks deeply, stuffing the lighter back in her pocket. She stares up at me, smoke boiling out of her nose and mouth. She takes another drag, her eyes narrowing. It's a Mexican standoff, except that I'm elevated at least ten feet above her head.

She squints, then raises her hand to shade her eyes. "How'd you get up there?" Her voice is harsh, accusing. "That's my place. It's where I go to meditate."

"Really. Nice view."

"Stop it. Just stop. What do you think you're up to? Just get the hell down here."

The stairs are only a few steps away, but I have no desire to be on equal footing with her. Especially when I don't know where Paul is. Or whose SUV is parked in the access road. I widen my stance and fold my arms, knowing I'm driving her crazy.

"C'mon, Carol. It's my Focus Day, remember? You hauled me out of bed yesterday and told me to expect the unexpected. So, here I am. What're you doing here? Don't you usually leave this kind of yard work to Guillermo and Olinda?"

"You think you're so funny, don't you? Why do you always have to ruin things for me? You've always got to horn in." She tosses the butt into water pooling near the table, her face pinched in anger. "I hate you! I'm sick of you grabbing everything for yourself. For once, everything is going my way! Can't you back off and give me a break? Get out of here!"

Stunned by her fury, I step back, imagining Carol rushing up the steps, going for my throat. "What are you talking about? What've I done?"

"God, you are so oblivious." She flaps her arms wide, in full operatic mode. "Whatever you want gets handed to you, doesn't it? No matter what I do, you get the whole damn works. The guys. The career. Am I supposed to stand around applauding all the time?" She kicks at the water, entangling her foot in the hose. She yanks free and kicks again, tears running down her face. "Damn it! Watching you play victim is really galling. It's sickening. Really sickening!"

"Carol, this is crazy. I don't get it. You've got everything you could want. What are you doing here? What about Sid?"

"You kidding? Who wants Sid? First you get Dirck, the sexiest guy on the planet. Or at least in acting class. He was amazing."

"Amazing? Wait, are you saying that you and Dirck—?"

"Yeah, so what? You were off doing a movie. Big deal." She grins and brushes the tears from her cheeks. "And in the end I get Paul, too. I'm the one he wanted, not you. He's mine!"

"You called him scum, Carol. You know what he is."

"Sure, but if you're looking for the perfect man, you couldn't do better than a con man. He's got it all figured out."

"I don't get it."

"You don't, do you?" She laughs, her eyes glistening, her face still tear-stained. "But you'll see—and he's all mine."

I freeze. "He's here?"

"He will be. You know something? It's worth it just to see the look on your face. Maybe I'm glad you did turn up. This'll be priceless."

"When is he coming?"

"Can't wait, can you? Don't worry. You'll see him. He won't be all that surprised you tracked him down. He knows you've been looking for him. God, everyone and his uncle is looking for him." She sloshes to a spigot hidden in the bougainvillea and turns off the water. "You know, I tried to warn you to forget about him, to move on. You could have spared yourself this humiliating little jaunt. You should have listened to me."

"When? If you knew what was going on, you sure didn't tell me."

"Oh, God, what an idiot you are! Your marriage was a sham from the beginning. I saw right away that he was way above your league. He was just using you. It's not my fault that he turned to me. You hadn't a clue what he was all about."

"And Sid?"

"What about him? He's in so deep he wouldn't dare make trouble." She looks up at me and grins, her confidence restored. "You never figured that out? Paul was fronting for a Russian outfit, pulling in high-end investors for the Mulholland development. Sid bought his pitch. Then Paul used Sid's connections and got him to handle the transactions. It all blew up when the housing market collapsed. A lot of people got burned, including Sid."

She laughs and begins yanking the hose, hand over hand, drawing its length into a coil at her feet. "Sid, always Mr. Big Shot, never saw any of the money. It was laundered and funneled back here through some Mexican contacts. By the time Sid got wise, he'd sunk so much money in—his own and other people's—there was no way out. With the feds breathing down his neck, he pointed the finger at Paul. Wrong thing to do." She tucks the last of the hose into the coil. "The feds can't touch Paul. God, Sid can be thick sometimes."

"So that's when you dumped him for Paul?"

"No need to be crass, Meg." She shakes her head, eyeing me with pity. "I looked out for myself. You didn't. Everything that's gone wrong for you is your own fault. How you could have missed all the warning signs is beyond me. You have to live with that." She picks up the hose, heaving it onto her shoulder. "You'd better also face the fact that Paul loves me. He's working out a deal so we can be together."

"Congratulations. I should probably look into getting a divorce."

"That would be nice. Sid's probably thinking the same thing, though I'm not sure it matters." Carol tosses the coiled hose into a trough near the bougainvillea. "You want a beer? Glass of wine?" She looks up at me, expectantly. "C'mon. Sun's over the yardarm, and we're closed Mondays. I'm having something."

"I'll pass, thanks." I take a deep breath and look out on the *Coop, Too* in the bay. An image of Rick Aquino aboard the *WindStar* flashes through my brain. He and his brother were probably involved in the money laundering. But who killed them off? Vladimir Ivanovich Proznorov would be my guess. Who's next? "Tell me, is it part of the deal that you and Paul stay here?"

"The finer points are under discussion, but seeing as how everyone seems to know where to find us, I doubt it. I hate it when people just drop in. We'll go somewhere else. Start fresh. Just the two of us." Carol, looking as carefree as a kid after a sun shower, splashes through the puddles. She stops to brush leaves off the walkway with the edge of her foot. "Hey, you're not afraid to come down here, are you? Believe me, nothing's going to happen to you."

"Why would it?"

"Right. The cards are on the table. No reason we can't be civil about this."

I can't resist taking advantage of Carol's affable mood while it lasts. Does she really know everything about Paul? Or is he lying to her, too? "So why can't the feds touch Paul?"

Carol brushes her hands on her shorts and shrugs. "He's got a long-standing deal with them. And he knows how to work it."

"Then why did he take off and fake a kidnapping?"

"Who says he faked it?" Carol lights another cigarette and squashes the empty packet in her hand. "When people get burned, they turn nasty, and that goes for Nat Wiggens. He was stupid enough to set Paul up for the kidnapping down here. But Paul's no fool. He did what he had to do to save his own skin." She exhales sharply, her eyes narrowing. "Nat Wiggens took the hit in the end. He deserved it. So did the kidnappers, a couple of beaners laundering money down here. They thought they could take over the whole operation. But these Russians don't play around when money goes missing."

"And Jack?"

"The feds didn't figure in until Sid blew the whistle. With all his damn maneuvering, Sid could've ended up like Nat. He doesn't know how lucky he is." Carol spreads her feet and exhales a trail of smoke. "Are you coming down or what? I'm getting a little tired of this long-distance grilling. You want to talk, get yourself down here."

I move slowly toward the stairs. "And Jack?" I repeat.

"Nice guy, don't you think? And he can't lay a hand on Paul." She takes a last drag, then flicks the cigarette into the muddy stream flowing off the patio. "Hold your friends close, your enemies even closer. It always pays off."

"That includes me, right?"

"C'mon, you've always been a friend. You know, I really meant all that stuff about your chart. If you'd listen to me, you'd be way ahead of the game." She laughs and stuffs her hands in her pockets. "Besides, Sid told me the other day you were living on the street. What's that about?"

"I'm not! That's ridiculous!" Finally she gets under my skin, and I almost lose it. "I don't know where Sid got that idea."

"Yeah, I figured. Just Sid feeling sorry for you again. You do know how to play the victim card, I gotta say."

She shrugs, waiting for me to reach the bottom of the stairs. She steps forward, taking advantage of her height to look down at me. "And Sid thinks he's got Jack in his pocket, do you believe it? What a lunk." She slowly shakes her head.

"Pluto must be taking good care of you, too."

"Better than you could dream, speaking of big changes. I did Paul's chart, too, and we're on the same course." She pulls the elastic off her ponytail and shakes out her hair. "Okay, you want *cerveza* or *vino*? I've got Pinot Grigio stashed in the cooler. C'mon, when did you ever turn down a glass of wine?"

"Sure. A glass of wine." I wait until Carol turns and walks toward the tiki bar, then follow. "Sounds like you really have a handle on all this. Did you happen to come across a woman named Lucy?"

The name barely escapes my lips before Carol whips around, eyes glittering. "Yeah, some cheap grifter who latched onto Paul when I wasn't on the scene. He used her, then flipped her to a Russian kid. Now she and this dim-wit have some two-bit deal going in San Diego." She brushes my arm with a backward slap. "Greg Proznorov's an idiot, but he suits Lucy. She likes young flesh and heavy metal."

"She liked my earrings, too."

Carol stares at me, her eyes losing luster. Or maybe it's the sun going down, casting shadows. She bites the inside of her cheek, then blinks at me. "Okay, that's one thing I'm really, really sorry about. Get mad at me if you want, but we had to give her something."

"My earrings?" Realization dawns even as I ask the question. "How did you happen to have my earrings?"

Carol chews her lip. "This is the part that's not so nice, okay? That call Paul asked you to make after he was kidnapped was to Vladimir Proznorov, his partner. He sent me to make the pickup. It wasn't easy to sneak out of the house without Sid knowing."

"The bag on my front steps?"

"Yeah," she breathes, radiating Bambi-eyed wonderment. "I honestly couldn't believe you'd fall for something like that. The only call Paul could make was to you—and he had to somehow alert Proznorov. I was shocked when I picked up that bag and saw what was in it. Even the Cartier pin I gave you for your thirtieth birthday. How could you? Jesus. All of it just dumped in a crummy Safeway grocery bag—"

"Obviously, he knew me better than you did. I would've done anything to save Paul."

"Don't get ratty on me," she says, her voice harsh. "I was sick with worry. I just wish I could've been the one to pick up Paul that night instead of Lucy. He should have called me!"

How ironic that while I sat waiting for the kidnapper's call, a tug–of-war was going on between Lucy and Carol about which one would pick up Paul in La Paz. I swallow hard, recalling that I told Jack how sorry I was that it hadn't been me picking him up. What was I thinking? I watch Carol stroll to the bar, confident and back in control. She's right. I missed all the warning signals. But even now, with so much explained, I'm not surprised I behaved as I did. I loved Paul. I would never have believed he would betray me like this.

Carol flips a switch next to the bar. Gelled lamps glow around the dock, resetting the scene. Fairy lights bloom in the bougainvillea, illuminating the patio like a stage set. It strikes me that I missed all the warning signs in Carol, too. When we were both studio contract players, I knew she was making a play for Dirck, and I brushed it off. She was too obvious to take seriously. No matter how outrageously she behaved, I gave her the benefit of the doubt.

She sets two wineglasses on the bar, humming to herself. Then, her manner girlish and confiding, she says, "All the poor guy ever needed was someone to believe in him. I do. I love him, Meg. I've loved him since the first time I laid eyes on him. We're so good together. Listen, I even got his cholesterol down. No more gravy biscuits, you know?" She laughs. "God love 'em, Kentucky boys love their ham and grits."

"You mean West Virginia boy, don't you?"

"What? Man, you really didn't know him at *all,* did you?" Her laughter rings across the patio. "He's Louisville, Kentucky, darlin'—born and bred."

"No, Carol. Whatever he told you, he's from West Virginia."

"Kentucky!" Carol thumps her hands on the bar and grins. "What the hell, we'll ask him when he gets here. Want to lay a bet?"

"Sure. Name it."

"Okay, but what? You don't have any money—and I already have Paul."

"So it appears. You're just going to run off with him?"

"Actually, I already did. But I went back. It was Paul's idea that I keep a lid on Sid for a while so he wouldn't spill everything. But I managed to visit my mother a lot." She winks. "Okay, that's the bad part out of the way. I hope you're okay with it. To tell you the truth, I probably saved Sid's life. These Russkies don't have a lot of patience. They'd kill as soon as look at you." She sighs and reaches into the cooler for the bottle of Pinot Grigio. "There's a lot I'd just as soon not know. Let's drink to getting all this behind us."

I pull a stool away from the bar and perch on the edge. "It's hard to keep up with you, Carol. One minute you hate me; the next you're my best friend."

"You just can't move on, can you?" she snaps. "I said I was sorry." She grips the bottle, her eyes frosty. "It's not that I hate you, but you do get on my nerves sometimes. You really do. If those stupid earrings mean that much to you, I could try to get them back from Lucy. How's that?"

"You've seen her lately?"

"None of your damn business."

"Sorry, I heard she'd disappeared."

"She tried to rat out Paul. So did Erica." Carol eyes me coldly. "You know, I don't expect any gratitude from you, but I probably saved your life, too. I don't know why I bothered."

A deep-throated burble sounds in the distance. Carol's eyes flick toward the bay. "He'll be here soon."

I slide off the bar stool, turning to look across the water, shimmering in the last slivers of sunlight. Squinting into the glare, I barely make out what appears to be a cabin cruiser.

Behind me, Carol's voice is low, distant. "He's mine now, Meg. I just wish I could trust you."

I turn back, a chill crawling up my neck. I catch a flash of Carol's arm swooping high, her hand gripping the neck of the bottle like a tennis racquet. In the instant it takes me to duck, her powerful stroke smashes the bottle against the wooden sign before it can hit my head. I turn away, wine and shards of glass raining on my back.

Above the bar, the heavy sign creaks and twists off its hooks. I blink, thrusting myself sideways, barely glimpsing Carol's wine-spattered face before the thick plank shudders loose and slams into her forehead. She screams and falls backward. I twist away, my hands flying to protect my head from the falling chain and broken bamboo.

I straighten up and glance down at Carol. Blood oozes from the wound on her forehead and seeps into her tangled hair. I heave the wooden sign from her chest, then grab a bar towel and press it to the bleeding gash. I dip another towel into the chilled water that remains in the overturned ice bucket, then mop the crimson flow pooling in her eyes and ears.

Once again I hear the deep burble of the cruiser's horn. I glance over my shoulder at the bay, silken and calm. Lavender hues have already crept into the deep crevices in the cliffs and the wilderness beyond. The day is coming to a close. What a strange place for friends of thirty years to discover how little they know each other.

Chapter Twenty-Two

"My God! You killed her!"

My eyes swing up to the boulder. Donna, wearing her smart St. John pantsuit with the shiny buttons, stares down at me. Her face looks bleached, her eyes horror-stricken.

"It was an accident. She's still alive, Donna. Can you give me a hand?"

"Be right there." She stoops to pick up my shoulder bag and jacket, then disappears from view. I sit back on my heels, struck by my own cold, dead calm. Was that really my voice sounding so detached? It seems like such a long time ago that I watched Carol, barefoot and humming, hosing down the flagstones. A disjointed sequence flashes through my mind, as jarring as images fragmented in disco lights, and ends with Carol's terrible scream and a shower of glass. Now, in a grotesque scene of fairy lights and gaudy bougainvillea, Carol lies in a pool of blood.

I hear Donna scrambling down the steps, hurrying across the flagstones. She wraps the fleece jacket around my shoulders and takes my hands in hers.

"You're icy cold, Meg. Are you okay?"

"I'm fine. Can you help Carol?"

"Is that who this is? I heard the scream." She leans over Carol, lifting her head slightly. I grab more bar towels and hand one to Donna, who slips it under Carol's head. Her fingers move deftly, taking her pulse. "We have to get help or she's not going to make it."

"I know. There's a motor boat pulling in, but—"

"I saw it. Maybe someone aboard has first-aid equipment. Or can call for help."

"It's Paul."

Her head whips around. "No! You're sure?"

I nod and stand up. "Carol was waiting for him. I know it's him. I'm going down there."

"You can't! When he sees what's happened—we have to get out of here!"

"You go, Donna. Please, let me handle this. I need to." I look into her anxious eyes, regretting more than ever involving her in this. "I'm so sorry. Please go. You can call for help on your cell phone. I'll look for you back at the motel."

"Meg, stop!"

I run across the flagstones, ignoring Donna's pleas, and conceal myself under a thick arch of bougainvillea. I touch my sticky hair, not daring to run my fingers through the silt of wine and shards. Tipping my head over, I gently shake the damp tangle of hair, then my legs and arms to dislodge flakes of glass from my T-shirt and jeans. Shivering, I push my arms through the sleeves of the fleece jacket, zipping it up to cover spatters of darkening red blood on my shirt.

For all my cold calm, a sense of urgency surges through me. The cabin cruiser, its engines throbbing, looms closer, shrouded in hazy twilight. I can't see Paul, but he could spot me limned in the glow of the gelled floodlights. He'll know it's not Carol, with her long legs and broad shoulders.

I squat down in the shadows, my eyes on the cabin cruiser. My stomach muscles twitch. It's a moment before I realize it's my cell phone throbbing on my waistband. I flip it open. Before I can say a word I hear Jack's voice, low and urgent.

"Meg? You're okay?"

"I'm fine. Sorry I didn't call—"

"Cut it. I know where you are."

"How?"

"Your cell phone. Easy to track."

"Great. I'm carrying around my own homing device." *One more thing Jinx didn't have to worry about.*

"This isn't funny. You have to get out of there. You see the dirt road behind you, to your left?"

"Hang on, you're *here*?"

"We just pulled in at the top of the road. You've got minutes to get out of there before Stephens returns."

"You mean Frank Cooper, don't you?" The abrupt silence gives me satisfaction. "You know, the Coop? You've been looking out for him all along, haven't you, Jack? Even before I met him you had him in some sort of witness protection, right? Trying to get him to turn on Proznorov? That's the only thing I can figure—"

"Meg, for God's sake! There's a lot more to it. We're working with the Mexican authorities here to take him in along with the whole syndicate—it's a lot bigger than just Cooper."

"Great, just swell. And then Paul gets another new identity, is that how it works? Come on, Jack. You play games, and innocent people lose everything."

"He'll pay, I promise you. Stephens was leading two lives. By the time we got onto it, he was hooked up with Proznorov. Meg? Can you hear me? Get the hell out of there. This is a big operation!"

"I've got one of my own to tend to." I glance over my shoulder, taking in the grisly scene on the patio. "Sorry, Jack. You couldn't even level with me about Carol. She's here, as I'm sure you know. She's got a bad head injury that needs medical attention. My friend Donna is with her up on the patio. They're the ones you need to get out of here."

"What happened?"

"No time, Jack. Got to go." I edge out from behind the rock, staying in shadow, and creep along a grassy verge toward the shoreline, the phone pressed to my ear. I hear Jack breathing hard as though he's running.

"Meg, what're you up to? Stay away from Stephens!"

"Too late for that. This is what I came here for."

I shut the phone and reattach it to my waistband. Huddling deep into shadow, I wait, my heart banging. The ghostly white cabin cruiser pulls into the dock and cuts its engines. A sour fug of diesel clouds suffocatingly around me.

"Hey, baby, you there?" Paul's voice, with its velvety twang, hangs in the air. I see him, his powerful shoulders visible in the wheel room. His hair, windblown and sun bleached, gleams in the light of an overhead globe. He turns toward me, his faded blue shirt pale against bronzed skin. "Carol? C'mon, baby! Give me a hand here!"

By now Carol would have waved and called out a greeting. She would be reaching for the ropes to tie up, as I would have done in another time and place.

"Carol, for chrissake!" The shadow of his head falls across the dock, touching the edges of my own patch of darkness. For a heart-stopping moment, we share the inky space. I hang back, holding my breath. He moves away. I reach out, securing the ropes, then ease myself aboard. Without a second thought, I fly up the steps in two quick bounds, my hands barely touching the rails. The moment my foot lands on the top deck, Paul whips around.

"Sorry. Carol couldn't make it." My chest heaves with the exertion, my lungs filling with diesel fumes.

"No?" His look of surprise doesn't linger. He smiles, his body easing against a teak panel. "Well, look who's here. Relax, baby. Welcome aboard. Catch your breath."

My eyes lock into the deep blue of his. I take in the weathered creases, the sunburned folds. He looks rugged, more raw-boned than I remember. The softness under his chin has vanished. A year on the lam has been kind to Paul—maybe because Carol got his cholesterol down? Too bad I slipped up when it came to his LDL levels.

"You were expecting me?"

"You might say." He folds his arms and tilts his head, his smile a sly pout. It's the face of the devil I fell in love with. I breathe in his salty warmth, marveling at how natural it feels to be near him again. In my dreams and most of my waking hours I've wondered how I would react to seeing Paul again. Now I know, and I'm relieved. I see him for what he is. He's playing me, but it's not working. My heart doesn't turn over. The butterflies are DOA. Paul looks confused. Did he imagine I would leap into his arms, lock lips, and maybe shed a few tears of happiness to be back in his embrace? It's not happening. He laughs, a big, boisterous, face-saving laugh that carries no mirth.

"Something funny?"

"Sure is, baby." He laughs again, even louder. "You're something else! You made poor ol' Greg hotwire his car, then got him traipsing off to a landfill for no good reason. Not knowin' what to do, he calls Lucy's cell phone—so I came up with a little change of plan." Paul chuckles and kicks the teak panel. His Top-Siders are unlaced, and altogether too familiar. "Now, come on, baby. Doesn't knowing that you sent Greg off to poke around in a city dump tickle you just a little? C'mon, where's that smile?"

I hate myself for it, but a smile tugs at my cheeks. "How did he manage to track me down again?"

"It wasn't hard to figure out where you'd be going, baby. Even driving a rental, Greg spotted you."

"So you had him stick a homing device on my car? Why?"

"Because I can. Because I have something he wants." He nods his head toward the bank of equipment in the wheel room. "I like keeping track, knowing where all the fish are. Besides, someone was riling you up, baby, just when things were settling down for me."

Regret clouds his eyes, seeps into his voice—but not regret for what he did to me. Regret that I was getting in his way and he couldn't seem to do anything about it.

I flinch as my cell phone begins to throb against my stomach. I double over, brushing my arm across my waist in an effort to flip the lid on the phone under my fleece jacket. *Please, God, let it be Jack!*

"What's the matter, baby? You going to be sick?"

I straighten up and look into the eyes of the man I once loved. "Sick? What do you think, Paul? You robbed me of everything, including our life together. How could you do something like that to me?"

"Pipe down, sugar. I hear ya loud and clear. You're steamed. I don't blame you." He shakes his head, his voice a purr. "I just didn't have much choice. I'd have made good on everything if I'd had a chance. You know it. My heart and soul was into that development up there. That was for you, baby." His eyes grow moist. He sucks his lower lip. "I would have been back for you as soon as I got things straightened out. You know I would, baby."

"I believed in you, Paul. You knew that. I think if you'd come into my life as Frankie Cooper, I'd have believed in you, too. And been there for you."

The muscles in his jaw tighten, but there's only the faintest shift in his eyes. "What do you know about Frank Cooper?"

I raise my voice, hoping Jack can hear. "A kid from West Virginia, known as the Coop. I talked to your ma—and Dorrie."

"You been doin' more snoopin' than I figured."

I shrug. "Just chance. What happened to you, anyway? How did you end up like this?"

Paul slings his arm across the wheel, a smile playing on his lips. "You want to know? I was running numbers back in Baltimore, and a mob guy caught me skimming. Bad move on my part, but I was too green to know better. The feds offered me a deal. I took it and testified, thinking I could use a fresh start. So they sent me to the boonies with six hundred a month and a job selling shoes. Can you see me doing that, baby? Living in some Sioux City tract house with a lawn to mow?"

He shakes his head. "Then I came up with a chance at some real money. Only every time I showed some enterprise, got a good deal going somewhere, they busted me. I don't think you would've bought in to that kind of life." He smiles lazily. "You're a class act, sugar. I think it's better you didn't get to know me back then. Besides, there's a lot of folks out there looking for the Coop, and that gets real tiresome."

"I'll just bet it does. I think I might've heard from one or two of them. What about Carol? Doesn't sound like something she'd sign up for, either. Did you bother to tell her any of this?" A look of confusion plays across Paul's face. "C'mon, Paul! Carol? Weren't you running off with her?"

He shrugs. "Yeah. So?"

I suck in air, trying not to dredge up my last gruesome sight of her. "Paul, this is crazy! She left Sid to run off with you."

"She told you that?" He looks at me with injured eyes. "If she and Sid hadn't gone off the rails, I could have been sitting pretty right now. The banks wouldn't have been any the wiser, and the law wouldn't be breathing down my neck. It's Sid who messed things up. I had everyone turning on me. Where the hell is Carol, anyway?"

I stare at him in disbelief. "The bar. She's in the bar."

A knowing smile plays on his lips. "Okay, got it. You two had it out. Man, it all comes down to a catfight, right?" He slaps his hand on the instrument panel, his voice taking on an edge. "No one's bringing me down again."

"So, what happens if someone does get in the way? I'm not familiar with this side of you."

Paul shrugs. "I don't know what you're getting at, sugar."

"Jeri. What happened to the waitress, Jerilyn?"

He whistles, his eyes darkening. "Not my style. Don't know how you could even think that of me."

"Then who killed her? Was she on to the mortgage scheme?"

"Chump change," he says breezily. "She could have messed things up over a nickel-dime deal. A partner of mine set his kid up and let little Greg play in the backyard to learn the ropes. He tried to impress Lucy and screwed up. So the old man stepped in. Turns out, the operation was worth something. These kids with their computers are something else, but they've got no experience." He smiles. "That's where I come in."

"Nat got in the way, too?"

"You might say." Paul sighs, his voice low. "He kind of outlived his usefulness."

"Like Sid?"

"Yeah, if he doesn't shut up." Paul laughs then. "Hey, why don't we join Carol up at the bar, have a drink?"

"Sounds cozy, but I should probably be on my way."

"What's your hurry?" His hands tighten on the teak panel, his fingers kneading the polished wood. "Can't even imagine where you'd be going, sugar. Stick around a while and you get to meet Vladimir."

"Proznorov? You're expecting him?"

"Anytime now. All part of a little change in plan." His eyes flick toward the bay, then settle back on me. "But no need for you to run. I got a little transaction to wrap up, then I'm hitting the road. Maybe you want to tie in with me again, now that you know so much. What do you say?"

"Instead of Carol?"

"Why not, sugar? I'm your biggest fan. Didn't you know?" He smiles as he flips over a photograph on the teak cabinet—the eight-by-ten glossy of Jinx in her top hat that I signed for Donna.

"How'd you get that?"

"You're sure looking good, baby." He looks back at me, a glint of menace in his eyes. "I missed you."

"Paul, how did you—?"

With a sudden movement, he yanks open the slatted teak doors. "Take a look, baby. You picked a helluva time to drop in." Lucy and Greg are crouched inside the cupboard, bound and gagged. Wearing the same outfit I saw her in a week ago, Lucy lies slumped against Greg, eyes closed, her breathing shallow. Greg stares at me with sullen eyes, his cheek bruised, his nose caked with dried blood.

"What're you going to do with them?"

He kicks the door closed. "A little bartering—one way of paying off a debt."

I nod, my brain grappling with this new twist. "You ripped off Lucy. Is that why she ratted on you?"

"And Erica. Lovely Erica." He sounds wistful, but his eyes are cold. "You just can't let a woman get the best of you, know what I mean? That's one thing about you, sugar. You never turned on me."

"I never got a chance to turn on you, Paul. You beat me to it. But no hard feelings." *Please, God, let Jack be hearing all this!* Meanwhile, how do I get out of here? I have no plan. No protection, no exit strategy. What would Jinx do? Divert attention, of course. I smile. "Hang on, Paul. I almost forgot. I have a little souvenir for you." Without taking my eyes off him, I back up a few steps and reach into my shoulder bag. "Just a sec—" I grasp the tubes stashed at the bottom of my bag and haul them out. "You went off and left your cigars—"

I sail the tubes over his shoulder. He turns to catch them as I grab the corner of the handrail and bound down the steps, my feet barely touching the treads. I hear a grunt of surprise, then laughter. "Thanks, baby, but where are you running off to? You've got nowhere to go!"

I hoist myself over the railing and onto the dock, crouching by the side of the boat. Paul appears at the railing on the top deck, then moves back into the wheelhouse. The lights go out, and darkness engulfs the lower portion of the dock. I move quickly toward the embankment, crouching low, trying to assess the best way to get on the other side of the inlet. A glint of light catches my eye. I strain to make out the flash of glitter bobbing near the top end of the dock. I crawl behind several oil drums and grab my cell phone, my heart racing. "Jack? Did you hear all that?"

"Yes, I heard. We didn't know about Greg and Lucy," he snaps. "But I wish to hell—we've been tracking Proznorov's boat, keeping everyone clear of the area. We're ready to move in. Where are you now?"

"Off the boat, near the oil drums. What about Carol?"

"She's not here. You got it wrong. It's your friend that's injured. A medic is with her. But there's no sign of Carol—or Sid. We picked him up on the road a couple of hours ago. He was cooperating with us, then he slipped away. "

"What? Wait, something's wrong. Carol was badly injured—"

There's movement in the reeds, a rustling. I freeze, clamping the phone against my cheek. I slowly turn my head to the sound. The unmistakable smell of vetiver hits my nostrils. I know it's Sid even before I see him lumbering onto the damp sand near the ramp.

I crouch lower and move around the oil drums, sliding the phone back down to my mouth. "I just saw Sid. He's maybe twenty feet away," I whisper.

"Let me know his movements. I'm just pulling up at the bungalow—are you still behind the oil drums? We've got teams ready to close in. I'll send someone in for you."

I swivel around, looking. "I'm closer to the lower end of the dock. Paul's still on the boat."

"Stay put! We'll find you."

"I'm not moving—"

"Who're you talking to?" I look up to see Paul, his face twisted in anger. He clamps my shoulder with one hand, the other coming down hard on my wrist, knocking my phone into the grass. On the upswing, Paul's hand crashes against my jaw, knocking me sideways. I cry out, pain shooting through the side of my face as I fall back against the oil drums. They clatter together, one of them toppling onto the dock.

"Carol! No, please! Don't hurt her!" It's Sid, his voice an anguished bellow. He stumbles and falls heavily against the ramp. "Let her go!"

"What the hell—" Paul swings around, pulling a gun from his waistband. I scramble back toward the oil drums, but not fast enough. Paul yanks me to my feet, clamping his hand across my mouth. "What're you doing down here, Sid?"

"Just let her go, please." Sid struggles to his feet, a pathetic, bloated figure silhouetted in the glow of the cantina. "All I want is to take her back with me. I've kept my end of the bargain."

"The hell you have!" Paul laughs coldly. He positions himself behind me, his grip on me tightening. I shift my head, trying to maneuver my face into the light from the patio so Sid can see it's me, not Carol. Paul pulls my head back, holding me against his chest. "You think we're bargaining over your wife? She wouldn't be here if she didn't want to be, Sid. I kind of think you know that." He laughs, then presses his lips to my cheek and makes a loud smacking sound. "What d'ya say, precious? Want me to give you back to Sid?"

"Let her go, damn you! Carol! For God's sake, tell him!"

Paul presses the gun into my back. "Let's just head for the cantina and talk it over. Go on, Sid. We're right behind you."

As I twist my face in Paul's viselike grip, I pick up a glint at the end of the dock. There's a slight movement, a glimpse of blonde hair. I know, without fully seeing her, that it's Carol—but how could it be? Then I realize that the silvery glint is a handgun. A sickening fear engulfs me. What has she done to Donna?

Sid, unaware that Carol is huddled in shadow no more than six feet away, lifts his hands, his palms white in the moonlight. "Please, I'm begging you. Don't hurt her. I'll do anything you want. Just don't hurt her."

"Then move, buddy. You want Carol, you can have her. My little gift to you, Sid. Just keep your hands where I can see 'em."

Paul shoves me forward. I stumble, then regain my footing. In the distance I hear the faint rumble of another cabin cruiser. I shift my gaze, a spark of light on the bay catching my eye. Paul glances back, too. It must be Proznorov steaming into the Harbor Queen Landing. I plant my heel on the laces of Paul's Top-Siders and sink my teeth into his thumb.

"What the hell?" He yanks his hand and stumbles backward, losing his balance. He's too solid to topple over, but while he regains his footing I drop to the deck and roll sideways. A shot rings out, then another, both slicing into the dock near Paul. I glance back to see Carol lurching toward Paul, gun in hand, screaming, "Bastard! Liar!"

I plunge into the water, grabbing a plastic float attached to a boat hook on the edge of the dock. I grip the metal handle and ease myself to the side of the dock, my feet settling onto a wide crossbeam. Carol fires again, this time striking Paul in the shoulder. He slumps onto the deck, breathing hard.

"Carol!" Sid lunges toward her as Paul raises his arm and fires. The deafening blast is echoed by a fierce scream. Carol falls at the end of the ramp with Sid crouching over her.

Paul raises his arm to fire again. I swing the boat hook, slicing it down hard on his wrist. I hear the crack of bone. He grunts with pain, and the weapon falls from his hand, clattering onto the deck. I grab the gun and kick away from the crossbar, struggling to reach one of the fraying rubber tires tied to the dock. I grab on, bracing myself against the side of the tire, the gun heavy in my hand. Paul is on his knees, his bulk slumped back on his heels. For an instant, our eyes lock. He stares, looking stupefied, his hand clutching his shoulder. Blood oozes through his fingers, darkening his shirt. I hold my breath, staring back, feeling no pity.

Gunfire cracks the air, and flares of brilliant light burst in the night sky. Mayhem thunders around us. Paul shouts something at me, but I can't hear above the drumming blades of a helicopter *thwack-thwack*ing above me. He twists his head in the direction of the cabin cruiser and tries to climb to his feet but falls back into the water. Blinded by the white light, I lose sight of him. Icy water numbs my legs and laps around my waist, weighting the fleece jacket. I wrap an arm around the thick wood pylon, my cheek pressing against its soft slime at the water's surface. One hand clutches the slippery tire ropes; the other is anchored on the edge of the dock gripping the gun. Whatever I know about firearms, I learned from prop guys coaching Jinx a long time ago, but I've got the basics down. All I'm missing now is a director calling "Cut!"

As the deafening storm rages around me, I spot Paul rising out of the water, his back to me. He shifts his weight, trying to pull himself up on the dock. I remain still, the gun poised in my hand, and watch him struggle. One shoulder is bloody, an arm useless, but slowly, with great effort he manages to lift a knee over a pylon and leverage his body onto the dock. He lies panting, then rolls onto his side, gasping. His head shifts as he looks around, then sees me. His eyes widen, then lock on the gun in my hand. "Don't," he grunts. His breathing is labored, his chest heaving with the effort to speak. "I'm hurt bad, baby." His eyes flutter, then open wide, his gaze shifting to me. I hear a guttural sigh and a faint voice whispering, "Help." I let go of the ropes and raise my arm onto the dock, bracing myself with my elbows, both hands holding the gun. My eyes are on Paul, his gaze frozen, his mouth still.

Gunfire ceases, and the drumming sounds of the helicopters fade into the distance. I hear Jack calling my name, then feel the pounding of feet on the dock. His arms pull me up, lifting me from the water. "Meg, let go. Let go of the gun." He pries it from my fingers, and I register a heavy thump as it drops on the dock. My hands are icy, my body numb, but I feel Jack holding me close. "Meg, look at me. Can you hear me?"

I wince at the pain throbbing in my mouth. "You're bleeding, Meg. Easy, there." He gently pats my lip with his handkerchief.

I nudge my face into the warmth of his hand and mumble, "Good to see you."

"You, too. Damn, you don't know how close—" He swallows hard, his voice choked. "You're cold and wet. We'll get you out of here as soon as possible."

I raise myself up and see men in flak jackets rushing onto the dock, two of them carrying a stretcher. "They're taking care of Paul?"

"He's alive, but I'm afraid Carol—"

"I know. I saw." Tears sting my cold cheeks. "It happened so fast. How's Donna? Please don't tell me she's—"

"Sprained arm, that's all. We need to get you checked out, too. Can you make it up to the patio?"

"Let's go. I want to see that she's okay." Jack helps me to my feet. My legs are stiff, but with Jack supporting me, we walk toward the patio.

I glance back at the cabin cruiser, starkly lit and swarming with agents. Paul is lying on a stretcher, his face covered with an oxygen mask. Two patrol boats circle away from a second cabin cruiser and head out of the inlet. "What about Lucy and Greg?"

"They're getting them out now. Both are hurt, but they'll be fine. So will Sid. They've taken Proznorov in custody, along with his key people. Sorry I couldn't tell you much before—"

"And I complicated things, but I'm not going to apologize. Anyway, you heard everything?"

Jack reaches in his pocket and hands me my cell phone. "Awfully clever of you, my dear."

I snort. "All in a day's work," I say wryly. "I can't imagine why I bothered with stunt doubles all those years."

"Easy there, hotshot," he says as I stumble on the flagstone patio. He steadies me, and we come to a stop under the arch of bougainvillea. He puts his hands on my shoulders and pulls me close, his eyes gleaming in the spill of light from the tiki bar. "I don't think you know how lucky you were in that crossfire. Thank God I didn't lose you, Meg." He leans down and brushes his lips on my cheek. "I want to see a lot more of you," he whispers.

"Good. I feel the same about you, Jack." I breathe in his warmth, my body relaxing in his embrace.

He strokes my cheek and holds me close. "I'll get a medic to take a look at you. I have to take care of a few things, but I'll be back as soon as I can." He hurries back down toward the dock, and I watch him climb aboard the motorboat.

At my feet, shards of glass glitter in pink-stained dampness. On the patio, strings of lights still twinkle around the tiki bar, but stools are overturned, and a blood-smeared sign is propped against a table. Near the tile-roofed hacienda, two attendants load a stretcher into an ambulance without any sign of urgency.

Donna, her arm in a sling, emerges from the hacienda. I start toward her, but she calls out, "Stay there. The medic's on his way." She reaches me, out of breath, her eyes fierce as she sits next to me. "Hope you're happy," she says in a rush. "I hear you damn near got killed. Just tell me what you were thinking, leaving me with that wounded Amazon? I thought she was dying, and then she wallops me. Completely knocked the wind out of me. I sailed halfway across the patio and have a skinned backside to prove it. My good pants are completely wrecked!"

"Donna, I'm really sorry. I was so worried about you when I saw Carol with the gun."

"Thank God she didn't waste a bullet on me." She shakes her head. "Next thing I know, some guy in a flak jacket hauls me off. I almost missed out on everything."

"I'm sorry you got hurt. It could've been so much worse. I promise I'll make it up to you."

"Never mind, okay? It'll be something to tell my golf partners. That's worth it right there."

My cell phone throbs in my hand, startling both of us. "UNKNOWN" flashes in the window. "Hello?"

"Oh, hey! Is this Meg Barnes? I hope I'm not calling at a bad time."

"Who is this?"

"Oh, it's you, okay! I'm Melanie calling from *The Morning Show* in New York, and—"

"What? It's got to be late out there. How did you—? Wait, you couldn't possibly know about this already—and I don't want to talk about it!" I cup my hand over the receiver and mouth "*The Morning Show*" to Donna.

"Oh, please." Melanie groans in my ear. "Actually, I'm in LA. I just have to let the guys in New York know before morning if you can help us out so they can start doing promos. Winston broke his leg shoveling snow yesterday, and we'd booked him for a segment next week, so it's like— Anyway, you were just terrific in *Holiday*. I used to beg my parents to let me stay up—"

"Wait a minute. What's this about Winnie?"

"Winston Sykes? The Magician with the really cool accent—"

"Of course. He's in Canada, last I heard. But what's that got to do with what's happened here—wait, what are you calling me about?"

"We were bringing Winston in for this special segment celebrating the twentieth anniversary of the series. The network is airing 'Valentine's Folly' next weekend, so we thought it would be neat to have you with Sondra and Derek here in the studio fooling around with the magic top hat, or something. I mean, we need you in person. We can't do a remote, so you'd have to fly in, okay?"

"You want me to fly to New York? When?"

"Next week. Maybe Thursday? Winston gave me your phone number. Do you want me to call your agent, or something?"

My brain churns. At the moment I can think of nothing I want more than to get as far away as possible. "Hang on a second, okay?" I cover the mouthpiece again and whisper to Donna. "Are you up for a trip to New York next week? Two first-class tickets and a nice hotel. We could see a show. Sound good to you?"

Donna blinks. "Sure. You wrap filming on Tuesday. Will it work?"

I nod. Even as I tell Melanie she can count on me to go to New York next week, and arrange for her to speak with Pat in the morning, my actor's sensibilities are already at work. In the midst of carnage I'm sorting out my future and mentally packing bags—hoping that what happens in Mexico stays in Mexico.

Chapter Twenty-Three

Chez Jay is packed. This seaside dive across from the Santa Monica Pier has been around for more than fifty years, much of that time clinging to a month-to-month lease on land owned by the Rand Corporation. High-rise hotels and posh restaurants have sprung up on Ocean Avenue, but Chez Jay remains as it was when Jay Fiondella, a sometime actor and avid sailor, launched his restaurant in a jerry-built shack that looked a lot like a beached ship's hull, complete with portholes. Next door, sharing a cracked tarmac parking lot, is the Seaview Motel, a faded pink-and-aqua structure with a '50s-era neon sign. Jack and I pull into the lot and grab the last parking space.

Jay has passed away, and I still feel a sad tug that he's not at the door to greet us. But Mike Anderson, Jay's longtime partner, runs the place now and has saved a booth for us. In a world that's shifted under my feet entirely too much lately, it's comforting to walk across the peanut-shell–littered floor and see that nothing has changed. The tables are still covered in red-checkered cloths, and Christmas tree lights remain strung year-around across the awning over the bar. A handwritten slate with the day's specials hangs on a hook next to a boxy TV set mounted on the wall. No flat-screen here.

There's no need to check the menu. Jack orders for both of us: a bottle of Cabernet, clam chowder, medium-rare pepper steaks, and banana home fries. Toasted garlic bread, hot from the oven, arrives with a retro dish of carrot sticks, celery, and black olives. It's not until the wine arrives that I realize Jack and I have been holding hands since we sat down. We relinquish one hand each to raise our glasses in a toast.

"To finally getting you here," Jack says and laughs. "Cheers!"

"To Jay and being here with you. Cheers yourself!" I know I'm grinning, and I can't stop. But so is Jack. We sip our wine, not taking our eyes off each other. I've been grinning since Jack called and asked me if I was free for dinner tonight. I hadn't seen him since Donna and I were whisked out of Mexico, but he'd warned me he would be busy wrapping things up. That was fine with me. I had two more scenes to film before I was wrapped at the studio. I wanted to start fresh with Jack, and I sensed that was his desire, too.

I also needed some breathing space to sort things out with Donna. I offered to move out, but she refused to hear of it—thank God. In the end, we knocked back a bottle of good red in her garden gazebo and decided a little honesty was probably necessary to keep our friendship on firm footing. Since I don't have much more to hide from Donna, I agreed. Besides, two women who have seen each other in Pepto-Bismol pink and sea-foam green shorty nighties are pretty much bonded for life.

There was also the little problem of dealing with press coverage from our escapade south of the border. Donna, ever the sophisticate when it comes to these matters, insisted some self-promoting lemonade could be squeezed out of what I considered to be very foul, past-their-sell-date lemons. "Been there, don't want to go there again," I told her, reminding her I had already shared front-page headlines with my con-man husband.

In the end, in a town without much in the way of print media, where hard news is hard to come by, Sid finessed a heart-wrenching tale about his blonde, beautiful wife—an innocent tourist in Mexico—murdered by warring drug cartels. The story grabbed headlines and proved excellent fodder for cable coverage. Clips of Carol in her most significant role as star of *Zombie Aliens from Outer Space* played repeatedly. Sid, buffed to a sheen (and with a plea deal in his pocket), stage-managed the coverage brilliantly, sparing both himself and me from undue press investigation. Carol's funeral, a subdued affair by Hollywood standards, took place the morning I wrapped my final scene on Soundstage 9. Alas, I was unable to attend the graveside service.

The one completely unexpected kicker was the phone call from Steve Dorfman, who rang just as I was about to hurl myself into the shower before meeting Jack for dinner. UNKNOWN blinked on my caller ID.

"Miss Barnes? Hi, this is Steve Dorfman. I'm a researcher on *Jeopardy*—your agent might have mentioned me? First, I'm a really big fan and was hoping to get you to sign a photo for me on Saturday, but you left the hotel early. Anyway, you were a category a few years back, and I'd love to do something again on Jinx."

"For *Jeopardy*? With Alex Trebek?"

"That's it. Since the twentieth anniversary of *Holiday* is coming up, I thought it would be great to throw in a few trivia questions about the show. You game, as we say?"

"Sure, and you must know Alex Trebek pretty well, right? I'd be happy to give you whatever you need if you could arrange for a friend and me to watch a taping. Could you do that? We'd love to meet Alex."

"Of course. In fact, I'll show you around our offices. I think you'd be astounded at the research we do here."

Mission accomplished. I've finally arranged a meeting with Alex Trebek—and a visit to the *Jeopardy* research office, the wellspring for all those questions Donna knows the answers to and shouts at her TV screen. This should make up for all the jeopardy I've put her through.

By the time Jack swings by to pick me up, I'm feeling as spunky as a puppy off leash. I bound out to his BMW, pleased to see he's put the top down. I don't give a damn about my hair, or much else. It's late February, but Southern California delivers on its promise of sunny skies, warm weather—and I'm back to believing in promises.

It was still early enough to go for a walk on the beach before dinner. We still had a few things to clear up—or rather, to put behind us. We parked along Pacific Coast Highway and strolled barefoot on an almost deserted beach. We stayed close to the hard-packed sand near the waterline, occasionally dancing back to dodge a drift of foamy water. Jack took my hand, entwining his fingers in mine. I only needed a few bottom-line answers, but I listened to him without interruption.

The gist, according to Jack, is that in a tight economy, with mortgage loans hard to come by, scams bilking the desperate and unsuspecting are on an upswing. Paul could have laid low when his development scheme unraveled, but that wasn't his style. He hooked up with a Russian syndicate targeting homeowners with forged documents that looked legitimate.

"It's almost impossible to trace," Jack said. "Internet webs with 800 numbers and sham bank accounts facilitate wire transfers to Mexico that inevitably involve drug cartels. Piecing it together is difficult and time consuming."

"And Paul?"

"He was in WITSEC, the witness-protection program. But under these circumstances, he'll be prosecuted."

"Will I have to testify?"

The smooth flow of words came to a halt. I was about to repeat my question, when Jack said quietly, "Against your husband? No, you are not required under law to do so."

Two thoughts sprang to mind. First, I wouldn't be filing for divorce anytime soon. Second, if I had been made to testify, I'd probably be eligible for WITSEC myself. What could be worse than living the life of a fugitive again, on the run, fearing strange phone calls and notes on my windshield, when my only crime was being a victim? Rage welled, and in that moment I determined that whatever happened from then on, I'd stand my ground. No one was going to steal away my life ever again.

Jack squeezed my hand. "Are you okay?"

"Never better. I could go for that pepper steak now. How about you?"

He swung me around, holding me so tightly that my toes danced in the wet sand. We kissed long and hard, then sweetly and gently, stopping often on the walk back to the car to kiss again. I glanced across at the kaleidoscope of lights blinking in the amusement arcades along the Santa Monica Pier. It occurred to me that after dinner at Chez Jay, Jack and I could stroll down the pier and take a ride on the Ferris wheel. Wrapped in each other's arms, we'd swing high above the glittering sea and look out on coastline, lit up and sparkling like fresh-tossed diamonds.

The Morning Show, Jeopardy . . . I was definitely on a nostalgia roll even as I looked ahead. It would be good to get out of town for a few days—and to appear on a nationally broadcast talk show to remind another generation that I'm still alive. Thank God I've just come off something fresh, a pilot for a new show. Of course, I'll also be expected to do magic tricks with the top hat. *Jinxed again!*

Acknowledgments

Deepest appreciation to Cynthia Manson, my agent, for her unfailing support and encouragement. Special thanks to Caitlin Alexander for superb editorial guidance and to Kelli Martin for believing in the project and making this book happen. Abiding gratitude to Rodger Claire, a dear friend who provided me with unstinting advice and assistance.

Hugs to my Brown Bag Book Club pals Diana Doyle, Katrina Leffler, Angela Movassaghi, Marian Power, and Raleigh Robinson. Many thanks to my friends and colleagues who offered encouragement and assisted with their professional expertise: Candalaria Aquino, Heather Cameron, Cheryl Carrington, Suzanne Childs, Sunnie Choi, Diane Clehane, Connell Cowan, Patrick De Blasi, Sandy Dumont, Jeff Fellman, Jo-an Jenkins, Bridget Hedison, Harry Hennig, Ben Martin, Robert Masello, Sheila McGrath, Mary and Chuck Rapaport, Mia and Peter Sasdy, Lucinda Smith, and Susan Sullivan.

Loving thanks to my mother, Hilda Kringstad, an avid reader and my unabashed booster, who offered wonderful comments after reading the first draft. Heartfelt thanks as always to my husband, Geoff Miller, for his inspiration, love, and delicious sense of humor.

ABOUT THE AUTHOR

DOUGLAS KIRKLAND

Kathryn Leigh Scott is best known for creating four characters, including Josette du Pres, vampire bride to Barnabas Collins, on the cult soap opera *Dark Shadows*. She is the author of several *Dark Shadows* memorabilia books. Kathryn's first work of fiction, *Dark Passages,* is an affectionate nod to her years on that '60s series and encapsulates the romance and innocence of JFK's Camelot era. Kathryn is also the author of *The Bunny Years,* a memoir covering her years as a Bunny in the New York City club, which includes interviews with other former Bunnies. As a publisher, Kathryn founded Pomegranate Press, which offers nonfiction and entertainment titles.